LINCOLNSHIRE COUNTY
RECREATIONAL

EVERY LAST CENT

Lovejoy is in serious trouble. For it appears that a local lad known as Mortimer shares his extraordinary talent for distinguishing genuine antiques from fake. Although perhaps that's not so surprising—as it is rumoured that Mortimer is Lovejoy's son . . . But there is one big difference between 'father' and 'son'—Mortimer's painful honesty, which is ruining the local antiques trade. And the dealers blame Lovejoy. Lovejoy decides to use his own gift to assemble a mass of antiques— with any luck he might be able to bargain his way out. But when he persuades one of his favourite ladies, the sculptress Bernicka, to help him, tragedy strikes. For he finds her dead, seemingly by suicide. Now Lovejoy is running scared. Particularly when the death toll around him starts to mount . . .

EVERY LAST CENT

Jonathan Gash

CHIVERS PRESS
BATH

First published 2001
by
Macmillan
This Large Print edition published by
Chivers Press
by arrangement with
Macmillan
2001

ISBN 0 7540 1609 9

Copyright © Jonathan Gash 2001

All rights reserved.

British Library Cataloguing in Publication Data available

LINCOLNSHIRE
COUNTY COUNCIL

Printed and bound in Great Britain by
BOOKCRAFT, Midsomer Norton, Somerset

For Beverley Cousins, and friends in America.

Thanks Susan

What is man,
If his chief good, and market for his time,
Be but to sleep and feed? A beast, no more

Hamlet, Shakespeare

CHAPTER ONE

An antique is an antique is an antique, but only sometimes. A woman is a woman for ever. When the two come together life is dangerous. Always remember my law of antiques: it's not the money, it's the price.

*   *   *

Have you ever been so cold that your feet simply aren't there, and the warm light in your middle threatens to go out? Standing in the undergrowth, two o'clock on a frosty morning, listening to a gorgeous woman making love to some other undeserving slob in my—*my*—thatched cottage, I felt even colder.

The frost worsened towards midnight. It crunched underfoot as I tried to get warm. I could see the log fire—my fireplace, my logs, their warmth—reflecting a reddish sheen along the windowsill. A couple of times I tried to peer in but the woman had pinned my threadbare curtains over the grotty panes. That's trust for you, I thought bitterly. One good thing: in the morning she'd pay. I'd be able to eat.

Her mewling and gasping got me down. When they reached ecstasy I got truly fed up and walked out of my moonlit garden and down the lane. Nowhere to go. Eleanor's husband was back from the oil rig this week. There was a new raving maniac of a guard dog at the White Hart pub so I couldn't doss there. Another hour to last out.

1

When you hire out your cottage to Borace those are the terms. Ten o'clock in the evening to three next morning. Life is unfair.

A while since, I used to drive one of Borace's love wagons. These were great pantechnicons, changed from their mundane furniture-removal functions into mobile bedrooms. This was the arrangement: suppose you're a bored housewife fed up with the usual grind (no pun intended). Let's say you meet Handsome Jack in a bus queue. But what then? You can't take him home on account of nosy neighbours. You can't snog in the park because of strolling families. The cinema's out these days. What do you do? Answer: you phone Borace. One of his mobile passion wagons trundles you to some quiet venue. As unsuspecting traffic roars past, you frolic and wassail with Handsome Jack in secrecy.

Borace supplies a luxury hamper, champagne, lobsters, and those little eats that never fill a tooth. Every mod con is provided, from televisions to smutty films and, rumour has it, a third person if required.

The vans had silly logos on their sides—WE MOVE YOU TO HEAVEN and suchlike—to protect the innocents (well, the illicit fornicators) within. Trouble was, a scandal rose. Some jealous geezer reported a pantechnicon one dark night. The plod arrived at the moment of the lovers' fulfilment. They broke into the wagon and caught our town mayor with the deputy mayor's missus in what newspapers used to call Certain Circumstances. I got blamed, arrested, fined, and beaten up, because I was the unlucky driver that night.

Passion wagons have vanished since then.

Borace has been reduced to what he calls Home For Abroad (*for a broad*, get it?), and now hires houses from anybody who can let their drum for surreptitious lust. In case this sounds like easy gelt, be careful. The rules are ominously strict. Stick to them or else. And that doesn't only mean you don't get paid. It means your legs get broken, and your house inexplicably catches fire at three-thirty the following afternoon.

Lust doesn't come cheap in East Anglia. In fact, it can make a cottage's legitimate resident wander the icy lanes and hedgerows all night instead of getting a decent kip. Like me.

$$* \qquad * \qquad *$$

As I plodded down the lane—it goes nowhere except to a river and a farm—I almost bumped into a huge motor parked in the moonshadows. A bloke's gruff voice exclaimed. The car's courtesy light came on. I saw a man's face. He'd been dozing in warmth and comfort, the swine.

The window whirred down. 'What you doing?'

'Nothing, wack. Just, er, walking.'

I scarpered. He was probably in the service of the two who'd come to my cottage. Borace's rule is that you don't see them, not even if you do. Keep out of their way.

The motor was one of these squarish-looking giants, all 1940s, like the car makers forgot to round their vehicles off. Rolls and Bentleys, I mean, with little mascots that collectors pay me for nicking. It made me hopeful, though the thought didn't even cross my mind.

One thing: if their driver was lurking in my lane,

then they'd be off the nest fairly soon. I trudged round Spring Lane and quietly stole into the rear of my overgrown garden. I nearly stood on Crispin, my hedgehog. He grumbled. Hate to think what the little pest eats, rummaging about all night. I feed him cat food when I'm in funds, but because cats eat those unspeakable tins of meat I get little Abigail from down the lane to dish it out for him. It's a nasty business. She says I'm being silly, but she's seven and knows everything.

So it was that I was trying not to freeze by marching silently on the spot near my derelict workshop in the brambles when the beautiful woman and her feller finally emerged. I saw them clearly in the light of my porch. They must have had a mobile phone because the motor came gliding up. They got in. The motor drove off with hardly a sound except for the crackling of gravel under the tyres.

Which left me astounded, thinking well, well, well. Who'd have imagined it was him? The American consul. I'd seen his photo at the Oyster Feast.

It's one thing to think that you've helped a stranger to an episode of transcendental bliss, but it's another to realize that you've just sanctioned a love tryst for the likes of him. The woman looked gorgeous.

Shivering, I went inside and sat on the edge of my crumpled divan bed. I've only this one room, with a curtained alcove as a kitchen, and a bathroom with a loo. They'd left the lantern burning, and the embers still glowed. I took off my shoes and extracted the soggy cardboard. The soles were both holed. My wet socks peeled off. I'd mend

4

their toes when I could afford some wool. My feet looked like albino prunes, the toes wrinkled and wet.

Then I noticed my forgery had been moved.

Normally I keep my fakes in one place. You shouldn't move a painting to catch a good north light, especially a portrait of an exquisite woman who'd died centuries agone. Artists call it 'chasing light'. I never do it, because it leads to terrible mistakes that show your forgery up for the miserable travesty that it is. Paint exactly as the Old Master did, and you might, just might, get away with it.

For a long time I stood staring at my forgery.

Definitely out of true. Somebody, and I knew exactly who, had moved it about the cottage to see it in different kinds of light. I could even see the scratch marks on the slab floor. They'd thought I wouldn't notice.

The bedclothes were tumbled. I was dropping from weariness, but stripped off the sheets. Eleanor would collect them in the morning. I'd borrowed them from her the previous afternoon, having to endure her suspicious questions and irritating jibes.

My belly rumbled as I scented food. I scavenged. The wine was all gone. I shoved the empty bottles into the hamper. I found a roll, some cheese, and some cakey stuff with virtually no substance. I can't see the point of baking cakes that vanish when you take a bite. I fell on the grub.

Some meat on a plate looked red raw, so I left that. I also ditched some smoked salmon strips because I never know if that means it's been cooked. They'd swigged all the coffee, but I put the dregs aside in my mug, hoping maybe they'd make a decent cuppa in the morning if I got some hot water. Six miniature spirit bottles rolled about the place, empty of course, testifying to the caring compassion with which my guests had frolicked with complete indifference to my welfare. I laid my wet socks and shoes on the flagstones near the warm grate.

My blanket was unsullied. I haven't got proper pillows, so I stripped, shoved my cushion into place, scenting the perfume of the woman whose body had voluptuously reclined there, promised myself a good long spell of hatred of the American consul in the morning, and slept.

CHAPTER TWO

Once, antiques and women were the only two aspects of life.

Then one day I learned there was a third problem just as brilliant and difficult. And now, I wouldn't be without any of them for the world. I need all three.

*   *   *

I was under the overhang of that chemist's shop in Pelhams Lane next morning selling stolen Christmas trees.

'Come with me, Lovejoy,' Sandra said. 'I've found some old panels. Vice's wood yard.'

'No, ta,' I said. 'I'm doing fine.'

I knew straight away it was a trick. Her smile

always tells you she's up to no good.

'They'll be worth a fortune to a forger like you, Lovejoy.'

They always say this, antique dealers. A bonny woman doubles the beauty and doubles the risk. It's one of my laws of antiques. Remember it.

'I'm making a fortune.' The shoppers surged past.

'Sold many, dear?' She looked me up and down. Frayed edges, shabby cuffs, patched jacket. I'd not eaten.

'Ninety,' I lied. 'Only three left.'

'It's summer, silly. And I've got what you want.'

Truth there. Sandra waited, her smile promising me untold wealth. What can you do? I left my bedraggled trees, ignoring the angry shouts of the other hawkers to clear up my rubbish.

*　　　*　　　*

Vice's wood yard stands back from the Ladies' Golf Course at Lettenham, a rural estuary six leagues away from my village. This is how local East Anglian folk still speak, 'Six leagues and a furlong, booy.' It took us thirty minutes in her enormous Jaguar.

'You're sure they're worth it, Sandra?' I kept asking.

'Two lovely old cupboards and a bench.'

'How old?'

She couldn't say, which should have alerted me. Everyone knew I'd been searching for old, aged wood to forge Old Master paintings. I'd combed the three counties and found nothing. I looked at Sandra. All antique dealers have a quirk.

7

Sandra Gainer is a compulsive gambler. Her marriage ended when she gambled her husband into bankruptcy. Frederick was a pillar of society, churchgoer, an eight-to-six commuter. She had him arrested for credit card fraud, on account of her (not his, note) gaming losses. The last honest bloke on earth, he's currently doing four years, out next autumn. Sandra looks well on Frederick's suffering. She'll sell anything—hers, yours, mine—to fund her gambling addiction. She once sold my cottage to a Bavarian tourist and lost the money before teatime on another infallible system. Three different banks each believed they were my sole mortgagers. I had a hell of a time evicting the Munich bloke. That's Sandra.

'Sand? Why can't people gamble on wrestling?'

'I tried. They won't take the bets.'

My trouble is an uncontrollable mind. It darts about, asking the unanswerable. Like, why do all the big peninsulas on earth point south, never north? Africa, India, South America, Malaysia, Baja California. And why did God, who loves us, invent malaria?

'You can keep your hand on my knee, Lovejoy, if you stump up for the three o'clock winner at Haydock.'

'Can I owe?' My hand was accidental.

'No kitty, no pity.'

Reluctantly I withdrew my hand to holiness. I'd made stupendous smiles with Sandra after her Frederick got collared, but grew alarmed when I found she backed losing nags all over the kingdom. Now I keep out of her way, except when I'm stupid.

We drove through depressing countryside, trees, fields, gentle rivers. Not an antique shop for miles.

8

Is it any wonder that rural pastures get you down? The only interesting thing we passed was Farlow. He was sitting at Stratford St Mary busily painting John Constable's famed *Loving Couple by the Stour*. Please don't complain that Constable never did such a work. I know that. Farlow knows that. But put one of his Constable fakes next to mine, his looks obviously a sham, and mine looks brilliant. It's called the match trick among the corrupt, when you pair a bad thing with a good. Customers assume the better forgery possibly isn't fake at all. Two tourists out of five will pay on the nail. Unless it's a woman buying gems, in which case it's four out of five.

You think it's a wicked ploy only done by antique dealers and other criminals? Wrong. Look in any boutique or jeweller's window. Everybody's at it.

'Here!' Sandra called brightly, pulling in to Vice's wood yard, tooting her horn. 'I got him!'

And handed me over to an aggressive horde waiting to do me grievous bodily harm. I alighted with a sigh to meet my doom.

'Lovejoy?' Dennis De Angelo piped. 'We're going to hang you.'

There were fifteen antique dealers, Dennis to the fore. Brains of a spud, and enough makeup trowelled onto his face to open a shop. He wants to start a fashion business without money. Antique dealers are a laugh a minute, but on the whole not frightening. You don't hang people who owe you money. I owed ten of these riff-raff serious gelt, but so? Life's one disappointment after another. Everybody has to learn.

The wood yard was quiet. Two workers whistled and laboured unloading a barge. Sandra eyeing their sweating forms. A dog dozed on the riverbank. No escape. It would have to be lies.

'Now, Dennis,' Margaret Dainty soothed. 'None of that.'

Margaret and me occasionally make smiles. A real lady, she's forever trying to hide her lameness. (Why? What difference does a limp make?) Her husband's always unseen. Sometimes, if I'm forced into a posh occasion, she lends me one of his suits. I'm lost in it, pea in a drum. Which should worry me, except five years ago she taught me a new way of making smiles. Until then I'd thought it was only in books. She saw me remembering and coloured slightly.

'We'll drown him instead,' Smarts said eagerly.

He's a Victorian jewellery freak. Wears all his stock on his person, earrings in great loops round his head. You can hear him coming if there's a wind. You never see him with fewer than two-score necklaces, bangles up his arms. He sounds like a small foundry. Smarts claims to be French but only comes from our village. Barmy.

'It's your by-blow, Lovejoy,' Jenny Blondel said. She really is French but says she comes from our village. Weird. She owns three falcons.

My mind went, who? I said, 'Who?'

Jenny's nice. I like her because she makes cider from my apples and has a secret lover called Aspirin who can do handstands when he's drunk. I admire him for that. I can't even do them when I'm sober. And I'm jealous because he's got Jenny. Aspirin is a defrocked vicar but nobody's supposed to know. He embezzled a church's antiques. He baptizes you when he's sloshed, whether you want to or not. Her husband Paul Blondel keeps hunting

10

birds.

'Your son, Lovejoy. Mortimer.'

I gave them the bent eye. Dennis squealed, darted back.

'I haven't got a son.'

'That Mortimer,' Jenny persisted. 'He's ruining our trade.'

'You lot already do that.'

'Arf arf,' Willie Lott said. No humour there. No compassion either. 'Stop him, Lovejoy. He's yours.'

Willie Lott really did worry me. Even a burp can sound threatening from Willie. He's been in one of those silent services, and says he hasn't. Pretends he's thick as a plank, but has several foreign languages. He looks like a street brawler, all crags and scars.

'Who, Willie?' I asked weakly.

Dennis got courage from Willie Lott and squeaked, 'Mortimer, your kid by that whore Colette Goldhorn.'

'What's he done?' I didn't admit a thing.

'He's divvying all our stock, free. Telling tourists which antiques are genuine and which aren't.' Smarts glared. 'He's frigging ruining us,' adding in his execrable French, for authenticity, *'Il est terrible, non?'*

Except he says the words just as they're written, ill esst terry bull none. Why do we all pretend we're different from our real selves? Women do it with cosmetics and plastic surgery, men pull their beer bellies in. We're all at it.

'Hang him, Willie!' Dennis, from the rear.

Jessica tutted. 'Shut it, Dennis, or I'll smack your wrists.'

Jessica is holy, runs a prayer chapel to bring us

11

all back to purity, and lives down the estuary with her son-in-law in a state of mortal (I sincerely hope) sin, wears enough perfume to stop a clock and slinks about the Eastern Hundreds in a full-length dress adorned with zodiacal symbols. I like her, too.

'Mortimer does no harm,' I said. Plant your flag and name the price, there's not much anybody can do.

Jessica took out a list. The waft of scent almost keeled me over. I leaned away for oxygen. 'He told the truth about these antiques in the Arcade.'

A groan arose, really heartfelt. I could have hired them out for a biblical epic. Antique dealers go weak when honesty sneaks in. Truth is death. Get any dealer tipsy, and he'll admit that only three per cent of all the antiques he's ever seen are genuine. Get him utterly kaylied, he'll finally admit that it's only one per cent. Which means, so you get the point, that ninety-nine per cent of all antiques currently on sale anywhere are forgeries.

'You want chapter and verse, Lovejoy?' Willie Lott said quietly. 'Marry-Me Burnside's fuddling cups, genuine slip ware? Jessica's papper mash genuine Henry Clay table?'

For genuine read fake. Dealers speak in fable.

'Two hundred items last week, Lovejoy,' Margaret said with sorrow. She loves me, a true friend. 'Speak to the boy. That's all we ask.'

'And Rose Madder's printed *Hours of the Virgin* on vellum—'

'He what?' I interrupted, because I'd done that fake medieval manuscript myself. Sweated blood on it, only finished it a fortnight back.

Vellum's not parchment, incidentally. It's a pig

to print on, slips and shuffles as the type comes down. It was a beautiful forgery, though I say it myself. I'd throttle Mortimer, the little sod.

'I never see him,' I said lamely. I'm really good at sincere indignation so I tried that. 'And who says he's my responsibility? How can I find somebody who lives wild?'

'By tomorrow, Lovejoy,' I got from Willie. 'No later.'

He slit my jacket from top to bottom in a movement so swift I didn't even see the knife. Hero that I am, I froze.

Tronker, one of Willie's goons, approached carrying my unfinished Gainsborough. He slashed it to ribbons. It made an odd sound, grush, grush. I watched stonily. More heroism.

They left then, skittering motors spattering me with mud. I looked at the slashed Gainsborough. Destroyed. No chance of marouflaging it. I gave them ten minutes, then walked to the trunk road and thumbed a lift home.

An hour later I was in my overgrown garden sitting on my unfinished wall by my old well. The robin came, saw I'd no cheese, flirted off with an angry cheep. Six bluetits did the same.

After a few minutes I spoke into the air. 'Mortimer?'

Silently he came out of the hedge and sat with me. Fifteen years old, thin, brown hair awry. Shoddy as me, but cool.

'I wish you wouldn't do that,' I said, narked. 'Can't you knock?'

'Sorry, Lovejoy. I didn't know they'd get mad.' He waited. 'I've found you a customer. Dangerous, but rich.'

13

'They go together.' I was so tired. 'Let's go.'

'What's a fuddling cup?' he asked as we walked down the lane. 'What's slipware? What's papper mash? Who was Henry Clay?'

'Shush. I'm thinking.'

Being with Mortimer was strange. I never knew what to say, how to behave. I mean, a child's a terrible thing. When you unexpectedly come across one who's fifteen, they're worse. Am I right or what?

They're also that third risk I mentioned.

*   *   *

On the bus, I pondered.

The dealers' vehemence seemed wrong. Okay, the antique trade is always chaos in search of a wardrobe. Frankly, it's mayhem. Lives are lost in the scramble for this gorgeous pendant, that perfect Chippendale. But lately the whole trade had been depressed. Antiques are riddled with calamities. An example:

Not long since, an elderly lady made her way, heart pounding, into a jeweller's. She fetched an old watch. Could the jeweller be so kind as to please value it? The jeweller's heart also pounded. He offered her a handful of zlotniks—fifteen to be precise, twenty dollars barring the handshake, enough for a meal. Not more, dear sir?

The dear sir regretfully said no, madam. Worth only scrap value. The lady took the paltry sum. Thank you and good day.

Normal business in the antiques trade, right?

The jury thought it shouldn't be, and said so at the trial. For it seemed the watch had quite a histoıy.

Cut to the ship that's always in the news, the Titanic. It happened, on the fateful day the great ship sank, that the waters closed over a certain lady. Horror! But two brave jolly jack tars hauled her into a lifeboat. Saved! She was the Countess of Rothes, and was eternally grateful.

So thankful was she, in fact, that she had two special watches made, engraved with the date of the sinking, a dedicatory inscription, and the sailors' initials. Two watches, then, eminently collectable.

Time passed.

The old lady's watch was one of the pair. The jeweller, a witness said, 'gloated'. A similar watch—presumably the partner—sold for a cool $30,000. Somebody blew the whistle. In came the plod. The jury thought the jeweller heartless. Guilty verdicts abounded.

What gave me a wry smile, though, was the front page headline, now famous among dealers. It read *Fears of 'fair price' precedent*. Get it? 'Fair price' was a threat! Suddenly antique dealers were terrified. When buying an antique from the innocent public (assuming there is such a thing) maybe they'd have to pay a 'fair price' for everything! Gulp.

Dealers call it the Southampton Case. Where antique dealers meet, the ghost of the Southampton Case lurks in their midst. And the commonest grumble of all? It's this: 'Whatever happened to *caveat emptor*, buyer beware?' Dealers sob into their muscatel, drop crocodile tears on their caviar. Cruel fate, making them behave!

Me? I think that Law, as ever, simply won't work. It never does. The innocent get taken to the cleaners, and the robber barons get the Rolls, blondes, and villas in Monte Carlo.

The bus trundled. I slept.

CHAPTER THREE

When I woke on the bus Mortimer gave me three home-made vegetarian sandwiches and a bottle of water. I had them, mourning my ravaged portrait.

*   *   *

The greatest portrait ever painted is that of a beautiful lady, *Portrait of the Artist's Wife* by Gainsborough. Some folk think that one woman's face is just like another. After all, what is a phizzog? Couple of eyes, mouth, eyelashes, whatever.

Untrue. For years I've been painting that same portrait over and over. I'm still at it. I'm the one who knows.

Go and see her. The painting just hangs there like all the rest in London's Courtauld. You may think, 'Hey, she's ordinary!' Disappointment! If so, you're looking wrong.

I admit she isn't young. She certainly isn't sprawled naked in a tangle of erotic satins. Her breast is modestly covered. She has a double chin at that, quite plain, holds back a mantilla in an awkward pose. Dullsville, no big deal. (I'm being honest here).

Except you're looking at the most beautiful portrait painted since the world began.

16

Others are fine, sure. Tell me that Rembrandt is superb, I'll go we-e-ell, ye-e-es. And I'll give you points if you're the indignant Hon Sec of the Michelangelo Appreciation Society. But are their works *the* greatest? Sorry and all that, but no. Not by a mile. Because out in front, winner by a street, is the lovely plain face of Mary Gainsborough.

Confront her. Let other viewers walk on. Imagine you are the artist himself, holding her gaze. Then wonder what sort of bloke was this Gainsborough?

Frankly, Tom G was a bad lad. If you say to local folk hereabouts, 'I'll pop over to Sudbury today,' something odd happens. They smile knowingly and reply, 'Lot of artists in Sudbury!' Sounds innocent, right? It isn't. They mean that Tom Gainsborough was wicked for the ladies. They still nickname a footpath Tom's Walk because there it was that young lusty Tom—and, in time, middle-aged lusty Tom—used to frolic with maids, matrons, wives. Anything in skirts. Plenty of unexpected little babes grew up to be astonishingly talented artists thereabouts . . .

He was the same in his London studio, when fame struck. He ordered his servants to keep gentlemen out. But if the next customer was a pretty lady, well . . .

Now look at Mary Gainsborough's blue eyes. She's not smiling, yet she is. For in her serene gaze there's genuine love for her randy husband, plus understanding too. But for me it's the glorious trace of humour that takes the biscuit. The entire masterpiece wouldn't cover your smallest window, yet that patch of daubed canvas defines what love really is. Her lovely smile is saying to Thomas, 'I know you, you devil. And about the ladies. And our milkmaid. And the grocer's wife . . .' And the love in her exquisite eyes dazzles so your vision blurs. She's just so beautiful. Okay, a portrait's only a blot on a rag, but even Sir Joshua Reynolds—no slouch—couldn't quite see how the brilliant Gainsborough had done it.

Is it any doubt that she had him for ever? He didn't paint any of his luscious tarts with anything like the passion that he lavished on that small portrait of his Mary.

It's genius. It was for yet more attempts on Mary's portrait that I needed the old panels. I use the same paints, same methods. And fail every time.

* * *

By the time we alighted at Saffron Fields I was well narked. Some schoolgirls on the bus kept giggling, daring each other to call come-hithers at Mortimer. The lad was only fifteen, God's sake. I tried glaring but they did that raised-eyebrows-lip-droop that means get knotted, you boring prat. Mortimer paid no attention. The schoolgirls bent heads to whisper. I could have pasted the lot of them.

Now, I'm no angel. I learned at an early age that there was more to gender than an apple in a garden. I was reaped in my early teens by a married woman who gave me a flintlock pistol (note that symbolism). It was my first real antique possession (I mean the flintlock). Her true gift, though, was excitement. Males and females, I saw in that first glorious thrill, came together, so to speak. Of course I didn't know what was going on. I only knew that life had arrived.

But Mortimer? Only fifteen, barely out of the egg. Surely he was too young to bother with the opposite sex? I'd never felt like this before. The schoolgirls alighted at Wickerham Lanes. They str-o-o-olled off the bus, then stood on the grass verge calling offers of what I can only term cohabitation. I fumed. They needed a good hiding, brazen young tarts. No discipline these days. I blame the parents—*what was I saying*? I caught myself, aghast. In shock, I glanced at Mortimer.

'Don't worry, Lovejoy. They know no better.'

'I'm not worried!' I blazed, then because heads turned at my vehemence whispered, 'Makes no difference to me. Get that in your head.'

We got off at Saffron Fields. The bus left us by the huge ornate gateway.

'Here? The customer's here?' It was his mansion.

He nodded. We started up the drive.

'Why's he staying here?' Now I was really out of my depth.

'They, Lovejoy. I leased the mansion and the estate.'

Mortimer, I should explain, for all that he's only a sprog, owns the entire place. That is to say, the manor house with its vast medieval acreage known as Saffron Fields, shooting rights, fens where anglers spend fortunes to drown worms in Mortimer's river, sundry canals, wharfage, estuaries, not to mention a marina near the Blackwater. Locals defer to him because he has one of these ancient titles nobody cares about these days. He likes living in a shed by the river. Which might beg the question how come Mortimer was

19

mighty throughout the land when I, alleged kin, was penniless and totting for a piece of old wood so I could earn a crust. Explanation: I knew his mum once. That's all I'll say. She is elsewhere; always was elsewhere.

Distant gardeners doffed caps. To my disappointment we went round to the servants' entrance. (See? Even I'm a secret snob.) An elegant woman was standing among rows of lettuces talking to a sandy-haired homely geezer.

Mortimer went all diffident. 'I fetched Lovejoy, missus.'

'I'm Mrs Susanne Eggers,' she told me irritably. 'You're late.'

'How do,' I said, narked at Mortimer's subservience, clocking her as American, bonny, dark of hair, and sharp.

'Come in. Not you,' she said tartly to Mortimer.

'Very good, ma'am,' said the lord of the manor, not quite tugging his forelock. I drew breath to tell her to go to hell but Mortimer's quick look warned me.

'You stay outside, Taylor,' she commanded the other bloke.

She swept in. Meekly I followed.

This terse lady was just into her thirties, given to flinging out Churchillian imperatives. I'd seen her the previous night emerging from my cottage.

'I don't suffer fools lightly, Lovejoy. Understand?'

I just said, 'Mmmh, mmmh.' Oscar Wilde's crack came to mind: America was discovered often before Columbus, but they hushed it up.

Tea was already served in the withdrawing room. She plunked herself down and gestured me to a seat.

'Tell me what you do,' she commanded.

In a way you have to admire Yanks. No wonder they're all millionaires and have ranches big as Berkshire. Okay, so other nations knock America. It's only envy. If we didn't have the USA we'd have to go around pretending there really was such a stupendous country. It's the nearest we shabbier nations get to paradise. Don't try telling me there's a lot wrong with America because I won't listen. Other countries live on dollar support. And we're all jealous of America's devil-may-care movies.

Humbly trying not to wobble my teacup and saucer, I sat and tried to please the lovely legs opposite.

'Not much, lady. I just like antiques.'

'Define a divvy.'

My tea nearly spilled. I can't drink anything hot, but tried a scalding sip.

'Er, I recognize antiques. I'm maybe just lucky.'

She nodded slowly, sipped her hellishly hot tea without a scream, but women can do that. Her eyes didn't even water.

'Is there such a thing as luck in antiques?' she countered.

'Folk say so.' I was lost. Mortimer hadn't told me a thing. Weren't children supposed to do as they were told? I'd clip the uncommunicative little sod's ear. Except, was I allowed or was that fascist nowadays? I could remember getting thrashed and being told it did me good.

'The idiot boy from the estate,' she said, replacing her empty cup. 'Who brought you. Lives in some hovel by the river. They say he's . . .' she looked askance a moment, ' . . . fey? That your

21

word for luck?'

It took a minute before I realized she was speaking of Mortimer. I almost belted her one: *Hey, missus, that's my son you're talking of, you ignorant cow.* But I remembered Mortimer's reproving glance and kept mum. I'd played the village idiot times out of number. What was Mortimer up to? With women I always feel pig-in-the-middle, that children's game.

'People hereabouts treat him like he is special,' she told me evenly.

'If you've got him, what d'you need me for? Two lucks are overdoing it.'

'Don't be flippant! A moron is no use to me. The land agent who rented me this place—some feudal cretin owns it; is travelling abroad—says the idiot boy finds antiques. He can distinguish forged antiques from genuine. I need such a person.'

She lit a cigarette, staring unblinkingly through the smoke, and eyed me. Not often you see eyes that hard outside a Steiff doll. Shapely, just the sort a bloke can't help wanting. A woman can entice more with a cigarette than virtually anything, but she was beginning to scare me witless. I mean, women are supposed to smile, right? And be charming or something. She seemed robotic.

'You have this divvy trick, Lovejoy.'

Want made me shrug, to show I could easily be bribed.

'Except you're unemployable, and I need an alternative to that idiot boy.' She snorted a laugh. 'So find me some better.'

Did she think divvies grew on trees? I was the only divvy I knew, but for Mortimer who was showing disturbing signs of having inherited the

22

trait. One and one only make two.

'Bring me several divvies so I can choose. What is your fee?'

For the unattainable? I could start eating, maybe get a jar of Gunton's marmalade. And Lancashire cheese! My belly rumbled. When this happens I press my elbows into my sides. It never works. I stooped into a hire-me grovel.

'Er, what does m'lady think adequate?' I croaked.

'I'll give you what I paid for that Cotman watercolour,' she said imperiously.

The plain little antique painting hung on the wall in a mahogany frame. Businesswoman that she was, she named half of what she'd bought it for. I knew she'd got it off Mirrorman Tate in St Botolph's Antiques Arcade. Incidentally, Cotman was the greatest at laying a sky wash. God knows how he did it, but it's always beautifully even, right down to the edges of clouds. It galls me. In fact, I'd taken four weeks to do this very fake, a sailing boat becalmed. I'd given in at the finish, worn out, and done an acrylic wash in despair, like most modern forgers. The old greats—Cotman, Turner, Sandby—mixed their own watercolours with gum arabic. Nowadays modern paints have so much gelatin in the gum arabic that overpainting, however lightly you do it, tends to leach out the colours underneath. It's one way of spotting the careless forger of old watercolours. *The Calm* by Miles Cotman is famous. It's used by water colour teachers the world over. One day, I'm going to steal the original from Oldham's Art Gallery and stare at it for life.

'Thank you,' I said humbly, half a loaf being

23

better than no bread.

'Leave your phone number and address, Lovejoy. Bring the best six divvies.'

'Very well, m'lady.' I gave her a mythical number knowing the phone company had cut me off for poverty.

Only by a stupendous effort of will did I manage not to back out, like they did from the tsarina. She was clearly off her trolley. The only other true divvy apart from myself and Mortimer had been one elderly French bloke who died years since. Apart from that, zilch. And here was this mad woman commanding me to round up an assorted half-dozen.

Mortimer joined me as I walked past an ornamental grove of evergreens. He wasn't there one minute then suddenly was.

'Stop appearing like that, you little burke,' I said. 'Why didn't you tell me she was crazy?'

'She's come to find a portrait. Somebody dead, she thinks. The cook overheard her say it.'

'Can't she get a private eye?' I'm never quite sure what the term means, but it sounds trendy American.

'Her second husband—you met Taylor Eggers— is an American ex-policeman. Into antiques.'

I have a special headache that can spot trouble a mile off. It saves itself for big occasions, like now. Every step I took jolted it up a notch. In silence we reached the main gate. It was coming on to rain.

'It's an opportunity, Lovejoy.' Mortimer left a space for me to speak, then did it for me. 'Bring actors. They can pretend to be divvies.'

I bleated feebly, 'I don't know any actors.'

'You painted the portrait, Lovejoy.'

24

'I painted a frigging *ghost*?'

The bus came. He helped me, a broken man, on board and paid my fare. I would have waved but the vehicle jerked noisily forward, so I just surrendered to the blinding agony. I'd had enough of fatherhood. Escape called.

CHAPTER FOUR

Outside the public library Paul Blondel stands. He's Jenny Blondel's husband. I watched him. He grows hunting birds, uses them to collect money for the St Helena Hospice on shopping afternoons. Saint Helena, incidentally, is supposed to hail from our town but didn't. They say she found the True Cross, but didn't. Paul Blondel, however, is one of the few genuine individuals in this make-believe mad world. He knows all about Aspirin, his wife's secret lover, but is a gentleman and pretends he doesn't.

A crowd of admiring shoppers congregated about Paul's wooden perches. He wears a huge leather gauntlet. Drop money into his bucket, you're allowed to hold one of his wicked-eyed hunting birds. People actually queue to do it. Unbelievable.

'Yes, you can stroke her.' Paul was smiling at some infant.

Today's brands included a pretty owl-looking thing with a white downy chest. The child reached up and patted the creature.

'Keep your fingers away from her face,' Paul warned. 'She has her eyes closed, but she can sense

25

something approaching and tends to snap.'

A large bird dozed on another perch, occasionally moving its feet so its bell clonked. It was hell of a size. God gets almost everything wrong in my book, but these two birds were exquisite, God on a good day.

'What do you feed them on?' some old dear wittered.

'Mice,' Paul said, pleased. 'And baby chicks. I tie a chick on a cotton and drag it along the ground.'

'How sweet!' sundry maniacs cooed.

'The hawk sulks,' Paul went on. 'I take him rabbiting and won't let him eat the little rabbits. I keep some for his supper. Gets really angry!'

Everybody laughed, a merry scene from English rural life. I felt dizzy and went to sit on Holy Trinity church wall, my forehead clammy. Nausea enveloped me. I came to moments later. A woman was dabbing my forehead with a damp tissue while her infant appraised me with scorn.

'Stay still, Lovejoy,' she kept saying. 'I get it too, all down my side.'

'He's scared of the birds,' the infant jeered.

'Shut up.' I tried to say it like Mrs Eggers, but it came out a bleat.

'Told you!' said the titch triumphantly. 'Cos they eat chicks.'

Paul came over with an owl. 'Sorry, Lovejoy. Didn't notice you, or I'd not have mentioned it.'

'They eat the eyes first,' the little psychopath remarked, swinging her foot. 'Paul shows us, don't you, Paul?'

'Miriam!' her mother scolded. 'Quiet, miss, or it's early bed. D'you hear?'

'Jenny told me about your trouble, Lovejoy,'

26

Paul said. 'They're gunning for you. When did you eat last?'

'Just on my way to Woody's nosh bar,' I lied, making to rise but the infant carnivore's mother restrained me. Other shoppers stopped to watch, contentedly reminiscing about other dramatic faints they had known.

Paul brought out a note. 'Order me some chips, okay? I'll follow on.'

'Right,' I said, letting him stuff the money in my pocket. I don't know about other folk, but shame figures largely in my life. Here was me, a grown man, cadging grub money off a bloke who was giving his all to collect money for the Hospice for the Dying. I'm pathetic.

'Stay still a minute more,' the woman advised.

Another of life's mysteries: a woman can give you a bit of advice and make it sound like Newton's Laws. If I merely suggest something nobody listens, not even children and animals. I looked up.

'Do I know you, missus?'

'I'm a friend of Eleanor's. We used to live next door to her in your lane.'

Oops. Eleanor is little Henry's mum. I babysit for him some afternoons. Uneasily I wondered if she knew that me and Eleanor used to make smiles. I remembered her now.

'Satina? Sorry, love. I got giddy.' Her husband Luke is a customs officer of singularly sour disposition, while Satina was always happy as a lark.

'This is my little Miriam, she of the sunny attitude.'

Genetics work, then, I thought, assessing Miriam's candid gaze. Got it from her neurotic

27

father, no doubt. Luke sees smugglers under every bed.

Satina hefted the pushchair round. 'Don't say I told you, Lovejoy, but Luke starts a special antiques investigation soon.'

Which explained why the town's antique dealers were gorilla about Mortimer.

'Lovejoy's scared about the chicks, Mummy.'

'No, darling. Lovejoy's just got a headache.'

I watched her go. Smart, attractive. Customs officers get all the luck. Warily I rose, testing my balance while Paul's hunting birds eyed me hopefully. I set off, trying to seem casual yet strong.

Ten minutes later I was wolfing fish, chips, mushy peas, and a ton of bread in Woody's nosh bar when Paul plonked himself down opposite and called for some chips. Woody does wonders with grease, fries everything in it except beans. His belly always shows through his unbuttoned shirt, black hair fungating up from below. Thick blue smoke hung in the air. His fag ash flaked down onto his rotting cakes. Why does TV never show places like Woody's, staple East Anglian nosh bar that keeps society going? TV cooks only tell you how to baste lampreys.

'Wotcher, Paul. Who's looking after your eagles?'

'My helper. Millicent.' He was lavish with the vinegar and brown sauce. 'She's especially good with harriers. They hunt in flocks, unlike the rest of—'

'Your wife Jenny,' I interrupted quickly. He had the grace to look sheepish. 'She and her pals threatened to hang me at Vice's wharf.'

'It's that lad of yours, Lovejoy. Mortimer's too

28

honest for his own good.'

'Don't you start.' I wondered why I'd come to find Paul in the first place, then my mind cleared. 'Here, Paul. You train your birds up Saffron Fields, right?'

'You want to see them fly, Lovejoy?'

'No, ta. You'll have seen the lodgers, posh Yanks?'

'Mmmh. The woman's a bit hairy. She's into the supernatural. Her husband Taylor Eggers is quite pleasant. He's into antiques, drops in the pub.'

But something felt awry about the Eggers. Or maybe I was just hoping to rile the bonny Susanne, seeing she talked Mortimer down.

'She one of these spirit mediums?'

'Definitely odd. Wouldn't like to cross her.'

'She doesn't mind your birds, then?'

Paul grimaced. 'She charges me a daily rate. Mortimer lets me fly them free, keep the rabbits down on the Short Tom pasture.'

'How come she doesn't know that Mortimer owns the place?'

'How come you don't know, Lovejoy?' he accused, then nodded understandingly. 'You're trying to keep out of the way, is that it?' And added, 'The boy's agents in St Edmundsbury do the letting. You know country folk, Lovejoy. They can keep mum for ever, if they want.'

Question two: 'There's some auctioneers who're twitchers, isn't there?'

'One bloke,' Paul corrected. 'He's a serious birdwatcher. You know him. Nice geezer, Lanny Langley-Willes. Sotheby's, Christie's, the rest.' He leaned close, the ultimate revelation. 'Birdwatchers hate being called twitchers, Lovejoy.'

29

And now the difficult question. 'Paul. What's Jenny looking for lately?'

His features didn't change when I mentioned his wife, but heartache always shows through.

'Regency and Victorian furniture. And some portrait.'

And now I really was worried. Antique dealers aren't secret. The trade can also be very laggardly. Yet all of a sudden the local dealers were ganging up to march on Rome, viz. me. Why? Something was going on, and I'd not heard about it. Worse, the slowest-selling antiques are always excellent Regency and early Victorian furniture. Check the auction records. It's true. Even the sale of a single scroll-pedestal card table would be talked of for days. Suddenly I wanted to ask if Jenny was still shacking up with Aspirin, but tactfully shelved the question.

'Does anybody know what the Eggers are after?'

'Some old portrait with a funny name. I'm just glad I'm not an antique dealer.' He looked at the coins I pushed across the table. 'Keep it, Lovejoy.'

'It's your change. Put it in your bucket. And ta.'

And I went in search of Rio Dauntless. If you want the truth, first find a liar. Nobody lies like Rio Dauntless, except me.

CHAPTER FIVE

Escape always looks greener on the other side of the fence. I sat on my doorstep trying to work out exactly *what* fence. My ancient Austin Ruby was just visible among tall weeds. Maybe I could sell it?

30

Except people complain because it lacks an engine, selfish sods.

Parenthood? Kids can keep it.

Children, I'd realized in my swift introduction to fatherhood, get into trouble (e.g. leasing Saffron Fields to loony Yankees) then drag you in so that it becomes your fault (e.g. ruining the antiques trade). And finally they concoct barmy schemes to make everything worse—'Hire actors, Lovejoy,' etc, etc.

I told the scrounging bird life, 'I'm off. Fend for yourselves, okay?' I ignored the reproachful stare of Crispin my hedgehog and left the lot of them to it.

*   *   *

The town nearest our village is ancient. Even its New Town area is old, so named because in AD 67 Queen Boadicea of the Ancient Brit Iceni tribe encouraged urban planning by razing the entire joint. I was glad to be leaving greenery and zooming back to civilization. Towns are safer. Sure, irate tribal queens may pillage and burn, but that's not half as creepy as a forest, it it?

A mile along the main road I got a lift from a pretty lady in a little whirry motor. She invited me for coffee. Eager to please, I accepted. Disappointingly it turned out to be a Salvosh sing-along hymn session in the Drill Hall. I didn't mind. In fact I felt quite good, swelling her numbers and doing my bit for God. He repaid my generosity by providing some cold bread pudding (which I can't stand) and fruit flan, which I like but which was horrible. I promised really sincerely to attend every

31

Thursday for ever and ever. See? Towns help. Countryside can do you in.

I wish I'd remembered that.

The market was just packing up when I got down Scheregate Steps among the barrows and awnings, and got hailed by Vi Anaconda on her market stall. She sells dry goods, which means dross like ribbons, children's plastic toys and suchlike tat. She sings—I use the term loosely—in taverns at night, doubling her money by brief sojourns in drinkers' motors before wending her way homeward like a good girl. It's where she gets her nickname. I like Vi.

'Wotcher, Vi.'

'Hello, Lovejoy.' She eyed me from beneath her striped cloth and the straggly balaclava she wears. 'Surprised to see you're still in one piece.'

'Misunderstanding, Vi.' My wayward brain talked me on. 'Hey, Vi. Why do birds' nicknames come last, and blokes' nicknames come first?'

'What the toss you on about?' She was stuffing her items into black bin bags.

'Well, Mirrorman Tate is Mirrorman, right? But you're Vi Anaconda. If you were a bloke, we'd call you Anaconda Vi, see?'

She paused to sigh. 'What're you after, Lovejoy?'

'I'm broke. I need—'

'A team of actors, right? Tina Maria Stevens says she'll do it.'

Everybody knows my business, except me.

'Er, look, love, I don't want birds.' Mortimer was only fifteen, for God's sake. Time enough for females when he was older. Also, I'd never even heard of a female divvy, so how could I make Tina

32

Maria into one?

'Stop it, Lovejoy.' Still narked, I glared while she sold some customer a flashing plastic sword and three flashing plastic bouncy balls. Then she said evenly, 'You're behaving like an outraged parent. Your lad's got more sense than you, twice your brains, ten times your savvy. Tina Maria lives near Saffron Fields anyway. She'll keep in line.'

Meaning tradition would control Tina Maria's potential lust? Tina Maria is neat, always brilliantly turned out, and has an antiques place called Tina Maria Interiors. She lives alone in a house—it's got a well in the living room; no, honest, it really has—and trades pre-Victorian gunge. She hungers to become an actress, which is like sinking on a rotting plank and hoping to swim to a different plank several shark-infested miles off. Thespians are a dodgy lot. I've heard that.

'Well, if there's nobody else.'

'How many do you need? I heard another four.'

'How'd you hear, Vi?' I was as secret as the UN.

'Some Yank in corduroys, been asking the market who's a divvy. Wants a naff painting of some crone.'

Mrs Eggers's bloke from among the leeks? I decided I needed some gelt to escape from this tangle.

'Ta, Vi. Look, could you lend me . . . ?'

She wouldn't half me a groat, stingy cow. Affluence comes in the door and charity flies out of the window.

Funny, but I felt odd, because something thrilling bulged a sheet on her stall. My chest bonged. A genuine antique within reach? Shoppers thronged. I could see nothing except that little mound. 'What've you got, luv?'

'Silver things, Lovejoy. Take a look.'

She uncovered a dozen items of genuine hallmarked silver. Knives, forks, serving and table spoons, fish servers. I drew breath.

'Sorry they're tarnished, Lovejoy,' she said apologetically. 'I've got a tin of scouring polish. Not had time.'

'Chuck it, Vi.' I frowned. They looked good, meaning silver that's supposed to be silver happens to be real silver, if you follow. 'How much?'

'For the lot?' Vi stopped bagging her crud and peered. 'You okay?'

I'd gone sick and had to lean against her stall, beads of sweat on my brow. She perched me on her barrow, propping me upright until I nodded that I felt fine.

'It's my cutlery, isn't it?' She gaped at the silver. 'I got them for a spade and three Cotton Easters.'

And I hadn't the wit to pretend they were worthless. All except one was standard 1930s stuff you can get anywhere. Tarnished but not deformed, they must have lain in a drawer, been sold as a job lot on some old biddy's passing. I winced as her fingers touched the one that mattered. She pounced.

'This?' she marvelled, holding it up. 'A frigging deformed teaspoon?'

'Be careful, you clumsy cow.' She dropped it into my palm, coming to ogle.

It's always other folk get lucky. Look for a short bulbous-bowled spoon with a straight rat's tail handle. (They fake them in Egypt and Turkey, so be careful.) Dealers call it a diamond-point, because its hexagonal handle ends in a faceted tip.

They also say its bowl is fig-shaped, which it's not—though you can always kid yourself in antiques. The main thing is the 'Arctic' leopard's head mark, in the bowl near the handle's insertion. I'd only ever seen one, and only heard of three.

'Is it rare, Lovejoy?'

'Edward IV, love, made about twenty years before Columbus sailed.'

She clapped her hands. 'How much?'

'It'll buy you a new car plus a round-the-world cruise. And,' I added, returning it like sacrificing a finger, 'leave some change to reward a helpful friend.'

'Great!' she cried. 'See you, Lovejoy. Good luck with the clowns!'

Help a friend, lose a friend, my old gran used to say. Tired, I drifted through the market, blaming Mortimer for getting me into this mess. Nothing for it, but to resume my job at the Pot Race Garden Nurseries, where I laboured on days that go horribly wrong. They'd be glad to see me.

*   *   *

You walk from town along the river until it goes under a bridge. There it forms a pool where a meadow slopes up to old people's bungalows. The Pot Race Garden Nurseries occupy a few acres, selling things to gladden gardeners. It's run by Merry and Tramway Adenath, who live in a troubled marital state. On quiet evenings you can hear their rage as far as Southwold. Their fighting script's unchanged these twenty years.

They divorced three (some say four) times, but remarried repeatedly from a deep longing to resume conflict. The reason is Merry wants herbaceous efficiency while Tramway wants uninhibited growth. Which means Merry wants the Eastern Hundreds sprayed with lethal non-degradables. Tramway wants chemicals banned. Merry stocks her shelves with sprays, toxins, and molecules of fearsome potency, all of them synthesized by evil alchemists and guaranteed to necrose Planet Earth for eternity. Tramway undoes this good work by propagating weeds. He develops sturdy dandelions and nettles resistant to every known herbicide, and grows them exactly where their pollen wafts onto Merry's potent sublimates. Marriage is total war.

Actually I'm on Tramway's side. You have to admit this couple is a good argument for bringing back duelling, though Planet Earth would lose out whoever won the shoot-out. I entered through the car park and reported for duty.

'Lovejoy!' Tramway was pricking out some desperately sick weeds into meagre soil. 'Good to see you. Sorry those dealers are going to hang you.'

'Wotcher, Tramway. I'll escape when I've a bob or two.' Hint, hint.

'Money? You're fired, Lovejoy.'

'Eh?'

He led me to where a few score of tiny trees struggled in dishes. I nodded, pleased. 'My handiwork. They're looking well, eh?'

'No, Lovejoy. They're ruined.'

'Can't be, Tramway,' I said proudly, not getting it. 'I repotted them.'

'Into?' he prompted, waiting. I noticed he looked more ferocious than usual. He held a stainless steel dibble, swung it to and fro in a

36

menacing manner.

'Into bigger pots!' I pointed. 'I used good compost, honest.'

'Why, Lovejoy?'

'They were stunted. Poor little sods were all gnarled. Give them a bit of sun and water, they'll grow like pantomime beanstalks.'

'They were priceless, Lovejoy. They were bonsai.'

'Eh?' I gaped. No wonder they'd seemed little.

'Yes, Lovejoy. Miniature trees, in pots. Some were eighty years old.'

'But their poor feet,' I said lamely, quickly edging towards the entrance where two children and their dad were lugging out some frondage.

'That's why I'm going to stab you to death, Lovejoy,' Tramway said, advancing. 'You owe me thousands for the damage you've done.'

'Let me help!' I called out, desperately trotting over and helping the dad and his kiddies. 'Car over there, is it?'

Screened by the little family, I reached their motor, then legged it. Merry jubilantly emerged to wave me off. I'd made a real pal in Merry by ruining Tramway's conservation programme, but maybe I'd spoiled her herbaceous skullduggery too. I couldn't risk it, so headed for the Antiques Emporium. Go back to antiques where you belong, you can't go far wrong. It's one of my more useless laws. I wondered if Tramway might give me some back pay.

Now all I could do was confront Mrs Eggers with a team of pretend divvies. At least I'd finish up with a bawbee and a bite. For me, that's a good day.

CHAPTER SIX

Gimbert's Auction Rooms were crowded. I was pleased, but worried Liza was in.

In prison slang, to 'chiff off' means to escape, slink away unseen, from the old word for a file or knife. Two years ago, sociologists did a survey on work defaulters. And who were the worst skivers? Answer: TV people—broadcasters, technicians. And second? The police, that's who. The sociologists didn't test themselves, clever old idlebacks that they were.

Liza used to be a posh sociologist before she clawed her way free to be a reporter. She has special links with the plod. Liza's a stringer, meaning she hangs about hoping for a political scandal, a train explosion, or some meteor to strike before her very eyes. Every reporter's dream. She distrusts me, unfairly, because of something that wasn't my fault. Gimbert has taken over the East Hill auctioneers and is now the biggest in East Anglia. He's a sombre grouser of ill fame who endears himself to all by upping his auctioneer's commission every millisec.

'Auctioneers win every time, Lovejoy,' Liza said, guessing from my expression. 'Today, he's going to charge buyers *and* vendors.'

'Wotcher, Liza. Any news?'

'Out, Lovejoy!' Gimbert called, imperious and testy, on his high seat. 'I'm not having you saying these genuine antiques are forgeries. Out!'

'I'm going, Gimby.'

Banishment didn't altogether displease me,

though I really did want to drift among the lots. In every auction, however tatty, musty dusty fortunes lurk, just waiting for me (or, less deservingly, you). Vague shapes of maybe brilliant Turners and Gainsboroughs hang on yonder cavernously dark walls. Cabinets of jewellery—currently the most prolific source of lucky finds—and grimy porcelains, all bring a different magic. My rule about auctions is that every auction contains gold. This is the reason that viewing days are like women, full of brilliant promise. Always have been, always will be.

The lads yelled delighted insults at Gimbert's command, the female dealers smiling silent jeers. I left, giving them all that backhanded wave the old Queen Mother had off to a tee, and went to stand on the pavement outside. There I annoyed Gimbert by pressing my nose against his murky window pane.

The reason I wasn't narked by this exile was that Mrs Alicia Domander was already halfway round Gimbert's load of tat and would be out soon. She always carries her dog. It's called Peshy, and is a special breed known as a Bichon something. She and I know that, lineage apart, little Peshy is truly special. It's a kleptomaniac, the cleverest thief in the Eastern Hundreds. Who suspects a dog?

Alicia herself wasn't a bad eye, for a human klepto, meaning that a good third of what she nicked was always decent quality. Like, if Alicia Domander casually inspected Fee and Brogan's displays of earrings, gems, necklaces, at our Saturday market, she'd be sure to come away with a dozen stolen pieces hidden about her shapely person, of which three, and maybe four, would be

39

genuine and not paste. I respect a woman whose batting average is that good. Usually 'stickers' (shoplifters, smalltime street thieves) only manage to steal one worthwhile item in twenty. It's their own fault. They don't concentrate. To a dyed-in-the-wool sticker the theft's the excitement. Alicia Domander once confessed that thieving was better than sex, which only goes to show how barmy some folk are.

'She'll not bring anything out, Lovejoy,' a familiar voice said.

My heart sank. Police, this early? 'Wotcher, Sep.'

Sep Verner had once been in the nick with me. I'd showed him how to paint like Van Gogh. To repay me and society he became a copper, CID no less. He takes bribes, to show that not all education is wasted. He's tall and languid, a better than average dresser, and hates blokes who wear earrings.

'Who's the Yank bird, renting Saffron Fields?'

'Eh? No idea, Sep.'

'Funny. Her husband gave your name to Grundy. Wants a search done on you. You should've heard us laugh.'

I eyed him. He grins friendly, but menace always does. I saw him kick a bloke nigh to death over an argument about a pop song. In another life.

'Search for what?' I said, just as Mrs Domander came briskly out, hesitated only slightly then walked on. Her expensive leather handbag was bulging. She wears the latest fashions. You never see her without a loony hat and lace gloves. She carried Peshy, who was looking smug.

'Past transgressions, Lovejoy. Come and be interviewed.'

Without a word to Mrs Domander or a gesture to the antique dealers crowding the auctioneer's windows, I entered his motor. We drove to the police station.

'This is a kindness on my part, officer,' I told Sep loudly as we disembarked. 'I only have a few minutes.'

Which was true. You can't be compelled to accompany the plod unless they arrest you. It's a mistake to go, because they keep you there, using all sorts of coercion, kidding you that they've limitless power when they haven't. (Incidentally, never let them into your home, either, because they're hard to get rid of. These are the forces of law and order I'm talking about.)

'This way, Lovejoy.' He walked ahead, entered a bare room. Somebody followed me in. I stood there like a prat. 'This the same man?' he asked.

'He's the one.' Taylor Eggers, still in garden gear.

'You still got it, Lovejoy?' Sep went conversational. 'Just give it back and this gent won't press charges.'

'Got what?' I asked, blank.

'His painting, the one you nicked.'

My eyes closed as headache struck. How could I nick an antique from Saffron Fields manor, when I hadn't, and my supposed offspring Mortimer was . . . ?

'Knock it off, Lovejoy. You were seen hanging around. It happens to be Mrs Eggers's ancestor. Show him, sir.'

The Yank brought out several papers, unfolded them. Receipt for an ancient portrait, shippers, customs stamps, import duty waivers, the lot.

41

'Better proof of honesty than the last opium shipment,' I joked feebly.

'Ha ha,' Sep said gravely. 'Where'd you cran it?'

A cran is a place where you leave stolen stuff. It can be a grand London auctioneer's warehouse, a remote godown amid tangled thickets, or simply a hollow brick in a disused garage. Mine is a tombstone corner in St Peter's churchyard on North Hill.

'Sorry, Sep. Never seen it. Sure, I went to Saffron Fields, to see . . .'

Oops. I petered out. I had a barmy job for the lovely Susanne Eggers, assemble several phoney divvies to suss out some antiques. This American bloke with the homely attire and greying hair, looking unflappable, was Mr Eggers. Presumably we were on the same side, but in which battle? And these Yanks thought Mortimer the village nut?

This is what I meant about families. Great invention, but they're chains of trouble.

'To see . . . ?' Sep prompted.

'Er, if I could get a job, Sep.' I shrugged, almost caught a nod from Mr Eggers. 'No luck, though.'

'Will you be bringing charges, Mr Eggers, sir?' Sep asked. I stared. Humility and the plod just don't go.

'You've been great, Sergeant,' Eggers said. 'I'll consult my lawyers. Thank you.'

We watched him leave. Sep exhaled a foul breath, truly naff. Paprika? Must be in the Police Training Manual; first get bad breath.

He clicked sundry controls. Tape deck off. No record of this next bit of chat.

'Bunce, Lovejoy.' He said it quietly. 'If you find the Eggers's missing portrait, I want a cut.'

42

'Money, Sep? I've got none.'

'Like me.' He gave a cadaver's grin. Yellow teeth. 'I need some. I'll be frank, Lovejoy. Got a bird in my sights. Married, though. Officer's daughter.'

'Birds are private. Can't help you.'

'You can.' We waited, some longer than others. He looked his old self, shifty, on the cadge. 'She's class. Her hubby's in antiques. Lame, though. I know I could get her—if I'd bunce enough.'

He wanted wealth, to lure an antique dealer's wife? Who doesn't? It never happens in real life. If I ever get a wadge, some bird dissects it from me. If some bonny woman happens along, I'm always broke. It's how life is.

'Why ask me, Sep?'

'This American woman's well connected. She's the ex of the American consul. He's called Sommon, official residence in Norwich.'

Yet Mr Sommon still frolics with his ex-wife, aka Mrs Susanne Eggers, currently leasing Saffron Fields with her new husband, the benign portrait-hunting Taylor Eggers?

'Find the portrait, Lovejoy. It could mean big gelt.' He must have noticed my mistrust, so added the robber baron's time-honoured incentive. 'You'd be doing me a big favour, Lovejoy. Fiddle it for me, I'd see you right.'

Unlikely. Hoods help police, sure, but police only help themselves.

'Okay,' I said, with what sincere honesty I could. 'You'll keep it fair, eh?'

'Honest,' he said, and let me go.

An hour later I traced Mrs Alicia Dormander. She was having tea by the fountain. She'd already

43

sold her thefts, to my disappointment. She stood me tea and a wad. A real lady. I honestly like her. The cosmetics on her face are always so thick that her face cracks when she smiles. Rouge, mascara, lipstick, foundation, it becomes a mass of craque lure, like an Old Master. You have to admire class.

'Look, love,' I said. 'Let me see your next lot before you sell it, okay? I'm running on empty.'

'How many times must I tell you, Lovejoy? There's only one deal—do a countrywide sweep with me. We'd clean up.'

'Whatcher mean, love?'

Her dog had its own plate and bowl on the table. It smirked.

'You suss out the viewings.' She smiled. Her mask crizzled. 'Tell me which antiques are genuine. Me and Peshy do the rest. Fifty fifty.'

'Lend us a few zlotniks, eh? I saw you coming out of Gimbert's.'

'The money's for Peshy's grooming session, isn't it, Peshy-Weshy?'

She clasped the smug little wart to her cleavage. I watched with envy.

'Okay,' I said, broken. I come second to a dog the size of a hamster. 'It's a deal. I'll say when, and where, right?'

'Travel expenses as we go, Lovejoy?'

I was so dejected I even agreed to that.

*   *   *

Rio Dauntless can lie his way into history books. He's famous. He's a bloke with squid eyes, hunched from stooping as he collects money for good causes. He adopts shabby gentility.

44

'Dress up, or too grubby,' he once warned me in all seriousness, 'they'll give you snot all. They think you're either rich or Fagin, see? Get it just right, and you'll have to open a bank account.'

He was a composer once, trained at Oxford's famed school of music. Except he wasn't, because he's been everywhere, done everything, and done none. Rio Dauntless was born a liar.

'Don't say liar, Lovejoy,' he rebuked me once. 'Say fibber. The difference is criminality. A fib's innocent, like you, like me. A liar is a criminal.'

'Like you, like me?' I'd asked. He only shrugged.

I found him collecting in the station caff. It's self-service. There he was, going from table to table, holding an official-looking collecting tin. He has a plastic identity-tag on a blue ribbon. He's quite small, looks dour yet quite spruce. I listened to his spiel.

'Good day. Please forgive the intrusion. I'm collecting for flowers, to mark the road accident last year on the northbound carriageway of the trunk road intersection. I want to lay a wreath. Poor girl. I'm only asking for your smallest coin. Just one. It was at the flyover, a foreign pantechnicon. If you do not wish to contribute, God bless you.'

It's at this point that Rio smiles and sadly moves away—only to be called back. People force coins into his tin. He demurs, then graciously gives way. Women usually take him at his word, one coin, but blokes are extra generous, because all small-car family men hate lorries. Astonishingly, they remember the tragic accident, even though it never happened. There simply is no trunk road intersection. Nor a flyover, no northbound

45

carriageway. Rio says people like a fable.

'Excuse me, sir,' he asked me, grovelling up. 'Please forgive the intrusion. I'm collecting . . . Oh, Christ. It's you, Lovejoy.'

'I heard about the tragedy,' I said loudly, not to let him down. 'Here you are, my man.'

I dropped a non-existent farthing in his tin. One good myth deserves another. I left then, to sit by the gaming machines. He emerged and joined me.

'Odd how many remember non-existent accidents. They get worked up. The women ask what flowers I'll get. It's hard keeping track. I told one old dear alstroemeria. She said get carnations, symbol of peace. Whatcher want, Lovejoy?'

'Who's these Yanks at Saffron Fields, then?'

'Her?' He gave a laugh, except his laughs only sound, never show. That's because he's in character. 'She's a psychic. Does tarot cards, the future.'

'What's she up to? Wants me to—'

'Get some actors? I heard. She was wed to that American consul Sommon from Anchor Key in Norwich. Her current husband is—'

'Got all that, Rio. She's after some portrait.'

'Dunno.' He searched his mind for scraps. 'The consul's a big London investor. They divorced three years back.'

Could that be? 'Yanks make their millions in New York and Los Angeles. That's why they're all millionaires.'

'He insures antiques. She recruits investors for him.'

'An antiques club?'

They were common enough. I'd not heard of a local one starting up, not at this level. Usually

46

they're small fry, everybody chipping in a shilling a week and hoping to get a cheap Rembrandt.

'Last I heard, Bernicka was seeing her. Trying to communicate with Leonardo da Vinci.'

Bernicka is enough to make a saint groan. I groaned.

'Nobody else?'

He looked askance. Like I said, squid eyes, trying to find a rock. He was an enemy to me once, hoping for neutrality. Finally, out it came.

'Remember Vestry?'

'Aye. Topped himself.' One of our local tragedies.

He came to a decision. 'Suicide. I'd look into his death, if I were you.'

'Sep Verner. Wasn't he Soco?'

'Scene of the Crime Officer? Yep. Don't say I said, eh?'

'Now, would I?' I said evenly. 'Is that it?'

I said ta, and thumbed a lift to town. Consistent rumours, then, but not much else. I'd been tempted to tap Rio for a few zlotniks, except it didn't seem proper, him collecting for flowers for that terrible accident . . . I caught myself. It's hard not to be dragged in when the lie—sorry, fib—is that good. I ought to have remembered that, too.

CHAPTER SEVEN

Nobody has worries like me. Mine drift behind like a vapour you're never free of.

In the early hours of the following night I was in a motor car with Olive Makins, parked on the edge of Riverside Park by the boating pond. After making smiles we nodded off. Olive's a buxom lass on her fifteenth fiancé (she never weds), and says this time she'll stick by him until death do them part, or at least until Easter Sunday. More importantly, she's secretary of the local auctioneers' group. She knows her worth, does Olive. Her betrothed Victor is a hard-working antiques valuer. Incidentally, never, never ever, trust valuers. The law won't protect you if they guess wrong about your house or anything else.

My leg had gone gangrenous. Olive was no lightweight. She'd crushed my thigh between her shoulder and the handbrake—don't ask for details. I groaned at the pins and needles. She burst out laughing.

'Honestly, Lovejoy! You're as bad as that Yank.' She snuggled closer, heavier still. The windows were misted. My leg thrombosed.

'What Yank?'

'He almost went comatose on me! You men!'

'What Yank?' I pretended to be offended. Women love jealousy.

'Now, now, Lovejoy.' She fluttered her false eyelashes. I could feel the gale. Like being in a wind tunnel. 'He'll go back to the US when he's done the scam. You've no need to worry.'

'Who is he?' I put on my feeble I'm-all-envy.

'He's very big—I mean powerful.' She tittered. The motor shook but managed to stay upright. 'He's an insurance syndicate.'

'Now, Olive!' I chided, as gangrene crept upwards. My waist, I swear, went numb. 'You know everything about dealers in the Eastern Hundreds!'

'No, honest, Lovejoy. His investors keep

48

themselves to themselves. You get kneecapped just for asking their telephone numbers.'

Mercifully the stress of thinking made her budge. She reached for her handbag, switched on the courtesy light and started trowelling on lipstick, mascara, moisturizer, powder. The air thickened. I wheezed. She munched her lips like they do. It always fascinates me. I keep wondering if make-up hurts. They say it doesn't.

'There was that prior, wasn't there? He was one. You knew him.'

'Look, daaarling. That bitch from Leeds who topped her husband was one. I met that ponce from Norway who inherited half their bleeding country. There's that Belgian royal who always has his hand in the till. And his ex-wife lodging at Saffron Fields. Them's the lot.'

'Shhh, Olive.' This time I was serious. Nobody stirred out in the dark, but you can never tell. 'They say her husband Taylor is decent.'

'Him? Weak as water. Doesn't even have the nerve to make his bitch do her bed work. You can always tell. He's another who came sniffing round.'

'He fell for you, Olive. Like me.'

'Him? Cold as a fish, lovey.' She clicked her handbag, turned smiling at me in the gloaming. 'Still, he dined me, gave me a diamond pendant. See it? Not bad for two photocopies and a list of addresses!'

'Of what?' I heard her snort of derision. I'd been too blunt. 'You could charm any man with a bus ticket, dwoorlink.'

'Do you really mean that, Lovejoy?' she purred.

'Course. Hang on, love.'

I hauled the pendant jewel from her cleavage, no

mean feat. I squinted at it against the glim. I sensed something, only by guess in the bad light, but I wasn't wrong. If the American bloke at Saffron Fields had used Olive, then he was a cheapskate. And here I was doing exactly the same thing.

'This is a diamond, love, but the tom trade calls these Light Brown Rejects.'

The tom trade means jewellery, from Cockney rhyming slang: tomfoolery, jewellery. In fury she switched on the interior light, revealing our clandestine meeting to the universe. I shrank in my seat.

'Not real?' she shrieked, as secret as Radio One.

I hadn't a loupe with me, but did the trick of squeezing together two fingers and a thumb to magnify sight in one eye. The diamond was stuffed with brown debris. Still genuine, but hardly worth a train fare. Diamonds are graded according to purity, flaws, size, other factors. It was my chance to maybe learn a bit more about Taylor and Susanne Eggers.

'This thing should be for industry.' I let go, and smiled my most sympathetic smile. 'They're the ones sold at multiple stores, dwoorlink.'

'The bastard!' she breathed. 'After all I did!'

'I'm sure he appreciated . . .'

'For two auctioneers' boxes and a list of dealers?' She was in floods of tears. 'He said it was a priceless effing diamond that the Queen once wore . . .'

And so on. I couldn't wait to get away fast enough, now I'd found out what I wanted. I know I sound horrible, but I'd a million excuses, most of them honestly nearly almost quite good. I tried to make it easier for Olive by telling her the tale.

'Listen, dwoorlink. What time is it?'

She told me some ungodly hour, still wailing.

'Look,' I said, all sudden brainwave. 'There's just time to get hold of Diamond Pease. He'll still be there! Quick, love! Go, go!'

'Who? What for?'

'He might change it for us. Into a valuable stone!' Some hopes.

She struggled upright and switched on the ignition, enthusiasm returning.

'Who's Diamond Pease?'

How the hell should I know? I thought, narked. I'd just made him up.

'Works in Hatton Garden, London's diamond district. An old pal. Might not be able to do anything, but at least we can ask, right?'

'Right! Right!'

We careered from the rural scene, me eager as Olive to reach civilization—that is, the town centre miles from the woods and fields I detest. As she dropped me at the war memorial I kissed her long and passionately, thanking her for a wonderful tryst. I asked to keep the pendant. She said okay. I promised I'd throttle the Yank with it if I bumped into him. Wish I'd not said that now, but what can you do?

Olive had given me enough to be going on with.

'See you soon,' I promised as she gunned away.

She called something that I wish now I'd heard, but I was already limping off down the road, my leg rediscovering circulation.

*   *   *

Who had the power to manipulate police, the

51

judiciary *and* all the local antiques dealers including auctioneers, plus the local hoods? Nobody, that's who. Meaning no one person. But there is one mob—note the term—that has. It is mightier than the sum of its parts.

It's called the raj.

Some people call it the tally, the old word for counting, as if they're a benign club of elderly gents, all quill pens and ledgers.

Wrong.

They say the raj began when Raffles was rollicking round the Far East. Or maybe in Hong Kong or India back in the days of the Raj proper when pirates—loyal and freebooters alike—rioted over the globe trying to keep one horizon ahead of a vengeful Royal Navy. Me, I believe the raj began in the horrendous slums of Seven Dials or London's evil Arches, or St Giles Parish where starving folk had to steal for bread.

Dealers speak of it with bated breath. I'd never met, as far as I know, anybody in the raj. There's supposed to be from nine to fourteen of the blighters. Who they are nobody knows. There was talk that Big John Sheehan was in. And that Willie Lott had tried to gain entry, and been rejected. I gulped. I was terrified of Sheehan.

Olive was supposed to be in the know. Now, I wasn't so sure.

The raj frightens me, like everything unknown. They're said to top, as in eliminate, three or four antique dealers each year, and to be involved with arms handlers, drug lords, and political taipans you don't mess with. They control some of the great auction houses but from without. That is to say, they charge each auction a fee to simply allow it to

52

go ahead, especially if it's going to change, say, the price of Impressionist paintings or early New England walnut furniture or Hepplewhite items.

I put Olive's pendant in my pocket and forgot about it.

* * *

For peace of mind, I paused to watch the Women's Institute making cakes. They're good at it. Occasionally I help out, shifting tables, lugging chairs. They give me edibles that have been damaged in transit, and a cuppa. I sat on the grass watching and thinking. I'd seen Susanne Eggers and Consul Sommon leaving my cottage. Ex-spouses, who'd left evidence of passion.

I reflected. Are we really the people we *say* we are?

* * *

We're a rotten species. Yet every so often something restores your faith, makes you think we're not so bad after all. Like the great Cash Dispenser Bonanza. True story, incidentally:

It happened just before the Millennium celebrations. A bloke rushed into a pub calling, 'Free money! Free money!' Folk thought, hello, old George has been at the ale again, and continued chatting, drinking.

Except it was true.

Across the dark street, nine o'clock at night, a bank's cash machine inexplicably started giving out *twice* what you asked for, and debiting your account with *half*. The crowd flowed across the road to

53

examine this curious phenomenon. Jubilation!

Within seconds an orderly queue formed. One bloke even took charge, calling out, 'Three goes only, please. Then return to the back of the queue. Keep in line. Please don't obstruct the pavement . . .' And would you believe, a police motor cruised by. The bobby asked was everything in order. 'Yes, thanks, constable,' the line replied, party hats at rakish angles, blowing razzers and laughing merrily. 'Happy New Year,' the bobbies said, driving off. The revellers replied, 'Thanks, lads, and the same to you!'

There was no riot. No shoving, no weapons, just people taking their turn with lots of, 'No, please go ahead, mate. I've already had a go,' and all that. There, in rain-sodden northern England, order ruled until the machine gasped out its last note, when the crowd returned to their wassailing.

Okay, people in effect robbed the bank. But the point is valid: people's good manners withstood the severest test of all, which is unbridled greed gratified free of charge. Hearing of the incident warmed the cockles of my heart.

When you are feeling down, though, your sourest convictions are sometimes confirmed. Like Rita. She's a legend in the Eastern Hundreds. Rita was a restless lady. I knew her distantly. She was alluring, evidently very rich. I'd have loved her given half a chance. She got through four husbands, accumulating investments. The trouble was, every penny was in her baby granddaughter's name.

Came the day when the world's watch collectors were stunned by the announcement that a Supercomplication was on sale. Rita snapped into action, announced that she was going to buy it for her baby granddaughter. We talked of nothing else for weeks. Antique dealers even applauded her as she swanned round. Rita was going for the Big One!

The Supercomplication?

Back in 1933, a firm called Patek Philippe in Switzerland made watches. Nothing new. Two American watch collectors were rivals. Henry Graves ran a bank, Mr Packard—*that* one—made cars. Being American, they were multi-millionaires. Obligingly the Swiss watchmakers set to, turning out ever more intricate and complicated watches to please the two friends. Until 1933, when the Henry Graves Supercomplication hit the road. It was almost impossibly refined: handcrafted, gold, nearly a thousand parts, it eclipsed all timepieces. It even gauged the wind, tides, moons. Clearly the last word. The rival Yanks called time, as it were.

This brilliant instrument was Rita's focus. She would buy the 1933 Patek Supercomplication for her baby granddaughter, who would be set up for life! Everybody loved Rita's devotion! The baby's trust funds were mobilized. Came the day when Rita embarked for the exciting Sotheby's sale amid an adoring crowd. I went to see her off on the London train, calling 'Good luck, love!' like the rest of the duckeggs. Jessica from Trinity Street's Antiques Nookery lit candles for Rita's success in Lion Walk church.

Rita reached London with her sack of money.

And kept going. And vanished.

That was the last anybody saw of Rita or the money. She never bid at the auction. She now lives with swarthy youths in Marbella, or on some Greek island, or Bali. Rumours vary. Jessica angrily sticks pins in a Rita doll every Lady Day. I organized a whip-round for her granddaughter, who is six now. Her parents run a garden centre out on the Ipswich road, struggling to make ends meet.

The lesson is that we're a rotten species.

Antiques make crooks of us all. Is it the notion of some thing for nothing? My erstwhile lady Maya, who sells antique cosmetic potions in the Arcade, says it's the terror of thinking that some worthless trinket—maybe an ordinary dress ring discovered on pantomime fripperies, or that ugly brooch from Auntie Mabel's bequest—will suddenly turn out to be a priceless heirloom. We argue about this. She says it's the risk of nearly having chucked out Grampa's valuable old rocking chair, or given Auntie Edith's dull old clip-on to some jumble sale, that makes everybody desperate. Calamity breathtakingly avoided, and the relief that cascade of money finally brings, is the cause of the joys and murders. 'It's like sexual love,' Maya says repeatedly. 'Bliss, ecstasy, triumph, disaster.' Maybe she's right. I dunno.

Vestry was the last antique dealer to die in odd circumstances. Rio Dauntless had reminded me.

CHAPTER EIGHT

She is prettier than most, but gets me mad. She's always apologizing for being fifty-three, then fifty-four, and so on as the clock ticks. I shouted hello, looked round the door, and saw that she'd really got on. The horse was now head height, ugly as sin

56

and all out of proportion. She sculpts it, dawn to dusk.

'You wish me happy birthday, Lovejoy,' she flared at me from behind the great statue's shoulder, 'and I'll strangle you.'

Bernicka (she made the name up; she was plain Glory once) is a sculptress, and loves Leonardo da Vinci.

'Never entered my mind, Bernicka.' I'd forgotten her birthday, was why. 'Looks good.'

It looked horrible. Who'd want that damned great thing? Terracotta clay, made of any old junk that solidifies, Bernicka slaps it on seemingly at random. I was amazed that it even looked vaguely equestrian. She does it in her husband's garage to rile him.

'You're gorgeous, Bernicka.' True, but women sense you're up to something.

She came round the statue, glaring. Coated in reddish dust, quite small, long hair, neat as a grape. She's solaced me several times, mainly to do her bloke down. She hates Jeb because he's not Leonardo da Vinci. He hates her for loving Leonardo.

'What d'you want, Lovejoy?'

'Nothing!' I beamed my sincerest. 'How did my portrait turn out?'

Last month I'd drawn her making her lover's horse statue. I drew her in sanguine—a kind of ancient reddish pastel I make myself with gum tragacanth. It was superb. I'd had to use skimmed milk because oxides are swine to shape into proper finger-long rods for sketching. Little Sarah and Charlotte from down the lane, eight and six respectively, shape them for me. They're so neat.

I'm not. It's galling to see infants fashion Conté pastels ten times better than I can.

'It's there.'

Against the far wall, among Jeb's derelict motors and bits of engines, was my framed portrait of Bernicka. I'd got her lovely eyes exactly. I'd done her (I mean painted) in that earthy brown-red the Old Masters loved. Nothing wrong with monochrome, incidentally, though it's currently unfashionable. The real trouble is that you fall for a woman when you paint her portrait. It's impossible not to. You have to gaze at her features, drink her into your mind. Peer into a deep pool, you fall in. Above my sketch was a photocopied drawing of Leonardo da Vinci, Bernicka's adored lover. That's why she's always going to mediums, psychics, spiritualists. She sends Leonardo messages. He fails to reply.

'Oooh.' She moaned with unrequited lust at Leonardo. She always does that.

'Still got the languishes for him?'

It's no wonder Jeb gave up. They sleep apart. She has a ton of love implements in her bedroom. All are devices with which a lovelorn lady might achieve solitary arousal. I once pointed out that Leonardo da Vinci has been dead for centuries, *requiescat in pace*. She says I'm too stupid to understand.

The horse is Leonardo's uncompleted, ill-fated monstrosity *Il Cavallo*. I hate the damned thing. He planned it in Milan after 1493, but only got to the model stage. Everybody thought it okay, except the French armies strolled in to depose Leonardo's boss, Duke Ludovico. Shamefully, the French soldiery shot it full of arrows—short of target

58

practice, you see. Milan's got a modern bronze replica of this giant horse, because making Leonardo's dreams come true is a money-making industry. Magazines these days are full of his never-were bridges, and buildings he built only in sketched fancy.

Next to my portrait hung several bowie knives. I eyed them uneasily.

'Knives,' she said. 'Some Yank bitch in Grand Rapids has made a crappy copy of *Il Cavallo*. I'll stab her when I get the chance.'

She means it.

'You do know that Leonardo's nag was going to be over three times taller than a man?' Way over twenty feet, in fact.

Her eyes misted. 'Yes. But I am unworthy of my master.'

Bernicka always was off her trolley. 'Don't run yourself down. Love's strong stuff.'

'No, Lovejoy.' Genuine tears made clean wadis down her umber-dusted cheeks. 'If my love were perfect, it would bring my darling Leonardo back.'

'Well, there is that,' I said weakly. Agree with everything, I might get what I'd come for. 'Your nag is really, er, nice.'

It wasn't. It was a mound of clay in a rural garage. Trouble is, Bernicka has no idea of art. She's tried her hand at everything. Her enthusiasms go in rushes. Last June it was encaustic Roman painting. July she was a dancer, with the co-ordination of a yak. September she took up the cello, tone deaf naturally.

Some women have this fatal attraction. Mary Queen of Scots had it, they say, so that even villeins kneeling in fear of their lives would lust after her.

59

Lord Nelson's Emma Hamilton, despite her eternally filthy unwashed hair, had it. Nell Gwynne, King Charles's gorgeous Cockney orange seller of Covent Garden, had it. And Bernicka. Other women hate Bernicka. Can't for the life of me see why. Us blokes adore her. The thing is, even after you've made serious smiles with Bernicka you're just as susceptible as if you never had, if you follow. A man's vulnerable to all women, of course, which is the reason that any woman can have any man any time she chooses, though women don't realize this. With Bernicka, popes and saints would come a-flocking if she simply beckoned. Where was I? Lying that her pot nag was really nice.

'Will Leonardo approve, Lovejoy?' she asked wistfully, gazing up at her hideous blob.

'I'm sure he would, will, er . . .' I gave up on tense. 'Does,' I concluded firmly. 'Look, love. Will you seduce a bloke for me?'

'How dare you!' etc, etc.

Twenty minutes later we finished a cup of tea on her couch and she was agreeing yes, certainly. By then she'd dusted herself off and was arguing her fee.

'Get me anything of Leonardo's,' she decided. 'From his very own fingers.' She moaned at the thought of his fingers.

'Impossible,' I said sadly. It was going as I'd planned. 'The few Leonardo items in our rusty old kingdom all belong to famous people.'

Daintily she blotted a tear. 'I know that, Lovejoy.'

'Bernicka!' I cried, doing my aggrieved horror act. 'You can't mean . . .'

'That you rescue my darling's precious creation

from some undeserving owner? Of course I do!'

That's women and morality. Love is the *Open sesame!* that rolls aside all ethics. To some birds, love is no more than a code word; say it and you're in, physically replete and thankful it worked. To other women, it's the solemn pronouncement of serious lifelong commitment. To Bernicka, it was run-leap-splash into the hot spring of life, as long as she could convince herself that da Vinci was in there somewhere. I don't understand it.

I asked, fingers crossed, 'You can't seriously mean Lord Orpen's parchment drawing of Leonardo's horse?'

'Does he have a Leonardo drawing? Yes, him then.'

'That's unfair, Bernicka!' I cried angrily. 'I might get caught!'

'Do it, darling, or I won't seduce anybody for you.' She caught my hand and pulled me down. 'Please.'

What can you say? Broad daylight, the parlour doors wide open, curtains not drawn, we made rapturous agreement. I awoke an hour later. She'd gone back to slapping clay onto her sculpture. I finished her biscuits and tottered off to catch the bus, shouting a *so-long* into the garage. I'd reached town before I realized she hadn't even asked the seducee's name. I phoned from the Zodiac Tea Rooms, trying to speak quietly so the elderly ladies sipping their Earl Grey wouldn't eavesdrop.

'Wotcher, Bernicka. I called to say ta for, er, tea and that.' Then I told her the Yank at Mortimer's manor. 'That's the, ah, beneficiary. Understand? You've been there to read tea leaves, I think. Taylor Eggers, your psychic's husband.'

She paused a bit too long. I felt a twinge of worry as she asked, 'Exactly why am I doing this, Lovejoy?'

'While you're, ah, resting, you can ask him what the hell he and his missus are up to. Ta, love. You're great. Darling? I just want you to know that I've never felt such deep emotion . . .' I listened. 'Hello? Hello?'

She'd gone. Leonardo's contemporary Vascari once said the maestro's every action 'was divine'. Evidently my passion hadn't matched up. Still, I should care. I felt marvellous. I'd received the ultimate gift from the lovely Bernicka, and my plan was one step nearer completion. I smiled weakly at the eavesdropping tea drinkers and made my way out amid the murderous traffic, where a bloke could feel safe.

*   *   *

Pets are a puzzle. Cats cause me anxiety because they eat birds; statistics say thirty million a year. Dogs have fangs, and eat cats. Horses are a big worry to me because they weigh ten tons. I fight unendingly against my garden birds' habits, because they scoff worms. Every dawn I feed the robin cheese, if I've got some, to wean him off various fauna. No hopes. He noshes what I give him then goes digging worms in my compost, dirty little devil.

So I was especially guarded climbing up the rickety steps of Cedric's wooden two-storey shack in the darkness that night. A snuffle sounded, very like distant thunder.

'Wotcher, Elk,' I called nervously. 'Get Cedric,

62

okay?'

Waiting, I couldn't help remembering Divina. She was one of these horsey lasses, very splendid in her pink jacket and jodhpurs. The trouble was the horse she bestrode. It was the size of Lambeth Palace. She used to do its skin with some sort of wire, hours at a time. Once, she made me— threatening celibacy if I didn't—come and see her polish the damned beast. It leaned against me, asphyxiating me by compression. While I gasped my last she exclaimed, 'Oh, Lovejoy! Animals really *like* you!' I was supposed to admire this monster for giving me a prolonged slobbering crush. See? The problem with pets is people.

A footfall sounded. 'That you, Lovejoy?'

'Wotcher, Cedric,' I said, then screeched as I heard a bolt slide, 'Don't open the bloody door!'

A chain settled to silence. I mopped my brow. Elk is a dog the size of, well, an elk, but with fangs not horns. It likes me. Elk's idea of a greeting is to place both its front paws on my shoulders and gaze into my eyes, its mouth open, fangs a-drool. Saying hello is an orgy, but resembles the prelude to a snack.

'Go down, Lovejoy.'

Relieved, I descended the swaying steps and he let me in. The workshop is beautiful. Most folk would hate it: cold, badly lit except for a bank of intense lights at the workbench. Untidy as hell, but definitely the place to be.

Cedric entered, wheezing and shuffling. He's eighty-four, and the classiest manuscript forger in the Eastern Hundreds. You'll have seen those certificates of provenance on those splendid antiques at London auctions. Well, Cedric turns

63

them out. Five a week, when he's really motoring. I like Cedric. Think of some old cartoon alchemist, floor-length robes, slippers, skull cap, specs on droopy wire, straggly beard, and you have Cedric Cobbold, Esquire, master forger.

'Evening, Lovejoy.' He grinned, gappy teeth, whiskers fluttering. A joke was on its way. 'I see,' he said, snuffling, 'they haven't hanged you yet!' He creaked and swayed. I helped him to a stool by the workbench while he recovered. He laughs like a distant zephyr. Unless you know him you think nothing is happening. I waited the riot out.

'It was only their joke, Ced.'

He sobered. 'Not so, Lovejoy. That Dennis is pressing for it. He's got into money trouble. A frightened man. And three others. Your son—'

'Mortimer's okay, wack. I've cleared it all up.'

'They mean damage, Lovejoy. That lady Mrs Eggers called the raj.'

My belly griped.

'How can she, for God's sake?' It came out as a terrified squeak. 'She's a Yank. She's no right. She can't.'

'She's got some contact in there.' He sighed, adjusted his spectacles. Respectfully I kept quiet, hoping. Instead the silly old sod finally came out with, 'The last full meeting of the raj last year was on the feast day of St Sebbi, King of Essex. I distinctly recall—'

'You daft old burke!' I yelled. A thunderous growl shook the boards upstairs as Elk stirred. I silenced. 'I meant, er, good gracious! That long ago?'

'Almost certain of it, Lovejoy. Though we can't take St Sebbi's date of AD 697 as altogether

64

proven, can we?'

'Certainly not,' I said, sweating, because my death sentence might well be hanging out there in the dark. 'Look, Ced. Sorry about this, but I need a drawing of Leonardo's *Il Cavallo*.'

'What in?' The old savant didn't turn a hair. 'Silver point? The Three Crayons? How much licence will you allow?'

You have to admire class. Here was me, disturbing this elderly sage at midnight, and he goes straight to the heart of the problem. True professionalism.

Silverpoint is a sharpened piece of lead or lead-tin alloy. Ancient artists drew outlines, leaving scarcely any indentation. They'd then maybe fill the sketch out using white chalk, black argillite or red chalk—*à trois crayons*, as the French have it.

'I don't want sepia, Cedric.'

There's a pathetic tendency these days among stupid forgers of Old Master drawings. They're all duckeggs, bone idle. They assume that if they make a dilute solution of some pigment—raw ochre down to burnt umber—then call it sepia and do a drawing on Woolworths' paper, it will pass as something dashed off by Michelangelo and be worth a million. Laughable. You see scores of these freaks in any country auction (and in sales in capital cities, I might add). Sepia proper is ink of the cuttlefish, only fashionable in the late eighteenth century.

'Leonardo, to modern innocents, means oak-gall and copperas.'

Cedric smiled affectionately at the bottles ranked on his workbench. I knew he loved Francis Clement's old slow recipe of 1587. It's long out of fashion, because modern forgers haven't Cedric's patience. They heat the ink with French wine and ox blood. Clement let it fester for days. See? Patience.

'You still use the old labels, Cedric.'

'I'm not stupid.'

We chuckled. Any intruder hoping to steal Cedric's precious forger's ingredients would be baffled by *Green Vitriol* and *Aleppo Originale* (only ancient names for ferrous sulphate and galls from oak trees). It's Cedric's game. For a few minutes we chatted about Hebborn, the modern English forger who used rotting acorns instead of galls and did pretty well. Then Cedric got down to it.

'Can I suggest bistre, Lovejoy? I have ancient paper. I could split a sheet, though that would cost dearly.'

Gulp. That warning was grave. Cedric was never cheap. Splitting a sheet of heavy ancient linen-rag paper is a fearsome risk, because you might ruin the priceless antique sheet altogether. If it's done just right, you finish up with two sheets instead of one. You then earn a fortune from both. It's done with two pieces of heavy felt and starch paste. See a true forger like Cedric do it, you can keep your Beethoven symphonies. They're not half so beautiful.

'Has to be, Ced. Aye, bistre's okay.'

This is nothing more than soot in solution, used as a kind of drawing ink by the Old Masters with their reed and quill pens. You can still buy bistre, but I like Cedric's. He burns willow, beech or pine branches out on the beach, and uses the charcoal and caught soot (on glass plates, incidentally, if you do it yourself). It sounds easy but it's not. He also makes his own quill and reed pens in the old way. God knows who'll have his skill when he finally pops his clogs.

'I'll use powdered pumice stone for lacing the paper, Lovejoy.'

This is an old way of dressing paper before doing a drawing. The ancients used it. I arranged a time to meet in Tolleshunt D'Arcy, where I would do the burglary for Bernicka, said ta and left before he could ask me for a deposit. He might have summoned Elk to enforce his request.

The rest of the night was spent peacefully, meaning lying awake, sweating at what I was drifting into.

CHAPTER NINE

It isn't only love that fails to recognize its own significance. It's everything. For instance, a theatre in the USA introduced the talkies twenty years before they actually caught on. Cameraphone opened one Monday in 1907. Despite the appeal of Victrola records scratching out audible sounds to match the film's action, the show closed on the Tuesday. It happens in antiques, too. The immortal Turner—greatest artist ever—had to argue with his housekeeper every morning when she brought out his palette because she was eternally stingy with his blue. Lapis lazuli cost the earth, so she eked it out in miserable amounts, driving the maestro to distraction.

Sorry for the digression. I'm making excuses, on account of the terrible thing that happened. Not realizing love is a flaw in a person.

St Peter's church hall stands at the top of North Hill. Tinker, my barker, sleeps in the churchyard on good nights. He tries to break in if it's raining, but Christian charity excludes vagrants and other poor. When he's sloshed, he kips in some antique shop and tells the police, should they bother to leave their snooker game and respond to the security alarm, that he's fallen asleep *in situ* after making a delivery. He was nowhere, which worried me. He's got a cough like thunder so I couldn't miss him. A group of folk huddled in the doorway as I entered the churchyard. The actors I'd phoned Tina for.

Dunno what it is about burgeoning youth, but they all look so blinking tired. In their teens they somehow become exhausted, bags under their eyes, drained of energy. Those that aren't skeletal are bulbously heavy, all floppy thighs. A bloke I know reckons he can date old films by merely looking at the body fat on the extras. Some smoked thin hand-rolled scraggly fags.

'Wotcher. Are you the actors, please?'

'That's us,' a bloke said, ready for a fight. 'I live in the park.' He was the scrawniest of the bunch, his clothes fraying, as if he'd left home and never washed since. 'I'm Larch. Classical and Stanislavski acting.'

'Larch.' Evidently a tree guardian from remote forests. 'Come in, please.'

'Tina told us wait outside.'

'Did she, now.'

Drill halls and church halls are the same the world over, musty, dusty, rusty, with the dank aroma of unswept floors. Tina was lazing on the stage while some bloke desperately urged everybody once more into the breach dear friends. She was reading a catalogue, casually shouted, 'Next, please.' The man, thirties and nervy, retired in shame. I felt sorry for him.

'Give me your modern piece,' Tina told a woman who stepped forward.

'It's an Oscar Wilde, Lady Bracknell—'

'Get on with it.'

The woman was weak, but gamely tried to be the frosty dowager. I kept quiet. Tina chatted to me, spoke ill of performers in general and ignored the auditioner.

'What's your name, love?' I asked as the actress finished.

'Wilhelmina. I trained at—'

'You're hired,' I told her. 'Where'd you get your shawl?'

'Shawl? My grandmother.' She picked it up from where she'd cast it before her audition. I lusted force nine at her garment, my breathing quickening. I felt hot and giddy. Her old shawl was worth a mint.

For in the Himalayas there lives the chiru, a long-horned antelope that's fast petering out. An ancient breed, it has made a few ghastly mistakes. One was to flourish in Tibet, a place desperate for hard currency. Another clanger was to be covered by the finest grade of wool on earth. The importance? Tibetan shawls made of the chiru's neck wool are the most desirable known to mankind. A wrap-around shahtoosh, a kind of shawl, costs a new motor. But a genuine antique Tibetan shawl (meaning over fifty years old, since Customs and Excise cynically decided that that

69

duration defined antiques for all eternity) will cost you an average house plus a round-the-world cruise.

Wilhelmina's garment was a truly ancient shawl made of chiru neck wool. As she shelled it to start her piece, it had folded like silk. No other wool does that. I've only ever seen two genuine shahtooshes, both in a boot fair. Caution: don't import any, no matter how cheaply you can get them while trekking through Asia. The whole world has banned the sale of this poor antelope's wool, so it's clink for you as you reach Customs.

Tip: the occasional shahtoosh is still around. You can still find a stray shawl. If you're in doubt, there's an important test. Take off your wedding ring and try to pass the long shawl *through the ring*. If it goes through without a single crease, buy it. Remember history? Back in the halcyon days, the Victorians did what they jolly well liked, for wasn't Mother Nature infinitely generous? And, the Edwardians reasoned, the Almighty surely must intend to provide Planet Earth's largesse for ever, in His perfect world. Like ivory, and like those stuffed animals that we admired so much that we made them extinct. Poor chiru. Poachers nowadays hunt the chiru with jeeps, gun them down in the headlights, then shear the corpses. They make aphrodisiac powder from the horns. The sale route is Hong Kong to London's Mayfair. (Incidentally, what exactly *did* Scotland Yard do with those twelve dozen priceless shahtooshes they collared so triumphantly not long ago . . . ?)

We're a rotten species.

'Am I?' Wilhelmina asked, stunned.

'Lovejoy!' Tina fumed, flinging her catalogue

down. 'She's not!'

I don't know why, but I felt rotten. Maybe the thought of all those dead antelopes. I mean, for Christ's sake, pashmina wool from Tibetan goats is nearly as fine, so why don't we use that instead and leave the poor sodding chiru alone? Whatever it was, Tina took one look at me and shut up.

'I'm in a hurry, Tina. Do it fast, you're in. I'll need you and three others. Bring that Larch bloke, Wilhelmina, and one other bloke.'

'Right, Lovejoy. What's wrong?'

Maybe I should have tried to buy Wilhelmina's shawl for a groat, but something was needling me, dunno what. I spoke quietly to Wilhelmina in a corner of the faded old assembly room, and told her about her granny's garb, chiru, the wool, the lot.

'You can't exactly buy your own theatre, love, but it'll keep you in clover until you storm the Old Vic. At least a year or two in a comfy bedsit. Go into any pub. Ask for Tinker. Tell him Lovejoy sent you. Take your shawl, if you want to sell it, to Blossom Arrance in Williams Walk in the Dutch Quarter. Don't sign anything, okay? Real antique deals are all done on the nod.'

She stared at the shawl in awe. 'Tinker?'

'You'll know him by his cough. It's like a foghorn.'

'The old man in the churchyard?' Her nose wrinkled. 'Who smells and spits?'

'That's him. Don't be snooty, love. He might not look much, but he's the world champ barker.'

'What's a . . . ?'

Listening to the others is painful. I couldn't stay to see the rejects banished, so lurked in St Peter's

71

until Tina came for me, scoffing.

'You're too soft, Lovejoy. Know that?'

'My granny always said.'

We assembled in the Castle Bookshop's upper room, where Heidi Pansock shut us away from pryers. I looked at them. Not much of an army.

'You'll be well paid. It's one hour's acting.' I extinguished the hope in their eyes by adding, 'Not a TV, er, movie.' I always try to sound American, and fail. I lied in a flare of genius, 'There might be one if this goes well.'

'Okay!' they exclaimed eagerly. Even Larch looked stirred.

'I'm Lovejoy. I'm the paymaster.' I chuckled. They didn't. Maybe they'd spotted that I hadn't a bean. I kept up my lazaroid grin. 'Names, please?'

'Larch,' said Larch. 'I kip in the park,' et angry cetera.

'Wilhelmina,' said the shahtoosh lady. 'I'm thirty-five, two children. A widow. My interests are the Romance poets, Tennyson and Ben Jonson with reference to . . .' and so on.

The nervy bloke who'd wanted us to go once more into the breach dear friends, was the third. I glanced at Tina. She avoided my eye.

'I'm Jules. I've been . . . away.' He coloured slightly, forged gamely on. 'I'm in the Refuge, no other fixed abode.' He waited anxiously, but nobody threw him out. The Refuge is a doss-house where violence holds sway, so I'd guessed right. He was newly out of prison.

'What've you done on the stage?'

'I did a series of leads,' he said, eyes shining. 'Ayckbourns, Shakespeare, two Cowards.'

'You're all hired,' I said. I'd placed him. I only

72

knew of one Refuge inmate. He'd starred in prison shows, had a past nearly as interesting as mine. He wasn't called Jules, though. Fine by me.

'The pay is basic Equity rate. It's . . .' I paused. I didn't know exactly what Equity was. And what style of acting, for heaven's sake? That Yank actor, who called his stage improvisations art. 'It's improvisation. Hidden cameras.'

'Where? On stage?'

'In a manor house hired for the purpose. You,' I said, pacing, well underway, 'must pretend. There's no script. It's, erm—'

'Off the top of your head,' Tina put in with a narked glance.

'That's it. Tina will lead. You're all supposed to be divvies in the antiques trade. The plot will evolve as we go, okay?'

'We're all interviewed together?'

'By an American lady with a massive track record in,' I coursed on in a blaze of inventiveness, 'Channel Eight-Seven-Zed in Hollywood. She's starred in thirty-one soaps and two major documentaries.'

They gasped. I smirked modestly, really making their day.

'What must we do?' asked anxious Wilhelmina.

'We go in together,' I explained. 'The lady will scrutinize us, and be especially rude to me. That,' I lied serenely on, 'is deliberate. You must pretend to be in the antiques trade. Wilhelmina, devise a background in an antiques shop down the coast. Larch, you're a hawker on the Saturday barrows. And, er, Jules, you're an auctioneer from the Midlands, okay?'

Jules looked at the floor. 'Thank you, Lovejoy.'

'Pretend that you're each a divvy. That's somebody who can detect genuine antiques by simply being near them. Right?'

'How on earth do we do that?'

'I'll have four test objects. You guess. I'll signal whether they're genuine or not. Tell you how on the way. Above all, keep in character. Any questions?'

'Will she be acting too?' Wilhelmina asked apprehensively.

'Superbly,' I answered. 'You won't be able to tell she's not genuine. There will be sixteen hidden cameras. If you start looking round, you're fired on the spot and don't get paid.'

'And what am I, Lovejoy?' Tina asked innocently.

'You're somebody who wants to be a divvy and hasn't got it,' I said cruelly, put her in her place. She was heading for a tanking. I wanted no loose ends. 'I don't know what script she'll choose. That's the scheme. I'll send to tell you when.'

'Like an audition?' Wilhelmina breathed, thrilled.

'No,' I said sadly. 'This is the real thing.'

*   *   *

Before I go any further, there's greed. Greed is a wish for success, ambition, secret romantic desires . . . In other words, money. There's a way of making it, from nothing.

Some things I can explain. Like, when Elizabeth, Empress of Austria, hunted with the Wynnstay Hunt (think Chester / Flint / Denbighshire) in the 1880s, she had herself stitched into chamois leather

74

knickers. Reason: vicious brambles locally.

Some things, I can't explain. Like, why is Russia's Great October Revolution called that, when it occurred in November? Did the Gregorian Calendar have something to do with it? Dunno. Or, how come the vast Wedgwood porcelain conglomerate forgot to renew its own name / title recently, and redfacedly had to make a deal with some eleven-year-old to *buy its own name back*? Or why all women don't realize that they can possess any man on earth, whatever their own age, shape, status. There are other inexplicables: Scotland has banned mystic William Blake's exquisite poem 'Jerusalem'. Sociologists, people who've never heard of a smile, have banned the children's game of Musical Chairs because it might be competitive (like life isn't). To most questions, I hold up my hand and say I don't know.

Antiques are different. And fakes are very *very* different. It's because of money. Don't read on unless you are prepared to consider a little bit of sin, okay?

Now, we're all greedy. I do mean *all* of us.

Let's say you happen to be a housewife—that honourable position now hated by every talk-show host in the known world. 'Housewife' was once a name for an eminently praiseworthy, all-knowing mainstay of society, pillar of common sense. Nowadays, though, girls spit the word with unequalled venom in bus queues. 'What, be a frigging housewife?' they snarl. Or they whine, 'Listen to my mum, you'd think everybody has to keep clean and do homework . . .' Parents please fill in the dots. You know the feeling.

Back to greed. Let's say you're a lady whose

daily round is well established. You've done the housework, seen the infants to school, had your snack (tomato soup for the hips, one sinful slice of bread, and tea without sugar). What now? Time on your hands, because soon George will be home, et mundane cetera, okay?

Your eyes light on a TV film. An old black-and-whitey, maybe *Brief Encounter* or some flashy 1950s thing where everybody has spacious motor cars and smokes themselves to death, the actresses gorgeously dressed, diamonds sparkling in every scene.

You watch, smiling. And you think how marvellous it would be just to have one day of that kind of life. Romance? Maybe. Affluent wealth? Oh, yes, very desirable. And you scan your own lot. Not with any kind of animosity. Because George is reliable, does his stint at that hellish factory. And the family, thank God, is healthy. No, nothing sinister.

But something starts whispering. It's gremlin-shaped, green. It is Envy. It talks quietly, as you flip through pictures of models who've earned a king's ransom just for dressing to the nines and standing still while society photographers take snaps for the centrefold.

It whispers of jealousy.

It says things like, 'Just look at her! In her baronial hall, gem-studded elegance and Vervainoo clothes! Never done a day's work in her life! She was always the idlest at school . . .'

Your envy grows.

In fairness, you reply to your gremlin, 'I'll bet her life isn't all cakes and lovers! I'll bet there are snags!' And (desperately making it up) 'Isn't she the one who had that terrible divorce in Monte Carlo only last month?' etc, etc.

Whoever wins—the Envy gremlin, or you—the greed seed is sown. You start to wonder what it would be like to suddenly shazam into a lottery win. *Or find a precious antique in the flea market!* (See where we're heading?) All are genuine possibilities. But what exactly are the odds? Phone them, and ask.

They'll tell you that the big lottery is fourteen million to one, minimum. TV quizzes are a hundred thousand to one. Better, your little green Envy whispers, to make money from nothing, *and keep that gelt coming*! Impossible, eh?

No. Antiques can do it. How on earth?

Forgery is the answer.

Back to our housewife, now listening avidly to her gremlin. Get some regular money, to spend as she likes! That's all very well, but she has a problem: she has no expertise in jewellery, porcelain, silverware. She couldn't knock up a Sheraton tallboy if she tried a million years.

Here's how she (no, you!) can do it. Today, buy a cheap set of oil paints or watercolours, cost a few pence. Take out a library book on Lowry's paintings. Copy any single one of his small 'Little Girl' pictures. Do it in watercolours, oils, and do it quickly. Never mind accuracy. Frame it. Pay a few quid to some printer to print a label of the Stone Gallery, Newcastle-upon-Tyne, stick the label on the back and date your painting (call it 'Little Girl in a Mini-Skirt') 1964 or so. I promise that you'll sell it, however badly you've copied the original, for a week's average wage. Trust me—or, rather, trust the greed that's making you do this. Sign it Lowry,

77

of course—many of his signatures are all but indecipherable. Don't worry. You're legally allowed. The Law, God bless it, says so.

One last thing. The dealer.

He'll be mistrustful. He'll say, 'This doesn't look genuine . . .' You'll lie that it's been in your attic for quite a while, and you agree that it *can't* be genuine, because your brother swapped a pair of old boots for it years ago. And so on.

The dealer will sigh (they all do a great sigh) and say, 'Look, love. I can't buy it as genuine Lowry. Tell you what I'll do. I'll buy it as a replica, okay?'

What do you do? You take the money and scarper. You needn't ever go back. You've been honest (well, almost) and so has he (well, almost). All's well. You have money in your purse! You get home in time to start your next Lowry lookalike.

Of course, you've been practical. You made sure your watercolours were dry (use your electric hairdryer) before you took it to El Superbo Antiquery Inc. And you tested the oil paint, to make certain it doesn't smell of linseed. (You can buy quick dryers if you're obsessional about it, or use various chemicals.)

Money for jam.

The reason I tell you this is so that you'll remember how easy it is to fake, forge, copy anything at all. Because if you can make multo zlotniks with no expertise at all, imagine what a master forger can do with a lifetime's skill and devotion to technique. Or a master cabinetmaker. Or a brilliant trained potter with a laboratory bulging with specialist kilns.

Remember, and beware. Message ends.

CHAPTER TEN

Dealers say antiques are a matter of life and death, but they're much more serious than that. I was becoming scared. Things were going wrong yet right. Women are supposed to get this feeling more than us. Like, a woman might wonder, is this dress trustworthy, remembering that she wore green at that disastrous party last Kissing Friday? Or, should she go out with somebody called Harold, seeing that her previous Harold spoke all evening about Aramaic translations? I knew that I'd made some calamitous mistake, but what? I'd only done as I was told.

As Tina locked up the church hall after a training session with our team, I heard a miraculous sound. It was a long rasping cough. It started as a distant rumble, reverberating so the traffic noise seemed to fade, then crashed to a shuddering crescendo that stunned us. It ended with a slurping expectoration that would have turned me nauseous, except I'd heard it before.

'Tinker?' A brilliant omen.

A heap of tat draped on one of the tombs rose. Wilhelmina screeched faintly and ducked behind Larch and Jules. It spoke.

'Wotcher, mate. Sandy and Mel're looking for you. Poncey bleeders.'

Filthy, wearing a dishevelled army greatcoat clinking with soiled medals, mittens blackened by desiccated food, enough stubble on his chin to card cotton, teeth corrugated brown crags, rheumy eyes and wheezing breath, he still was my loyal ally. I pay him in whisky, London gin, rum, and—more often—promises.

'If that horror's coming with us, Lovejoy, I'm off!' cried Tina.

'Tara then, love. Come on, troops.'

'Lovejoy!' she yelped, but I was too edgy for a bird's ire to take hold. If birds were kind now and then, maybe I'd respond. As it was, I'd things to do.

'Tinker, get us transport to Saffron Fields when I send word, okay?'

Then I heard it, the most daunting sound. By the yew trees a figure stood, waving proudly. It was Sandy, dressed as a glittering angel, frosty white wings, a dazzling magenta and cerise gossamer robe, a purple handbag and a circlet of electric lights rotating round his artificial curls while some electronic trinket played *Ave Maria*. The ultimate prat. My heart sank, the actors with me gaping.

'Yoohoo, Lovejoy! Come and positively *adore*!'

'Sorry, Sandy,' I called nervously. 'We're just off.'

'I shall tell that Yank bitch of you-hoo!' Sandy shrilled in fury.

Meaning Susanne Eggers?

Resignedly we plodded over. Several photographers were saying a little more this way, tilt your head. Sandy was loving it. 'Got my starlight eyes, sweeties?' and all that. I find him squirmily embarrassing. He thinks we all admire him. In fact we often have to say so, because he's a vicious antique dealer who'll stop at nothing to avenge a slight, real or imagined. His friend is Mel, a surly dealer who's always fuming. Mel was seated on a nearby gravestone. He looked away as we approached, fuming no doubt.

'Ooooh, Lovejoy!' Sandy held up a hand to stay

the photographers while he did lipstick in a mirror. 'You've started collecting *tramps*! How quaint!' He eyed Wilhelmina. 'And that senile cow over there—the one with the rotting hair—has stolen a shahtoosh! It's mine. Tell her it's mine. I'll pay her.' He struck a pose. 'Recommence, darlings!'

Stepping aside, I asked, 'What's this in aid of, Mel?'

'I shan't speak to him, Lovejoy.' Mel glared. 'He's launching a children's charity, Angels On Gravestones Trust. It's obscene.'

'I can see that. How'll it get funded?'

'That's it, Lovejoy. It's a con. There *is* no charity. He's going to use the money for buying imported antiques.'

Sandy was posing away. I noticed banners draped on two poor-quality stone angels nearby. They read GIVE GENEROUSLY TO THE SANDY AOG TRUST!, red on white. I sighed.

'Stop him, Mel.'

'Don't you think I've tried?' Mel is even less honest than the rest of us, but a glim of morality must lurk somewhere in his DNA. 'Remember the old folks' homes?'

The reminder made me wince. Sandy once invented a charity called Sandy's Antique Dealers All Giving. He and Mel conned old people out of their antiques, with the cock-and-bull tale that they would make a fortune. He got nerks to collect the antiques, of course, so he could pretend he'd been jumped by sinister dealers from France. He always blames Continentals.

'Don't listen to Mel, Lovejoy!' Sandy carolled, arms aloft in dramatic pose. 'He's positively *glowering* because I *might* have met a Greek

81

locksmith.'

'Oh, am I?' Mel barked, rising in fury. 'Well, Lovejoy, you just tell that absolute trollop that I have other things to do than sulk—' et cetera.

'Come on, people,' I said to my actors. I was too tired to play go-between for this exotic pair. God knows I try to keep friends with everybody, but some are just too much. 'See you, Sandy. Tara, Mel.'

'Come and see us, Lovejoy,' Sandy trilled. 'We'll sell you your ghost painting.'

That froze me in mid-flight. The actors bumped into me like dominoes.

He smiled, wafting his robe to and fro as photographers clicked away. 'We'll only charge you a hundred per cent commission.'

'Mel?' He had the grace to look sheepish. 'What ghost picture?'

'You did several, Lovejoy. This one was Vestry's. Sandy pre-empted it at the box sale last week.'

'Deal,' I croaked, making my exit. The lichgate leads into the High Street, traffic and supermarkets, pedestrians thronging. I almost walked under a bus but Tinker hauled me back in time.

'Tinker, get us to Saffron Fields manor by three o'clock.'

'Right, son. It'll be Jacko's coal lorry. Here, Lovejoy.' He sprayed the concourse with a cough that momentarily stalled the vehicles. 'We in trouble?'

'Vestry.' I drew him aside for secrecy. My actors stood, gazing back at Sandy glittering in the churchyard. 'What was it exactly?'

'Vestry hanged hisself in his barn, didn't he?

82

Month since, down the Broads. FeelFree and Horse found him.'

'Find out what you can, Tinker, okay?' I smiled at the team. They didn't look much.

'Don't you remember?' his foghorn voice gravelled out. Half the High Street heard Tinker's whisper. He thinks that by leaning at an angle— nothing new—he becomes the soul of confidentiality. 'Vestry hung hisself while you wus framing that neff portrait. He wanted it reframed.'

'Thanks, Tinker.' I could hardly see for the migraine thumping my sight sideways. 'Keep it secret, okay? You lot, see you later. Remember— be convincing.'

They chorused eagerness. My scheme was becoming as secret as the Opening of Parliament. I tottered off to find FeelFree Halsey. She and her bloke Horse claim to be Royal Doulton specialists who know when the world's going to end. For voyantes, they weren't very accurate the afternoon they found Vestry's cooling body at his private finale. They're also friends of Aspirin and Paul the birdman's wife Jenny. It was getting complicated. I could have throttled Mortimer for getting me into this.

First, though, a word about collectors, and how stupendous dreams come true.

*   *   *

Collectors are wonderful people. That's all they do, collect. They'll rob, plunder, sell their grandma, abandon the most prestigious job on earth, just to collect matchboxes, old wheels, pins, pieces of rocketry, coloured buttons, inkstands and—honest, no kidding—bits of tripe and olive pips. They might end up threadbare, living in cardboard boxes on the Embankment, yet become the proud possessors of hidden stores of toy telescopes or a thousand metal keys. For me, they are barmy yet beautiful.

Some manage to keep their jobs. Others go to the dogs while dreaming that one day—*soon*—the world will come a-thronging to worship their unbeatable collection of Victorian hats, limestone baptism fonts, or bronze camels. I like collectors, partly because they keep me alive by buying bits of junk that no sane person would look at twice.

Sometimes, though, collectors come a cropper. Like Vestry, *requiescat in pace*. I tried to think. He was a collector-dealer of gruesome old medical instruments.

I found Horse preaching in the shopping precinct. FeelFree was at the nearby open-air caff. She's gorgeous and voluptuous, just the sort I should win. It's no hopes, though, because she's hooked on Horse, a tiny desiccated clerk, all bulbous forehead and specs, but who has the undoubted appeal of being our only Existence Guru. An ex-convent girl, FeelFree reasons that she'll be able to square it with the Almighty in the nick of time. Her plan is theologically suspect, but what isn't?

'Wotcher, Feel. Having coffee, I see.' I swallowed, desperate for some. She moved her biscuits away and sipped with gentility. She knows me. I peered into an abandoned cup but somebody had drained it, stingy swine. They'd taken the sugar.

Horse was standing in our precinct's fountain,

84

thundering—well, piping—away to a crowd of two old ladies who listened approvingly to his intentions to inflict his hang-the-swine morality on a liberal country. FeelFree's eyes glistened.

'Isn't he wonderful, Lovejoy?'

Well, no. But I was starving and Maggie the waitress was questing for orders. A noisy family on the next table asked for egg and chips with sponge pudding for afters, not a thought for hungry folk near by. My belly rumbled as they whaled in.

'When does the world end, Feel? Soon, is it?' Asking for the latest bulletin on Planet Earth's chances always cheers her.

'No news this week.'

Thank God for that. 'Sad about Vestry, eh, love?' The tact of an axe.

Horse was working himself up to a shrill denunciation of Satan, who this week was making us all hard-hearted materialists. This, note, from a dealer who establishes, then defrauds, antiques clubs. (Get the clue, from Rio?) The clubs invariably go bust, leaving his members destitute and him in clover, with (as such clubs always claim when they mysteriously go bankrupt) 'unexplained financial losses'.

What happens is that Horse starts up an antiques collectors' club, then exhibits the antiques he's bought with members' subscriptions. The members are delighted at the porcelains, Georgian silver, Regency household items, Portuguese colonial ivories, whatever, and chip in more investment gelt. (Greed, see?) Horse sends round an urgent circular, and guess what? A rich American tourist has asked to buy the club's antiques! Quick, quick! He sails on Tuesday . . .

Who can resist? The club hastily agrees, yes, sell for God's sake, don't let him/her get away . . . The club's antiques are sold. Then, horror of horrors, the cheque bounces! The club is broke. And who's the saddest and brokest of them all? Why, none other than the Hon Sec, for didn't he lose more than anyone?

In fact, no, he didn't, for there never was any rich American tourist. There was only some crooked pal (read FeelFree) who drives the antiques north and sells them on that motorway service station beyond Hawkshead. It's Horse's (and every other crook's) favourite venue.

That's Horse's scam. He's worked it four times so far. FeelFree is named from her patter: 'Feel free to cheat me,' she says with a glamorous smile. 'Offer me half the price. I'll starve . . .' and draws her clothes tightly round her voluptuous form, and lands another bargain. She does Horse's driving, sees the trips north as her rightful (not righteous) holiday entitlement. I'm being cynical, saying that all antiques investment clubs end in tears. I don't mean it. I only mean the vast majority. Except I've only ever heard of one honest one. Not two. One.

'Vestry?' Religion lapsed as she swivelled her exquisite eyes on me. I almost fell into their limpid blue. Women make you forget what you're up to, don't they? 'Please don't mention him, Lovejoy. It was ghastly.'

To my alarm her eyes filled. She wept genuine tears.

'Ignore him, love,' a passing crone gave out. 'They're not worth it and I've been wed these forty-six years,' et dronesome cetera, daft old bat.

'How come you were visiting him, Feel?'

Her eyes narrowed. She made no reply while I worked it out.

Antiques dealers are creatures of habit. They're worse than serial killers. (I wish now I'd not thought that.) They'll stalk every country auction after making one superb find. In fact, they'll sacrifice the rest of their lives in hopes of repeating a one-off success. As in the old music-hall song, where some lass danced with a man who danced with a girl who danced with the Prince of Wales. Now Horse wouldn't be seen dead (sorry) with Vestry. Nor would FeelFree. In fact, their paths never crossed. They ran on different tramlines. The row was all over, believe it or not, a piece of toast. Literally. Toast.

Some antiques are as ancient as the planet. Others are so-called 'tomorrow's antiques'. (Tip: avoid these at all costs. They're never, never ever, worth buying, because everything today will be antique in the future, right?). But some very mundane antiques are priceless because of their rarity.

I get narked, because it's always others who find these genuinely desirable items, never me. Somebody finds a priceless 26,000-year-old woolly mammoth planted in the Siberian ice. It's some undeserving rambler.

This piece of toast. It was found in the Yarnton pit near Oxford, together with a biggish flint knife, hazelnut shells, a few apple cores, some toasted cereal, bits of pottery, and a few tools. It turned out to be barley bread, like the stuff my gran used to make, but baked in 3,485 BC, give or take a radiocarbon burp. Unimportant? Yes, until you realize it's a mite older than Stonehenge, and

87

antedates all other antique breads by a cool 2,500 years. Now, Vestry was always a scammer, never honest like me. And Horse and FeelFree are nothing but no-hope scammers working the investment club game. Vestry claimed he had some ancient toast from Yarnton, complete with authentic radiocarbon dating certificates. Worthless? Hardly; find some, it means a cool five years of affluence in Monaco, blondes and beer thrown in. Horse sensed profit. He tried to buy Vestry's archeological relics for his current antiques club scam. Vestry refused. Word was he'd been scared of drowning in the tide of litigation that always threatens to submerge Horse and FeelFree's manky clubs.

'What I mean, Feel, is why would you two supposed Royal Doulton collectors race to the Fenlands to buy some antique barley bread?'

'Money, Lovejoy!' she said with scorn, tears drying instantly. 'Heard of it?'

'You shunned Vestry after that Beethoven business.'

This is what I mean by luck. In 1817, the great Ludwig had a young English visitor called Richard Ford. In the way of geniuses, LvB dashed off a string quartet for him. The original manuscript lay dormant in some attic, only coming to light when money called its siren summons. The whole thing was dated, and in Big B's own hand. Ecstasy! Sotheby's auctioned it, musicians fought to play it, and harmony soared on wings of song while the rest of us, forlorn and deprived, drooled and sobbed. Needless to say, the ancient house in Pencarrow, Cornwall, where the manuscript was found, is now the focus of many a braggart dealer's imaginings: 'I've got a Dickens manuscript from that attic in Pencarrow. The end of Edwin Drood, for the right price . . .' Vestry tried this on with everybody in the Eastern Hundreds, and got nowhere.

'Vestry made us a special offer,' she said lamely. 'He chucked in a French pottery fake.'

'Nobody trusted Vestry. He'd the knowledge of a gnat.' And the luck of one.

'We did!' She tried to sound indignant. 'Horse is clever!'

I didn't believe a word of it. Horse wouldn't know how to market Stone Age toast any more than fly. He didn't know porcelain from pork. Clever? This was the man who, unbelievable to relate, once sold a dinner service, not spotting that the gungy old chipped plates were actually copies done by Edmé Samson of Paris, the immortal copier. Samson's creations often cost ten times the originals. Samson started as a faithful honest duplicator of broken pots, and ended up making brilliant fakes of Meissen, Chelsea, and Chinese *famille rose* by the million. Pretty good they are, too. Incidentally, moulds taken from Meissen originals are almost invariably smaller than the originals (a useful tip, this) owing to shrinkage in firing, so watch out. And the base of Meissen figures of, say, 1740 to 1750-odd, is always supposed to be a flat unglazed 'buff' hue, whereas fakes are practically white, though I've never found this much use because there are exceptions. If I have a fake porcelain anything, I offload it onto Horse and FeelFree because they know nil.

Hence FeelFree was lying, telling me Horse and she were doing a deal with Vestry. But why?

89

'Did you tell the police this, love?'

'Should I? We just popped over. He was our friend. We found him hanging there. It was horrible.'

She burst into sobs, hands over her face, peeping between her fingers to see how I was taking her falsehoods.

'God rest him,' I said, sick now.

'Leave her alone, you brute.' The same vicious old bat advancing threateningly across the square made me get up with ill grace.

'Sorry, love,' I said loudly to the crone. 'She's an alcoholic junkie. Spare a copper for her junkie friends. She's not had a drink for almost an hour.'

I fled the contumely.

CHAPTER ELEVEN

I believe that women love a scrap. For what reason? Nobody knows. I used to know this placid woman. Placid, that is, until one day something went wrong at work, heralding a terrible fight next morning. 'Sorry, love,' I sympathized. Eyes shining, best dress on, she swung joyously from my cottage that Monday dawn, the songs of angels on her lips. And that evening arrived home blissfully replete. She'd had the ghastliest fight. Somebody else had got her comeuppance and retreated in tears. See? They love it.

It's the same with my understanding of people—lack of it, I mean. Some folk don't accept the obvious. 'Oh, it's raining!' this bird Nia once exclaimed, halting at the door. 'I said it would,' I pointed out. She rounded on me. 'Oh, *you*!' she spat, furious. 'Weather isn't my fault,' I told her, because it isn't. No good. She blamed me because she got wet.

Which brings me to Quaker, seeing I was in trouble and didn't know why.

First, I called at a shop in Long Wyre Street and got a small silver cup. Cost me the earth. Engraving was extra. I also bought—my next four days' meals—a silver trophy depicting a kite, the sort you fly on windy days with a string. I caught the bus, and eventually reached Quaker's house by the Quay, where the theatre is.

'Quaker? You in?' I knocked.

He is always in, seeing he's in a wheelchair and won't go out.

'That you, Lovejoy?'

I entered diffidently, hoping Maud wasn't home. She was, and came all a-bustle. She bakes cakes for church bazaars, orphanages, supports starving donkeys. Her father's a bitter brigadier, retired from lack of wars. (You'll see why in a sec.)

'Wotcher, Quake. Thought I'd bring your award, seeing you were too damned idle to collect it yourself.'

'Lovejoy! What a treat!' Maud engulfed me, flour leaving her mark on me like an exotic printing device. 'It's been so long! Cake and tea any moment!'

Here came Quaker, trundling in his wheelchair. Specky, stout, wheezing, he shoves the wheels. He's only thirty-one. Won't see a doctor, won't accept that he can't walk, run, jump, swim, sing, dance, fly, or any of the above.

'You just caught me, mate,' he said, his face

rapturous. 'I was just off out. I'm in the sculling finals!'

'Don't miss the start because of me, Quake,' I called, but he'd pumped himself quickly into his room.

'Lovejoy,' Maud murmured.

'Shhh,' I said. Do lame folk hear better, or is that blindness? I needed Quaker's help, couldn't risk wives' whispers, though I like Maud.

'I'm going shopping at two, Lovejoy. Meet me in the Corn Market.'

'I'm in trouble, love. Quaker can help me.'

'Help me, Lovejoy,' she whispered huskily.

Quaker rolled back into view. I sprang away, hoping he wouldn't notice Maud's new flour imprint on me.

'They'll wait half an hour,' he said happily. 'Just give us time for a chat.'

'Who's your opponent this time, Quake?'

His face clouded. 'A bloke called Matterheim. Dolomite champion. He's in the Olympics.'

'Christ, Quake,' I breathed, anxious. 'You'll have your work cut out.'

He spun with extraordinary dexterity. 'He's odds on favourite.'

Into his room we went, Maud dashing to the kitchen to bring sustenance.

Not everybody gets to see Quaker's private room. It's vast, a specially extended part of his bungalow. You can see rowing boats on the Stour, canoes and things, sculling past this long picture window. Big as any classroom. At the far end, a glass wall. Seated in the conservatory through there, in the adjoining bungalow, sat the brigadier, Maud's dad, looking at me with sardonic eyes. I'm

92

not quite sure what sardonic means, but if any geezer on earth's sardonic it's Brigadier Hedge. He acknowledged me with a nod, which from him is like a tournament. He wants his beloved daughter Maud to leave Quaker and get a life. She says no because Quaker needs her. Brig says Quaker's off his trolley, she should cut her losses. She says no. Joining the dots in the argument can wear you out. It sends me mental.

All round Quaker's walls are shelves covered with trophies, cups, bowls, vases, silverware, gold chalices. All sham. There's hardly an inch of wall that isn't stuck with plaques, shields, crests, ornaments that Quaker has not won hang-gliding, sprinting, shooting, swimming, high-diving. There are Olympic medals from the 1985 Mogadishu Winter Olympics for downhill slaloms and ski jumping. Quaker led our triumphant assault on Russian dominance of the downhill cycling races in the 1989 Honolulu Olympics. He collared the trophy for architectural Millennium designs. In fact, it's increasingly difficult to think up a new frigging sport or championship every blinking time I come.

He's done none of it. He's a dreamer whose dreams mean more to him than reality. Hence my pathetic purchase of my kite trophy. Best I could do in such a rush.

'What is it, Lovejoy?' Quaker asked, spinning to face me.

Behind him, the brigadier rolled his eyes. I looked away. I always feel embarrassed at this stage.

'I feel a fraud, Quake,' I said. 'I've never ever won a thing.'

'No, no. It's okay.' Shining eyes on my parcel.

I unwrapped it, stood there like a duckegg with my glittering phoney cup and the silver kite model.

'It's your award, Quake. Eastern Hundreds Kite-flying Champion. They asked me to accept it for you at the National Awards Centre.'

He smacked his forehead.

'God, I clean forgot! Thanks, pal. You got me out of a real mess!'

I donated the award. He received it, eyes moist.

'Sorry, Lovejoy. It's just that I remember how Bushido looked after the match. Japan always held the title until I beat him in the playoffs.'

He sniffed a bit. I welled up myself. It's not often you meet a dynamic champ who is decently sympathetic about the chap he's defeated.

'Was Bushido there?' he asked sadly.

'Yes,' I invented. Well, I'd invented the championship, so I'd a right to invent who turned up. 'He looked pretty down. Said he'd give you a run for your money, next world championships.'

'You know, Lovejoy,' he said seriously, fondling his cup and the trophy, 'I admire that. Taking defeat on the chin.'

'So do I,' I said fervently. I know defeat.

The brigadier couldn't hear behind the glass wall, but guessed the conversation. His headshake was graphic.

Maud entered at a sprint with a tray of edibles, thank God, all her own making. She was defloured, so to speak, in a clean pinafore and gave a smiling wave to her dad who nodded and returned to his newspaper. We settled down facing the river. Folk walk along the riverbank footpath into town. They pretend not to look in Maud's window, sometimes.

94

They must wonder at Quaker's array of trophies and guess which sporting over-achiever lives there.

'How marvellous of you to bring Quaker's new award, Lovejoy!'

'No bother, love.'

Maud's grub is legendary. She cooks from Mrs Beeton's *All About Cookery* for the homeless of Suffolk. It's a wonder they don't all die from clogged arteries because it's heavy suety stuff. Or maybe that's the Council's plan? Some charity buys the raw ingredients for her. I like Maud. She and I started making smiles soon after Quaker took to his wheelchair, but I got worried. Anyhow by then I'd met Georgina from Stoke. There you go.

The whole point of this is that Quaker doesn't even do sports that he can do. Doesn't shoot, no Paralympics, doesn't sketch or study ornithology. He just accepts awards.

It's all myth.

In fact, even The Day Quaker's Legs Got Crushed In That Accident is also a fable, invented for reasons nobody knows. There is no paraplegia. Quaker is as fit as a flea. He could jump up and ramble his riverbank with the best of them.

We all deceive ourselves. Which raises the question of his missus.

This is Maud: thirty-six, palish hair, blue of eye, shapely if a bit dumpy. Nice legs, and what the county set call 'good bones', though I should think that all bones are pretty decent things to have around. Features pleasant, smile animated and alert. A bright compassionate woman is Maud Quaker.

She knows Quaker's a fraud, and told me about him when we were resting after having tired ourselves.

'Quaker's not to be blamed, Lovejoy,' she explained along the pillow. We were in my cottage, my chair propping the door because the lock needed mending.

'Why not?' I'd asked, mystified. 'He's a total con.'

'We all deceive ourselves. You. Me. My dad. Government. Why only blame Quaker?'

'Because he sponges on you,' I said, offended.

'So do you, Lovejoy.'

She pointed out that she paid for my food. She lent me her motor. She kept on about it until I got narked.

'At least I do a job,' I said heatedly.

'So does Quaker,' she'd said to my surprise. 'And he doesn't just scrounge off women and faint when he looks at silly old antiques.'

'What job?' I challenged. 'The idle bugger just sits in his wheelchair making up imaginary bloody trophies while I'm slogging in muck and bullets.'

I don't usually get narked, especially with blokes who've thought up a good scam. I too am an idleback. People who live in glass houses and all that.

It was then that she started to speak about Quaker really for the first time. Reluctantly, both of us naked as a grape, she told me in whispers. Afterwards she seemed scared, and swore me to secrecy. I promised, hand on her heart. And kept silent for ever and ever. Until now.

*   *   *

'Quaker's the conduit for the raj,' she'd said.

96

'Eh?'

My mind wearily chugged its synapses into action. Nerve ends groped. Electrons flickered.

'He can't be,' I got out. In fact, I almost laughed.

'He is, Lovejoy,' she said firmly, blue eyes looking at me that day in my divan bed. 'So take back what you said about him.'

'Quaker? He's the raj's brainpiece?'

Then I did it, made her mad. I really did laugh, rolling in the aisles at the thought that Quaker, that deluded bloke who lived a total sham, actually was the pivot for a—no, the—biggest club of investors in antiques.

I'd heard of women's devotion to dud blokes, of course. In fact I'd had plenty myself, but that was no fault of mine.

'Quaker?' I rolled in the aisles. 'He wouldn't know what the raj is.'

'No?' she spat. 'There are nine of them. Quaker knows. Who do you think he's seeing now, while you pleasure his wife?' She spoke with bitterness. 'And how come a foolish woman like me puts up with a neurotic like Quaker? Do you think I'd stay with him a minute, if he was only what he seems?'

'Stop it, love,' I said, wiping my eyes. 'You don't have to convince me. I like Quaker. And you know I worship you.' I propped myself up on an elbow, looking down. 'I take it back, doowerlink.'

She gazed up at me, took a deep breath as she reached some decision.

'You want convincing, Lovejoy? Then listen: the raj decides which antiques to buy. And who can steal which antiques. And who's allowed to get away with it. Who can rob museums and who can't. Big John Sheehan's one.'

97

My smile faded. Women don't know these things as a rule. She must have read some article in one of those antiques glossies that get names, dates, and antiques wrong.

'Bet you Quaker's never even heard of the raj.'

'No? Ask me, Lovejoy.' She waited. I stared. She was deadly serious. 'That trio of motor car dealers who stole those two Constable oil sketches? They tried to sell them last New Year in a hotel. They were caught, weren't they?'

I turned my head to align with her face, see directly into her. She looked sincere. But birds defending their blokes always are.

'Ask me about any antiques crime, Lovejoy. Including your theft from that place by the Minories.'

'Here, nark it.' I did my best indignation, but it didn't wash. Her triumphant gaze saw she'd hurt me. 'Nobody knows I did that!'

'You stole a sixteenth-century linenfold-patterned jointed chest. It was Thursday night. Tinker your oppo didn't bring the motor on time, so you had to leave the chest in the monastery garden until Colin Service went for it.'

Suddenly I wasn't laughing. Nobody knew about Colin. He's an ambulance driver, uses the health authority's wagons to collect stolen antiques.

'You're guessing,' I said feebly.

'Am I? Then I won't know that you complained to your dipper about the way the muntin to the left of the chest's lock had been damaged. You swore blind you didn't do it. You whined that Colin must have done it, collecting the chest from the herb garden before the rush hour.'

I think I paled. If I didn't, I should have. A

98

dipper's a contact man, the one who checks up after you've done a job. He decides if you've obeyed right, so that you get paid. Antiques are stolen to order nowadays. The raj tells the dipper. The dipper tells you. You do the steal, and that is that. A muntin is the straight vertical piece of wood between panels in a joinery chest front. Before that came in, in ancient times, everything was made of plain planking. That's why so few of the old pre-Elizabethan boarded chests survive. I gaped, partly because I didn't know that Maud knew a single antiques term.

'How the hell?'

'How the hell could I know that, Lovejoy?' Her voice didn't even waver. 'The same way I know about the Ashmolean Museum's cat snatch. Remember that? The whole country was aghast. New Year's Eve celebrations. Fireworks. Dancing in the streets of Oxford. Students in fancy dress.'

'You saw it in the papers.' Feebler and feebler.

'He used a smoke bomb. Single-handed, shifted nine roof slates to cut a hole. Dropped through with a nautical rope ladder. Let off the bomb, wafted the clouds with a battery-driven fan. He visited no other room. Cut the Cezanne from the frame. Left his holdall, scalpel, gloves behind. And danced off amid the crowds.'

No laughs now.

'The raj told him to penetrate the Ashmolean Museum through the new Sackler Library building site, because the University of Oxford can never—and I quote, Lovejoy—"make up its mind about agreeing with its benefactors". The raj deducted twenty per cent of his thiever's fee because he dropped his gloves.'

Now I was gaping. The *nine* slates hadn't been in the papers, nor the *nautical* rope ladder.

'The painting?' I croaked.

'*Auvers-sur-Oise*, by Paul Cezanne. The only Cezanne the Ashmolean had. He ignored the Leonardo da Vinci because the raj ordered him to. And the Picasso. You want measurements? Dates? Anything else?' She smiled, power to womenfolk.

For a second I had a terrible urge to scarper, clear off and never see her again. I must have looked shaken because her eyes took on that hard glaze when a woman sees a man's terror. I'm not a coward, honest, but the raj tops people for eavesdropping. Actually kills. I could name names. All dealers could. Maud smiled.

'Lovejoy. Why d'you think he's in a wheelchair? There's more technology in it than the parson preached about. Everything he says is recorded. He has transmitters to spare. Get the joke?'

'No.' I didn't get any joke.

'His phoney cups, trophies, all his fake awards. People laugh at him. The joke's on them, because nothing *they* own is secure. Any instant, he could simply advise the raj, and somebody would lose every penny piece. I mean you, the British Museum, America's Metropolitan, anywhere that owns anything.'

I sank back, laid my tired head on the pillow. She came over me, smiling down, her breast in view.

'Are we being broadcast?' I bleated, frightened.

'No, darling.' Her face clouded slightly, then cleared. 'No. Impossible. Quaker wouldn't do that.'

What man wouldn't keep track of his missus, though, if she kept sneaking out to see a scrounging ape like me? My throat dried. Quaker could say the word and I'd get found in a ditch, victim of some hit-and-run. Nobody would know. I'd be forgotten in an hour, that old Lovejoy, serve him right.

'Come on, darling,' she said, smiling as her confidence returned. 'You're forgiven. I know you're Quaker's friend. The only one he's got, truth to tell.'

Thank God for that, I thought but did not say.

'Course I am,' I said instead. 'I always am. Always will be.'

I said it for a gillion hidden cameras and tape recorders in my fertile and terrified mind. We joined, Maud and I, and made smiles. My smile was weak, but no less heartfelt.

*　　　*　　　*

'Tea, Lovejoy?' Maud asked, teapot poised, as Quaker smiled fondly and decided where his new trophies would go. 'Scone or cake?'

Ten of each was the right answer. 'Please.'

Quaker laughed. I kept my eyes off his electronically loaded wheelchair. Probably emitting signals to Planet Mongo, where menacing minds were judging every syllable. I felt weak so fell on Maud's grub. I love a bird like her.

'Wish I could eat like you, Lovejoy,' Quaker said wistfully. He slapped his protruberant belly. 'In training, see.'

'Ever think of retiring, mate?' I asked, mouth full.

'No.' He looked sad. 'I know what people say about me, Lovejoy.' I hoped I didn't look stricken

101

with terror. Even Maud froze for an instant. 'That it's an addiction, me striving to achieve things when most blokes just have one hobby.' He sighed at his dazzling array of awards.

'Well,' I said heartily, 'they expect it.'

'True,' he agreed eagerly. 'Today, there'll be TV cameras all along the river to watch me scull. Interviews after. That Frenchman has a reputation.'

His opponent had been a Bavarian minutes ago. He'd forgotten. Too much on his mind, cluttered up with antique robberies? I wondered for a second whether there was a way of finding out where all his information was kept.

'Next week I'm boxing.'

'You're fighting again?'

'Lovejoy,' he said gravely, the light of lions in his eyes. 'I couldn't let the Lonsdale Belt go to Czechoslovakia.'

'But you might get clobbered.'

He smiled nobly. 'Then I'll go down fighting.'

We made similar merry chat until it was time to go. I said ta for Maud's grub. He never shakes hands, says that's for Americans and other foreigners. Nor do I, come to think.

'Oh, Quake,' I said, clumsily bringing in my panic as I rose to leave. It was the reason I'd come, after all. 'I hope you don't think less of me.' It was awkward. I shifted from foot to foot. 'Over my, er, lad. They're saying,' I explained for the recording devices Maud had told me about, 'that this lad Mortimer from Saffron Fields is my son. He's causing trouble, telling tourists which antiques are genuine and which aren't.'

'Your what?' he said, playing astonished well

enough for the Old Vic.

'Your what?' Maud exclaimed, with hatred.

'It's said,' I amended. 'He's fifteen.'

'Good heavens!' Quaker almost offered his hand in congratulation. Maud did no such thing.

'Who is she, Lovejoy?' she asked in a voice of sleet.

'Only, I have no friends as such.' I almost moved myself to tears. 'Not ones I could trust.'

'It's all right, Lovejoy,' Quaker said. 'We understand.'

'He's not poor or anything. I'd like to think somebody like you might look out for him if . . . he needed anything. His mother frolics full-time in Soho. His dad—who brought him up—is dead. He might need somebody.'

'Tell him we will, Lovejoy,' Quaker said. 'You're our friend. If a cripple and a cook from the soup kitchen will do?'

'Ta, wack.' I was really—I mean *really* really—moved, and retreated as Maud showed me out. They could have said go to hell, but hadn't.

'Lovejoy,' Maud said urgently on her doorstep.

'Shhh,' I whispered, though what good's whispering when modern sound booms might be concealed in every twig? I added in a voice of thunder, 'Tell Quake good luck with the, er, boat.'

'Friday, Lovejoy,' Maud whispered, bussing me so-long. I left, exhausted.

To find the brigadier waiting for me at the bus stop.

'Isn't it time, Lovejoy,' he said without preamble, 'that you made an honest woman of Maud?'

People in the queue turned to look. He has a

delivery like a Shakespearean herald: now hear this, oh world. I went red.

'Sorry, Brig,' I apologized. 'She's married.'

'That doesn't stop people these days, Lovejoy. And from what I hear—'

'Brig,' I said, broken. 'Ask Maud. If I were you I'd just fall into line.'

'She's living with a dud,' he boomed. 'He's not even a genuine dud. He's a sham dud, for heaven's sake. All that let's-pretend lameness, when he actually floats off in his punt at all hours. I reckon he's got another woman anyway, so where's the harm?' He eyed me wistfully. 'I'd like a son-in-law like you, Lovejoy. No mockery. And something would keep happening.'

'The bus is here.' It wasn't.

'I wish the silly bugger really *was* lame,' he said sadly. 'You see, Lovejoy, my world has changed. If there are floods in Mozambique, or a new miracle genetic rice gives some coolie the bellyache, then my generation's very existence is up the creek. Our Defence Weapon Procurement makes a trivial mistake, another chunk of my life shreds. A passenger plane crashes, and more of my generation becomes penniless. It's true, Lovejoy. It's that serious. I'm closer to the edge every time I open *The Times*.'

Seemed a bit pessimistic to me. I said so. And what could a penniless antique dealer do to straighten earth's calamities?

'You know the theory, how mankind started?' For a second he seemed deeply moved, but how could that be, him a stalwart brigadier and all?

'Which one?' I'd heard dozens, each as unbelievable as the next.

'Three million years ago, primitive australopithecines living in the rain forests divided. One branch stayed vegetarian and are still monkeys. The others became carnivorous and learned to make war. They're us, Lovejoy. Man. Just remember that's all we are.'

He looked sad. I blurted out, 'Cheer up, Brig. Anything I can do, I will.'

'Thank you, Lovejoy. See me Friday, then. No later. Chin chin.'

I thought of saying toodle-pip, but he'd had enough disappointment in one visit. He looked a tired old man weighed down by desperation. How could I help a rich man like him, for heaven's sake?

'Tara, Brig.' I caught the bus. Things to do.

CHAPTER TWELVE

It was the most peaceful scene; village girls practising the maypole dance with ribbons, folk feeding ducks on the White Hart pond, no rain for once. Couldn't be better. Dealers were chatting all about, readying for the auction at Bledsew's. I wasn't restful. Inside I was in turmoil, with the worst of all feelings.

Hesk was trying to get me to endorse some fake Georgian drawings—Roman women seducing lovers in baths, frolicking maidens at it under arboreal fronds. I was waiting for Mortimer. Hesk narks me, always trying something on and getting it wrong. If he'd only take trouble, he'd be a classy forger. His drawings were not bad, just copies of those rapacious Pompeii scenes.

105

'Your black-letter Gothic inscriptions are wrong, Hesk,' I told him. 'You included the word pornography in, see?'

'It *is* porn, Lovejoy!' he cried, the prospect of a fortune dwindling. Two dealers, Becky and her mate Tony who deal in Jacobean (approx) glassware (approx) sniggered. Derision is the way dealers express sympathy with others.

'No, Hesk,' I said patiently. 'The word pornography wasn't coined until Dunglison put it in his medical dictionary in 1857.' Hesk had dated them all Pornography 1813–1816.

'Oh.' He looked close to tears. 'Should I change it?'

He left, glumly studying his drawings. Suddenly Mortimer was there beside me on the bench. I managed not to infarct at his abrupt manifestation.

'Keep your voice down,' I managed to say when my heart resumed. 'There's a dozen dealers about. *What* ghost painting?'

'You painted four, Lovejoy.' He gave me a second to adjust. 'The ghost was a lady.'

'I remember.' The portrait was of a seated woman, an oval canvas. Pretty good. I'd auctioned one, done three duplicates, and had eaten real food for almost two months.

'Didn't you sell one to your friend Ferdinand?' he asked.

'Children are the pits,' I told him, resigned. He looked puzzled.

Once, a pal of mine Ferd had the happiest life imaginable. Bonny wife, decent job, twins—pigeon pair, boy and girl—could life be better? One day hankies waved, and off the twins went to university. 'We're independent now,' they told their parents, beaming. Ferd and Norma his missus sighed fondly. Brave children, off into the big wide world. Peace in the old homestead! Not a bit of it. I met Ferd the following week and asked him for a lift.

'Can't, Lovejoy,' he said. 'No motor.'

The twins had returned carrying sacks of washing for Mum to do. 'They carried a sack of clinking pots,' Ferd told me gloomily. 'And two bicycles to be mended.' When challenged about this novel version of independence the twins said heatedly, *'Hey, Dad, who's got the washing machine, tools, and the dishwasher?'*

The visit was brief. They emptied the fridge of everything edible, ordered Ferd to fill his motor with petrol, promised to return at weekends, and drove away to continue being bravely independent in London's Soho, that well-known raw frontier. The daughter instantly shacked up with a penniless andromorph guitarist, her brother with a gorgeous lass hooked on anorexia who claimed, with a certain accuracy, to be a street juggler. Norma's washing load quadrupled, the bills became a Danegeld on the hapless Ferd. The twins' monetary demands soared. ('Hey, Dad, aren't we allowed to smoke, drink, have fun?' etc, etc.)

Ferd, once a Foreign Office diplomat, began to long for the halcyon days when his children had been completely parasitic infants at home while he slogged like a dog in London. 'They're so-say independent now, Lovejoy,' he told me wistfully, 'and I'm broke. Norma's out of her mind. We're worn out.'

Sadly, Ferd did the unthinkable. He cashed in his pension to open an antiques shop. The horrible trade joke is, 'Leap off a cliff, play Russian roulette—but don't do anything really dangerous like going into antiques!' Except it isn't a joke. Recorded history is crammed with famous wars, but Man's unwritten odyssey is littered with the wreckage of failed antiques businesses. One of those was Ferd's. He had a nervous breakdown after bankruptcy. His children were outraged ('What on earth is Dad thinking of, falling ill when we're deprived?' etc). Norma now goes out cleaning, four zlotniks an hour, to maintain Ferd in his silent despond while the twins, now a sturdy, booze-swilling twenty-two years of age, smoke their heads off in the idle manner to which they have become accustomed. Occasionally I visit Ferd, teach him watercolours; I've heard it's a good cure-all. Doesn't work, of course. Usually I paint while he gazes in silence, and that's it. But a friend has to try.

'See what I mean?' I told Mortimer defiantly. 'Independence for some is parasitism to others.'

'I'm not a university student,' he pointed out quietly. 'I don't smoke or drink. I protect you more than you do me. And I'm not a twin.'

Doesn't it nark you when other folk are reasonable? One less troublesome zygote, however, was good news. I said this with bitterness. He took no notice.

'Just stop ruining the antiques trade, please. They're threatening me.'

'Sorry, Lovejoy. It's not fair. Dealers pretend everything's genuine.'

Give me strength. I gave him the bent eye.

'Isn't Ferd the man at Tolleshunt Knights? His wife used to wheel him down the water with a radio?'

'That's Ferd. Ruined!'

'Not now, Lovejoy. He's better.' Mortimer didn't quite smile. I had the uneasy feeling that I was being manipulated. Odd that he'd twice brought up the name of somebody he'd never known.

'Can't be. Ferd's gone doolally, prey to his offspring.' I said this pointedly, still irked at this sprog getting me in bad with that Mrs Eggers and her barmy scheme. 'I saw Ferd only last week.'

'Go and see him *this* week, Lovejoy. Follow the Rolls-Royces.'

Which was how I came across a reincarnation, and some ugly bits of the jigsaw fell into place.

*   *   *

I hitched as far as Maldon, always easy to get to. There, I phoned Ferd. A startlingly bright Norma answered, gushed that she'd come for me. She arrived in an electric blue Rolls the size of our church. Humbly I got in.

'You don't look like a cleaning lady any more, love.'

She sparkled. You know the way women go when they're on top of the world? They become radiant, elated, their clothes priceless. They zoom down to twenty-four years of age when really they're over fifty. She dazzled. Except she'd dazzled me a week ago when she was in scrubber's clothes, and we'd made do with a tin of soup for the three of us. I wondered uneasily if my visit was superfluous.

'One thing, Lovejoy,' she said, concentrating on the steep hill down to Maldon's titchy river bridge. She blushed charmingly. 'Before we reach home.

Ferd's made a miraculous recovery from depression. Totally fit. So whatever happened in the past between *any two persons* mustn't recur. You do see that?'

'Erm . . .' Being baffled is nothing new, but this was exceptional. First the Rolls, then a Cinderella transformation without the mice, and now Ferd has shazammed into wealth plus the Olympics?

'You mustn't, Lovejoy.'

I mustn't what? Then I twigged. She meant ravishment was out of the question. Ferd was hale and vigilant. We hadn't made smiles as routine, honestly. But Norma had utterly lost her spirits, gone from being comfortably off to eking out the pennies, her husband a broken man while she skivvied for neighbours. I didn't blame her for raping me while Ferd dozed and twitched in his deckchair. I was the only bliss she'd had. Back then, of course; no longer.

'No ravishing,' I translated. 'Right?'

She coloured deeper still. 'I was weak, Lovejoy. Naturally I was grateful. You were the only friend who had the decency to stay loyal to Ferd while . . .' et pious cetera.

Join those dots for the usual cop-out. I honestly don't understand why women think like this. They believe in words too much, assume that feelings have to be spoken aloud, every twinge detailed. The opposite is true, but they just don't get it.

Once, I was subjected to a long diatribe by a lady I'd only just met. I'd taken her a jump-up. This is a lovely antique baby chair with a little tray that stands on a small beautifully edged table so the chair can't fall off. Lift the baby down, and you have a table and chair set! The Victorian joiners of

High Wycombe made these. They're still unbelievably cheap, a mere three hundred zlotniks in mint condition, though by the time you read this . . .

That particular lady spoke for a full hour, staring past me at the middle distance, gradually encroaching on my bit of her couch until we were virtually seated in the same spot. The inevitable happened, and we made smiles. See what I mean? Too many words, when a simple beckoning gesture would have done. Where was I? Being warned off Norma, by Norma.

'I understand, love. No groping.'

'Lovejoy! Must you say everything straight out?' Which from her . . .

We drove in silence the rest of the way, me the scruff, she the brilliantly lovely fashion goddess at the wheel of her cruiser. At Ferd's house I saw an instant transformation.

One of those huge Scandinavian wooden sheds had been erected by the dwelling. A new shingle drive had been laid. Notices proclaimed FERNORM ANTIQUES, INC in flashing neon. Two lasses dressed as Edwardian housemaids were busily enticing customers in from the main road while pretending to arrange antique furniture on the cloistered forecourt. A week ago, note, it had been the usual unkempt grassy shambles of the impoverished sinking classes. I wondered where the buildings and curved drives had sprung from. We alighted.

'Ferd's inside arranging antiques,' Norma said a little breathlessly, leading the way. A fortnight ago they couldn't afford to run their TV.

The maids chorused a welcome. Two dealers I

recognized stalked among the antiques, hardly gave me a glance when I called a hearty wotcher.

'Hello, old friend!' Ferd boomed, advancing.

He too had changed. From a morose shaky old man he'd filled out, smartened, become the village squire in tweeds and plus-fours. Everything he'd ever dreamed of, in fact.

'Wotcher, Ferd. No painting session today, then?'

He boomed, actually boomed, a hearty guffaw and shook my hand in a grip of iron. I yelped, lacking manly pride.

'Heavens, no, Lovejoy. I'll show you some antiques, old fruit!'

As I followed I marvelled. Norma avoided my eye, said she needed to see the housekeeper, and left me to it. Servants, wealth, new buildings, a thriving antiques business, all in a matter of days?

'Look at these, Lovejoy!' Ferd was intoning. 'Who says you can't make a splendid living from antiques, hey?' He actually said that, Heyyy? like calling the first round at boxing.

'Well, I do,' I said, but it was a weak quip. I stared.

The main shed—grander than the word tells—was about twenty strides square, crammed with antiques. There were two small back rooms. One was an office, the other he opened with a flourish.

'Seen anything like this, Lovejoy?'

There's a saying among antique dealers that 'before 1750 nothing came out of Ireland, but that after 1750 everything did'. Meaning that older Irish antiques are virtually non-existent, whereas after the mid-eighteenth century you find plenty of Irish artefacts. Irish furniture isn't to my liking, not

112

unless you like massive masks on your Georgian yew-wood furniture, weird faces carved on to table edges and the like. They went in for bog oak, even dyed mahogany to resemble it. Can't understand it myself, but whatever turns you on. The room was crammed with Irish furniture. I gulped, sweated, felt my chest thump and my hands go clammy. It was genuine. I reeled, made the door and onto the grass, inhaling cooler air.

He followed.

'What, Lovejoy?' He hadn't lost confidence. 'You're not saying it isn't genuine?'

'No, Ferd.' I gradually came to. 'Antiques do that to me, set me off.' I edged away from the shed, glancing back at it as I did so. The place must have cost him a fortune. The Rolls, the assistants, Norma's clothes. The main room was also thickly strewn with mixed antiques and junk, fifty-fifty. I was witnessing a resurgence, a miracle. 'Where'd you get the pier tables?' There'd been two.

'Oh, around. Got a backer.'

He smiled modestly, waved, and a maidservant approached with a chilled bottle of white wine and two glasses. Ferd led the way to a wrought-iron table with matching chairs. We sat. He raised his brogues, placed the heels on a chair, graciously allowed the lass to light his massive Cuban cigar.

'You'd need a backer, to afford them.'

Pier in antiques doesn't mean that thing sticking out of a seaside town into the sea, for the populace to stroll and take the air. It's the architectural term for a bit of the wall between two windows in your withdrawing room. From Queen Anne's time on, ladies became specially concerned with it as a feature. So 'pier glasses' were produced by London

113

craftsmen. These were mirrors especially designed to occupy that wall space and give an illusion of space. A lady's talent could be gauged by her adept use of furnishings that didn't make her parlour piers look daft. So pier tables came into being, small semicircular pieces that stood against the pier, unfolding into round tables with a superimposed leaf. And very lovely they are. Now, in Ireland, walls of Dublin's town houses lent themselves to slightly different pier tables, so you find 'typically Irish' (meaning exquisitely rare) pier tables *that are more of an ellipse than half a circle*. Find one in mahogany, mint, you're into your next world cruise, three times round. Find a pair, you can retire.

'Got a superb backer, Lovejoy!' He tasted the wine, nodded so the serf could withdraw to her slavery. 'See my potato rings? Two!'

'Aye. You've done well, mate.'

Dealers call them that, but they're properly termed dish rings. They're never much to look at, just a curved circlet of silver a few inches tall. You put them on tables then lodge your hot serving dishes on top, to stop the table getting scorched. What goon first called them potato or spud rings I don't know. They're hollow, of course, the silver quite thin, cut to depict flowers, birds and villeins doing their stuff. One dealer I knew sold one cheaply, thinking it was merely a dressing-table stand for ladies' necklaces. While Ferd expounded on life's gracious turns of fortune I heard motors drive up, car doors slam. Norma came to sit with us. I noticed her gold ring, her lovely sapphire and diamond. She'd had to pawn them three months since. Now they were back. Affluence is as affluence does. She looked brilliant. I wanted to eat her, but the thought of chewing her thighs honestly never crossed my mind.

'Who's the backer, Ferd?' I asked.

He smiled and wagged a finger roguishly. 'Now, now, Lovejoy.'

'Sorry.'

You don't ask three things of any dealer: how much, where from, and who else. (Why, is always self-explanatory, for we all know why, or so we believe.)

Norma was smiling. I noticed she'd donned a lovely cold green pendant in gold. Risky, but on her effective. The gem was demantoid, a semi-precious garnet. (God, how I hate that term. You wouldn't call a diamond a semi-opal, or dawn a semi-day, so why are gemstones called semi-precious? We think of everything as money, that's why. I reckon it's an insult to gemstones.)

Demantoid: think of an emerald trying hard to be peridot, wash out more than half of the colour you have left, and there you have it. I love demantoid. It's actually a very pale clear green variety of andradite, but has a luscious lustre. Heaven knows why women don't go more for this exquisite stone, but they don't. Maybe they don't like the name. She caught me looking and had the grace to blush. She carolled a covering laugh.

'Lovejoy's noticed my new pendant, Ferdinand!' She fingered it. 'I got it from a maiden aunt who died.'

Possibly in the Soviet Union, when there was such a country? Because that's where demantoid and andradites mostly come from. The gold mount was devised to resemble niello, a Russian form of

115

decoration.

'God rest her,' I said politely, as if I believed her.

Ferd looked amused, full of himself. Some pleb called out for him and he waved nonchalantly. Mortimer was right; this was a transformation the like I'd never seen. From defeated relic to a mercantile prince all in a week.

'Can I help, Ferd?' I asked. When I'm broke I start whining. I'm rubbish. 'I'll sort your incoming. I'll divvy for you,' I added recklessly, though it always gives me a terrible headache, sorting genuine antiques from fake.

'No, thanks, Lovejoy.' He rose, stretched, waved to his minions that he was coming. 'I've got everything I need.' And strode off to his burgeoning empire, monarch of all.

'Leaving two green bottles hanging on the wall, love.'

Norma said, 'Shhh. I told you, Lovejoy. No more.'

'I'm glad he's got a money partner. Is it permanent?'

A shadow crossed her face. You can always tell. No clouds in the skies, yet something darkened her eyes very like a portent. It happens more with women's eyes than men's, because women look close. Men gaze afar.

'Yes. As near as we can tell.'

'At great cost, love? Or does he come free?'

'It's a partnership, for heaven's sake!' She rose angrily. 'I knew you'd start the minute I heard you on the phone. You'd better go now. And take your ridiculous daubs with you! You're never anything but trouble!'

Off she stalked, leaving me alone. My ridiculous

daubs? She meant my watercolours that I tried to cheer Ferd up with when he was ailing. No need of them now. I looked after her. She even moved alluringly in high heels on her greensward, which takes some doing. I waited until she was gone, then cadged a lift back to town with Openers, a shabby little geezer from the street barrows. He makes lunatic starting bids at auctions to rile the auctioneers. 'Penny-farthing for openers, guv,' is his usual squawk. He never laughs, though others do.

On the way I asked him what he'd bought from Ferd's magnificent new storehouse.

'Nil,' he groused, surly. 'Where the hell could I get money to buy that sort of kite?' Kite is antique-speak for quality. 'Especially with Sandy and Mel buying everything for Ferd that's not nailed down.'

'Eh?' Now, Ferd and Norma hated Sandy, wouldn't do business with him for a knighthood, yet here was Openers saying that Randy Sandy was Ferd's new backer. A headache began.

'Here, Lovejoy. Can you help me?'

'Hardly, wack. I'm on my uppers.'

'It's my wife. I promised I'd pay for her wedding if she'll divorce me. Let me say we're doing some deal, eh?'

'Oh, right,' I said, blank. 'Er, it'll be her third husband?'

'Course,' he said, like it was the most usual thing in the world. 'She's fixed on splicing with him before Bonfire Plot. She says it'll be unlucky otherwise.'

'Okay, if it'll get you out of a hole, Openers.'

'Ta, Lovejoy. You're a pal. I owe you.'

Some debtor. Openers had never been solvent.

I've always had an eye for a bargain. He dropped me at the war memorial, so I decided to go and scrounge from Alanna, a reporter who broadcasts falsehoods to the sealands on local stations, which only goes to show how desperately worried I was.

CHAPTER THIRTEEN

I like the way women look. I mean the way they glance, stare, peer. They look even when they're not looking, if you follow. Mostly they do it at other women, sizing rivals, is she likely to cause trouble or just a stain on the backdrop. They're interesting because they're interested.

There's a species of frog that lives in trees, if you can imagine anything so daft, that generates chemical molecules called splendipherin. It's a sex pheromone that makes the male frog become gorgeous with tones, hues, colours, so the female *Litora splendida* gives him a glance and thinks, hey, what a dazzler, and clambers to his branch to make smiles. We blokes need something. We're a pretty dull lot. If I could bottle that stuff I'd make a fortune selling it in our market.

My actors' army made me sigh. I'd seen better routs. The Duke of Wellington's crack came to mind: 'I don't know what Napoleon will think of our new recruits, but by God they frighten me!' and other anecdotes. They stood there, nervy and shambolic. The nerk called Larch, like me lacking splendipherins, had tarted himself up in dark leathers, obviously borrowed to impress. My gran used to say, 'Fashion today, fool tomorrow,' and it's

118

true. Pictures of 1920s flappers in their cloche hats and strapped bodices make you exclaim, 'They wore *that*?' and roll in the aisles. And those wide Windsor bags, trousers with creases unbelievably pressed sideways—the late Duke of Windsor's only contribution to civilization, 'tis said—make you think, 'God in heaven, who donned those?'

'You know the drill?'

I'd gone over it as we'd driven over in Jacko's coal wagon, him my last resort singing bad opera as we clattered across East Anglia. They were still dusting themselves down, Tina and Wilhelmina—mercifully minus her shahtoosh—were angry. So was I, because they'd made a special dress effort when I'd told them not to. On a scale of ten, I felt twice as narked.

'I thought it was a real production, Lovejoy,' Larch said. Jules was quiet, sensing my desperation.

'Larch, it's more real than you'd ever imagine.'

'I'm nervous,' Wilhelmina whispered as Taylor Eggers came to the door and smilingly beckoned us. 'What if I forget the signal?'

'You won't, love.' If she'd podded off her woollen and done as I said, she must have serious gelt. The thought of all that profit from her granny's shawl made me realize how lovely she was. I felt myself redden as Tina caught me looking. (See? Women's glances.)

Susanne Eggers was waiting, smoking elegantly, seated in the library. I recognized a silver-framed photograph of Arthur Goldhorn, RIP, and his missus with a bonny baby boy. The boy was, is, Mortimer. His mother lives in sordid but affluent sin among muscle dancers in Soho, Bondi Beach

119

and other exotic climes. I don't really miss her.

Mrs Eggers was reading a volume set on a wooden Moorish stand, beautifully carved. I'd sweated blood carving that from Resak wood for Mortimer's parents' wedding. I don't really like paler woods; the dark brown smooth varieties are a delight. Seasoning Resak drives you mad, of course, but it's the carver's friend for hard, heavy, classy joinery. Her book was modern and therefore gunge, meaning printed after 1939.

'Wait,' she commanded, not looking.

We waited. Mr Eggers smiled, bustled, nobly held himself back from offering us chairs or tea. Larch, Tina, and Wilhelmina were frozen in awe of the money lady. Jules used the moments silently sussing out the room's antiques.

He'd done five years, three with remission for good behaviour, mainly for seducing the Countess, whenever she commanded him to do so. He used to drive her pantechnicon to Eastern Europe. It was loaded with relief supplies to the Balkans after mayhem set people refugeeing all over the place. Sounds rum? Not really, because charities are the biggest ripoffs on earth. (You know the scam: please send us money so we can feed the Hungry Out There, et phoney cetera.) If in doubt, check any major charity. It'll have splendid offices, highly paid staff living in tree-lined suburbs with swimming pools and servants. Think of the United Nations and the World Bank, and there you have it. I call the lot of them Crooks, Inc.

The Countess is a major antiques dealer near Long Melford. She funds ('from my profits, daaahlink!' she always says at her trials) heart-rending charity runs. Folk—meaning you—donate

120

clothes, money, medical supplies, and off the great vehicles go. One convoy's leading lorry was driven by Jules. It got stopped because some well-meaning Customs blokes wanted to give some medicines to the convoy, and discovered that Jules's wagon was ramjam packed with antique furniture, silver, porcelain, and paintings, not a single crust or a bandage. The clean lorries went on. Jules earned the vilification of the entire nation. The Countess naturally went scotage free ('Ay didn't know a thing, daaahlink!') and still lives on donations nicked from her charities, antiques, and men, more or less in that order. Local dealers felt almost nearly sincerely sorry for Jules, but secretly rejoiced that a rival dealer was removed to where he couldn't compete, namely in nick. Ten minutes after his conviction, the entire trade was back dealing with the Countess. This was why I'd told Tina to pick him, from sympathy. Always a duckegg.

'Right.' Mrs Eggers closed the book with a thud and surveyed us. She looked even better today, a superb royal blue satin dress, with baroque pearls that must be Scotch naturals from Perth, earrings to match, gold bangles. She was worth the county, me thrown in. 'Names.'

'I'm Lovejoy. This is Tina. Wilhelmina. Larch and, er, Jules.'

'You're all divvies, I believe. Score these antiques correctly. Some, I'm told, are forgeries, others not.' She crossed to a sofa table, its leaves raised for maximum space. On it stood four antiques. Straight off I saw her ploy: choose right, you were in; get one wrong, off with your head. 'Men first, women next, in,' she commanded icily,

121

'order of age. Cards and pencils.'

Taylor smilingly handed out cards, beaming. 'They're numbered from the left. Put a tick or a cross,' and retired grinning like a Cheshire cat. I wished he'd frown. I distrust smiley folk the same way I hate charmers.

Jules stepped forward, walked along the four antiques, marking his card. He initialled the back and handed it to Taylor. Larch took his time. Tina then Wilhelmina followed suit. I didn't like the way Larch posed, swirled and pondered, mmmhing and fingering his chin. Silly melodrama stuff. Wilhelmina tried for some mythical part in *Rebecca*, hoping the non-existent cameras were catching her best side.

'Lovejoy?' To my stare Mrs Eggers said angrily, 'Go on, dolt.'

Me too? I got a card, went along the row. The sofa table was not genuine, though somebody had had a high old time doing french polishing, kidding us it was a genuine sofa table of about 1820 that had been fopped up in late Victorian times. More crud, by definition. To check, I leaned down as if to adjust my shoe, and looked along the grain. The surface was entirely without pores. Now, you can't have this, not by the original french polishing techniques, so somebody had cleverly used an alkyd wash. This spreads out of its own accord, giving you the pluperfectly level finish. Then you can polish any way you like to your heart's content, because the lovely table will come up like a genuine table that some Regency lady would use for tea while reclining in languor on her sofa to the admiration of her visitors. I'd signalled it false to the others, but I gave it a tick, for genuine.

122

A pewter drinking goblet was early Victorian. Some burke had tried to clean its patina off with potash or soda (some nerks use ammonia; they should be gaoled). It was genuine right enough, but I grew angry for the poor little vessel. Homemade, probably, or recast by some wandering tinsmith. They went from village to village in the old days, remaking battered pewter cups. If you *have* to clean pewter, and I recommend that you don't, please put it in a simple hay bath—three pints of chopped hay into a big metal pan. Fill it with water just too hot to touch, then immerse the pewter in it for seven or so hours. Please promise you won't use solvents or hot sand, no matter what professional books say. I couldn't help glowering at Taylor Eggers. Mortimer was daily providing fresh evidence of being a true divvy, so I knew he wouldn't be the vandal who'd ruined the goblet. I apologized mentally to the poor genuine thing. I marked it a fake.

A little marble statuette of a faun was tagged Number Three. Nigh on two hundred years old, Italian from the look, but some hard-hearted swine had etched a mark on its foot with some coarse cleaning agent, probably oxalic acid, to ruin the patina and make a casual observer assume it was a reproduction. Such blemishes are common in fakes. So Susanne Eggers must have thought it worthwhile to injure a genuine antique just to make her test more effective, the rotten cow. I ask you, what morality is that? Now I'd hate her for ever. She must have been desperate about something vital. I scored it fake, to be wrong again.

The last object was an earthenware galena-glazed moneybox shaped like a hen sitting on a crude nest. Three hundred years old or so, these things are highly valuable. They have a slit for coins. Full, you simply smashed the pot and totted up your loot. (Hence our saying, 'nest-egg'.) Very few have survived, though we—I mean dishonest forgers and fakers, not me—make them when desperate for gelt, hoping some buyer will jump to the wrong conclusion. This was genuine, making real bongs in my chest. Worth a decent motor on a good day. So I scored it a dud.

'That it, missus?' I gave Taylor Eggers the card.

'Wait outside,' she ordered. 'This is confidential. Understand?'

We swore eternal fealty and trailed out to stand on the gravel. I felt embarrassed. They'd done really well, got every one correct. I was the only one to get them wrong.

'Are we still in character, Lovejoy?' Wilhelmina asked in a whisper.

'Not any longer,' Tina said, smiling fetchingly at me. 'Did we get your signals right, Lovejoy?'

It took a millisec to answer. She'd just proved she was a treacherous bitch.

'Aye, well done all of you.'

'Will she tell us straight away which of us gets the part?'

'Maybe she'll want everybody.' I tried to do one of Taylor's hearty beams, on the theory that optimistic lies are best.

'That'd be superb,' Larch said to Wilhelmina. She smiled at him. I realized he must have overheard my spiel about her priceless shahtoosh. I sighed inwardly. So near and yet so far.

'Lovejoy?' Taylor appeared at the door. 'Thank you for your services. Mrs Eggers will send word.

You will each get expenses.'

One last beam, then slam. We looked at one another. I wondered if the deal was off, whatever it was. Maybe Susanne Eggers's mystery ghost had its own way of working. I led the way in silence to the road and we clam bered aboard Jacko's lorry. Only because I was looking, I saw a shadowy figure in the shrubbery by the huge ornate gate. It raised a thumb and little finger, sign of the telephone. I just nodded.

We drove back to town while Jacko sang that high C thing from *The Daughter of the Regiment*. I hummed along but, unlike Jacko, in tune with the composer's intentions until Tina snapped at me to shut up. Jacko bawled atonally on. Well, it was his lorry. Larch and Wilhelmina talked quietly. Tina then settled down, smiling inwardly at a good job done, the traitorous cow. Jules only once was careless enough to catch my eye and swiftly looked away. He too knew we'd been had, maybe guessed who by.

We alighted at the war memorial. I told Tina to give me a list of phone numbers where I could reach them. It was only then that I wondered how the hell could I phone Mortimer like he'd signalled, if the phone people had disconnected me. We split up, and that was the end of a perfect day until I was reminded of a death, the only one in recorded history that was not my fault.

CHAPTER FOURTEEN

The Welcome Sailor was crowded. The dealers raised a derisory cheer when I entered, 'Watch your wallets / women / pints!' in various combinations, all that. I was surprised to see five auctioneers in, because they're like kestrels. You only see one at a time, unlike other birds of prey I could mention.

I went about trying to cadge a drink, not because I was thirsty but because it would legitimize my presence and I could see who else was in. Failing miserably, I went into the saloon bar where I found Jules losing to himself at dominoes.

'Ta for that, Lovejoy. Made me feel a lot better.'

'Give over. Seen Susanne Eggers before, have you?'

'Once,' he said. I showed surprise. 'She tried to buy out the Edgar Allen Poe bloke. Remember that Prague business?'

I remembered all right. 'Your bit of coffin?'

'Before I went on holiday.' He meant gaol.

The Poe bloke is secretly famous. We all know that he's English, obsessed with the long-dead writer. Very like some sculptress I could mention who's emotionally involved with Leonardo da Vinci. It takes all sorts. The Poe bloke arranged a vast EAP Festival in Prague, of all places, and actually pulled it off. He assembled Poe's clothes, gear, books, etc, etc. Jules here reckoned he'd contributed a chunk of Poe's actual coffin. Most dealers claim this kind of thing, given half a listen.

'What did she have to do with it?'

'She tried to pinch his idea, see? It failed.' Jules put his arm round his glass as if to shield it, the mark of the soldier squaddie and the lag. 'I saw her the day she got her team together. One of them's a big Yank diplomat.'

'She had quite a mob, then?' Remember what I said about antique dealers flocking? Think

126

vultures, not budgies.

'Not really.' He was watching the tap-room door as if waiting for somebody. 'Ferd and Norma, the Countess, Sandy and Mel. Horse and FeelFree wanted in but got the sailor's elbow, nudge splash. Vestry was going to try but shuffled the coil.'

A strange group. My voice croaked twice before it got going. 'How come you wanted to audition, you having met her before and all?'

Nobody was within earshot. Two middle-aged lovebirds by the door were having one of those terrible whispered arguments, all thin lips and white knuckles. I didn't know them.

He smiled sadly. 'She's never seen me before. I was the Countess's next bloke after you, Lovejoy.' I went a bit red. The Countess has lovers like restaurants do servings. 'I was in her Antiques Emporiana.' In case I'd forgotten, he added helpfully, 'You turn off through Long Melford—'

'I know.' Who didn't?

'We were in her stockroom when they all came to decide the chop. Ferd and Norma, Mrs Eggers, Sandy, a bloke I'd never seen before.' He winced. 'The Countess shoved me behind a curtain. It covers the doorway into—'

'I know, I know.'

Chop is the division of the spoils. I was embarrassed, that curtain. Uneasily I wondered how many of the Countess's former lovers had hidden behind it while she sallied forth to awe customers.

'I heard about you wanted actors so I changed my name. That's it.'

So Susanne Eggers was a would-be international buyer. My pathetic brain felt it was clip-clopping

127

after Derby runners. 'She must have money,' I bleated feebly, as if a Yank lady who could rent a country estate and assemble a team of antique dealers might possibly be destitute.

'She's loaded. The Countess was in raptures.'

'What happened?'

For it had changed. Instead of a respectable mob of well-off dealers, she'd finished up with a penniless dolt, namely Icky Tod, me. I felt risk closing in. Thank you, Mortimer.

He said scornfully, 'Vestry took the drop, didn't he? That's what happened, Lovejoy.'

My imbecilic mind went, trying to trick me with the obvious, hey? It was then that I realized I was simply putting things off. I'd known what to do for some time. It was time I got on.

'Ta, Jules.'

Now I knew that Susanne Eggers was dedicated to something long-term and multo vital. She was a trier and a stayer. All the clues were somewhere there. She wanted to assemble a task force, and failed. She'd tried to nick a successful international festival, and failed. So she was scraping the barrel, namely me, that well-known success story.

Desperate from hunger, I went to find my talented ex-friend Alanna, who now hated me because I once made smiles with her mother. Please hear me out, because it wasn't my fault. I postponed the burglary I was going to do for Bernicka. I'd just got time to reach the rubbish tip.

There stands Marjorie.

*　　　*　　　*

Law compels our rural councils to run a rubbish

dump. It's called the Regional Council Recycling and Hygienic Refuse Disposal Central Facility. It only means a tip.

Among waste containers loaded with old clothes, tins, bottles, and stacks of sodden paper are vast heaps of smouldering ashes spread over a desolate landscape. There's a hut where workmen play cards and doze, a prefab office where the boss watches cricket on a TV nicked from the chutes, and that's it. Except for Marjorie, she of the biggest customized Aston Martin you ever did see. She is fiftyish. (Her age doesn't matter. I'm only trying to explain how things turned out.) She was, is, always there on weekdays, dressed to the nines. Fox fur (ugh), elegant high heels, lovely figure, a quite splendid hat and kid gloves, she stands and watches the macabre terrain. If the weather turns foul she sits in her motor listening to the radio. Usually she's merely there while folk drive in, ditch their rubbish and exit smiling. And Marjorie leaps into action.

Sometimes, folk throw out things that aren't quite crud. It's then that this serene, charming figure moves with the alacrity of a decathlete and scavenges like a terrier. I've seen Marjorie actually fight—not merely squabble or rant; I mean fisticuffs and talons—over a broken side-table you wouldn't shake a stick at. It's ugly. Is there anything worse than a drunken woman, or two women brawling over detritus? I was fascinated by her when first we met. We both were trying for a leatherette case that looked hopeful. I was on my uppers from an episode of financial ruin, and had grown desperate. Challenged by this harridan, I made a chivalrous withdrawal. Marjorie turned on

129

me such a lovely smile of triumph that I was quite dazzled. The dress pouch she won held a lovely articulated Regency fan with a perfectly preserved silk leaf painted with Parisian scenes, about 1778 give or take a yard. I fell head over heels for Marjorie on the spot, and wooed her with instant passion, of course hoping to nick the fan.

We made smiles, the lovely scavenger Marjorie and I, for quite three days. Long time, especially as I never did get the cased fan. Our pure love was ruined when her daughter woke us, hollering what the hell was I doing in her mother's bed. The affronted offspring was Alanna, she of the golden hair, who is a broadcaster, meaning she sings those jingles trying to get you to buy face cream and toilet rolls, and fills in when the newsreader's too sloshed or stoned to sit erect. I'd given Alanna the best years of my life for a fortnight once, so knew her temper. The story got around and for a month or two my name was mud. Paradoxically, things move apace in antiques. Apart from a deluge of jokes at my expense the affair was soon forgot, though I still sob over that Regency silk fan. I could have bought my cottage for it, and lived there honestly.

The lovely Marjorie was there, beautifully attired in the lunar landscape. She wore a pastel blue suit, the skirt hem defiantly lower than fashionable, a capellone hat with flowers on its sweeping brim, gloves and a chic veil. A queen amid jetsam. On hot days she carries a frilly parasol. I noticed an old Singer sewing machine in her brilliant Aston Martin. (Who'd lifted it for her? And who would lift it out?) I peered as I approached. It wasn't a Kimball Morton Lion treadler of 1868, thank God, or I'd have been really narked because one would buy a new car. (Tip: the head of this sewing machine rarity is cast actually like a lion, its bottom towards the bobbin.) You can't miss it, yet folk still chuck them out. I heard of one old lady who actually paid a dealer to take hers away. Dandy Jack, down the Arcade.

'Good day, Lovejoy.'

'Wotcher, Marjorie. Trade good?'

'Slow, Lovejoy.' She appraised me in silence as cars arrived. A bloke hefted out a bundle of hedge cuttings. She smiled at him as he drove off, her investment in an unknowable future. 'It's time you and Alanna got back together, Lovejoy. She's at Eastern Hundreds TV down Pelhams Lane.'

'Chance'd be a fine thing, Marjorie.'

'For somebody who reckons he's clever you're stupid, Lovejoy. Tell her you were only trying to make her jealous.'

I tried to work out what she was on about. Women, lacking any legal or social accountability, are basically greed machines fuelled by whim, yet they do have a certain paralogic that occasionally works, though you can't use it yourself without a detailed instruction manual.

After a few minutes I asked, 'Jealous of what?'

'She was seeing a Cambridgeshire bobby. I didn't approve, Lovejoy.'

'Alanna was?' I seethed with indignation. 'Seeing somebody else? The rotten two-timing bitch.'

'You were sleeping with her mother, Lovejoy,' Marjorie said. That old reason trick again. It shows how underhand women can be.

'I'll try,' I said, giving in after sulking a bit. I badly needed Alanna's help. 'Ta, Marjorie.'

'Here.' She passed me a note. 'Have something to eat, for God's sake. And don't be such a bloody fool. I won't bite if you call in.'

Accepting a loan on a rubbish dump doesn't seem quite so humiliating as anywhere else, does it? I trudged off, leaving the stylish Marjorie standing there, queen of her domain.

*   *   *

The shoddy Eastern Hundreds TV studios are in a side street near Trinity Square. I waited in the anteroom among tatty magazines and soiled plastic cups. Occasional girls and bearded wonders strolled in, went through by tapping in some code on a panel. They looked hung over, arrivals from a shop-soiled protest march. I said hello to one or two and was ignored. They were marauders acting out a corporate conspiracy against TV viewers. Some called out vigorous greetings into the squawk box, of the tally-ho sort that foxes know so well. My Auntie Agnes wouldn't have let any of them across her threshold. She'd have given them all a good scrubbing.

Alanna angrily emerged after an hour. She must have seen me on the closed circuit and finally lost patience.

'What do you want?'

Nobody about, nobody to overhear.

I blurted, 'Whyn't you tell me Vestry was murdered, Alanna?' And thought, *what* did I just say? I stared, aghast at my exhumed suspicion, gaping inwardly as much as out at her radiant gold hair, because she recoiled in shock, eyes wide.

Quickly she glanced about, closed the panel

132

bchind her. She slowly sat. I tried to adjust, get things back to normal.

'This place always pongs of armpit.' I didn't manage a smile, just worked those levator muscles without reassurance. It was a wonder she didn't run.

'Why didn't I *what*, Lovejoy?'

People in broadcasting are of two sorts. One is the wireball, as they call those blokes who trail flexes and wear earphones to shut the world out. The other is the scripwit, some nerk who sits before the camera's red eye, tries to sound original and look as if they're not being screamed at down headphones by some frantic producer exasperated at their stupidity. There's no other sort. Alanna was a scripwit, couldn't speak to camera without the idiot board. The only thing gets her going unprompted is finding some penniless git in bed with her mum, but whose fault was that? Marjorie had nicked my antique cased fan, after all.

'Vestry. Remember him?' In for a penny. 'You guessed there was something wrong, didn't you?'

She occasionally does work—I use the term loosely—for the *News Come Nine* team. She harbours hopes of becoming a national TV figure, like miracles happen. By instinct I went for her ambition's jugular.

'I knew it,' I said with bitterness. 'You were too smart to be taken in.' Soulfully I raised my eyes. 'I had suspicions all along, but thought I was the only one to realize it must have been murder.'

'Murder!' she breathed, the light of promotion in her eyes.

'Just as you suspected, Alanna,' I repeated, narked that she wasn't moving as fast as I hoped.

133

'You were clever, keeping your suspicions to yourself. Why didn't you tell me?'

'Well, I, ahm, you see—'

'I know, Alanna.' I turned aside, irritated that I couldn't see her reflection in some handy mirror, see how I was doing. I tried for a hurt kind of anger, the sort of thing women themselves act so brilliantly, but couldn't quite make it. Instead, I tried words, always a poor third to silence and passion. 'I know why. It was because you'd sussed me out, wasn't it?'

'Was it?' she said, quite lost.

Give me strength, I thought in temper. Do I have to do all the blinking work? I waxed lyrical to egg her on.

'Of course.' I uttered it coldly, deeply hurt by forsaken love. 'You always did see straight through me, Alanna. You knew I only ingratiated myself with your mum Marjorie to get even with you for going out with that horrible Cambridge copper. You saw I was trying to make you jealous.' I did a bitter laugh, nearly choked myself. Acting just isn't for me. I honestly don't know why I do it. I always lose conviction halfway through, like suddenly forgetting a poem.

'I didn't know,' she said, astonished, too many unscripted prompts in her mind. 'I honestly thought—'

'Very well.' I stood, Mr Darcy before his fireplace, perfidious women all about. 'I shall leave, but it ill behoves . . .' I stopped. I never say behoves. I hardly know what it means. 'If you won't help, then I'll go.'

'Wait, Lovejoy.' She saw the chance of a scoop and took my hand. 'Maybe I did misjudge you. You can't really blame me. I'll be in the Steps Caff tonight. I get off about eight.'

Relieved, I left with a murmured Mr Darcy adieu. If I'd had a lace hanky I'd have bowed. See? Tricking myself into being somebody else. One day it might be the end of me.

CHAPTER FIFTEEN

The market was already closing down Scheregate Steps, so the cheapo grub Filtho Shaughnessy cooks there to pollute our internal organs wasn't available. He packs up earliest of all the stalls because he's a lifeboat man down the estuary. Instead, I went to Princess Beatrice's Splendid Tea Shoppe on North Hill.

Bea Willing, no pun intended, runs it. With Marjorie's money I ordered a plate of scones, seven jam tarts, a pot of tea, a heap of toast, Lancashire cheese, and a plate of fried bread. I felt really proud. Bea served it with enough serviettes to stuff a mattress. Every one of her four minute tables held posies of flowers. The curtains are chintz. Portraits of Princess Beatrice (whoever was she?) adorned the walls. The name was spelled out in flowers over Bea's counter. Souvenirs were on sale near the fireplace, miniature busts, lace hankies 'as worn by our beloved Princess Beatrice!' and suchlike. I like Bea, who used to be in antiques but is now going straight. Princess Beatrice appeared to her in a vision.

'Can I tempt you to subscribe to my canonization fund, Lovejoy?'

'And help religion? My grampa'd have a fit.'

'No, dear. For our beloved Princess Beatrice!' Bea's eyes filled. 'I've got her really close to beatification!'

However hopeful, it's all hopeless. I felt sorry. Bea doesn't have a cat in hell's chance of getting Princess Beatrice made a saint. The process used to take a century, until Pope John Paul II started the modern sainthood epidemic. I knew—know—little about sanctity and less about princesses. Anyway, it's only women who can answer lineage questions—like who was ninth in line to the throne in 1935, and so on—on those tiresome quiz shows where you can win a million but nobody ever does.

'Wish you luck, Bea.' I started wolfing my grub.

She affects rustic dress, long russet skirt, smocked apron, lace mobcap, lace bertha when she has to go through to the kitchen. Bea has a pretty granddaughter aged eight dolled up in matching Victoriana who helps out during a rush (meaning when any two customers arrive simultaneously). Polly chews gum and hums Top Ten tunes. I have a lurking suspicion that Polly secretly enjoys spoiling Bea's Splendid Tea Shoppe ambience.

'Lovejoy?' Polly came to watch, swinging her foot. 'You eat fast.'

'Wotcher, Poll. I'm hungry, that's why.'

'I got chewing gum in my hair again last night.'

'You get it out okay?'

I once showed Bea how. You warm some chocolate in a pan, rub it briskly on the gum stuck to the child's hair, and it slides off like a dream. The butterfat, see? Continental chocolate doesn't work half as well. I made a lifelong friend in Polly, who sticks chewing gum into her hair every chance she gets to win a free boost of chocolate. The chocolate trick also does for chewing gum stuck on antique carpets. (Incidentally, for gum stuck on to small firm items, like a wooden carving or picture frames, put the antique into the freezer, if it'll take it. The gum lifts off clean as a whistle. It works for your best Northampton shoes as well.)

Polly is also my spy. No fewer than four antique shops are on North Hill near Bea's caff. One elderly gentleman was in, reading *The Times*. He wore a hearing aid, the flex dangling. Safe.

'Spied anything, Polly?'

'Yes. A lady came with the police.' And as my heart griped, 'They raided Sandy's shop.' She bent her head to spare the old colonel and whispered, 'Sandy's queer as a square frock. Did you know?'

'Watch your language, miss! You're only eight, you little sod.'

'Granma!' Polly rushed through the counter flap. 'Lovejoy sweared.'

'Tell him to stop it this instant!' from Bea's voice, distant in the kitchen.

The wretch had done it just to get me in trouble. Polly returned glowing with satisfaction and started to eat my fried bread. She cleared it almost as fast as me. It became a race. You wouldn't think a shrimp her size could engulf grub that fast.

'When?' I asked.

'Last night. I had to watch from upstairs because there was something bad on telly and Granma said I'd to sleep quick.' She swung listlessly in her little russet dress. 'Don't you want to know what happened?'

'Yes, please.'

'They took Peter Myer away. He's got nice ears.

137

Nobody got shot.'

'Doesn't sound much of a police raid without shooting.'

'It wasn't bad,' said this connoisseur of crime. 'They've left some police inside. I think they're being kept in because they didn't do things right. Like detention, see?'

'How many?'

'They come with seven, and four come out. Four from seven leaves three.'

'So it does.' Three police still in Antiques Antics across the road. Sandy owns it. Well, well. Spies have their uses.

'They sent for a lot of televisions. And,' she added, 'wires and things. And long guns. Why've you no marmalade?'

Long guns to Polly might well be some kind of telescopes. What Polly saw as TV sets might be CCTV consoles for closed circuitry cameras. Were they harking to me and little Polly even as we spoke?

'Good idea. Miss, could I please have some marmalade?' I asked. Such is our game.

'Yes, sir.' She fetched it by climbing onto a stool. We resumed our meal. She has three sugars in one cup, hardly room for the tea.

'The police motors followed a horrible American woman. I hated her teeth. She came in for some Gentleman's Relish yesterday and said Granma charged too much. She has terrible hair.'

'Where is Peter now, love?'

'He's poorly. He went in an ambulance. My kitten went in one once for its ears. They grew pus and one nearly fell off.' I stopped eating. 'Gangrene,' said this little angel. 'It rots cats' heads.'

I left soon after, smiling and waving to Polly at the door and shouting ta to Bea. I didn't even glance at Peter's double-fronted antiques shop, nor did I look at the other three on the steep slope. It leads down to the old North Gate of Roman times, long since crumbled and now encrusted with terraced houses and small shops. Quite pleasant old pubs by the river. But why had Peter been done over, and the police called, to lurk behind the curtains? Almost as if they expected somebody to come burgling.

Which raised the question what did he have that somebody needed so badly, that the police also were interested in?

I was halfway through the shopping precinct when a motor drew up alongside me and a lady's voice told me to get in. I obeyed, because that's what I do.

'Your money, Lovejoy. And for your divvies.'

'Ta.'

She still hadn't learned to smile. I decided I wouldn't, either. Take that, oh wicked one. I didn't count the gelt, just said to drop me anywhere.

'Stay.' She wasn't driving. Her husband Taylor was at the wheel. He did enough beaming for the pair of them, like it was his part of an understood bargain. 'You'll work for me. It'll take one week. You get a share of the take.'

'None of the others any good?'

'I've rerun the home movie, Lovejoy. The sofa table, the earthenware coin box, the marble faun, the pewter. Taylor had three cameras. It took him quite a while to spot your signs. Any noise—cough, clearing your throat—was a warning to say false,

139

right? Silence was approval.'

'What gave us away?' I asked hoarsely. Besides Tina's betrayal, I thought.

'The silence of the rest. They stood looking from you to the antiques, learning what was good and what bad.'

'Who blemished the marble?'

'That old thing? Me, of course. Don't worry, Lovejoy. There's much, much more at stake than those bits and pieces.'

'When?'

'Soon. Out.'

Out? 'Oh, right.' I stood on the pavement, worrying whether to say thank you or not. The motor revved, shrank into the middle distance.

For a while I looked down North Hill. Sandy and Mel actually owned Antique Antics. They lease it to Peter Myer for a peppercorn rent. Don't ask for reasons. Now, I thought as I went for the bus, Peter Myer and Sandy might be colluding with the plod, or Peter was under arrest. But what was worth setting up a police surveillance unit for? The plod never stir far from the TVs in their social clubs, unless forced. Besides Bea's teashop the only thing directly opposite was an insurance agency— 'Registered Speciality at Lloyd's of London!'— belonging to Timothy Giverell. I vaguely knew him, and his wife Florence. Dull as you'd ever get.

Then I thought oh what the hell, and decided to call on the Countess. Then the forger. Then I'd do the burglary. Keep things in order. My mind was getting so cluttered I was starting to lose the plot. Actors say that a lot.

CHAPTER SIXTEEN

The Countess is the antique dealer to top all dealers.

*   *   *

Life must be so easy for women. I mean, if they've to meet some bloke, they simply get glitzed up knowing they'll be in supercontrol. Whatever happens. Whoever the bloke might be. Women rule.

But for the man it's so-o-o-o different. If he's to meet some woman he's on edge, worried sick. What'll she think? Will she cost more than the few pence he possesses? What'll he talk about, for God's sake? Will she see that he's a wimp who doesn't pump iron? That he hasn't a degree in astrophysics? That he once had trouble with his credit card, hasn't got a Rolls-Royce? What has he got to offer?

There's a reason for this.

It's beauty.

Beauty is power, total and immutable power. And every woman has her own beauty. Old, young, fat, thin, lame or wick as a flea, spectacled or with the limpid eyes of Cleopatra, she's on the box seat and the man is a mere supplicant down there in the splashy mud begging a lift. That's my Law of Gender in a nutshell. It's the reason that a woman—*any* woman—can have any man any time, any place. She wants some rich, handsome polyglot devil? He's hers for the taking.

Not so the other way round. *No* man can get a woman without inordinate luck, astronomical wealth, stunning teeth, immense physique, the patience of a saint, the morals of a crook, the charm of the devil, the brains of Newton, total fame, global influence, and perennial youth. And if he does succeed? It's temporary. She'll depart on a whim—and women have whims like grass grows worms.

(Sorry if this seems cynical, but I've studied these conclusions a lifetime. And I've tried, I've tried.)

It follows that a man can never escape a woman who sets her cap. He's trapped. Permanent. A man can't leave until she gets rid. Until that day—and it will come, what ever poets and drink and optimism might say—you're in thrall to her for life. No good moaning, because it's natural. A bloke has to make the best of it.

The only thing we've got going for us is that women don't believe this.

For some reason, they think beauty is in expensive lotions, the designer label, costly garments and the breathtaking charges of fashionable hairdressers. Why they're hooked on trendy colours, silly styles or daft shoes I honestly don't know. They believe the myth that these cunning devices are necessary. Wrong, wrong. If they went out uncombed and shoddy, women would have exactly the same success rate, and that is total, hundred per cent. Failure rate: nil, zero. If they once tried it, they'd end the entire fashion industry in an afternoon.

To summarize: any woman can get any man. A man can't leave a woman unless she says get lost.

On the hour-long bus journey out of town, I reconsidered these inflexible laws. And alighted, ready for the Countess.

*   *   *

Some folk have the knack of resuming conversations exactly where they left off months, maybe years, before. I'd last seen her on Braggot Sunday, the old mid-Lent day when you give ladies a present of honey-brewed spiced ale. We were pretty close, until a horrid moment when she'd had two of her whifflers drive me from her door by the simple technique of pointing a digit. No reason, no logic. And God knows I'd slogged to gain her a fortune in antiques. Okay, so I'd reportedly been seen in the motor car belonging to Hepsibah Smith, our church's choir mistress, on the Coggeshall bypass, but was that my fault? Women aren't fair. When I please one woman, the rest get narked. What is it with them?

When the fatal sly note-of-hand was dropped in front of the Countess by some kind friend she'd opened it, read slowly, then raised her eyes. With a snap of her imperial fingers she'd had me bundled out into the path of a farm tractor. At the time the Countess had been reminiscing about Russian nobility over Lipton's tea. She had been one of them in a former incarnation. Now, she was phoney like the rest of us, becoming somewhat bloated (like the rest of us) and indolent and guessy (LTROU).

You'll have got my drift. In life, female stands for every thing that matters, whereas in antiques wealth means everything. Now think of a dealer

143

who is a titled lady *and* has untold wealth: that's the Countess. We'd been close once, or have I already said that? I think I've gone on about her a shade too long to convince me that I didn't care any longer.

Countesses don't have simple antique shops. They own Antiques Emporianas and Antiqueries A La Modes. This joint had a workshop making Special Customizations (read fakes) at the rear, and others on her two balconies that did varnishing and assembly work. Porcelains were being fired outside. Metalwork was done in a forge with two small foundries tacked on to the side of her building. It was more a small industrial town.

In the centre seated on a regal chaise-longue under a tester embroidered with gold reclined the Countess. She always feasts on grapes, fruits you never know the names of, and is wafted and cooled—if not warmed—by two youths dressed as blackamoors straight from some Manet painting.

The place was crammed with antique furniture. Most of it was fake, though I felt the vibrations of several authentic pieces. On the balconies I could see the silhouettes of her artisans labouring at lathes and workbenches, hear boots crunching wood shavings. The scent of varnish was pure aroma, stirring my heart as much as the woman I had come to see.

'Lovejoy,' she said, bored. 'Out.'

'Out,' a nerk the size of Wolverhampton repeated, chucking me into the road. A motor screeched. The driver got out, badly disturbed, and asked if I was all right. I told him yes, ta. He drove off shaking his head.

This made me think. I rummaged in a nearby

dustbin for a newspaper, and borrowed a passing postman's ballpoint. On the paper I wrote, 'BANKRUPT YET?' and propped it against the window.

The hulk let me in. I walked towards the Countess, not genuflecting in spite of the impulse. She was lovely. Okay, plump and florid, hair piled up into a Carolean landscape and features a thick mask of cosmetics. I could see where the layers began. I'd never seen so much blue caked round a woman's eyes since I'd met Dame Barbara Cartland, God rest her. Lipstick thickened her mouth to a tubular pout. Earrings spread over her shoulders like epaulettes. She wore a dozen necklaces of heavy gold links, each with assorted pendants. Her toes shone with scarlet varnish and diamond rings. Lovely to see a real woman making the best of herself. I'd never seen anything so beautiful. I felt a pang. I had lost all that pulchritude.

'Russia, in the days of the Soviets,' the Countess said, resuming where she'd left off yonks since, 'nationalized reindeer. Can you imagine the barbarity? And guess, Lovejoy. Which country has the most American one-hundred dollar bills?'

'Russia?'

'Who else? More than America. When Russia needed a bank to launder several billions of dollars, how long did it take those Cossack ruffians to find crooks with sufficient expertise? Guess.' And when I shook my head, 'One hour! What a stupendous, horrifying country!'

'Indeed, Countess.' Me, dyed-in-the-wool humility.

'Come and sit down, dear boy.'

145

This is how teachers speak before they clobber you, hitting you hurts me more than it hurts you. I advanced gingerly and perched on a low stool waiting to be scurrilously treated. The hulk stood by, a landslide in search of a victim. She made a sign. He receded, to be a thundercloud darkening the yard window.

'Countess. I accept that I was to blame, and acknowledge that your dismissal of me was perfectly just. I apologize.'

I'd worked out this tactic from TV. Half the soaps thrive on blokes apologizing to birds. In fact there's no other plot on telly. What's the average number of 'Sorry-sorry' lines per thirty-minute soap? Four. Count them. TV scripters have one maxim: never mind logic, go for the grovel. The ratings will soar.

She smiled. 'You are correct. I do not accept, Lovejoy.'

I rose. 'Well, Countess. I'll leave. Thanks for the . . . er.'

I'd already turned, when something really strange happened. She said, 'Stay. Sit.' I obeyed, which wasn't the oddity. It was that she'd changed her mind. Countesses don't.

'Do you see the painting?' she asked.

'Where?'

There in the corner was a portrait. It was at an angle in the top corner, exactly where people who can afford electricity and air conditioning site their gadgets. And like Russians anciently placed their icons of saints or the tsar. No vibes, so not a genuine antique. It was in shadow.

'Who is she?'

'Is not a woman a remarkable thing, Lovejoy?'

146

the Countess mused. She sipped at a glass of white wine, offered me none. 'So exquisite, so fatal! She was Princess Zanaida. Of course, her husband Prince Volkonsky was an animal. She only married him to hush up her affaire with Tsar Alexander, with Goethe, Pushkin, Rossini, Donizetti, others. Do I believe she took the pope as her lover? No!'

She screamed the denial so loudly I jumped.

'I don't either, Countess,' I said quickly. Princess who?

'Do you know why I *know* she was pure, Lovejoy?'

Pure? If she said so. 'Enlighten me, please, Countess.'

'Because she only fornicated with honest men! If that sordid pianist Liszt had wooed her, she would have had him beheaded. Why? Because he stole every composition he called his own.'

Well, everybody knows that Liszt was a thief. Hear a tune, he'd 'compose' it himself next day, like a certain modern English composer I could mention. She glared at me. I hurriedly smiled to prove I wasn't Liszt.

'Anyway,' she said with scorn, 'Franz Liszt was Hungarian. Can you get lower?'

She snapped her fingers and a youth appeared with a silver basket of sweets and chocolates. She selected one, inserted it into her mouth, and accepted a fresh glass. The youth retired.

'You admired the silver basket,' she said with satisfaction.

'No, Countess.' To her withering glare I said candidly, 'Its handles had been clumsily removed. Your silversmith—is it still Yosh? He's losing his touch—hasn't concealed the marks very well. They

147

catch the light.'

On safer ground, I added the really important detail that silver table baskets tended to get shallower as more and more people afforded them. They started about 1730. Oddly, they were mainly a British thing. You find them made of clever silver wire, and in Sheffield plate, adorned with loaves and sheaves of corn. I suppose they were mainly decorative centrepieces. Fraudsters file the handles off to make fake silver trinkets for high prices, because then lab oratory tests will reveal the trace elements of Georgian silver instead of crummy modern stuff. If you're ever offered an antique silver basket without handles, look at it in subdued light, to see if there are the marks left by missing original handles. It's sensible if you're a crook, because a handled basket will net you only a fraction more money than a handle-less one, whereas a few seemingly genuine artefacts made of ancient silver bring in a fortune.

'Have you got any old dies, Countess?' You need old silversmiths' dies for best forgeries, though possession of them in England is forbidden by law.

She suddenly laughed, white teeth on display, her cosmetic layers shivering into craquelure. I was stunned by her beauty. Women never lose it, do they? Her varicose veins were painted out. Real class.

'I really do miss you, Lovejoy! Antiques are the only things you remain honest about!' She leaned forward confidingly. Her breasts moved. I was almost enveloped in her cleavage. Gold chains sagged against my forehead. Perfume almost asphyxiated me.

'Thank you, Countess.'

You even have to address her by her title in bed. (It got bizarre sometimes: 'Lie over me, doowerlink.') I suppose she insisted on it with all her blokes. There's grounds for a sociological survey on the subject, if any university out there is at a loose end. It would take time, though. There's plenty of us ex-Countess languishers about.

'You don't see the painting's resemblance, Lovejoy?'

'No, Countess.' I craned. Was it herself?

'You poor fool.' She didn't sound sympathetic, just a mite relieved.

'Have you got anything you want me to divvy?'

She seemed to wonder about laughing, decided I wasn't worth it.

'If I do another large shipment, Lovejoy, I'll send for you.'

'Thank you, Countess.'

I left then, no wiser. Odd, I thought, waiting for the bus home, that she'd commanded me to stay, when she'd only wanted to see if I could recognize a musty old portrait of a lady. I honestly couldn't. After confessing ignorance, I was banished among her cast-offs. Funny, that. I tried to forget her. If she summoned me to divvy one of her priceless frigging export shipments from Sotheby's or Christie's, I'd refuse, see how she liked it.

Actually, I'd come running. Like I say, pathetic. I waited by the bus stop, got hungry after a while, saw the village schoolchildren come out in droves. Saw the start of the village rush-hour, namely three motor cars, a farm cart and two bikes. No bus.

A car I'd seen before—but who remembers motor cars?—emerged from the Countess's antiques empire loading yard. A whiffler stood in

149

the road to signal it out. An old Ford. I was too far off to see who was driving, but the driver had the look of Jules. Observation is overrated, I always think.

The bus was cancelled. I finally walked four miles to a neighbouring village to catch the shoppers' bus.

It rained.

CHAPTER SEVENTEEN

Bernicka was furious when I said she had to do the burglary with me.

'Why?' she demanded, in her grotty studio with that flaming horse statue. It was worse than ever. 'You were going to do it on your own.'

'Look, love.' I smiled with great sorrow. 'Who knows *Il Maestro*? You.'

A woman can't resist being told that she excels in understanding love. She calmed. 'That's true.'

'How else could you have created this great, er, thing?'

'You're right.'

'How could I possibly detect the hand of the Master,' I said reasonably, 'in what I steal, unless you're there to give me proof?' I acted more sadness. 'I'm good at antiques, Bernicka, but we're talking of Leonardo's very own work. And he,' I concluded, my voice breaking with emotion, 'needs you, Bernicka.'

I tried to gaze adoringly up at the shambolic heap of gunge she'd splattered together, but couldn't manage it. She patted my shoulder.

150

'There, there. I understand.' Her eyes filled with tears. 'I didn't know you were so sensitive, Lovejoy. I'll come.'

Gone eleven o'clock, we hit the road in her motor and reached Tolleshunt D'Arcy just about midnight.

*   *   *

A great crime writer I used to know lived right in the village. We were friends, Marjorie A and me, despite her mangy blinking dog. Her husband was a sponging duckegg, tried to finish her uncompleted novels after she passed away, total failures of course. The house near the war memorial belonged now to Sir Jasper Haux. It has an enormous walled garden. I got Bernicka to park on a country road where manic anglers do night fishing, a mile from the village centre.

'You know what to do, Bernicka?'

'No.' She was nervous now she actually had to do some thing. She'd complained all the way, what am I doing here, I should be at home in bed.

'Wait forty minutes. I'll walk there, burgle the Haux mansion, find the Master's drawing. You come driving slowly past, and give me a lift, okay?'

Her face shone like a green ghost's in the dashboard lights.

'Do I have to, Lovejoy?'

'Yes,' I said, cruel. 'Are you beginning to doubt your love for Leonardo?'

Honestly, women drive me spare. Here was I trying to help her, at enormous risk to life and limb, not to mention the plod, and she starts dithering. I filled up, overcome at the sacrifices I

151

was making.

'What if the village bobby catches me, Lovejoy?' Then quickly added, 'I mean, catches you.'

This is typical: when they want to prove how daring and brave they are in the cause of True Lerve, you've to do it for them. If you're caught, you're on your own. There was a girl climbed Everest a few years back single-handed, with no help except skilled climbers and a camera crew. They made a TV documentary—carefully avoiding mention of twenty-seven tourists already at the summit.

'The cover story, doowerlink, keeps you in the clear. I phoned you for a lift.' I smiled with admiration. 'I think this is a truly courageous romantic thing you're doing, Bernicka.' I said intently, 'I only wish I was as worthy of love.' And walked bravely into the night.

Twenty minutes later I was outside the village pub. It's supposed to close by eleven, but keeps going. I caught Cedric Cobbold just downing his umpteenth gin. He came straight away with his Elk. The three of us stood in the car park. Elk slobbers and scares the daylights out of me, whom it adores. I keep patting it, hoping I'll get my hand back. It rumbles. No more to be said, except that it likes tripe. I can't honestly see the point of him, but wisely keep such thoughts to myself.

'Got it here, Lovejoy.' It was in a velveteen case. 'You won't be disappointed. Leonardo used very dilute sanguine whole—'

'Ta, Cedric. Great.' I'd no time to discuss techniques.

'Money first, Lovejoy.' The old soak wouldn't let go. I gave him a roll of notes—well, a few strips of newspaper in one genuine note, but he'd only done ten minutes' work, for God's sake. Make the price match the job.

'Get gone, Cedric. The mark'll be along any minute.'

I left him quickly, crossed the road and nipped over the huge Haux wall. It came on to drizzle then, of course, so I had to crouch down covering the precious fake so it didn't get wet. I heard car doors slam, folk calling cheery goodnights, heard a couple pause under the branches of a London plane tree. For a second I wondered what on earth such a big tree was doing in East Anglia—shouldn't it be in London? Then I heard the couple's mutters. One familiar voice said, 'Did they recognize us?' The bloke replied, 'No. We were lucky. It was only old Cedric and that crook Lovejoy.' The female voice worried, 'Are you sure?' 'Positive. Can I see you tomorrow? Take the Bures road, in case Paul's back early. I'll take the coast road.' And so on, while I stayed hunched, rain trickling down my nape and blotting itself on my one shirt.

They left after a few sighs and mmmhs. I'm not proud of eavesdropping this way, but whose fault was that? People foist their private hangups on me all the blinking time, then I get blamed. That word crook stung, though, rotten swine. Paul, though, gave me a clue. I remembered the woman's voice. It was Jenny, Paul the birdman's wife, who was having a torrid affair with Aspirin, he of the drunken handstands. Except I know Aspirin's voice, and I'd never heard this new, cultured, decisive voice before.

Cars drove away. They all sounded run-of-the-mill motors, no sibilant Rolls-Royces whispering homeward. I was tempted to stand up amid the foliage and peer, but dared not take the risk. I heard the pub doors lock, the chains across the forecourt clank in place. The village silenced. I stayed put, listening for Bernicka's car, feeling really down, wondering what I was doing. The scent of food had made me so hungry I went dizzy. I grew bitter. The landlord would be whaling into the remains of the pub grub while his missus readied for bed. To them that hath shall be given, but not me.

A car approached at walking speed, changing gear every throb. It could only be Bernicka, devil driver. Its cogs ground maddeningly. Unbelievably it notched into an even lower gear, stalled, took three goes to restart, and crawled nearer. I sighed. One cliffhanger after another. I heard the door open.

'Lovejoy?' Bernicka called loudly. 'Are you there?'

Secret as an invasion. A wonder she didn't sound the horn. I creaked erect and clambered over the wall, huddling my precious forgery, and ran to her car as if the bailiffs were after me.

'Off, Fangio.'

She drove off almost at jogging speed. On the way to her studio I told her how I'd burgled Sir Jasper Haux's mansion ('Those drainpipes; his library on the fifth floor, see?' etc, etc) and lied how I did over the electronic protection units ('They're the new Eight-Nine-Nine model—used by the SAS . . .').

'Is that it?' She stared apprehensively at my velveteen parcel.

'Yes, Bernicka. Keep your eyes on the road.' I've often noticed that women turn to look at you if you speak to them while they're driving. Blokes don't. Dunno why. 'I was very, very scared, love. I did it for you, doowerlink.'

'Oh, Lovejoy! You're so brave! Leonardo's own hand!'

She filled up. I almost did, too, because burgling the Haux manor house would have been really risky if I really had done it. I might have been arrested, put in a dungeon for years. I remained manly and bold.

'It's all right, Bernicka.' I gazed soulfully at her profile. 'You know I'd do anything for you, doowerlink, honestly . . .'

She got us a take-away meal at Bluebell's roadside caff by the main A12. I wolfed most of hers as well to help her finish it. Then I stayed at her place the rest of the night while she ogled the Leonardo drawing Cedric Cobbold had done for me. I was too worn out to stay gaping at his work, though it looked pretty good, nearly better than mine. Maybe, I thought grudgingly, I'd pay him in full next time.

*   *   *

After all that, I reached my cottage worn out and slumped on my unfinished wall. The village children were skipping up the lane on the way to join the school bus. They were singing the little girls' ancient skipping-rope chant:

Fair is foolish, short is loud,
Long is lazy, black is proud,

155

Fat is merry, lean is sad,
Pale is pettish, red is bad.

It predicts their eventual lovers. Elizabeth, seven, is their leader and knows everything.

'You didn't come home last night, Lovejoy,' she said in condemnation. 'Dirty stop-out!'

Little Marie came to rifle my pockets. She's five.

'I got tired,' I improvised. 'And stopped at a friend's.'

'You sleep on Mrs Newcastle,' Jane explaining to the rest.

'No.' Elizabeth was annoyed at being contradicted. 'He sleeps on Mrs Vullamy. Her legs go in the air. I seed through his window.'

Christ, I thought. Little Marie glared. 'You've no toffees, Lovejoy. And no money!'

Everybody knows my business except me. Wearily I searched and found her a coin in the lining. She confiscated it without a word of gratitude.

'What am I?' I demanded. 'In your song.'

Elizabeth snorted. 'Untidy.'

Little Marie said, 'You're hopeless. My mum says.'

They went off up the lane trailing their skipping ropes. Little Marie walked backwards to shout, 'You're not in the song, Lovejoy, coz you're poor.'

'Charming,' I called bitterly. I like them, the pests.

'There's a new auntie hiding in your cottage, Lovejoy.'

Elizabeth too had a parting shot. 'She's got horrible shoes. And her frock's crap.'

Was this a godsend of an alibi? I went in, stiff as

a plank. The woman was seated on my stool, handbag on her knees, prim and primed for action.

'Wotcher, missus.'

'How do you do?'

Her frock didn't look that bad, and I quite liked her shoes. Gloves, neat skirt, the right side of forty. Mind you, women can't have a wrong side of forty.

'The children said you were my auntie.' I wanted her to shift over so I could sprawl on my divan and sleep. I've only one mug, so tea was out.

'It's what I told them, Lovejoy.' She sounded schoolmarmish, no-nonsense-from-you. 'Infants harbour wrong conclusions.'

'Indeed.' I hoped they hadn't blabbed about Mrs Vullamy's aerial legs.

'I called to ask you how I can conceal an object.' She avoided an exchange of glances, addressing the middle distance. 'I want antique dealers not to see it.'

'I don't understand.'

The way women present themselves to the world is admirable. Blokes aren't worth looking at. Not exactly poor, she'd get a mention in Elizabeth's skipping song any day. Weighty wedding ring, earrings pricey, but some jeweller had made a terrible mistake with her pendant, a blue topaz set in oval gold. Still, it wasn't pale lavender, which would have been dearer but worse.

'It's a painting of a lady,' she explained. 'Done by Geoffreye Parlayne.' She took my aghast silence for awe and smiled. 'It is rare and valuable.'

'Oh, good,' I bleated faintly. 'Can I lie down, please? I've had a hard night.'

'Please don't dissemble, Lovejoy. I heard what the children said about you and Darla Vullamy.'

'Never heard of the lady,' I gave back, sagging onto my divan.

People have a right to anonymity. I know I'm in the minority in thinking this. Nowadays, every model having a one-nighter with some film star thinks it the height of propriety to hurtle for tomorrow's headlines and tell, sell every gasp of pillow passion. I regard it as a modern ailment, like Value Added Tax and vile clergy, and hope it might pass.

'She's my neighbour,' the lady said, doing the thin lips.

'I trust I might meet her one day,' I returned politely, thinking *what* frigging painting by Geoffreye Parlayne? Because that renowned Cromwellian soldier-cum-artist, 1599 to 1658, is actually me. He didn't exist. Still doesn't. I'm the forger who coined the name and stuck it on a dreadful daub I did one drunken month. I called it *A Portrait of Lady Parlayne*. The picture, almost a spillage, was astonishingly bought at Selpman and Coater's auction by a London dealer. I dined out, and in, until I got with Eve, who runs a fingernail shop (honest, there is such a thing. Eve sells gruesomely false fingernails). After a week of Eve I was broke. When I'm desperate I forge yet another version of his Lady Parlayne. I've done four. The point is there's no such geezer as Geoffreye Parlayne, Cromwell's warrior artist. It's only me in a bad spell. My career can be logged by troughs and depressions, the nadir marked by portraits of Lady Hypatia Parlayne.

Never, never ever, buy art by Parlayne. He's the Dauber Who Never Was. All his paintings are forgeries done by me and skilfully aged to look Old

Mastery.

Which is why I gazed at her bonny features and pondered.

*   *   *

You think folk are honest? Think again.

True story, to convince skeptics. Once upon a time, a bloke died. The eccentric millionaire Mr Digweed, sad to relate, passed away in a tent erected in his living room. He actually left his fortune to Jesus Christ. A proper will, legal to the hilt. Hearing this, we might just smile and think what a charming old geezer. After all, the English are known eccentrics. Nary a ripple on the pond of life, right?

Not a bit of it.

Claims flooded in—from Jesus Christ! Within days, the Home Office was knee deep in letters claiming Digweed's gelt. Letters from whom? From JC, no less, duly signed and witnessed. They poured in by recorded delivery, with Address of Sender solemnly filled in, giving bank accounts where the money should be forwarded. The HO is still wondering what on earth.

I don't read the *Church Times* or the Vatican's daily newspaper, so maybe a Second Coming has occurred and I missed it.

My point is, logically there could be only one truthsayer, maximum. And most bookmakers would give odds on all those Jesus Christs being duds. (Incidentally, if you're the real genuine Claimant, the correct Home Office form of application is 319(b), and good luck. But I suppose you'd already know that.)

Stark truth? We're all on the make, crooks, the sinful lot of us. I honestly don't mean you—just me and everybody else. We're bad hats.

Hence me, exhausted on my creaky divan, wondering what the hell.

*　　　*　　　*

She told me gravely, 'I am Mrs Thomasina Quayle. I approach you because you are, I believe, the most evasive of the local dealers.'

Evasive? Daft, I found myself wondering how little Marie would fit that into her skipping chant, *Lovejoy's evasive* or some such. I was just tired out.

'Who d'you want to evade?'

'Buyers, dealers, auctioneers. And,' she added prettily, 'thieves.'

'They're usually the ones I hunt down.'

'No flippancy, if you please.' From her handbag she withdrew a purse, gave me a thin wad of notes bound in bank paper. 'This is for the first month.'

'Where's the painting?'

'It is already in your shed.' She meant my workshop, but was too proud to say it. 'I shall expect a written report concerning its preservation from marauders each Sunday noon.'

'Why this malarkey?' I asked, reason struggling to the surface. 'Sotheby's, your bank, some dealers, they all have impregnable vaults. I don't.'

'Can they be trusted, Lovejoy?'

Another headacher. She had a point. 'Not by me,' I said grudgingly.

'There we are, then.' She rose, poetry in motion. I thought, *I measure time by how a body sways*, then wondered who'd said that. He must have known

160

Thomasina Quayle.

She left then, and like a pillock I rolled over to sleep, my silence implying acceptance of the dumbest con trick I'd ever fallen for.

CHAPTER EIGHTEEN

Susanne Eggers didn't deign to drive. Her husband Taylor drove us in a motor so plush I almost nodded off. We went to the River Deben estuary, a favourite site for lovers. Not today, though.

There's a seaside hamlet near one of the large boating centres. Nearly a marina, it has an old Martello tower. These squat edifices were built to resist Tyrant Bonaparte. Now, they're little museums or trendy caffs. This one I already knew. All candles, purple chintz and gothic silver, with waitresses dressed like young witches waiting for the Black Sabbath. Purple lipstick, kohl eyeliner, chalk-white features and niello jewellery. It isn't exactly teatime at Frinton-on-Sea. I once had a long smileship with a bird who used to take two hours doing her face like this. Daft, when she was gorgeous to start with. Forty-three years of age was Bliss, shapely plump, yet a born worrier. We used to come out to this very place and spend summer evenings watching the boats while I'd tell her about antique scams I'd done.

'Stop that smirking, Lovejoy.'

'Sorry.' I hadn't known I was.

Her bloke dashed round and opened the door. The only time I did that for Bliss I fell flat on my face and she rolled in the aisles.

'I said stop smirking. You look Neanderthal.'

'Sorry, sorry.' Do women know when you're thinking of a different bird? It makes them ratty.

We alighted. The foreshore was coolish and breezy. A delivery van was parked by the side entrance, a youth in overalls unloading crates. Two cheapo motors in the little car park. And, three-four furlongs off amid tussocky grass and dunes, a large dark motor. Nobody in it. Nobody fishing on the breakwater. So why was it here?

Inside, the place hadn't started serving. A senior man was sitting at the far end, last table. I felt odd. It was Consul Sommon, the bloke who'd made serious smiles in my cottage with Mrs Eggers that cold frosty night. The mighty American. I glanced anxiously at Taylor Eggers, but he simply went to stand by the entrance. We serfs are prone to do that, attend humbly on our betters while they live life.

The gent signalled us to approach. I'd seen his face in newspaper photographs, so I was sure. The waitresses were laying tables. A musician was tinkering with those black sound boxes that deafen you, cables everywhere.

'This is he,' Susanne said.

He? How come I was he? I felt his eyes peel my features away. His gaze roamed my skull, ferreting out hidden allegiances. A politician to be scared of.

'Hello, sir.' I didn't fawn or grovel, but showed I was that way inclined.

'How?' the man growled.

Close to, he had large jowls, baggy eyes, impeccable attire, and modern cufflinks that would see off our national debt. Definitely the same man from that cold night. I almost asked how what?

162

'I tested him with some others,' Susanne said. 'He got every antique wrong. The others got every one correct, on his signals.'

The man almost smiled. She sat, shivered in a sudden draught as the delivery man opened the door.

'Clever.' He fixed me. 'Why?'

He meant why did I try to fiddle the results. This meeting was already hard work and I'd only just arrived. When all else fails, try truth.

'I was scared.'

'What of?' He froze the place with a wintry smile. 'One little lady?'

'I was out of my depth, sir.' Too many sirs spoil the broth. I saw his contempt. He knew I was buttering him and he wasn't having any.

'Your suspicions were what, exactly?'

'Posh is trouble.' No sir this time. Take that, you arrogant diplomat.

He didn't like my mention of trouble. 'What trouble?'

'I've no money. You need it to deal in high antiques.'

He didn't quite glance at Mrs Eggers. At last a clue.

A waitress emerged carrying a tray. She set it down. I stared at the porcelain as she distributed it. I felt queer, my chest bonging and my hands clammy. I'd never seen so much wealth come out for coffee. One plate was the rarest. I'd never seen one before in any open market. It was a rare early Meissen, meaning from New Year's Day of 1710 and the few years following. Tip: they're the first really honest European (non-Chinese, I should say) hard-paste porcelain, and are a grubby white, sometimes an even grottier fawnish hue. They're priceless. It was so genuine I almost cried out.

'What?' The man was interested, watching me.

'I feel a bit odd. I don't like driving. Twisty roads,' I explained, pretending.

The waitress returned bringing a coffee pot, cream and milk jugs, sugar and whatnot. All costly modern gunge. I almost apologized out loud to the three genuine antique pieces, them keeping such crappy company.

'Tell.' A man of few syllables.

'Tell what?'

He reached out and hit me. Actually gave me a swipe with his clenched fist so I flew off my chair. Susanne gave a loud cackle. My only thought was for the porcelain. Slowly I clambered back. We serfs know our place.

'Which are they? And no trifling.'

It was the shell game. Find the pea under the walnut shells and you win. I shook my head.

'Sorry, mate. I've had enough of your games.'

I got up, glanced at the heartbreaking loveliness of the three porcelains, and strode from the place. At least I started to. His voice halted me.

'Do I break it?' he called.

I halted. Mr Eggers, arms folded, sadly shook his head. You're a fool, his expression said. Just go along with it. There's no other way for the likes of us kulaks. Back at the table, the consul was holding up the modern Doulton sugar bowl.

'Why ask me?' I said, always the idiot.

He dropped it, ground his heel into the fragments. It was a pity, because Royal Doulton's classy, though the poor bowl was only made a fortnight gone.

The plate he lifted next, though, made my heart stop. The Meissen.

'How about this, chum?' He made a prolonged insult of the appellation, the way American gangsters do sometimes on film, like they sometimes say toodle-oo. I felt like clobbering him back, but for an old geezer he'd fairly swung his weight, and that big motor out on the dunes told me he never travelled alone.

It took me two attempts to say, 'What about it?'

And he dropped it. Smash it went, on the marble floor. I looked at the fragments. I'd not even had the time to gasp, let alone dive to save it. Pieces were everywhere. To gather them up would be a waste of time. Nobody would want a relic, as we call such desperate repairs, however valuable it had once been. In a split second it had gone from a perfect Meissen genuine hard-paste porcelain to nothing. Murder.

'Look at his face!' Susanne Eggers shrieked, rolling in the aisles.

The murderer grinned, exhibiting massively even white teeth. What is it about American politicians? They all have superb incisors and canines. Darwinian selection, I shouldn't wonder.

'Sit,' he said. I obeyed.

Susanne patted my arm. She found all this hilarious. 'Don't take on, Lovejoy. Just do as you're told and we'll get along.'

'Pick them out,' the killer commanded. 'And say what.'

For a second I sat and thought. He wanted confirmation. Yet it was weird. If he'd wanted to be sure of the Meissen plate, he could have called in any expert and got a million certificates of authenticity. But he hadn't. Therefore I was somehow vital. His cause, shared so intensely by Susanne Eggers, must be pretty desperate. It wasn't just romantic love between this fetching lady and him, passion on the sly. Despite his cool he was desperate behind his tombstone teeth and natty attire. I wondered if he was one of the antiques raj. Would they let a politician in, though? Except nowadays they might take anybody. After all, they accepted that Continental, Prince Whatsisname so they'll accept any crook. Or so people say. (I've got to add that, to prevent more law suits.) And the antiques raj didn't do their own clobbering. You'd never see their fist coming.

It was now a question of saving the other two porcelains from this maniac. I cleared my throat.

*   *   *

Search among your pots and pans. Wander through the village boot fairs. You might get lucky.

Continental porcelain is all the rage. The saying is: *You can sell any antique in its own sector, but you can sell antique porcelain anywhere anytime.* It's true. It means that you'll have no real difficulty selling paintings to a collector of paintings, jewellery to a collector of jewellery and so on, but that everybody falls for porcelain. Forgers know this, incidentally, so pay heed here.

The humble punter who drops in at some auction hoping to find a dazzling antique Continental dinner service going for a song has little chance. Remember a few tips, however, and you might narrow those odds.

Leave aside English wares. Leave aside Japanese

and Chinese. Think of Continentals, as I was having to do for this lunatic. And remember these snippets:

There are three biggies. (Correction: there's two whales and one tiddler.) If a dealer makes a mistake and passes up one of these mainstreamers, he might as well give up, because he'll be a laughing stock.

First and most splendidly, there's Meissen. Its story's pretty horrible, but if I tell it quick it'll help to fix it in the mind.

Once upon a time, all European porcelain was duff stuff. Compared to Chinese, it was crud. Why? Because it was soft paste, that's why. Oriental porcelain was hard paste. Simple as that. The Continentals and the English kept trying to copy the Chinese. Year after endless year, they failed.

Enter a clever youth called Johann F. Bottger, alchemist of Prussia. He was obsessed with changing base metal into gold. The King of Prussia, Frederick the First, was a greedy swine. He heard about Bottger. Cunning, he decided to hire young Bottger, which he did by simply locking the alchemist up. The trick of turning dross into gold would make King Fred the one true world power. That's politicians for you.

Young John Bottger got out and fled sharpish. The poor deluded bloke hurtled to Saxony, where Augustus the Strong offered him sanctuary. *The young alchemist believed him!* And simply finished up in a different dungeon. King Augustus was another greedy swine, you see, and thought, tomorrow the whole world will be mine when Bottger pulls off the gold trick.

The enslaved John F. Bottger laboured away in

clink. No gold, but he discovered how to make hard-paste porcelain. The world of European ceramics was born. Meissen china made Augustus the Strong a fortune. (Poor Bottger died young, of course, from hardship and booze, the way genuises do.)

At first, Dresden and Meissen were interchangeable names in England, seeing there's only a dozen miles between the two places, both in Saxony anyway. In January 1710 the factory started up. The first pieces look like they're trying hard to be pure white but never quite make it. They're unbelievably rare. But that doesn't mean they're not out there waiting for you. A faint fawnish hue is said to be most typical.

Look for the crossed-swords mark. It doesn't prove Meissen, but it's one clue. Some pieces, like the (genuine!) over-decorated 'Snowball type' flowery bottle-shaped vases, look ghastly and foolish though they still cost a king's ransom. Still, Meissen rules Continental hard-paste porcelain, whether or not pieces have the crossed-swords mark, with or without the dot, star, or pommel. In the figurines, I always look at the stripes on the maiden's skirt, which you've got to be a real cracker to fake right. Tip: a numbering system was brought in about 1763. The numbers were incised, like when you write on wet clay with a tooth pick, so an overly neat stamped number suggests forgery.

Then there was the piece this killer American hadn't yet smashed to smithereens. It was a Sèvres plate. These French pieces were soft paste, but so what? Their gilding is superb, and the enamel looks somehow about to sink into the glaze. The two crossed-letter L marks look like they're trying to make a bell shape. That's all, but they're beautiful. The flower decorations are unequalled.

Those are the two whales. The single tiddler is Vienna. Good stuff, to be sure, and worth a fortune now, but still a minnow in comparison to the two giants.

Odd how rascals and rogues abound in the story of porcelain. They thrived, especially in Vienna, where in 1717 folk began to hear of the wonderful events in Meissen. By bribery, Vienna procured a Meissen worker to nick all the manufacturing secrets. (Didn't pay him, of course.) The outcome was Vienna hard-paste porcelain and multo bad feeling. There are supposed to be lots of clues to its authenticity—the greenish tint to the thin glaze, the perspective of the painting and so on. Here's my only tip, unless you're an expert: *every single feature* of early Vienna porcelain looks copied from some other style. The square handles are phoney Oriental; the rims are Japanese ideas; the masked feet are copied from silverware of the period. It's a giveaway.

Beware, for the tiddler costs a fortune too.

*   *   *

'So it isn't all vibes,' the killer said in his best senatorial voice. 'It's knowledge as well?'

'No. It's the chimes.' I was torn between the Vienna piece and the Sèvres. The French porcelain is always higher regarded in London's auction rooms, because the decoration is bonnier. They sat there amid the modern garbage—I meant us, not just the crockery. 'What bits you pick up—dates, names, tricks to tell other dealers—are just gilt on the gingerbread.'

'What dealers?' He barked the question so loudly I jumped.

'Whatever dealers will stump up for a meal.'

He ran his eyes over me slowly, like I was for sale. My frayed cuffs, my battered shoes worn down to the welts, my shredding collar.

'Broke, huh?' He seemed pleased. He shot Susanne a glance of approval. She almost purred. 'I'm glad he's a bum, Suse.'

'I've had a bad streak lately.' Pathetic to sound so defensive. Maybe when I got as fat as him I'd feel the same scorn for the impoverished. Until then I'd no choice.

'How about a retainer, Lovejoy? To divvy.'

Money, now? I must have looked astonished because he barked a laugh, a seal coughing offshore in a salmon glut.

'Suse, you picked a moron here.' He fixed me, finger pointing. 'Listen up, Lovejoy. When the Antwerp High Council gets flak from do-gooders who whine that crooked African politicians are selling blood diamonds to finance some peanut war, you think it ends there? Hell, no. Some body like me picks up the tab when the diamond market goes through De Beers' floor.

'And if Sotheby's and Christie's come unglued, everybody turns to me. When smuggled "economic migrants" die in container lorries, or some ship gets impounded—you think the owners just smile and pay up? Shit, no. They turn to the insurers with their hands out. You know what they want? They want money. Every fucker insures against their own sins. The Church against their own perverts, inept footballers against losing. Tobacco manufacturers

170

insure themselves against the Feds in Raleigh, North Carolina, detecting their own tax-evading smuggling rackets. You with me at last?'

I surrendered and said resignedly, 'What do you want me to divvy? Where?'

He lit a cigar, though smoking wasn't allowed in the restaurant. Taylor Eggers beckoned me. I left. No tea, no grub, though it was all served ready for a hungry bloke like, say, me. No money either. Taylor still beamed. A cuckolded husband always smarts, even at the point of murderous revenge. Don't try telling me different. Taylor, however, smilingly walked me along the promenade to a stall. There we dined on pasties and hot spuds and tea thick enough to plough. He paid, thank God.

'D'you know where I'm to do the divvying, mate?' I asked him.

'Don't know what they're on about, Lovejoy.'

'Whose are those antiques?' I meant the Sèvres and the Vienna piece. No good asking about the Meissen, *requiescat in pace*.

'Mine.'

I stared. He spoke in tones of faint regret. Not heartbroken, note. Merely a bit of hard luck, losing that priceless plate.

'My only three genuine antiques,' he said, like easy come, easy go.

'He's the consul, isn't he?'

'Don't, Lovejoy.' He stared out to sea. 'Hear no evil, speak no evil. Just go along. There's no other way. The powers are too great.'

'Right,' I said. Then, 'Can I have some more tea?'

171

CHAPTER NINETEEN

The lads were having a whale of a time reminiscing when I reached the Welcome Sailor in the teeming rain. Big Frank from Suffolk was especially creased. I went in grinning, hoping it wasn't the usual what-about-Joe-in-prison malarkey, got a pale ale on the slate from Unis, and sat by the fire to let my soaked jacket steam dry. My gran always said that's the way to catch a chill, but never did explain how to keep dry if you'd no raincoat.

'This bloke actually believed the rounder!' Big Frank howled.

Roars of merriment. Big Frank is always moving on to his next wife. Friends run a book on how long his new marriage will last. The longest is nine months (a significant duration). I honestly don't know why he keeps getting married. I tell him to just fall into romance, and so cut out the middleman. He says no, marriage is like flu, you can't stop it happening.

A rounder, incidentally, is a phoney antique that dealers know about and recycle through auctions. Do it often enough, the fake takes on a kind of allure, escalating as it goes from catalogue to catalogue. Everybody starts to think of it as nearly almost practically genuine. Sooner or later somebody buys it, for a high price.

'And he was the frigging auctioneer!' Peggy Price screeched, falling off her bar stool.

Peggy Price 'is to be admired', women say. She poisoned her bloke once (well, you can't do it more than once, can you?) who beat her savagely, put

172

her in hospital. He was a junkie, drunkard, gambler, and idle. None of us liked him. The final straw, though, was when he stole the only genuinely real antique she'd ever had from her tatty little antiques shop down the sea wharf. He tried to sell it in Stepney.

A Minton fruit and nut dish might not sound much—to go and poison a whole bloke for, I mean—but it was true as a saint. I can see it now in my mind's eye: painted, not printed, those gorgeous florid colours of 1805 with Thomas Minton's interlinked stroke marks just like the Sèvres device that Minton liked to imitate. Hearing about the dish, well, all the collectors and dealers in the Eastern Hundreds finally took Peggy's side. 'You can only go so far,' the lads sympathized. Our women dealers said things like, 'Well, you can only take so much, can't you?' We all gave evidence at her trial. The judge let her off with two hundred hours of community service. That only meant that when she came to sweep the market she didn't need to lift a broom. The stallholders simply kept their pitches clean.

Justice isn't often so straightforward, though.

Luckily, among the revellers was Cromwell, for where Peggy Price comes can Cromwell be far behind? He sat in his breastplate and gauntlets, smoking a churchwarden pipe. He sometimes speaks daft Ho There Sir Knave stuff. Dunno why. He was once prevented from tethering his nag outside the pub. I spoke up for him at the town council. They claimed there was no need to ride to the tavern on a horse these days. Walking and motor cars were good enough.

I claimed in evidence, 'His nag knows the way

home, your honour.' I got pretty heated. 'Even when Cromwell is drunk as a lord, your, er, lordship, his horse carries him home safe. Cromwell himself was allowed to ride here.'

'Confine yourself to facts, please,' the judge said wearily.

It was Mrs Finisterre, a distinguished battleaxe with lovely legs. She shouldn't wear purple skirts. She should try tan or beige. I sold her a lovely Wellington chest once, and charged too little because I knew she was a famed lawyer. See what good it did me.

'I am, missus!' I'd bleated.

'Lovejoy. This plaintiff is not Oliver Cromwell. The Lord Protector died in 1658.'

Just like a woman, slipping truth in. They're sly. This particular Cromwell was the Rt Hon St John (say Sinjern or people think you're common) Featheringshay Popperinghe, late of the diplomatic corps. He can speak twenty lingos. Once, he put 'Polyglot' for his occupation on a dole claim form, and got a letter from some thick civil servant, 'Dear Mr Polyglot . . .' And we pay their wages.

I'm in good with Cromwell. I got his fiancée off his back once. Literally, in a dancehall scrap. My intervention escaped him to Lancaster where his sister lives with a clergyman. Also, I didn't tell his lass where he'd gone, so earning Cromwell's undying gratitude. By the time he came back Feya had married a French bargee on the River Rhône.

'Whose rounder are they yakking about, Cromwell?'

'That birdman's wife owned a fake Sisley, one of the Impressionists.'

Paul Blondel, the kindly wild-bird keeper.

Cromwell meant his wife Jenny who was shacked up with Aspirin.

'It went for two thousand, right?'

'Tom Keating did it, they're saying. Hence the joviality.'

Tom Keating, RIP, was my old friend. A master faker of paintings, his stuff is actually pretty ropey and wouldn't deceive anybody, though they did mucho deception in their day. Alfred Sisley ('the English Impressionist') is probably the greatest of the Imps. The paintings he dashed off in the open air are the best ever. Faker Tom was always broke. Running out of expensive oils, Tom used poster colours blended in decorator's white. I often saw him scumble schoolkiddies' powder paint into house-painter's white. In fact I helped Tom more than once. The point is, you can't mistake modern acrylic for antique French oil paint. They shine differently. If you're too idle to look, you deserve to be ripped off.

'Cromwell,' I began with humility, as befitted asking the Lord Protector, 'what diplomat's knocking around East Anglia?'

'That Yank consul,' he said with bitterness. 'Wald Sommon by name.'

Cromwell got drummed out of the diplomatic for being found in a cupboard with an honorary consul's wife one Europe Day. A guard heard whimpers of ecstasy and wouldn't accept a bribe, which only goes to show how far standards have sunk since we gave away the Empire, thank God. Cromwell got drummed out of the Brownies without pension rights. He runs on hate.

I injected a little bitterness there myself. 'He ran over a cat near Stalham.'

175

'The bastard!' he breathed.

Cromwell judges local cat shows, loves them in fact. I was making it up, but so what? The bloke had almost knocked me senseless.

'It was a big American motor. Diplomatic plates.'

He actually trembled with fury. 'Did you help the cat?'

'Eh?' I hadn't seen any bloody cat. Now I had to play out this sympathy. Wearily, I made up a cock-and-bull tale of some poor feline dragging itself, broken and bleeding, along a country road. 'I shouted. The swine drove on.'

'What did you do?' he asked, appalled.

'I was seething. I carried the poor thing to a farmhouse. They promised to look after it. But,' I added brokenly, because I was really welling up, that poor moggie all bloodied and everything, 'they didn't hold out much hope.'

'Give me their address, Lovejoy.'

To my horror he took out a pencil. The dolt wanted to drive to the cat's rescue. I felt like yelling, 'There isn't any bleeding cat, you silly sod.'

'No, Cromwell.' I gripped his arm. 'I was trying to shield you . . .'

'It passed away?' Tears dripped from his chin.

I felt bad, especially after the way I'd struggled to save the poor cat, carrying its broken body to the dimly lit farmhouse. Except there wasn't any frigging moggie. No accident. No thoughtless diplomat. My imagination will get me in trouble one of these days.

'Yes.' I looked into my empty glass, sighing. 'If only there was some way to get back at him. There never is, is there? You'd need money. I gave my last

176

groat to the farmer's wife. The poor kitty deserved a decent burial.'

Cromwell took my glass. 'What'll you have, Lovejoy? Have you eaten?'

'If you insist,' I said. 'Ta. Ask Unis for a full nosh, please.'

And settled back in the warm to listen to the gossip.

*   *   *

During that pleasant evening—the last quiet spell for some time, though I didn't know it—Peggy Price brought me a glass to divvy. Cromwell had gone to phone somebody. I was drowsy after two meals and wine. Peggy offered me a refill, but I couldn't help thinking how she'd sped her late husband on his way with a fry-up sprinkled with sundry vitriols. I declined. She rummaged in her bag.

'This glass, Lovejoy.'

No wonder I'd gone wonky. She brought out a drinking glass in one of those bubbly plastic cases that protect against breakages. It was a beautiful piece of Anglo-Dutch soda glass, engraved with a coat-of-arms. Seventeenth century, it felt typically lightweight, its cup thin as a wafer. The surface was crizzled, all little cracks that make the glass look frosted. I used Peggy's loupe. Sure enough the engraving was shallow, mere scratches engraved with a diamond point.

'The foot's flat as a fallen arch,' I joked, giving myself time to get my breathing back. 'These Anglo-Dutch drinkers are always flat across. Anglo-Venetians have an inverted cone space

177

underneath.'

'It's genuine, then, Lovejoy?' Peggy breathed.

'Say that the bubbles in the stem "exhibit the freestyle glassblower's art", or some such junk,' I advised. 'Buyers expect it.'

This actually means that if there are any bubbles in the decorative swellings in the stem, they'll be asymmetrical. This isn't a stunning instance of brilliant artistry. It's just that the glass they used in those days cooled at speed, so the glassblower didn't have time to get it even all round. It's off kilter.

She bussed me enthusiastically and asked, pen poised, 'How much, Lovejoy?'

'Hardly anything, love. Sorry.'

It had two chips on its thin rim. The flat wide foot was also chipped. A scale of glass had fallen from the bowl—water can creep into the crizzles, you see. If the glass isn't dried in the warm, the water might actually freeze and lift away a flake of the actual glass. It's heartbreaking, the way people treat their glass. Worse even than women with pearls, and that's saying something. The worst crime of all, though, is to put them through a dishwasher.

'Don't get me started, Peggy,' I said, sadly returning her glass. She was mortified.

'Will you look at some more stuff for me, Lovejoy?' she asked. 'I bought a job lot in Norwich last week, a commission for Mr Eggers. He's American, staying at Saffron Fields.'

'I've heard of him,' I said, wondering what now.

She coaxed, 'I'll stand you supper.'

Supper with our poisoner? 'Er, ta, love. Some other time.'

It was then that Unis called me over and gave me a bulky envelope.

'A street busker brought it for you, Lovejoy. Feels like money.'

'Just some newspaper cuttings,' I said, wondering who was sending me messages at this time of night.

As soon as Peggy had returned to her bar stool I slipped a finger into the envelope and saw more money than I'd ever had in my life. I put it away, casual, but Peggy was watching.

When she went to the loo I ferreted out the message, shielding it from curious dealers. It read, *Dear Lovejoy, Come this instant! Sandy.*

As if I wasn't in enough trouble. The gelt was presumably the retainer Consul Sommon had mentioned. And Sandy was confirmed as heavily involved, because he never paid even legitimate debts.

That was my last peaceful evening before the deaths. None of it really was my fault.

CHAPTER TWENTY

That night I slept badly. Actually I'm not big on sleep. I think sleep's a trick. God made night so we'd wear ourselves out worrying, then gave us days to be exhausted in. My mind was in turmoil. I felt something frightening coming.

In all this was Mortimer. I had to protect him at all costs, never mind why. The lad was an innocent, hardly out of the egg. He didn't know that inexplicables ruled in antiques. It was the antiques trade's fault.

Antiques is an army of scroungers hunting for dross. In short, antiques is chaos in search of a wardrobe. See, I've no illusions. At the upper end, however, stands the antiques raj, that eclectic club of hoods who control everything. If the International Court of Justice grouses about looted heritage, you can bet that justice will fade before the ink is dry. And why? Simply because the antiques raj will make sure that art and antiques don't move out of their hands. The corollary is this: what you see in museums, galleries, or famed auction rooms is merely the residue that the members of the raj can't be bothered with and allows to remain untouched. For a fee, of course.

The money Unis passed me in the Welcome Sailor was a fortune. I stared at the notes. I could eat for years, get some shoes without holes in, socks, fit myself out in Willie Griffs. And a hat! I'd always wanted a hat, look like a gent. Gloves I tend to lose, but with so much gelt what's a lost glove?

Sandy, I knew, had society connections, the sort that only fashionably weird individuals have these days. He sold them antiques. Many were ultra rich. In fact, there'd often been rumours that Sandy was a raj bloke, but I didn't believe it. They're unseen, and Sandy thrived on attention.

There was no doubt, though. I was now firmly yoked to somebody's plough. Everywhere I went, dealers were working for Susanne Eggers. Directly or indirectly. Like Ferd, with auctioneers arriving in posh motors itching to do deals. And his missus Norma, warning me off now that she was in ladyland—riff-raff lovers need no longer apply, so get thee gone, ye varlet. Never mind that I'd been

Ferd's only pal while he was mental, and kept Norma in groceries and emotion. And Olive Makins, secretary of the local auctioneers, was used—forgive the word—by Mr Eggers *et al.* to sweet-talk auction lists out of her.

Also, the matter of my forged portraits. Not long since it was hard to give them. Now they were in demand. They were clear fakes, yet dealers were scouring the kingdom for them. Worse, Mortimer had begun lobbing the stone of honesty into the tranquil pond of fraud, threatening me.

So here was me, sitting on my let-down divan in my cold, bare-flagged cottage with a bundle of bunce like I'd never seen. Handed through some pub's back door by a street wino. I was retained by some American consul geezer. Foolishly, I'd blundered off to ask Cromwell, because he was the only ex-diplomat I knew. My logic always finishes up bizarre. Just as it had, in fact, when I went to see Quaker and Maud. I'd thought I was boxing clever, but finished up being talked into a risky tryst with Maud, learning nothing from Quaker, then stupidly agreeing to meet Brigadier Hedge. Only dedicated duds like Hesk, the would-be faker of Georgian art, were left out.

There was a huge scam on. The public would suffer, of course. They always do. Whatever genuine antiques they possessed would be collared, fiddled, stolen, and they'd end up with barely a farthing. I woke with a splitting headache, took half an aspirin because I hadn't any more, drank some water, and went to the village shop with my wealth.

At nine o'clock I made a hearty breakfast—cereal, eggs, those veggie sausages that give you heartburn, fried tomatoes, a stack of bread, tea. I diced some Lancashire cheese for the bluetits and the robin, and put an egg, cracked, by the cottage door for the hedgehog. Mother Nature, a scrounging harridan, could share my affluence.

'To labour, folk,' I told them, took a ton of the money, hid the rest and caught the bus.

Ginny and Ox were already out working the Liveridge estate when I arrived. I'd spent a mint on Visbee's taxi, guessing where they'd be this morning. Visbee reckons he has a brilliant sense of direction, but hasn't. He bets on a mobile phone while trying to chat up some housewife not his own. I spotted Ginny's motor near the livery stables and told Visbee to let them finish their con.

She's boss, so Ox can be ignored. Except, fraudsters need somebody who looks the part, don't they? Ginny is executive pretty and computer smart, twenty-five, smiles like an angel. Ox is thick, but tall, elegant, can make a cheap suit look Jermyn Street. He says nothing. Ginny rings your doorbell and stands there exuding charm. The con trick (soon to your door!) is this: Ginny smilingly offers you a free security check. She'll show you printed cards, credentials, has a security ID pinned to her ample bosom, and offers you letters from dignitaries. You, in all this charade, are the householder soon to be done out of every trinket, your furniture, porcelain, your savings books and credit cards.

Both Ox and Ginny carry gadgets. They're actually micro-camcorders that photograph your locks, windows, doors, and anything worth stealing. Needless to say, there is actually a real security firm should you check up—it's only her cousin Ditch, to whom she is very, very close. He has an electrical shop near Ipswich. The actual burglar is a violinist called Felly, works from darkest Hammersmith. He sells the stolen goods along the M18 motorway, like everybody else. I'm not in favour of Ginny's con trick, incidentally. But needs must when the devil's hard at it. I like to know what antiques they've stolen, keep abreast of what's safe.

'Wotcher, Ginny.' I flagged them down as they left the avenue.

She brightened. 'Hello, Lovejoy. So early, this bright dawn?'

'It's eleven o'clock, love. Where's Sandy?'

Her face clouded. 'Slumming, Lovejoy?'

'Desperate to unravel the plot, love.'

She examined my expression, let it go and alighted. 'Ox, drive to St Edmundsbury. We'll follow.'

'Which way is St Edmundsbury?' he asked, synapses clanging.

'Try the St Edmundsbury road,' she suggested.

And off he drove, we trundling behind in Visbee's motor. I asked her about Sandy. She could be trusted, for Sandy had done her down in a way I daren't repeat. It was foul, sinister, and marked Ginny's mind with permanent grief. Luckily, a woman never forgives. My sort of ally.

'If I tell you, Lovejoy, will it be bad for him?'

'Very bad.'

She smiled. 'Brilliant! Sandy's doing one of his morning showtimes. A hired audience and Eastern Hundreds TV, hoping to break in to *Look Eastward*.'

'Who's financing?'

She nodded at the pertinent question. 'You're right to ask, Lovejoy. That evil queen won't spend

183

tuppence. Some American. You're bound to've heard of *them*.' She meant because of Saffron Fields and Mortimer.

'Sandy's got one of my Geoffreye Parlayne portraits.'

'How come?'

Her question cheered me up.

'Dunno. If you find one for me I'll be your best friend.'

She smiled. 'I can do more than that, Lovejoy. We've got one. It's there.' She nodded to indicate the boot of Ox's limo up ahead. 'Felly handed it back last night.' She laughed. 'It was the only thing he couldn't sell up the motorway because it was spav. You can have it for a favour or two. Ox'll hand it to Tinker.'

Spav means rubbish, tat so dud nobody would even give it house room. Stung, I found myself arguing heatedly that it wasn't as bad as all that.

'I know,' she surprised me by saying. 'She has a lovely face. But she's that ghost, isn't she?'

Which was where I came in. I think.

＊　　　　＊　　　　＊

The village hall stood a few miles from St Edmundsbury. Cars and an excessive number of motorbikes filled its car park. Inside, gusts of laughter. Three massive pantechnicons filled with cables and TV crud darkened the double doorway. Sandy can't sing, can't keep time, doesn't dance, can't tell a joke, yet believes that he is God's gift to the world of entertainment. I went in alone. Two goons accosted me.

'Ticket?'

184

'Sandy told me to stand here and wait for his signal.'

Sandy was on the stage. Lights hurt my eyes. He looked whitewashed. He was dressed in a showgirl's feathers, glittering bodice, plumed head-dress, silver train, high heels, his face set in a ghastly rictus under panto makeup. I always feel sad for him.

He was dancing, singing, waving, in complete disregard of the efforts of musicians in the wings. The audience was howling, laughing. Some two hundred, cheering him on. Sadder still, I knew they were only there because they'd been paid. Not even extras got from some film company register, just anybody who wanted a free beer. Mel was seated by the door, glowering. I didn't blame him.

As Sandy did an inept vah-vah-vah-voom, the crowd helpfully calling the drumbeats, Mel said sourly, 'You were supposed to come yesterday, Lovejoy. Money works when all else fails, it seems.'

'I find that.'

In the screaming crowd, I saw Olive Makins, trying to look beside herself with glee. There was a hullabaloo when Sandy's attire lit up with multicoloured lights. The musicians despairingly tried to keep pace. He was in raptures.

'Has she come, then?' I asked Mel quietly.

'Who?' He gazed at me blankly, then his brow cleared. 'No. Not today.'

Odd, that. If Susanne Eggers wasn't financing the entire scam, then who was? The Yank consul surely couldn't, wouldn't, risk such an obvious scandal. I couldn't think of anybody else. The Countess? I didn't know anybody else so heavy. Except Mel had been momentarily puzzled when

185

I'd assumed it was a bird, not a bloke.

'What's this show in aid of, Mel?'

'Sandy wants to be a chat cat. Y'know? The TV *Antiques Trailshow*. This will impress TV producers. He'd give his all for it. Has, in fact.'

Yet more bitterness. They keep leaving each other. Last time, Mel fled to Sark, the little Channel Isle, but returned in a sulk when Sandy threatened to try to buy the island from the Dame of Sark herself. They are the shrewdest, sharpest antiques dealers in the known world. Except for Big John, I suddenly remembered with a snap of my fingers.

Big John is an Ulsterman. The saying is Ulster for soldiers, and John epitomizes it. Enough nous to start a war and win. I did him a couple of favours time since, but you can't always count on his memory. He believes he's hard done by if something happens and he doesn't get a percentage. Despite this I like him, though he puts the fear of God in me. He had the clout to start a scam this size.

'Are they here?' I asked, meaning TV producers.

Mel definitely paled. 'Leave it out, Lovejoy.'

For the first time since I'd known him his Cockney accent came through. I was surprised. He always cracked on he was Welsh.

The audience was what folk these days call camp. Pink garb, feathers, T-shirted, many crew cuts, alchemic gothic studs and emblems. They didn't look the kind to tempt *Antiques Trailshow* producers. I said I'd wait outside as Sandy started a striptease to the audience's howls. As I turned I saw somebody else also singularly out of place. He caught my eye and glanced away, reddening.

186

Timothy Giverill and his wife are your dyed-in-the-wool sober suits. Sunday church, councillors both. To cap it all, Timothy is in insurance. He has the insurance shop next to Bea Willing's Tea Shoppe on North Hill, facing that Antiques Antics that Peter Myer ran for Sandy. The shop little Polly told me the plod had taken over for surveillance. A clue?

The Giverills too were also ectopic, and stood out like sun in a pit.

Outside, two drivers chatted to a couple of TV technicians. Don't know why, but TV units always bring supernumaries. I have a theory that they need numbers for supportive psychotherapy, seeing they've no real job. The more turn up, the more convincing the charade.

'Wotcher,' I said idly. 'A right do in there, eh?'

'That poof goes on, dunnee?' one said. He smoked, his head clamped between earphones, wires trailing.

'You on that *Antiques Trailshow*, then?' I asked, gormless. 'He's going to present it, they say.'

One barked a laugh, lit a new fag from old. 'Him? Never. Camp's okay, but idiocy's not.'

They cackled. I drifted, and saw Timothy Giverill following me.

'Lovejoy?' I'd never seen anybody so worried. 'I'm glad to see you here for the meeting. I don't mind telling you, I'm at my wit's end.' He gazed at me with bottled eyes, his Clarke Gable tash quivering. 'Who'd have thought my world would crash this way? Insurance seemed so safe. And where will this Sotheby-Christie business end?'

'Who knows, Timothy?' Not me, that's for certain. What meeting?

187

He looked helpless. 'Four others are coming from the Midlands.'

'Well, as long as something happens.' What the hell were we on about?

He smiled tentatively. 'With you here we've a chance, especially with antiques.'

Me the arbiter of fair play? 'Always look on the bright side, Timothy.'

I felt sickened the way his expression cleared. 'Thank you, Lovejoy. Florence and I always liked you, despite your insurance trick on my company.'

'Here,' I said, narked. 'That wasn't my fault.'

'Say no more,' he said, smiling, and went back inside to Sandy's riot.

*   *   *

The insurance trick was one of my lucky moments. I'd found an old lady weeping at the Norwich bus stop. She'd had her bag stolen, containing hairdressing implements with which she eked out her pension undetected by marauding taxmen. She'd hoped to get her old husband a seventieth birthday present, and look what had happened.

'Two lads simply took it off me,' she'd sobbed.

'Good heavens,' I said. 'Leave it to me.'

Using the emergency number, I phoned East Anglia's finest, who told me to sod off—it was our Eastern Hundreds Crime Squad's snooker finals, when crime doesn't get a look in. So I phoned Bright Hawk Star Insurance from a phone box.

To Timothy—our first encounter—I explained. 'Two robbers knocked on her door and simply grabbed the brooch.'

I swore it was a genuine Edwardian bow-and-swag design (meaning all fragile loops and things) with lots of miniature rose-cut diamonds.

'Relatively cheap, really. It could have been frightfully valuable.' I kept cool. 'Typical early twentieth century. Incidentally,' and I lowered my voice, 'I happen to know she hasn't got long to live.'

To help, I described the imaginary brooch. Tip: Edwardian jewellery always looks slender, with lacy or bow-and-swag shape. Jewellers back then loved lots of small gem stones instead of one great rock. Remember that the style isn't the bonny later diamond cut. 'I recall it particularly because it was my great granny's.'

'No,' the old lady put in helpfully. 'It was my father's side . . .' I hissed to silence the old crab.

Timothy started his insurer's resistance. I slipped in the casual threat that I was a by-liner for *The Times*. Mr Giverill promised a settlement cheque on receipt of a statement. I posted one off. The following month, learning who I was, he tried to get me arrested. I eeled out by threats of wrong publicity. Luckily, his Florence thought what I'd done was sweet. The old lady's still doing her hairdressing. That was how I encountered the Giverills.

You get the point? My rescue of the old lady was fair. Timothy Giverill saw it as doing down Ordered Society, though much later he asked for advice about an antique swing-topped table Florence wanted to sell.

What were they doing here, fish out of water? I wandered among the cars and motorbikes as Sandy's performance reached a tuneless crescendo. Lot of costly motors. Plush leather, wooden dashboards, a couple with chauffeurs who frostily wound the windows up when I approached. No limos of the sort I'd seen at the Martello tower, and none with diplomatic plates.

Funny expression Timothy had used. What was it, *Who'd have thought my world would crash this way?* There was another: *the Christie-Sotheby business.* Had he really said that? Timothy had never done anything else except insurance, and they're all zombified. You never meet a happy one, like farmers. And his gripe, *Insurance seemed so safe.* They make money out of everything, don't they?

'Time they ended, eh?' I said to one limo driver.

'Two more hours. It'll be sodding dark.'

He spoke in disgust. I thought, hell fire. I had to meet Quaker's Maud for a genteel snog, perhaps, or a heart-rending tears-and-jam butty out in the sticks. Holy people, Henrietta for instance, think my attitude's reprehensible. But holiness doesn't know that life is basically any port in a storm, and being without a woman is a truly terrible storm. What can you do? I'd been deprived since Olive's feats in her motor. I thought, aha.

A quick search of the adjacent tennis courts and I found a frayed ball in the undergrowth. I borrowed a penknife from a driver, and slit the ball into hemispheres.

'My girlfriend's car,' I explained to his knowing grin.

Olive Makin's motor I knew well. I shoved the half ball flat over the lock, driver's side, and let it resume its shape. Couple of goes, the lock sprung. I got in and lay down to kip on the rear seat. I thought of switching the radio on but that would have meant scraping the wires. I wanted at least one week without a split nail.

Sleep came easily.

CHAPTER TWENTY-ONE

Everybody wakes differently, don't they.

There was somebody talking, somebody whose scent was familiar answering back. Was it a row? I was back hearing my parents rowing. I was five, and she was going to be absent when my brother and I returned from school that night, though I didn't yet know it. That wasn't right, though, because she wasn't screaming hate. And the man wasn't Dad, who never raised his voice but just took what was coming.

When dreams go wrong, slip back into the doze and maybe when you start again things will all come right. It's what I used to do when I was little, so I tried.

Male said in tones of iron, 'You've got any alternative, Olive dear?'

'No, Mel.'

'Then what are you saying? That you've discovered oil under your pseudo-Mediterranean patio? Or a hundred new Names clamouring to come aboard?'

Silence, then sounds of a backhander. Olive yelped. A fleck of spittle fell cold on my closed eyelid. The motor rocked. Mel and Olive in the motor with me, but doing more than bickering. It had all the sounds of a lover's tiff. That couldn't be right, my sluggish brain went, because Mel and

191

Sandy are . . . And Olive and me had been . . .
Suddenly I didn't want to hear this. I wanted sleep
back.

'You'll be witness, dear.' Mel at his most vicious.
'They'll start home the minute Sandy waves them
off, capeesh?'

Silence. A sudden bounce in the motor's
suspension, and Olive whimpered. Mel swung at
her, three savage slaps, his voice shaking with rage.

'You . . . shall . . . do . . . it.'

Olive wept and cringed. My eyes opened. Mel
was the beater in the passenger seat, Olive the
beatee. I'd never heard him speak with such
venom. The jokey waspishness of the avowed
person of his proclivities, the barbed wit that
amuses women so and always sounds audience-
aware, made for titters. But this? Savagery.

Outside was dark, except for slashes of yellow
glim from the village hall. I didn't want to be
discovered.

'Promise, dear.' That *dear* was the frightener. As
bad as Big John's quiet voice.

'Yes.' Her whisper didn't please him because he
sighed.

'I can't hear it, Olive, dear.'

'Yes, Mel. I'll do it.' She sounded so weary.
'Look. If—'

'No, Olive. There's not a single *if* left. Not since
Lovejoy's by-blow scuppered us all. Understand?'

I thought, Mel means Mortimer. I almost got up
and clobbered him but wanted more.

'We're all in it. You too.'

He opened the passenger's door and to my
horror the interior light came on. I froze, wishing
I'd had the sense to cover myself with a blanket.

192

Except Olive never does carry a blanket in her motor, the stupid cow. See the trouble you get into, depending on women?

'Let the Giverills drive out of the car park, then follow.'

'What do I say when somebody asks me what I saw?' Olive sniffed.

'Use your head, you stupid mare.'

He slammed the door, almost perforating my eardrums. The light dowsed. I thought, God Almighty, I'd never heard Mel speak like a gangster before. A betrayed lover, sure, when Sandy was doing what Sandy gleefully calls pub rubber, or taunting Mel across crowded auction rooms when they'd disagreed on some colour scheme. We all go embarrassed and look at the floor. Mel gets bitter and sulks for days. Sometimes he storms out, even drives off to his cousin's shack near Cherbourg, yet always returns.

The most remarkable thing was, he threatened Olive Makins! Olive, doyenne of affairs of the heart and wallet, the one woman who you'd put your money on to survive. Queen of cut-throat competition, she ran the local auctioneers' society, and was a hard-dealing contract agent for most. I'd heard Gimbert himself call her Mother Shark. Hard as nails, I'd seen her sack two women for simply getting tired in the Mile End central office. And Olive was a serious investor in trust funds, where you pay in monthly and bankers pretend they've made you a fortune that's always smaller than they promised. I've seen her throw ledgers in a high street bank.

That was the lady currently weeping at the wheel while I hid. If I sat up, might I try pretending I'd

193

just woken up? I'd never get away with it. Maybe I could eel out, then stroll up and beg a lift to town? Except the light would come on.

No. Stay put. Maybe she would go to the loo? Or go and find Sandy, try to argue him out of whatever course of action he was bent on?

I heard Sandy call, 'Byyyeee peoples! Missing you alreadeee!'

Not far away an engine fired, small motor by the sound of it. It slowly rose in pitch. I heard the motor falter as it took to the highway. Hardly Fangio driving, more your staid middle-of-the-road elderly bloke who'd wax the bonnet to a gleam every Sunday after church . . . A horrible thought took hold and I almost sat up, but Olive turned her ignition and moved off, tyres crunching. As the car tilted and picked up speed, I heard Sandy give a shrill scream of laughter.

Well, in for a penny. At least I'd find out what promise Olive had made and who else was involved.

The motor hummed, trying to lull me to sleep. I made myself stay awake. Easy, because the mention of Mortimer—it *was* Mortimer he'd meant, wasn't it?—had scared me badly. I felt clammy, this time not because of antiques. Maybe Olive secretly realized I was in her car and, sly cow, was chortling away, bent on exposing me at some horrible moment.

Except she had other things on her mind. She started crying again as she turned onto the main arterial road, sniffing and coughing. I heard her handbag click open. Getting a hanky? The last time she'd made that same click, I thought guiltily, was to find something else in her handbag when we were making smiles. I began to hear lorries and heavy wagons overtaking. Olive was not driving fast, so the car she was presumably following was trundling along the same.

Once or twice I heard an HGV irritably sound its horn as it thundered by, its airwave shoving Olive's light car slightly. She was driving slower than usual, following a slow motor. I wanted to risk a quick glance, but Olive might see my head in her driving mirror.

We'd been going fifteen minutes, I thought, when she spoke quietly.

'I see.'

She slowed. No sudden braking, just let the car lose impetus. I felt her motor nudged aside as something larger and heavier created an overtaking wash of air. A light swamped the car. The larger vehicle swished past.

'Oh, oh,' Olive moaned, and braked. A grinding sound filled the night.

There's nothing worse than the sudden squeal of car tyres. It always makes me tense up. Stupid. A scream of twisting metal took maybe a second, perhaps two. A fantastic screeching noise, endlessly drawn out, horns going, lights and shadows swirling in the car's interior—I could only really see the ceiling material from my position on the back seat. I was thrown forward.

Olive cried out, 'No, no, no . . .'

She braked a second time, harder, her tyres making a long sound as if they were tearing the ground. My back almost broke as something slammed into Olive's rear bumper. My head jerked, and I thought, Christ, I'm going to get killed, we've had it. We jerked forward, abruptly

195

seemed to crunch against something massively inert, and spun round, halting almost nose down. Her headlights dowsed. People started shouting, car horns going everywhere. Her engine raced futilely. Olive was keening, 'No, no, no.'

For a long time I stayed put. I might have broken bones, my neck fractured at some vital spot. What if the car doors locked by some slick anti-theft mechanism so I couldn't get out? I heard somebody shout, 'There's somebody down there!' And another man call, 'I'll go down. Looks like a woman.'

'Is there anybody else?' a man yelled.

'Never mind that,' a bloke boomed in a deep bass. 'Give us a lift here.'

A cry for ambulances rose. Horns blared in a cacophony. The sound of engines was deafening. I worked out that Olive's car must be in a ditch beside the trunk road.

Olive, still whimpering, opened her door and climbed out. I heard her shoes slither on the sloping bank. Bracken crackled as she blundered. I felt myself for injuries. I should have helped her, but who was in a worse state, her or me? Survival of the fittest. She had a job to do. Now that events of the night had dictated their own grim logic, I guessed that Mel had simply instructed her to be a biased witness to a rigged accident. It had all the hallmarks. I felt sick.

The door on which my head rested was down. Olive had climbed to get out. Therefore I had to go upwards. I had a sudden terror of explosion. I could smell petrol, and without worrying about broken bones I frantically scrabbled round, never mind who saw me, reeled the window down and heaved myself through into undergrowth.

Hawthorn bushes and sloes always go for my eyes. I was in a right state by the time I reached the road.

An ambulance was slowly trying to get through the array of wagons, pantechnicons, cars and vans crammed along the carriageway. An AA man's van was in the thick of it, having somehow come via the ditch. He was trying to get the traffic moving, signalling with lights, his reflective yellow jacket gleaming. Men were struggling with two motors that were concertinaed against trees. I couldn't see Olive. People were stooping over forms lying on the ground. I couldn't see, dazzled by the kaleidoscopic lights and the flashing ambers of security vehicles pressing in.

The noise was indescribable. What the hell were all the engines revving for? Blokes in heavy goods vehicles leaned out calling questions. It was mayhem. I sat on the running board of a lorry. I had a bad headache.

I could have prevented this somehow. And hadn't. I could have lied to Mel that I knew what he was up to. I could have confronted Sandy, demanded what the hell. Or gone to the police. I could have seized Olive's wheel, flagged the mark motor down and warned them. I hadn't done a frigging thing.

A lorry driver came. 'You okay, mate?'

'Aye. Ta.'

'You look rough. In one of the motors, were you?'

'No. Thumbing a lift on the verge.'

'See anything, did yer? Here.' He gave me a swig of tea from his flask. Hot, thick, sweet.

197

'Ta. No, saw nowt. Anybody hurt?'

'Two people in a motor bought it. The other motor isn't too bad.'

He was a crew-cutted bruiser, but often they're the kindliest people on the road, do anything to help. He sounded Merseyside.

'This'll be a long time clearing,' he said. 'Get in my cabin and watch the telly if you like.'

'Ta,' I said, and did.

The plod came with their loudhailers, filling the night with questions.

They asked what I'd seen. I said I recalled seeing a motor driving past and swerving. I was trying to thumb a lift, but nobody seemed willing to stop in the darkness. Something gave me a thump. I fell, heard tyres screeching, found myself down in the ditch.

'I climbed up the bank to the road,' I said.

'I gave him some tea and sat him down,' the lorry driver said. 'I wondered if he'd been thrown out of one of the motors. I've seen that happen.'

They let me go after an hour. I got a lift to civilization from the driver. I have an idea he knew my tale was made up, but that's the same for pope, poet, and peasant. We're all fibbers.

It took me a couple of hours to walk down to the river and up the footpath to my cottage. I made tea and pulled the divan down. I stripped and went to bed.

The tangled mass of Timothy Giverill's motor, crumpled against the tree in the lights, was with me as I closed my eyes and waited for the night to pass and bright day come with its new sequence of hauntings. I should have wept for what I'd done, but my senses wouldn't play my silly games any

198

more. They just sat in me, eyes, hearing, touch, the rest, just knowing what a worm I really was.

*   *   *

In sad moments the past comes niggling, making you feel bad about things long forgot. Melancholy blamed me for the tragedy. I remembered Trudy and Betcher.

It was all down to unrequited love.

Trudy was an accountant. 'I'm no oil painting,' she said jestingly. She did tax for antique dealers. Wisely she never learned the trade, or what dark deeds were done. Or, indeed, how much income flowed silently along the night hedgerows of East Anglia. I liked Trudy.

Enter Betcher. Extrovert, noisy, chatty, a caricature of the wartime spiv of old black and white films right down to the padded shoulders and natty trilby. He was called Betcher because of his gambling. 'The Derby's been run exactly for three hundred years, betcher ten quid,' and so on. He never owned a thing, simply gambled wildly. Losing a bet, he'd bet his way out: 'Okay, so it's Sheraton and I lose,' he'd say, spirits instantly lifting as something else caught his eye. 'Then that tallboy over there. Betcher it's Chippendale. Double or quits?' He used me as referee, seeing I was the only divvy around.

There was a problem. He longed for Trudy and hadn't the nerve to tell her.

'Trudy's got everything, Lovejoy. Bright, bonny. I'm rubbish.'

Tact seemed the best tack so I said, 'You frigging burke. Ask her out, God's sakes. This isn't *Jane*

199

Eyre.'

'Help me, mate.'

I get uneasy in affairs of the heart. I'd lately been in trouble with Big Frank's new betrothed lady—his fifth wife, maybe sixth—and I didn't want to be anybody else's go-between.

'Look, Betch, I'm pushed at the moment.'

'She likes that thing. I could win it on a bet.'

He described a pendant that Trudy admired in Fookleston's window. Fookie is a cadaverous, stooping bloke of immense height, bespectacled and thin. He inherited our town's best jewellery shop, and spends his profit in the bookmaker's in Head Street. Another gambler. I'd never known a bloke like him—well, I have, but you've got to say that. Fookie gambles serious money. With Betcher gambling's a mere introductory spiel leading, he hopes, to better things.

'That spinel?'

'Isn't it a sapphire?'

'No. Fookie's just trying it on. It should only be a tenth of the price.'

People let themselves get carried away by simple points of recognition. Men do it with women—she's got a terrific shape, so she must be desirable / holy / honest / kind / trustworthy, etc—and women invariably do it with jewellery. They see something prettily mounted and blue, and think, 'Egad! A princely sapphire in twenty-four carat gold! Astronomically priced, so it must be terribly valuable . . .' and so on. A spinel can be red, through blue to black. Most people think that so-called 'noble' spinel (only means gem quality) is always red, which isn't true. Okay, blue spinels are sometimes cloudy and not so bonny, but when you see transparent violety or frankly blue stones, they don't come any lovelier. The great 'Black Prince's Ruby' in our Crown jewels is secretly a spinel, not a ruby at all, but don't let on. Blue and red spinels have been substituted for sapphires and rubies over the centuries.

Like a duckegg I decided to help Betcher. I got Fookie to sell me the blue spinel pendant for a fraction of his asking price. I sold it on to Betcher for exactly what I'd paid. He wooed Trudy, heavenly violins soared and angels sang, and we all waited for wedding bells to chime. No such luck. The sky fell in. Trudy abruptly resigned and went to Manchester. Betcher sank into profound dejection, recovered slowly to his usual, 'Wotcher, Lovejoy. Betcher that new cat of Chrissy's gets lost within the week, ten quid on it?' I thought, oh well, lovers' parting is such sweet sorrow and all that. I'd done my bit so was it my fault?

Needless to say, yes it was.

One day I was in Manchester collecting some fake English secretaire bookcases—lovely mahogany, narrow, finely dovetailed drawers. Manchester repros are by far the best anywhere on earth. They're dead ringers for 1795. Dunno why, but Manchester craftsmen take the trouble of matching wood grain top and bottom, banding the same. Other forgers are too damned idle, don't do a proper job . . . Where was I? Manchester, bumping into Trudy in an antique dealer's.

She still wore Betcher's spinel pendant. In fact I recognized it before I even looked at her. We said hello. I stood shuffling, waiting for her to get mad over something I'd done / hadn't done, the usual female response to me. Until she said, 'I'm married now, Lovejoy. A little girl, twelve months.'

'Oh, good.' What can you say?

'It didn't work out with Brendon,' she said wistfully. I remembered in the nick of time that was Betcher's real name. 'I waited, but he never said anything. I saw it was hopeless.' Sorrow pained her eyes. 'I just had to leave.'

Betcher had been too much of a dope to speak out and I'd been too thick to bang their silly heads together and tell them to get on with it and stop annoying us. A classic tragedy, English reserve versus ardent longing.

The question was, what to say? Tell Trudy the truth, that Betcher had always loved her, now she was married with a family? Or reveal all to Betcher? Or let things slide? Being me, I took the easiest, saddest route. When next I met Betcher he said wistfully, 'Back from Lancashire, eh?' And asked, heart in his eyes, 'Betcher didn't see Trudy, Lovejoy. Tenner on it.'

'No,' I lied evenly. What else could I say?

So Betcher languishes and Trudy languishes and me helping made it shambolic. And that, said Alice, was that.

The lesson? When I help, things get worse. My gran used to say, 'Lord save me from helpers.' She meant me.

*　　　*　　　*

There's no doubt. Morality's punk, dud from start to finish. I believe there's only one moral problem in life. It's this: if you could save somebody's life and you don't, then you're a murderer. That's the only moral dilemma since the dawn of man, like

202

Brigadier Hedge's australopithecines question. Except it's no problem, for it's solved before you even utter the question.

Whoever else was responsible for Florence and Timothy Giverill's deaths—plus the deaths of whoever else had died in the crash—there was no doubt who was the real culprit. It was me, as surely as if I'd driven Timothy into that tree.

No sleep that night. The bluetits knocked on my window at seven as usual. I got up, filled their thing full of nuts, diced cheese for the robin and scattered a load of gunge for them to get on with. The plod came and took me in. I wasn't quite ready for them, but answered as I'd worked out during the lantern hours.

CHAPTER TWENTY-TWO

It was a different office. I prefer uniformed plod these days. Once, I used to think they were the worst of a myriad evils. Now, I think maybe they're the least, though you've still to watch them.

'Eh?' I asked Sep Verner.

He showed his teeth. He believes it looks like smiling, but so far he hasn't learned how. When he was in clink and I was showing him how to paint like Vincent—I told you about that—he was a quiet, withdrawn geezer on remand. We all make mistakes. I believed he was human, or at least lifelike, capable of emotion and everything. I was well wrong. He shook my hand, I remember, when I got sprung, and told me ta for helping him through. A blink of an eye, and there he was a rising star in the plod's firmament.

'This fatal accident in which you were involved, Lovejoy.'

'What accident?'

No lie to tell him my head hurt. I'd no mirror at the cottage, but knew I must look frayed at the edges. I had a bump on my noggin, though I'd bathed as usual in my tin bath and got blood and mud off.

He sat in his chair, rocking and swinging. I'm sure he copies American gangster films. He's prognathous, teeth like that cowcatcher device that Babbage invented for the front of railway engines. I'll bet he got called names by his pals at school. Is there anything worse than the cruelty of children?

'What was that about children?' he asked sharply, his chair slamming down. He leaned forward, fingers linked. Whoops. Must have spoken my thoughts. I'm always doing that.

'Sorry,' I said. 'I'm still woozy from the accident.'

'What accident?' he asked softly.

'That's what I asked.'

He flicked open a slender file. My name. I must have started a new one, for legal goings-on instead of the usual messes.

'Last night, Lovejoy.' He stared beyond me, gave some newcomer the nod. 'You were injured. Two people were killed. An antique dealer, one Mrs Olive Makins, was injured along with three other drivers. You were an eye witness.'

'Olive Makins? I know her. Is she all right?'

'Fine. Just grazes.'

'Thank heavens,' I said piously. 'She's the auctioneers' secretary.'

'We know.' No grin now. 'Which raises the

204

question what you were doing so late thumbing lifts on the trunk road.'

'Trying to get home, I suppose.' I furrowed my brow, trying to help him against the odds. 'I remember some event in a village hall. Was it Beccles?'

'How did you get to the main road?'

'I don't remember. All I can see is . . .' I did the same patter, tyres, vehicles braking, me down the embankment. 'Then this truck driver was saying there'd been an accident. From Liverpool,' I added helpfully.

The newcomer spoke. 'You're not pulling the wool over my eyes, Lovejoy,' she said, coming round the desk. My heart sank.

Sep Verner made way as Petra Deighnson seated herself and gazed at me unsmiling. Petra, incidentally, means rock in Latin.

Deighnson missed her vocation. She could have been human given half a chance. No, I mean it, could have been a real functioning *Homo sapiens* with friends and a life to lead. Don't misunderstand. She looks the part, is always well turned-out. Smart, my generation would say, suited, good legs and high heels, only one item of jewellery and that a spanker with an ultramarine— my favourite gem—at its centre. High Victorian, it's what posher antique dealers call *en tremblant*, meaning shivery, always on the go. It's one of the few brooches you can tell a mile off.

It had all the marks of pricey craftsmanship; not flat, but different planes of the brooch standing proud. Class. This, I knew just from looking, would be as superb when you turned it over as it looked from the front. Only one gem, set in fragile leaves

205

made of diamonds in silver and platinum. It made my mouth drool. I'd never seen her wear any other jewellery. Blouse, neat white gloves, jacket and skirt matching, she looked you-shall-go-to-the-ball. She's known for it. I daresay the lads at the nick have a score of spiteful names for her. They say she'll go far. I don't doubt it. When first we met she was a lowly come-here-do-that. Now, she's the one they stand up for. Always wears white gloves, but not for what you think. I've actually seen her hands, and they're beautiful. No split nails for our Petra.

'Do be seated, Lovejoy.'

She has a pleasant face, lovely eyes. I couldn't imagine her doing the three-minute basic police training, Kevlar vests and guns. Petra seems remote as monarchy. Rumour puts her at Oxford reading classics, pure maths, divinity. Whatever, she's hard to fool and harder still to oppose. She looks the sort of plod that fashionable actresses are always trying to emulate in those tiresome TV mayhem-and-murder episodes. I was once being questioned when somebody rang her up and asked if she'd be willing to let some TV actress come and see her work. She'd replied, 'Don't be silly,' and rang off, continuing the questions without breaking step.

That's Petra Deighnson, vicar's daughter from Northampton. Oh, and big ranker in the Serious Fraud Office. She used to be in the local plod, but saw the light of promotion in the galaxy and jumped ship. The SFO has nicknames—Seriously Flawed Office among variants—but you dursn't utter them in dear Petra's hearing. Local dealers call it the Silly Failure Orifice. The SFO's useless, despite our Petra. It rattles sabres at robber barons like Robert Maxwell, then lets them get away scotage free while the rest of us sit seething and the tabloid newspapers thunder Why Are They Allowed? It's the little bloke who gets done, for forgetting half a groat on his tax return, or the old woman who forgets to claim her pension. They wistfully wonder how the huge-haul thieves get away with everything. The SFO alone knows, and does sweet sod all.

'Lovejoy. You witnessed an accident last night.'

'People keep saying so.'

She didn't smile, but something in her changed as if she was pondering a smile as a possible strategem for some future reincarnation.

'Won't you answer the question?' she said, quite pleasant.

'What question?'

'You watch it, Lovejoy!' Sep spat, itching to rise and belt my head in, his form of psychotherapy. Showing off before the pretty lady, more like.

'Leave him. Lovejoy's quite correct, Mr Verner. I didn't ask a question.'

He subsided, glowering. I'd made a pal.

'Sorry, missus. I've a bad head.'

'Can we offer you anything? Would you like to see a doctor?'

'I'll be okay as soon as I get back to work.'

Verner sniggered. She half turned and he quietened, staring at me with pure hatred. I wondered, not for the first time, how close he and Susanne Eggers actually were. Thick as thieves, to coin a phrase.

'If I remember anything, I'll phone in.'

'Very well.' She rose. We rose. 'I'll take you to hospital.'

'I'm not as bad as that, missus,' I said in alarm.

207

'To visit your friends.' I gaped at her as she wafted past. 'The Giverills. Do come.'

We drove to the new hospital in Gosbecks in a superb saloon that must have cost us taxpayers a mint. She had the grace not to charge me a penny fare. I was almost fainting from relief. Timothy and Florence were safe! All along I'd assumed that Olive Makins had been there to bear witness to their murders in a rigged road accident. I felt so grateful, to everybody—God, police, the ambulance, the AA, oddly to Sandy and Mel.

La Petra seemed to know the hospital corridors, leading the way with clicking heels. I wondered if, once folk rose to some requisite rank in official bureaux, they were trained to walk like a fieldmarshal. Patients and nurses melted before us at the Intensive Care Unit.

I'm scared of these places. The doctors look into you, obviously working out where the next needle must be drilled in, and nurses look like they're weighing how heavy you'd be to lift onto a bedpan. It's demoralizing when you're just a visitor.

The place was all glass cubicles, like some crazy computer game where a little figure has to make it through a castle dungeon and gets hoodwinked by hidden assassins. I was told to wait. A doctor came, looking at the floor while he spoke to Ms Deighnson. She held a small transmitter thing. The doctor shook his head, shrugged, finally nodded. She beckoned.

'Go in, Lovejoy. He wants you.'

'Who? Is it Timothy Giverill?'

She didn't quite shove me, but I felt propelled. Somebody gave me a green hat and a mask—what the hell for? Was I to operate? A green gown

208

enveloped me, the arms gorilla length, the tapes trailing on the lino.

'Sit there, please.'

I obeyed, stricken. Timothy—was that him, for Christ's sake?—was in a floppy transparent tent. Gasses hissed. Screens blipped green lines and spikes. I felt ill. I could hardly look. The nurse, garbed the same as me, warned me with a glare, but of what exactly? I didn't want to be here.

'Lovejoy?' A whispering gnat.

'It's me, Timothy. You okay?' Then I could have kicked myself. What was he supposed to say? Of course he wasn't frigging okay. He was smashed to blazes, his face swathed in bandages, plasters keeping tubes in place and see-through muzzles on his mouth. It was obscene.

'How is Florence?'

'She's fine, wack,' I said hoarsely, thinking well, nobody's told me different.

'Lovejoy? It's not her fault. It's mine, you see, old chap.'

'Don't worry, Timothy. You're going to be fine.'

'I asked for you.' A long pause. I looked to see if I could take his hand, maybe save his weakening breath by letting him signal by squeezing fingers. I'd seen a film where folk communicated like that, when one of them was poorly.

'Lovejoy? I trusted the contracts.'

His unsmashed eye caught me. I nodded agreement.

'Well, you would,' I said feebly. Contracts?

'I went in thinking it would be so splendid, being a Name.'

'That's natural, Timothy.'

'It would have gone all right. Hugo started it all.'

209

He seemed suddenly desperate, tried to move, failed and sank back. He searched, found me as I moved my head to be in slightly better light. Bloody wards are all lit by the Prince of Darkness. I'd have glared at the nurse but didn't want Timothy to waste his energy.

'Lovejoy. I didn't really do anything wrong, did I?'

He sounded pathetic. I shook my head emphatically.

'Course you didn't, mate. Not you.'

There was no reply for so long that the nurse began to tell me to clear off. As she gestured, Timothy spoke almost with his usual clarity, quite as if in the middle of a normal conversation.

'You see, old fruit, it's the promise, isn't it? Like the man said after the earthquake. Every last cent. Wasn't that his phrase?'

'Yes,' I said, baffled. 'That's it, Timothy.'

Into the silence I said eventually, because he'd gone abnormally still, 'Some bloke, eh?'

Then in the clearest voice he said, 'You'll look after my Florence, Lovejoy.'

A statement, not a question.

'Until you're up and about, mate, course I will.'

Silence. The monitors blipped industriously. I rose, ahemed.

'I'd best be off, Timothy. Florence, er, sends her love. She'll be in to see you about, er, nineish, if that's okay?'

The nurse glared. The monitors bleeped. I left, saying so-long. Hugo?

Downstairs as we headed for the main concourse Petra spoke to one of the doctors. Mrs Giverill was on life support. They spoke for hell of a time. He looked a frazzled ten-year-old. I saw his name on his white coat and remembered it.

By the time he'd finished and Petra Deighnson looked round for me I was among the parents in the paediatric queue, crouching down and chatting with a titch bent on unscrewing his toys. We mangled two, to the little lad's mother's amused tut-tutting. I heard the doctor's bleep go and he hurried off. Sickened, I eeled out, went down past the mortuary where nobody ever checks the exits, and opened the wooden door into St Mary's Lane. I hurried through the back doubles, thinking straight and fast for the first time. What I'd learned was dire, grievous, horrid.

All previous plans—if I'd had any—had to go. I phoned from a public phone box by the multi-storey car park behind the hospital. I had to dash back into antiques, where I could make / break some rules of my own and let everybody else's go hang. I needed a lot of small, neat thefts of exemplary accuracy. It wouldn't matter whose antiques got nicked, as long as they finished up in my sack. When your own skill runs out, hire the very very best. The greatest thief in the Eastern Hundreds was downing her pink gins in the Welcome Sailor. I got her on the phone.

'Alicia? I need help, love.'

'Who gives a toss, dear?' she purred.

'Money does.'

'Money?' She sharpened her mental claws. I could hear them honing on her stony heart, swish swish.

'Multo bunce, doowerlink. Some of it's for you.'

'For little me, dwahling?' She giggled. 'What do I have to do?'

211

Pubs have ears, so I said, 'Come out of the side door and walk down to the war memorial. I'll want you to do an antiques sweep, like we said. I know that some of your pals use that new shoulder—whatsername, Confetta from Manchester—but I want proven class like you, Alicia.'

She made a sharp intake of breath. I heard it. Now I knew that she had a rival 'shoulder' (read thief) she'd be less inclined to blow the gaff. That was the best persuasion to secrecy I could manage, over the phone.

'See you in twenty minutes. Take note who's in the pubs you pass, okay?'

'For you, anything!' she cooed, and rang off.

The one thing that proves irresistible to any skilled artisan is asking them to display their expertise to an admiring throng. Even if that throng is only me, it still attracts the skilled thief. Nobody could steal like Alicia.

Like I say, an expert. She was there on time. She was carrying her little dog Peshy. She held it up for me to kiss. I turned aside.

'Oh, pwease say hello to daahling Peshy, Lovejoy!' she trilled. It growled. I gave it a half-hearted pat. It snapped. Normally animals love me, spotting a pushover, but this canine must have thought I was muscling into its ample niche.

'I hope Peshy's on form, love.' I was in enough trouble without a bad-tempered mongrel the size and shape of a cheap brooch.

'Of course!' she warbled, clasping the animal to her bosom. 'He's a pure bred. And he's a Bichon Frise, Lovejoy, not an *it*. He helps mumsy-wumsy to borrow *such* lovely shinies from those nasty greedy dealers, doesn't he?'

Keeping a weather eye out for Petra Deighnson and her plod squad, I walked Alicia to her husband's motor and told her the name of a farmhouse near Norwich.

'It's where we're going for a few days, love,' I explained. 'If you can nick as I want, then we're partners. If you get caught, that's your lookout. Agreed?'

'Caught!' She said the word like I'd mentioned some distant asteroid. 'I've not been caught since before you were born, Lovejoy.'

'Then don't start now, eh?'

'You'll be delighted with my performance, Lovejoy.' She fondled her dog, gazing into its eyes. 'Won't he, my little woofie?'

'We're going to assault a number of auctioneers and antique shops, Alicia. We'll raid the whole of Suffolk and Norfolk, et al. I've allocated a fortnight.'

Her eyes closed in rapture. She said huskily, 'And you'll pay? Lovejoy, bless you from the bottom of my heart. You've just promised paradise!'

She chuckled all the way to my village. I like Alicia, always have, but being with her makes me sigh. Times were getting rough when the one person you could trust was an arch thief. Mind you, the Lord found that. Am I right or am I right?

CHAPTER TWENTY-THREE

Alicia dropped me at the chapel. I skulked down the lane. I'd told her to pack, tell our destination to

213

nobody, then drive to the nosh van on the Ipswich road.

No bobbies lurked among the hydrangeas, no sudden rustling in the ivy. The door was fastened by the same old twists of wire I always used. La Deighnson hadn't caught up with me yet. Safe! I eeled in, smiling, and halted.

The woman stared at me. Same person, ankles primly crossed, gloved hands on her lap. I thought, I've seen you before.

'Good day, Lovejoy.'

She spoke like teachers used to, fingers drumming. 'I'm waiting . . .'

'Er, refresh my memory, please.'

Even as I spoke I thought, she's the bird who asked me to guard that painting I'd forged, wanted a report every day, week, whatever.

'Look, missus,' I began, clearing my throat. Making dud excuses always makes me nervy. 'I've had a lot on. I think you'll have to find somebody else. I've to go away a few days.'

'You have entirely forgotten, have you not?'

She actually said it like that, Have (pause) you (pause) not (pause), then a long time afterwards came that ? I was left admiring, but conscious that I'd been soundly told off. She was the woman who'd given me my forgery of Geoffreye Parlayne's wife, Lady Hypatia Parlayne of that ilk. I plundered my feeble memory through mental murk. This was the woman who believed that her—my—forgery was in fact a Cromwellian masterpiece. I was to protect it against thieves. My headache came like a wolf on the fold, slamming my temple and making my eyes uncertain of gaze.

'Er, certainly not! You're, er . . .' She wore a

wedding ring. Hadn't she said she was a neighbour of Darla Vullamy? Something like that.

'I am Mrs Thomasina Quayle. I paid you to protect my rare antique portrait. The contract is legally binding.'

'Er, sure it is!' I said brightly through a mask of pain in half my head. 'You want to see it?'

'If you please, Lovejoy.'

She followed. I led the way to my workshop, asked if she'd wait a sec as I went in. I crossed to the far end and hauled up the old flagstone. It isn't a trapdoor like the one in my cottage. It's just a simple flat paving slab with an iron ring in it so you can lift one end. There's nothing beneath except a level metal tray, for whatever canvas or antique I choose to lay in it.

Nothing.

I stared, my heart banging. I lowered the slab with a thud, retraced my steps, returned, lifted the damned thing a second time, gaped. Zilch. Nil. Empty.

I thought back to when she'd come. What did she actually say, that day? 'It's already in your . . . shed,' when I'd asked her where her portrait was.

After she left, I'd gone to the workshop, seen it leaning against the wall. I'd examined it, still thought it pretty neff, then gingerly laid it down, covering it with a pink bedsheet some bird had left. Now, there was the selfsame sheet neatly folded on the old beech easel I use for landscape forgeries. (Folded neatly? Moi?) The security tricks I normally use—threads on the earthenware floor, dust sprinkled around the easel—were undisturbed. So how in God's name had the thief nicked the portrait, in its frame, from beneath the flagstone? The cobweb I'd layered over the iron ring hadn't been disturbed. You get the cobwebs on dewy morning grass, and it's a good trick—until now, foolproof. It was just gone.

'Yes, Mrs Quayle!' I cried, emerging brightly. 'There it is! Perfectly safe!'

She didn't move, stood there by the door.

I said gaily, 'I didn't even offer you a cup of rosy. Let me make amends!'

Eyes of stone. 'I must see it, Lovejoy.'

'I can assure you . . .'

'I paid. I want to see it. Now.'

The last word was like a pistol shot. The bloody woman wouldn't budge. What is it with these people? Suspicion, suspicion, suspicion. I swallowed. 'Actually, missus, there's been a bit of a problem. I happened to notice that the surface of the painting had bloomed a bit in one corner, so I varnished it—perfectly free! Gratis! I've improved its net worth. I can't move it for a week.'

'Show me my portrait,' she said quietly. That same terrible spaced speaking chilled me, every word a mile from its neighbour.

I noticed the mobile phone in her hand. She hadn't had it before. She was transmitting. I suddenly didn't like Mrs Quayle. Still stunning, like all women, but I was scared. The thought came that she might serve the antiques raj.

'Right!' I said heartily, for the phone's benefit. 'I'll take you to it. Can I change first?'

Not a flicker. 'Where is it?'

I pointed down the lane. It only leads to the river and Seven Arches where the railway line runs.

'Eleanor's bungalow. I use an old garage. A minute's walk.'

216

'I shall accompany you, Lovejoy. Don't leave my sight.'

'Very well.' I found myself saying it like she would, syllables slow and spaced. Nobody catches accents quicker than me. I led the way into the cottage, asked to be excused a sec while I went to the loo. I closed the door, humming a catchy tune, stood on the edge of the loo and prised open the loft trapdoor.

Ten heartbeats later, I dropped from the thatched roof—several startled bats flapped a bit, disturbed having their nap—and was off, haring up the footpath to the main road. I wasn't defrauding Thomasina Quayle by escaping. Give me a few days, I'd knock her up half a dozen of the damned portraits. They're all as good as each other. I should know. God's sakes, who better? I caught the bus at the churchyard and sank down in the rearmost seat until it reached St Peter's on North Hill. I caught Tinker on his trek from the Bugle Horn to the Welcome Sailor. He likes to be precise, law and ale money permitting.

*   *   *

'Here, Lovejoy,' he said, nervous. 'What we in here for?'

The Old Court Coffee House is the best coffee place in the Eastern Hundreds. Quiet, no mayhem, a living antique with a proper fire in the grate and decent chairs. It's a family place. You can get a swig of wine with your nosh, and nobody hassles you.

'We won't be spotted here, Tinker.'

'We in trouble?'

'A bit.' I told him about the accident to Timothy

217

and Florence Giverill. He heard me out.

'I heard. Gawd rest the poor sod, even if he was in insurance.'

'Timothy?' I said, stricken.

'Dead an hour since, poor bleeder. Just heard in the Bull.'

For a while I said nothing. He understood, coughed a sympathetic cough that quivered the old rafters. I looked into the fire. Time I started thinking instead of running away. I told him I was leaving town with Alicia Domander.

He cackled, nodding. 'She'll see you right, Lovejoy. A right randy cow, her, but you already know that.'

'No, Tinker. An antiques run. Me and her'll sweep Suffolk, Norfolk.'

'Then what?'

'Scare everybody, stir the swine up. Unload every single item in Gimbert's Auction Rooms, a special one-off.'

'The lads will hate that, Lovejoy. It'll attract London bidders. Big money.'

'With Alicia and Peshy doing the shoulder, I'll have vanloads.'

'You're wanted, son, so watch out.'

'Who by?' I asked, uneasy.

'That poofter, Sandy. And some tart who talks like the telephone. And that Maud, Quaker's missus—here, you back to shagging her? And that American bird. And that actor geezer, calls hisself Jules now he's out of clink. And Tina, the one with that bloody great well in her house. And—'

'Tinker,' I said wearily. 'Shut it. You've got a job on.'

'Work?' he said. 'I can't, Lovejoy. My wound

218

plays me up.'

'Get me an antiques kit. They'll be watching the craft shops. I can't go home and get my own. You know that tin biscuit box I carry about.'

'Right, son. What you want in it?'

'What I've had in it ever since Adam dressed, you ignorant burke. The essentials for examining antiques.'

'How the hell would I know?' he gravelled out, hawking up phlegm and spitting into the fire. It sizzled. And they say elegance is dead.

You don't need much to suss out antiques. Very few things are any use. My kit is lightweight. Anybody can make one. It saves many a mistake. They're mostly household things, easily got: a tape measure showing inches and centimetres; a x10 loupe (higher magnification is more nuisance than help); a colour chart (I use a Daler-Rowney one because art shops give them free—I pencil in dates the actual colours came in); a midget pocket calculator because I'm thick doing sums; a miniature pencil torch. The only valuable instrument in the entire kit is a McArthur microscope. There are cheap plastic versions, but if you can afford a unique original, get one. It's worth its weight in gold. You simply put it down on anything—wood, stone, metal, material, silks, whatever—and switch on. You look in, and it shows you a magnificent detailed view of the surface, just as if you were in a pathology laboratory. Then, in a tissue, two broken lenses from polarized sunglasses—essential for jewellery.

Lastly, I carry a little packet of carob seeds. That's it. Doesn't sound much, but that little kit will save you a fortune in avoiding mistakes in antiques. The seeds incidentally are anciently the *Ceratonia siliqua*, supposedly the 'locusts' eaten by John the Baptist when he was doing his thing. Remarkably, they have hardly any variation in size or weight. For this reason the carob seed became our 'carat' in measuring precious grades. They serve as a reminder, in case I feel any bidding madness come over me in auctions.

'Leave it, Tinker. I'll gather my own, once I'm on the road.'

Gloom took hold of him.

'I don't want you to leave town, son. What'll I do for a drop or two with you tarting around the Hundreds?' He looked piteous. 'I've got me bad chest back.'

'Excuse me, Lovejoy,' the lady called from behind her counter. 'Is the old gentleman not well? I could always make him a hot toddy, if you like.'

Tinker brightened instantly. 'Ta, lady. That's real—'

'No, thank you, love,' I said quickly. It could become an orgy in seconds. 'He'll be better in the fresh air.'

'Here, son. Nark it.' Tinker was outraged. I hauled him to his feet.

'You're coming too, Tinker.' I said so-long to the lady and got him outside, peering about like a cartoon cat to check the gardens were empty of foes. 'Here's a wadge. I'm heading east. Follow me on. Be there tomorrow noon.'

'East? But everybody says you're going to Stalham, Lovejoy.' He cheered up, feeling the bunce I'd given him.

Did the world know? Anyhow, I had to avoid that route now, or I'd get nabbed in a trice. 'No.

220

East. I'll do Harwich first, them three antique shops near the Hook of Holland ferry. The nearest pub, dinner time, okay? Another thing. Find out who Hugo is.'

'Who the hell is—?'

Give me strength. I left him hawking up phlegm. I slid between the old post office and the theatre, and briskly walked the Roman wall to the railway station where I could get a taxi. It was all go. No sign of Thomasina Quayle. I vaguely knew that she'd said something important, but couldn't for the life of me get it straight. Luckily children were thronging from North Street School as I reached the river bridge, so I wasn't unduly worried about getting caught by my sundry creditors. I still had more money than I was used to. I could keep Alicia and her blinking Bichon Frise in luxury until we'd done the antiques sweep. Not enough money to burn, you understand. Just stealing enough to become temporarily rich.

On the bridge I bought a posy of those little blue flowers, the sort I like that grow wild in my garden. I dropped them into the river, watched them out of sight among the ducks. They were for Timothy. I'd settle the rest of the obligation later.

Then headed out.

CHAPTER TWENTY-FOUR

It was next day. The antiques shop in Harwich was set back between a natty tailor's and a fishing place. I didn't know the proprietress, only that she wasn't the expert she thought she was. I'd seen her miss a small occasional table that would have kept her a year, maybe more, but she was too proud to kneel and check underneath.

'It was glass,' I told Alicia as we readied to do the first robbery. She would shoulder, I'd be safely elsewhere.

'A glass topped table?'

'No. The entire table. Osler of Birmingham made glass furniture, right down to the pedestal. Not a splinter of wood in sight. Some loon had painted it a hideous green, wanting it to look like wrought iron. I got it home and stripped the paint off.'

'Christ, that sounds ugly.'

Osler's glass furniture factory kept going from Trafalgar times, but failed in the 1920s. Oddly, they sold best in Calcutta and Hong Kong, God knows why. Too little sun in England, and the perennial brightness in the Eastern Empire, might explain it. Victorian ladies loved them in their conservatories, where light could pick up the gleams. Folk chuck them out these days, thinking it's a neffie modern fashion. Wrong. It's a stylish art gone from us. If you see one, buy it. Collectors and fashioneers are starting to cotton on.

'Ann Fosstitch, as ever was.'

The woman entered the shop, her great saloon motor illegally parked. Soon after, another woman scurried away, and La Fosstitch appeared in the window arranging her wares.

'What do you want me to uncle, Lovejoy?'

Uncle to mean nick, from Uncle Dick, nick. Hence, steal. Alicia's Cockney rhyming slang shows through when she's keyed up. Peshy woke, yawned, and stretched, ready for action.

'Anything good. I can't decoy for you, so take care, love.'

She left, walking the dog on its string. It bounced along like a ball of fur. I'm told that breeders can change their shapes. If so, they've let the Almighty down. Peshy was a travesty. What on earth could a dog like that do? Hunting was out. Guarding somebody's castle was not on. Pulling some sledge was a ludicrous thought. I think people with fancy dogs are odd.

They vanished into the shop, Alicia carefully picking Peshy up and pausing in the entrance beforehand, presumably asking if the shopkeeper had any objections to a mongrel. A traffic warden knocked on the window. I opened it.

'Will you be parked here long, sir?'

'Only a minute,' I said, affecting boredom, though my heart was racing. 'My wife just wanted to do a bit of shopping in that tailor's.'

He smiled in sympathy. 'Then five minutes, sir.'

He strolled off. I was dreading Tinker's arrival. With his mighty cough and tatty appearance we'd get arrested on sight, hanging about this busy port. The water looked par ticularly cold today, the ferries hustling, cars streaming past to the Continental terminals. I'd chosen well. I didn't like La Fosstitch. She'd once complained about a children's playground.

Ten minutes, me getting anxious, Alicia emerged and walked. It was only a few yards to the corner. I drove quickly off, parked near a shopping mall. Alicia opened the door and slid in.

'Lovejoy,' she exclaimed as I pulled out into the traffic. 'What an absolute cow! What a mare!'

I was pleased, my judgement confirmed. 'Get

223

anything?'

Alicia simply held her hand over the back seat where Peshy was wagging and yapping, noisy little sod. It nuzzled in its frothy fur and dropped a little plastic packet into her hand. I almost shunted a big Ford up ahead in astonishment.

'Who's a clever little Peshy-Weshy!' she cooed, fondling the mutt. It gave a few self-congratulatory yaps. 'Are they any good, Lovejoy?'

There was a lucky parking space near the turn-off to the wharfs. I took the earrings out. Our first theft. They were chalcedony, almost classical William IV in style. This means light-looking, drop-stone earrings, one gem with fancy detailed settings. Chalcedony's a lovely stone, though people turn their noses up at it nowadays because it's only quartz and not diamond, but so what if it's beautiful? If chalcedony's got a 'typical' colour it's a cloudy bluish white, virtually impossible to shine a narrow light through.

'Lovely. You did well. Brilliant.'

She was pleased. 'You're working with the best here, Lovejoy.'

'Could you put them away, love? The back of my neck's gone funny.'

'Oh, has it!' she suddenly asked, eyes hard. 'Wait.' Her lips set in a thin line. She said quietly, 'Peshy.'

Silence from the back seat. I turned. Peshy was staring out at the cars.

'Peshy?' No response. What was going on? The dog kept its back to us, gazing out. Her voice cracked like a gunshot. *'Peshy!'*

'Christ, Alicia. You made me . . .'

The Bichon slowly looked round. I wouldn't

224

have believed that a dog could look, well, hangdog, but this managed it. Head down, eyes avoiding Alicia's, it nuzzled into its fur and brought out another sachet. Caught red-muzzled.

It waited, maybe hoping things hadn't quite gone horribly wrong, but Alicia wriggled her fingers, palm cupped. The dog looked at her hand, the plastic jewellery envelope in its mouth.

'Give! Hand it over.'

'You keep making me jump.'

'He's got to learn, Lovejoy.'

The dog surrendered. Alicia slapped its nose and gave it a right telling off, lecturing the miniature hound on obedience, trust, fairness, honesty, and Doing Right By Your Mistress. Much of it was in incomprehensible dog-speak, 'Does he want his toysie-woysies in his beddie-weddie . . .' etc, etc, but Peshy looked thrashed.

'Sorry about that, Lovejoy. He keeps some things back. I've to watch him.'

'The dog's a kleppie?' A blowsy shoplifter and a kleptomaniac dog. My antiques sweep round the Eastern Hundreds was looking dodgy. I blotted the plastic. If we got stopped, I didn't want my fingerprints on the stolen goods, only Alicia's. Fair's fair. So far I'd skated inside the law.

'He's mumsy-wumsy's little helper, isn't he?' she crooned, patting him. 'All is forgiven, isn't he, Uncle Lovejoy?'

Uncle Lovejoy could have strangled the bloody animal, because if we got apprehended an animal's collar is the first place the plod would look.

Peshy had stolen well, though. It was a mourning brooch, Victorian, with MEMORIAM in gold gothic lettering, unusually in white enamel, and a white

225

agate cabochon embossing the centre. The reverse was hollowed, the locket containing a wisp of fair hair.

'It's wrong, isn't it, Lovejoy?' she said, leaning heavily across to examine it with me. 'Shouldn't it be black, mourning jewellery?'

'Somebody young, unmarried, happen a babby, some times got white stones. They're rarer and more valuable.' Purple and even dark blue brooches became acceptable as the Victorians' obsession with mourning reached its height and craftsmen turned their skill to ever more varied displays of grief.

This robbery mingled two emotions in me. Respect for Peshy's unerring eye was one, but it was submerged in pity for the sorrow at the brooch. For an instant I felt almost choked. Poor Timothy Giverill. Poor Vestry found hanging. Poor who next?

'Where to, Lovejoy?'

'We'll do an auctioneer's. There's Balance and Knorr's place by the open market, isn't there?'

'Their whiffler used to be a plod, Lovejoy,' she warned.

'If he's on duty, come out.'

We agreed. It was getting on for noon, always a good time to do a shoulder in auction rooms because security blokes' fancies lightly turn to the nearest boozer's pies and pints. It was viewing day, saving us the awkward drive to Dovercourt.

She got her midget wolfhound and went in, Peshy all excited at thoughts of more thievery. I stayed out of sight. She emerged after half an hour, some young bloke opening the door for her and handing her a free catalogue. Getting anything free

226

from an auctioneer's the equivalent of a peerage. I admired her. She swept off down the pavement. On a good day, when she's on song, feeling particularly bright and well dressed, Alicia can charm the birds off the trees. Other women don't like her much, because she looks a bit blowzy and showy.

I remember Nell, a bird from Bristol. I used her for repairing Art Deco ceramics, until she went ape with a Mauritian singer. Nell went for Alicia because she wore colours that clashed, as women say. Nell's tiny shape was dwarfed by Alicia's ample figure. She said caustically, 'Alicia, dear, don't you know the old saying about colours? *Orange and yellow make folk bellow.* And *blue and green must never be seen*!' Alicia swept past Nell like a ship in full sail saying loudly, 'What crap dwarfs talk!' They never spoke again. Personally, I think Nell was wrong, because Alicia always wears tons of makeup, like a woman should, and dresses really colourfully. Sometimes she wears every colour you can imagine, all together. That's real style. I can't for the life of me think why women hate her. My only worry was that people tended to remember her more than most.

We met up by the shopping mall and I drove to a tavern on the north road. She did her lipstick from a handbag that I could have dossed in. The car's interior filled with scent and powder clouds. She asked how she looked.

'Stupendous, love.' How else? I could tell she'd struck oil because I felt giddy like a cold was coming on.

'I hope you like it, Lovejoy.'

'Silver.'

Three little silvers were hauled from Alicia's

cleavage while Peshy looked on, possibly working out how on earth he could compete with that. One was a disappointment, being a modern silver pepperpot, but two were lovely.

When tea—best drink in the world—became cheaper as imports flooded in, it became unnecessary to lock tea caddies, as they used to until later Victorian times (ungrateful servants nicked the precious commodity, you see). This was an important step, because ladies used the caddy's silver lid for measuring out the tea leaves. Getting it exactly right was an indication of a lady's skill. Still is. So tea-caddy spoons came in. There are leagues of caddy spoon collectors all over the world. Rare examples are almost fought over.

Sadly, here's one of my grievous laws: where collectors thrive, forgers follow. The most evil trick is when a forger (sometimes a skilled silversmith, so watch out) nicks the silver case from some genuine old watch. By beating it out into a bowl shape, it can simulate a caddy spoon *complete with a genuine silver hallmark*! Add a crescent of silver to its edge, and there you have an antique jockey-cap caddy spoon. Impress a contour, and you have a vine-leaf or a commemorative map of some island just added to the Empire. The giveaway is that the hallmarks are all clustered in the reshaped bowl, whereas they aren't on the really genuine antique. One of Alicia's pieces was like that.

'Still, never mind.' I showed her. 'People'll be taken in.'

The other was a winner. It was a pair of grape scissors, the most useless implement ever made since Neanderthal man dressed. They never quite cut, which for scissors is a bit of a handicap. You'll never find any equally useless antique so costly, though. They often have rings for the lady's finger and thumb at the end of elaborately chased handles, its useless blinking blades pivoting on a fancy screw. Victorians tried inserting a sliver of steel into the hopeless blades, but even those never work, not even on a grape. Like I say, they're stupid. I can't imagine why ancient craftsmen went to the trouble of making the damned things. Until you ask the price, when all of a sudden your admiration for these exquisite antiques leaps a-bounding from the breast, because the cost of a genuine pair—silver plate, parcel gilt, silver—stuns you.

These were hallmarked for Birmingham in the 1840s. They were 'clean' as dealers say, meaning nearly mint. They were still warm from being inside Alicia's blouse.

'Love, you deserve plus for these. Well done.'

It was a superb beginning to the sweep. Okay, I knew Alicia was trying to impress, but she'd excelled.

'Thank you, Lovejoy.' Even Peshy looked smug.

We went to the restaurant.

'One thing, Lovejoy.' She gave me a look. 'You stayed in your own room last night.'

'Er . . .' I reddened.

'I expected you to come in. A nightcap, possibly explain why we're roaming the Hundreds like this. And why you picked me.'

I said lamely, 'I got a bit weary, thinking things.'

'You lying swine. You're never weary.'

'Look, love.' I decided to come clean. 'Don't get mad. It's just . . . It's your wolfhound.' From politeness I didn't mention Peshy's name.

229

'Peshy?' she said, astonished. 'What's wrong with Peshy?'

'Nothing, nowt, course not!' I shrugged apology. 'Only, you don't, well, sleep with him in bed, do you?'

She laughed, her whole form shaking with merriment.

'Lovejoy, you're ridiculous! You mean you lay awake next door because you thought—? You stupid man. Of course not! Peshy has his own bed. It's my big leather case. It unfolds into a splendid snuggly-wuggly . . .' She turned to include the mongrel in the conversation, which thereon became meaningless.

I sighed with relief, got out of the motor and walked inside. She could make her own arrangements for the dog. She followed, insisting on a special steak cooked just so for Peshy. He dined in a children's high chair. I asked not to face him. Alicia said I was being stupid. I finished before she did and went to collect Tinker, agreeing to return in about two hours to carry on westward. I phoned Norma and Ferd in the meantime, to ask if they had heard anything about Timothy.

Norma was in tears telling me the bad news. I said how sad, and rang off. I phoned the hospital, asking for the doctor by name, pretending to be a doctor from Suffolk. Florence was still in intensive care, the doctor said.

'What are the prospects of recovery?'

He reeled off a string of numbers with a load of terms I couldn't comprehend. Finally he asked, 'Who is this, please? Did you say . . . ?'

That should do it. I rang off. They'd know it was me. That system of tapping in a number to find the number of the person who's just rung is a godsend in some circum stances, but highly dangerous in others. This was either, maybe both.

Tinker was in the pub when I got there, happy waiting and almost kaylied from booze. I got a jar and took it across. He'd gone back to smoking his old pipe. Eight empty glasses were on the table. He must have been waiting half an hour at least.

'Wotcher, Tinker. All right?'

'Fine, son. Did that fat old bint nick some good stuff?'

Cruel description of Alicia Domander—plump she might be, but age never comes into it.

'I think so. Had anything to eat?'

'Thought I'd let my thirst go down.'

'You'd best have a bite before we go on.'

I made him eat a couple of pasties, and had one myself for luck. I handed him the yield, wrapped in bubble plastic.

'Buy a couple of postage boxes from the post office and get them to Eleanor's house, in my lane in the village.'

Eleanor is nothing to do with antiques. She just has Henry, a little baby I mind while she's out. She knew to keep unexplained parcels in her garage until I returned. It would be the first of many. I badly needed as many as I could get, and the more famous the thefts we did the better.

'Did you find out who Hugo is?'

He belched. The tavern shuddered. People all about stopped talking, wondering what spaceship had just effected re-entry.

'There's a bloke called Hugo mends old Lancaster engines down Romford. He's nearly ninety, not done a hand's turn for a decade.

231

Nobody else.'

'Keep trying. Be in that tavern where Tandy's knock-out ring meets in Acle, you know the one. Eight o'clock tonight. I'll phone you, tell you what to do.' I gave him another two notes.

'How many more you going to do today, then?'

'Eight or nine, maybe double figures, give or take.'

I hoped our thefts would make the *Antiques Trade Gazette* by the following week. Things were looking better, except for absent friends.

*   *   *

By afternoon I was worn out. Planning ahead always does this. I had a splitting headache, and the Bichon Frise—what a name for a species; sounds like a fried egg—was getting on my nerves. Alicia Domander's good cheer and pride in her artistry was unfailing. I warmed to her. You can't help admiring a real pro. We really got going.

We did three antique shops in Ipswich and one auctioneer place. Then I said to cut across country to Norwich, while I dozed in the rear seat and Peshy sat upright grandly staring out of the windscreen from the front passenger seat. All he needed was goggles to be Biggles.

In Norwich Alicia knocked off a few items from those posh antique shops near Norwich Cathedral. She even got a painting out of the Black Horse Gallery in Wensum Street, and two small silvers at the adjacent place. All genuine, too, which goes to show that the real stuff isn't only in Sotheby's and Christie's. That thought worried me because it called something to mind, except I was too tired to remember exactly what. I shelved the moment and dozed.

That night we stayed on the outskirts of Norwich. I phoned Tinker in his Acle bar, got another definite negative to my Hugo question, and told him to go to Cambridge, see him in St John's Chapel at noon tomorrow.

'There's somebody come here asking if you're booked in, Lovejoy,' he gravelled out in an attempted whisper. 'Some bird. I said you were in Southwold. That all right?'

'Good, Tinker,' I told him. 'You did well. Keep going, okay?'

'Right. Tara, son.'

That night Alicia came into my room, leaving her midget mongrel asleep in her room. We made smiles, me with relief and she with joy in her ample heart. It would have been a peaceful start to next morning, except there was an envelope under the door before the girl brought morning tea at seven o'clock.

There was a note:

Dear Lovejoy,
    Please confirm soonest to me your next precise location. I regard your default on our contractual arrangements a serious breach of trust, and do hope this transgression is not repeated.
        Yours sincerely,
        Thomasina Quayle (Mrs)

Alicia stirred and groaned, looked at the bedside alarm clock.

'Christ Almighty, Lovejoy. It can't be day.'

233

'Up, love. Lots to do.'

She whimpered. 'Lovejoy, I didn't even know there was a seven o'clock in the morning. I thought it only came in the evening.'

'Stop it, Alicia. Think of Peshy.'

'He'll be fine. He doesn't get up until nine even when he's working. And he doesn't really wake up properly until after his elevenses and his walk.'

So much for an early start. I went back to bed, burrowed in beside her. And that was that until nine. I didn't tell her about the warning note. We'd have to move faster, dog or no dog. How the hell had Thomasina Quayle traced me that fast?

CHAPTER TWENTY-FIVE

The fifth evening me and Alicia noshed in a tatty restaurant near Cambridge. It had to be neff, because Peshy had to come too. It swilled Earl Grey tea and steak, all in one bowl. I could tell that Alicia was working up to a question.

'Lovejoy.' She twiddled her earring, like they do when they're trying to get away with something. 'Will you answer a question?'

'No.'

'Pwetty please, diddumsy-widdumsy?'

I honestly think that pet people aren't right in the head. I told Alicia that. She answered cryptically, 'That from a tart-exploiting rough who chats to antique furniture, Lovejoy?' Which I thought unfair, but that's women.

'What?'

'That cow Biddy, from Blue Barn Mansion,

Suffolk.'

'Don't know the woman,' I lied.

'Come on, Lovejoy. Tell me.' She leaned over the table, candlelight into contours. 'When we drove past there the other day I suggested we pay a quick visit. It was open to the public. We could have lifted a few nice things. You got shirty and made me drive on. Why?' She smiled, licking her lips. 'Was that scam you?'

'I was in clink when that was burgled,' I said, cold. 'How could I?'

She leaned further. The boggle-eyed waiter poured us wine practically into her cleavage. His hand shook.

'Okay, I'll tell you.' Otherwise she'd go on about it.

The story was simple enough.

Once, I stayed at a posh lady's house. County set, daddy in parliament. Biddy was dynamite, went skiing in those resorts where avalanches kill you. She seemed to own most of everywhere we went. When, scared, I stammered something about money to pay for the hotels and things, she hooted with laughter. She owned a string of shops. They sold—wait for it—lipsticks and bras. Can you imagine making a living out of that?

Anyhow, Biddy had a dozen guests to dinner— which is your evening nosh to the rich, instead of midday grub like to us plebs. During it, she said out of the blue, 'Lovejoy, be a daaahling and bring some Barolo from the cellar. The best year. Gavain is busy.' Gavain the butler. At the time I thought it a bit odd but obligingly went. Blue Barn Mansion was terribly grand, stuffed with antiques that the public paid to see. As I left I heard her giggle.

235

In the corridor I paused to look at a small oak side-table that stood against the wall. Maybe I have a burglar's silent walk or something, dunno, but I have the hearing of a bat. This table was lovely, with typical non-circular pegs that stood proud of the surface, the way old ones really should. No drawers, but so what? Genuine seventeenth century.

I smiled my thanks to it in case it thought I was being cheeky mauling it like I had. Suddenly I heard Biddy—nicknames are go, in the county set—say, 'Honestly, isn't he an utter boor?' to trills of laughter. I froze. Was he me?

'Honestly, Biddy, dwaaahling,' somebody drawled. 'I don't know why you pick these tramps up. Aren't we rough enough?'

More laughs.

'Did you see him when I asked him his opinion of the new champers?' Biddy tittered. 'He went red as fire! What an ignoramo!'

Yet more merry hoots as they fell about. In the cellar I seized the first bottle that came to hand. I took it up. Their faces were composed when I re-entered, but you can tell when everybody's laughing. I realized then that, coming to stay with Biddy at Blue Barn, I'd made a bigger fool of myself even than the Almighty, and he'd had a good go. I'd been blind from wanting her so badly. I'd been on show, the clown everybody laughs at. I'm pathetic.

'Sorry, Biddy,' I said. 'I couldn't see in the gloaming. Is it right?'

'Absolutely, daaahling!' she crooned. 'Except we *rayther* expected Barolo to be red.'

Everybody hid smiles. Talk began of tomorrow's

riding party. I'd already learned that I didn't know how to ride anything except a pushbike.

That night Biddy and me made the usual smiles. I rose silently in the early dawn and left before she or anyone else was awake. I felt ashamed.

A week later I drew detailed plans of her residence for Pogger, a Manchester burglar. I chose him because of his photographic memory. It took him an unbelievable eight minutes to scan the drawings, then I burned them. On an agreed day I got myself arrested by deliberately causing an affray in Gimbert's Auction Rooms. I was in clink awaiting trial when somebody—nobody knows who—burgled Biddy's famed Blue Barn Mansion. It was such a tragedy. Burglars stole the furniture, paintings, cutlery, silver, glassware, antique flintlocks, wall tapestries, even the carpets. One odd thing, though. Standing all alone in the centre of the emptied dining room—the scene of Biddy's giggling dinner party—Pogger had left a charming gift for the lady of the house.

It was a bottle of expensive red Barolo wine.

Naturally, I was accused. It was very unfair because you see I was in pokey, unable to raise my bail. I waxed indignant behind my bars, saying it was obviously somebody trying to fit me up. See how wicked some people are? Always ready to believe the worst of folk. There's no honesty these days.

Biddy's hysterical accusations were the sort that give antique dealers a bad name. She screamed untruths at the media, newspapers, the police, anybody who would listen. 'Oh, dear,' I said sadly when TV people came to interview me in gaol. 'I'm really sorry for Biddy. Usually she's so good-

237

humoured. Why on earth would anyone burgle Blue Barn Mansion? Everything there is modern reproduction, including those fake portraits and silver . . .' Which effectively barred her from claiming on the insurance. It was so sad. I mean that most sincerely.

From hardship, she got wed later that year to a rich bloke she hated. The happy couple returned to Blue Barn Mansion. Her husband, a fat old banker, is trying to restock the mansion with antiques. Our local dealers sell him tat, because neither he nor Biddy have a clue and are, of course, too proud to seek advice.

Alicia loved the story. She'd heard it from some pal of Gimbert's, only guesswork gossip but almost true in every respect. Strange how things get around.

'Served the bitch right,' Alicia purred. She relishes such tales. 'You should have . . .' And proceeded to embellish, suggesting new ways to do Biddy down.

She did tell me one thing I hadn't heard, though.

'Had you heard? Biddy's shops have gone bust. Some insurance thing. They turned her down and she had to sell for a pittance.' She eyed me after checking that her wolfhound was replete. 'When you said we should leave Blue Barn Mansion alone, Lovejoy, I wondered if you still had feelings for her.'

'Not those feelings, love. She's only got dross.'

She brightened, but I gulped. I supposed it was my crack about her possessions all being fakes and repros that had made the insurers turn her shops down. Well, that's what luck does, changes good to bad. If only we could control things as we go on, wouldn't life be wonderful?

That conversation set me thinking. That night I was especially good value for Alicia. At least I tried to be, except all I can think is yippee. But I did have a go, and even bought her animal a tin of unspeakable grot that it wolfed for its supper, and told her a load of tales she hadn't heard. I had her laughing. Then we slept. I like Alicia, and Peshy is all right too. We were quite an effective team, really.

Next day, though, life bungled things badly.

*   *   *

Alicia and Peshy started the morning off doing a shoulder in Cairhirst and Thremble's, the big auction rooms north of Cambridge. The security there's never been any good, so I felt at ease leaving Alicia to it while I went to the railway station to phone Bernicka. She answered the phone sounding terrified.

'Hello, Bernicka,' I began. I was so sure of myself, for hadn't I bribed her with a genuine (well, forged) drawing from the hand of her beloved Leonardo da Vinci? 'Did you see that Yank? What did you find out?'

'Lovejoy,' she said, her voice a gnat's whine. 'I don't know what you're talking about.'

'I'm talking about Leonardo da Vinci!' I croaked, thunderstruck.

'I want nothing to do with him. I posted your drawing back.'

She rang off.

Stunned, I stared at the receiver.

She *didn't want* Leonardo? Now, this was a

239

woman who once stood in the rain all night gazing at a poster outside a village hall where somebody was going to talk on Leonardo's handwriting. (He wrote backwards, mirror writing.) Get the point? Bernicka risked pneumonia to see a frigging poster slapped on a billboard simply because it had her beloved's name on it. And reneged on a dozen highly paid careers, to make dud copies of Leonardo's non-existent works.

She *didn't* want . . . ? Worse, *she* didn't want?

Badly shaken, I sat on the railway platform. Don't incidentally try this yourself, because Eastern Network Railway's taken away all the seats in the interests of efficiency. You've to sit on the floor and catch your death of cold. Logic told me that Bernicka had been bullied. The persuaders must have been pretty potent, because nothing dissuades a woman in love. Passion simply changes her universe. Her whole life goes overboard. I too had been given the sailor's elbow, that terrible nudge-splash farewell, when Bernicka tumbled head over heels for *Il Maestro*. The world and everything in it suddenly came second. I shrugged and went on with life. Bernicka didn't, because Leonardo had taken over her soul.

Yet now she blithely tells me that Leonardo can get stuffed, sod off?

Impossible. I didn't know much, but I knew that.

Tough on Alicia and Peshy, leaving them unaided in the auction rooms, but what can you do? I got Alicia's motor and drove off. Well, I reasoned, I was in a panic but Alicia never was. And Peshy, not me, was her expert accomplice, the thieving little swine. They could get on with it. I'd already told her where to book us in, so she'd come

240

to no harm. I hoped.

Three hours and a nervy nosh in a motorway caff later, I parked a mile or so away from Bernicka's studio and walked footpaths to her place. I didn't want anybody gossiping that she'd at last got herself a live bloke instead of a dead memory. Her house stands near a wood on the outskirts of Hawanthorpe, a titch of a village. Since falling hook line and sinker for L da V she'd had this studio built. It dwarfed the family home, and even had two outhouses, said to be for mixing gunge that sculptors like.

Coming on the place, I heard voices. Any visitor's motor would be parked at the front, so I wasn't forewarned. I stopped in case they'd heard my approach, but they kept talking. Your own name springs out of conversation.

'Lovejoy's in serious trouble,' Olive Makins was saying. 'Worse even than the rest of us.'

My mind went, *the rest of who, exactly*?

'I'm sorry.' Bernicka was in tears.

'You understand? There's no way out. We must do as we're told, Bernicka. It's civilization or the Dark Ages.'

'I understand.' Sniff, sniff.

'If you don't toe the line, Bernicka, all your precious works of art will go to collectors. Oafs, dolts, vandals. Can you imagine, Leonardo's greatest creations in some barbarian's brothel?'

A strangled cry of, 'Don't, Olive!'

'Even Lovejoy has come into line. He's just phoned. He'll start divvying for them tomorrow.' There was silence, then the soft command, 'Do it, Bernicka.'

'Yes, honey. Think of it as a simple misfortune,

241

like Hugo.'

Bloody Hugo was getting on my nerves.

The day was gloomy, a steady drizzle coming. I went slowly round the side of the house, saw Olive's motor. Nobody else about. I slid in the side entrance. Bernicka had a cat, one of those grey things that looks a bit bald. It kips in a giant furry shoe thing, didn't even stir as I went to the corridor. I heard Bernicka sobbing. Something smashed, thudded. There started a constant crackling and shuffling. I thought, what on earth?

'No, Bernicka. Harder. Get going. It's survival. Sandy will be furious if you default. What was that? Is somebody out there?'

Maybe I caused a draught, made some noise. Footsteps came smartly across the studio floor. I darted out across the grass to the outhouses, trying to cover distance before Olive reached the door and saw me. I dodged round the first outhouse. The second was a tumbledown, crumbling thing. Its rotting door was marked GONG, the letters crudely daubed in faded gothic script on the door. I had a hard time yanking the door ajar enough to eel inside. Gong is old English for loo, a privvy, of the ancient sort they used before Sir John Harington invented the flush lavatory—with moving working parts! Short of racing to the shelter of the trees, it was the one refuge.

Breathing hard, I pulled the door to. It was an old earth closet, disused, weeds snaking in, rime on the brickwork, dank as a Candlemas cauldron. A slice of daylight cut across me. I prayed I hadn't been seen. Distantly I heard that thump, crash, thump resume, and Olive's reassuring voice insisting, commanding, accompanied by Bernicka's

242

faint wailing. I thought, what the hell's going on? Me to do whose bidding, to the benefit of everybody, because Sandy says Hugo insists?

No place to sit. Don't laugh. Rickety old boards were placed over the loo. Sir John had written a whole treatise on his flush gadget in 1596, calling it *The Metamorphosis of Ajax*, bragging that it required merely 'a cisterne, not a whole Tems [Thames] full . . . to keep all sweete . . .' It's a document that collectors go mad for nowadays. He made one of his loos for his godmother—she happened to be Queen Elizabeth I—and installed it in Richmond Palace, love his heart. Did more good for mankind than all the doctors and politicians before or since. He forgot to take out a patent, incidentally, but a clockmaker called Mr Cummings patented it nearly two centuries later and made a fortune out of that unique S-bend. A lesson for us all. The brilliant Joseph Bramah perfected it in 1797—hence our slang word 'braumer' for anything superb.

Where was I? No place to sit in a gong.

No place to sit because of file boxes resting on a stack of papers. I looked. They weren't old at all. How very odd. A hiding place for modern documents? The last place anybody would think of looking, right enough. The instant I heard the activity resume convincingly in the studio I had a shufti. I mean, who wouldn't? I'm a great believer in privacy, but Bernicka had put me in this mess by heartlessly breaking her promises. Okay, so I'd betrayed her trust, but whose fault was that? Well, mine actually . . . I paused and thought, hello, what's this? I caught sight of a name I loathed. Good old Hugo? I pulled it out. A summary of a

243

creditors' meeting in London.

The boxes and the stacks of papers moved to the grassy floor, in grand style I sat to read.

*   *   *

Later, the daylight starting to fade, I slowly emerged from the outhouse. I'd heard a motor start up some time before, but thought it best to read on. I replaced the files and papers very much as I'd found them. You can't do much about a trodden grassy floor.

No sign of Bernicka. No light on upstairs, though it was fading day. I crossed to the house. If she caught me, I'd lie that I had shouted and knocked. The cat was gone. I did my burglar's tread and peered into the studio.

The horse statue was smashed to smithereens. Nothing left except a heap of plaster. The structure was a mass of twisted wire. Tools lay all about. Wire cutters, hammers, mallets and a crowbar. My respect for Bernicka rose. Don't cross a sculptress. Bernicka could have fought a war with that tackle.

Then I remembered her weeping, that terrible wail and gulping sound she'd made as she'd destroyed her beloved Leonardo's sculpture while Olive had cajoled her. Uneasily I tried to shout upstairs but had no voice. The house was eerily quiet. I toured the ground floor, kitchen to front door, hall to living room. She wasn't there. Bernicka would never leave without locking up.

Finally I cleared my throat at the bottom of the stairs and called up, 'Bernicka? It's me, Lovejoy.' Then another effort, almost louder this time.

'Hello, love? You up there?' I tried humour. 'It's

me. I thought I'd see how your, er, horse was getting on. You okay?'

In case she was in the bath or anything, 'Can I come up? It isn't anything, just something I'd like to ask. About,' I improvised stupidly, 'er, *Il Maestro*. Shall I come up? Only, I think your cat's poorly. It looks a bit off colour.'

Nothing. There was no cat.

Then I got frightened. I started on the stairs, one at a time, calling.

'Did you say to come up?' I bleated. I could see daylight seeping from an open door onto the landing, a towel on a handrail. 'I'm coming.'

Another step. 'Is it okay?' Step. 'Me coming up, I mean?'

Finally two steps, bravely one more. 'Right?'

A sandalled foot hung over the edge of a bed. No movement. Was this bad? Or was she in a fuming temper at Lovejoy who'd betrayed her with a forged drawing?

Did it look pale? I was unable to recall whether she had pale feet. Where I come from you never go to bed with shod feet, like you don't dare put shoes on a bed. It heralds death, so watch it. I once got thumped for nearly doing that when I wasn't even three. Not knowing superstitions was no excuse.

'Er, Bernicka?'

A leg. I craned to see. The other leg came into view. Sandalled. She wore a working brat, no gloves. Her cat lay on her. It looked stiff. I'd run out of stairs, stood there in her bedroom doorway.

'Bernicka, love. It's me.'

Nothing. I think you can tell. The cat didn't move either. Bernicka didn't breathe. Her features, usually so vehement and coloured—she's really

245

into emotion—looked drained and still. So utterly still. 'A mirror,' I said aloud to her, like she'd helpfully hand me a mirror to see if she was still breathing or dead.

In fright I raced downstairs and dialled 999, managing to drop the phone twice. I got a snatch of the *Cuckoo Waltz* played on some bloody cinema organ and an automated voice telling me I was in a queue, hold on please, the world of emergency services was champing at the bit to help but would respond as soon as they could be bothered. Translation: they were still at that snooker match.

After a full year hanging on, couldn't have been less, somebody bored said, what? I told her to send an ambulance fast because a young woman looked dead. I ran back upstairs, budged the cat aside and tried shoving Bernicka's chest like they do on films. I think I got some air puffing in and out but wasn't sure. I tried counting like I'd seen in those American hospital serials on TV, but what was I counting and how fast? I stuck at it.

An aeon later ambulance folk rushed in. They wore thick uniforms, very macho, yelled a lot and undid cables. I left them to their game. I don't honestly know if their tardiness made a difference. The real delay had been mine, waiting in the decrepit outhouse, reading those hidden files, giving myself priority instead of coming out and taking a risk that Olive Makins might see me.

Instead I'd dawdled while Bernicka went upstairs and took whatever drugs she'd had to hand and dosed her cat so it came with her too.

While the ambulance lot did their thumping rituals I went to look in the studio. It was a ruin. Sketches of *Il Cavallo* were tacked to the walls, with the portrait of Leonardo looking down. A candle, thick and stubby, burned before it. How long since it had been lit? Two hours, three? Drawings of mock-ups were pasted to the door. A bunch of flowers, suspiciously new, stood in a vase amid the crushed plaster. Bernicka must have gone into her garden and picked a bouquet for her bloke's picture. She may even have walked past the outhouse.

She'd known what she was about to do.

Had Olive Makins known that would have been the consequence, Bernicka's suicide? Her life's work for da Vinci had fallen apart because of what Olive said. I pondered this, while the goons upstairs rushed in and out.

Now, whatever else she'd been, Bernicka was that troublesome thing known as a woman in love. Okay, forget that she'd had the odd bloke now and then—she wasn't going to go short of physical love while she was a slave to Leonardo. Fine.

That being so, why take that terrible final step? The logical thing would be to sweep up and begin anew, right? To look, as I was doing that instant, at the heaped chunks of her statue and then start again. The Bernicka I knew simply wouldn't give in. Just like any woman who, deterred because her embroidery colour suddenly looks wrong, undoes the whole thing and simply restarts. It's what birds do. It's also what blokes do. They curse that blinking wrong gadget, strip the engine down, and set about making new cogs for that steam engine they've set their heart on. It's human. Annoying, maddening, but human.

So there was something else. Something lethal. And Olive Makins, instrument of Bernicka's death

247

as she was for Timothy Giverill's, knew what.

And now, after my slothful reading in the outhouse, so did I.

Time to see Sandy, to get my ghost paintings back, and find Mrs Thomasina Quayle.

A policeman strolled in, wanting to take a statement. I pointed into the house and said, 'The bloke who phoned the ambulance? He's waiting in there, mate. I'm with the ambulance.'

And walked away from my dead friend. I'm good at that.

CHAPTER TWENTY-SIX

The motel was grottier than I'd expected. She'd booked in her name, Mrs Alicia Domander, which worried me a bit because I didn't want anybody trekking after us who shouldn't be doing any such thing. The usual trick in the antiques trade is to give a hyphenated name. London antiques auctioneers—and I do mean those in Bond Street—do it, whenever they illegally pretend to sell an antique that nobody wants. They say, 'Sold to Barnshaugh-Smythies,' or some such, which tells their staff that the bidder doesn't really exist.

The restaurant had almost finished serving supper as I bowled in. I was famished. Grumpily they agreed to dish me up some grot. Alicia joined me, saying nothing until I started to slow down. Then she spoke, full of reproach.

'You look like death warmed up, Lovejoy.'

'Had a poor day, love.'

'You think I didn't?'

'They don't give you enough spuds in these places.'

I had to fill up on gravy and bread. I felt I'd not eaten for a week. Peshy glared, supercilious because he'd been slogging away thieving while I'd been whooping it up on the Riviera.

'You haven't even asked what I lifted, Lovejoy.'

'What'd you shoulder, love?'

'A Sheffield plate jug. A fake Lalique glass. An assortment of jewellery, and the ugliest porcelain figures you ever saw.' She stared at me as I wiped the plate with my bread. I started straight away on the pudding, a thick treacle sponge and knobbly custard you could have skated on. Her eyes slowly filled.

'You didn't even phone the room to make sure I was safe, did you, Lovejoy?' No answer. 'How do you think I felt? I came swanning out of the auction rooms loaded with stuff, and you weren't there.'

There was no tea. In dud motels you only get your coffee when you've eaten your greens all up, like school dinners.

She stayed bitter. 'You don't care, Lovejoy. Peshy and me could have been collared and you wouldn't have cared.' She blotted her eyes. Peshy licked her tears. Ingrate.

I couldn't tell her. Anyway, it's women's game to get you saying sorry. Look at TV soaps, or have I said that?

'You did well, love. It sounds good shoulder. Can I see it?'

She told me the room number and asked me for her car keys. I handed them over. I saw a couple of geezers give each other a grin as she wafted past.

249

That narked me. Okay, Alicia doesn't exactly look a picture of purity, but did they? Fine, people say Alicia doesn't dress clever and joke at her frothy chintzy stuff. But she was here being my friend when others weren't. I'd suddenly had enough. I rose and crossed to their table, stood looking.

'You okay, lads?' I could hardly see for rage.

'Yeah. What's it to you?'

'Detective Sergeant Henriques, City Met Div, CID.' I was making it up. If they turned out to be plod, that was my hard luck. I was past caring. 'Which one of you's the thief?'

'Eh?' They stared. One started to rise. I kicked his heels and he sat with a thump. 'We nicked nothing.'

'Car keys.' I wiggled my fingers, palm up. 'The Lincoln. Hand them over.' I didn't know what a Lincoln was. I'd heard of a motor by that name talked of on the radio driving back from Bernicka's.

'We come in an Alfa Romeo.' They said it almost together, Flash Harrys the pair of them. One pulled out his ignition keys and showed them.

'Okay.' I nodded slowly. 'Okay.'

I left, them shouting sneery comments after me, but careful like I really might have been a ploddite out for trouble.

In the gloaming I smashed the headlights of the only Alfa Romeo, a bright electric green job. For quiet, I did it through a piece of old tyre—there's always a chunk lying about in car parks; wagoneers change their burst tyres, too lazy to shift the rubbish. Then I did the tyres by sticking a matchstick into each nipple. The posh vehicle squealed gently as it settled.

Up in the room Alicia was weeping, surrounded by her wares. I couldn't take any more glares from Peshy, so I felt round underneath his collar and pulled out a horseshoe brooch, gold and pearl, Victorian of 1884. The dog looked chastened. I started to get mad with the damned kleptomaniac mutt, but Alicia decided to ballock him herself, though not so's you'd notice, going, 'Oooh, who's a naughty little Peshy-Weshy then?' and so on.

While she sent for his caviar and steak I had a bath, and emerged feeling definite vibes from the stolen goods she'd arranged on the coffee table for me to look at. An impressive haul.

One thing here: I don't see that me and Alicia were doing much wrong, not really. We were only lifting from auctioneers, and they're in the trade more for sleight-of-hand reasons than anything else. I think of them as estate agents, realtors, and insurance agents, who share the same warped morality. So they must take the consequences when Alicia and her slick-pawed pooch drift in for a gander at the antiques—genuine or otherwise—that they're trying to exploit. We understand fairness. They don't.

Trying to give her a convincing smile, I sat on the couch.

'Not bad, Alicia.'

God knows how she'd managed to nick the Sheffield plate coffee jug. I didn't ask, though every shoplifter I've ever known will talk about techniques till the cows come home. They're the only thieves that will. Incidentally, most are female. They do it better, and play the sympathy ploy with more assurance than blokes.

'I felt under the rim, Lovejoy,' she said

251

anxiously. 'No ledge that I could flick with my fingernail.'

'Don't worry, love. There's not many ledges on a thing this shape.'

You have to feel sorry for Sheffield plate. I do. It was always seen as a second-rate cheap substitute for real silverware, even back in the 1740s when it started. Yet the minute an even cheaper lookalike came in—it was electroplating—the hard-hearted public instantly switched their affections and lovely, clever Sheffield plate vanished like snow off a duck. It's so sad. Everybody forgot it quick as blink, though it's now regarded as a genuine antique. I think the inventor Thomas Bolsover was a hero, even if he was only a Sheffield cutler. People made (and still make) the calamitous mistake of polishing his plate so much that the silver layer gets worn away to the copper beneath.

Even so, genuine Sheffield plate is fairly easy to tell. Alicia meant that if you trail your fingernail under the rims and you feel your nail catch on an edge, then you've found where one sheet of silver-sandwiched copper joins another. There's no such edge in crummy old electroplating. I don't like electroplate, because it's simply 'German silver' or some other miserable alloy that has been lobbed into an electroplating tub. People talk of it like it's artistic, but it's only them trying to sell you junk. It's usually a stamp-cast thing that's been coated thinly with silver by being hung between two electrodes. Big deal. Real Sheffield plate has the mellow, milkier sterling look instead of the harsh pure silver coat of electroplating.

Love the real thing. It does no harm.

'Brilliant, love. Ten out of ten.'

The porcelains were simply forgeries of old German wares. One was so neatly faked that I almost filled up, remembering Consul Sommon who'd smashed the Meissen to teach me a lesson. He'd succeeded. I wasn't sure, but I blamed him for Bernicka's death.

'What's the matter, Lovejoy?'

'Nothing. Shut up.'

Still, they were decent fakes, and you can always sell good forged porcelain. I told her this, though she was disappointed. She was still looking at me, suspecting emotion, when she ought to have been listening and learning. My main worry was, why exactly hadn't she used a phoney name when registering us tonight? Almost like she was deliberately leaving a trail.

'You said this was dud. It's real Lalique, Alicia.'

She stared at the glass pot. 'Is it?' And smiled. 'I'm better than I thought! I thought he never used blue.'

'No. It was that horrible raspberry red he loathed.'

The moulded glass vase didn't look much, but its thin collar and graded opalescence were class. I think Laliques are seriously over-priced, but whatever opens collectors' wallets . . .

Unbelievably, she'd got two copies of *Vogue*, that magazine everybody now raves about, depicting 1920s women. I like Art Deco things. The Art Nouveau turn-of-the-1900 look I find a bit macabre.

'Alicia, you're brilliant.'

Well, being only 1927 and so not antique to me, the two magazines meant nothing. Collectors would go berserk, though, and pay through the nose.

'Really?' Her eyes widened. 'I thought you'd get cross. I could have lifted two prints instead, but wanted to read the fashions.'

'You did right. Genuine prints are only worth a fifth of the magazine.' Another antique oddity. 'Anybody can fake them. You stencil them in gouache, make a decent living. That girl Vestra does them down Brightlingsea.'

'Bitch,' Alicia said, without irony. 'Sorry about the porcelain, Lovejoy. I thought you'd say they were real Frankenthal figures.'

'No. Their hands are too accurate. Genuine figures have bigger hands than they should, and the bases are wavy, not level like these.' I turned one over, a huntsman, hound and dead deer. I winced. 'These that you nicked are soft paste. See where it looks sandy instead of smooth, where the porcelain is left raw and unglazed?'

'Thank you, Lovejoy. One thing.'

'What?' I asked, uneasy. She had that distressed look. I waited. She gathered herself, bridling.

'I feel I have to tell you this,' she said finally. 'I don't resent many things, Lovejoy. But I really must rebuke you about your choice of words.'

'Eh?' I was frankly done for. My friends were dropping like flies, and here she was yakking about what, exactly?

'You continually say nick, steal, thieve.' Her lips set in a thin line. 'I find the terms singularly distasteful. I am a shoulder expert, not a thief or a robber. I also know that Peshy resents your tone. He is highly sensitive to nuances . . .'

I'd lost two, if not three, of my pals, was on the run from God-knows-what, and she lectures me on

254

the finer feelings of a kleptomaniac midget canine?

My mind shut down. I was worn out. It wasn't the right time to tell her about my—well, Bernicka's—day, in case we got nicked before posting the goods off to little Henry's mum Eleanor. So I apologized profoundly to her and, can you believe, her mongrel. We saw that he had enough raw meat to feed a zoo, then went to bed. We made smiles, me utterly done for but desperate not to lose the chance of love. You can never tell where your next passion's coming from.

During the night she spoke, knowing I'd be awake because I often mostly usually nearly always am.

'I know I'm not much, Lovejoy,' she said quietly. 'You only brought me along to do the job. I'm not deceiving myself. I know it isn't because you're head over heels, me older than I say . . .' etc, etc.

She went on, running herself down. I dozed a bit while she rabbited on. Why women deplore themselves like this I don't know, but they do. She catalogued her defects—overweight, fingers too thick, low-quality ears. Finally I managed to open my eyes and rouse, the monster from the Black Lagoon.

'Shut up, you silly cow,' I told her drowsily. 'You're just right. Can't you tell? You're the only bird I can depend on.'

I felt her turn in the darkness. 'Am I?' she asked in amazement. (See? Astonished that somebody liked her. Beats me.)

'Silly mare,' I said. 'You miss the point. You're the one I'm in bed with. It's a clue.' I can't honestly work out what women are on about. It's a flaw in their character.

Next morning I was up early. Sure enough, there was an envelope under the door. Good old indefatigable Thomasina Quayle (Mrs), asked if she might prevail on my good offices to appraise her of my movements 'for the convenience of all those concerned'. Quickly I hid the letter before Peshy nicked it.

We had breakfast in our room, though room service always embarrasses me. Then Alicia went and booked us out. I eeled out of the rear of the building to the trunk road. She picked me up at the crossroads. This was in case those two blokes were looking for me. We were in Kings Lynn by noon. We posted off the goods to Eleanor.

The central library was open. I made Alicia promise not to nick—sorry, to shoulder—anything from the mall and left her and Peshy window shopping while I went to the reference library and looked up everything I could lay hands on about Hugo.

At last I knew where I was.

CHAPTER TWENTY-SEVEN

Reflection time.

Somewhere, it seems to me, I harbour a deep suspicion that God is having us on. Just look at the state mankind is in. It's not just our own messes—wars, pollution, famine—it's everything God starts us off with. Like our shapes, for instance. Like having to gulp slices of dead plants and animals just to keep alive. Having to go to the loo is another winner. Could anything be more pointless? Or sleeping. Stop what we're doing, to lie flat and become unconscious for hours, just to do it all over again. Daft. I reckon God was a beginner. God wanted to create a brilliant computer but never read the manual.

He's as hopeless with animals. Think of parasites. For heaven's sake, whatever was God thinking of? Every spring I worry for the swallows. Poor little sods have to fly all the way up the entire world, hang about East Anglia for the summer, then migrate all the way back to South Africa and just make it in time to start back again. Where's the sense in that? For God's glory? I ask you. It's time God got his act together. Please, oh God, next time read the instructions on the box before reaching for the screwdriver. Better still, leave us alone. We're thick, but we're not total duds like Somebody Up There I might mention.

Except for one thing.

Remember greed?

*　　　*　　　*

Once upon a time, back in darkest old London town, coffee houses flourished. Everybody loved to forgather in smoky old seventeenth-century streets, Greenwich to Hampton Court, and swill the new tarry stuff. Coffee even had streets named after it. It was believed to be so-o-o healthy. In those dens you could meet gentry, famous society beaux, politicians up to no good, empire builders. You might chat to Dr Johnson, harken to admirals, notorious gamblers, saints and sinners all.

And businessmen.

Years passed. Coffee dives specialized. Some

257

tended to cater for literary buffs, others for society. In cramped old Tower Street, one Edward Lloyd charged penny a swig for his brew. This wasn't all that cheap in those days, incidentally, when it took 240 pence (each penny worth four whole farthings!) to make one pound, coin of the realm. Lloyd kindly chucked in ink, quills, paper and free spills for you to light your churchwarden pipe as you sat by his fireplace and penned messages about your mercantile enterprises. At first, ladies frequented the coffee caffs but, as this place and then that place became teeming outhouses of London's free-wheeling markets, the ladies drifted to fashion-conscious emporiums to gossip over cakes and furbelows, leaving the men to deal.

London's insurance market was born.

Insurance wasn't new. Long before 1 AD, traders bargained on the shores of North Africa when insuring cargoes in Mediterranean galleys. But the sheer global range and intensity of London's maritime activity was beyond anyone's imagining. And nowhere was it more boisterous than in Edward Lloyd's little coffee pad. They called it assurance at first, then standards slid as the underwriters—who inked their names at the bottom (under-writing, see?) of agreements scribed in Lloyd's nook—started plain gambling. Besides ships, they bet who would win wars, who might survive if the Black Death returned, who'd marry and when. You could drop in Lloyd's coffee shop and insure yourself against losing at cards or the chances of rain on your new daffodil. Anything, in fact.

Deceit flourished.

Something had to give. A cluster of sober

merchants hived themselves off. Still identifying themselves by Edward Lloyd's moniker, they became, in effect, a dedicated insurance market, the great Lloyd's of London. Its humble messengers became magnates in their own right, flourishing by part-time spying for the Empire as Napoleon did his tyrannical stuff and navies fought and fleets foundered.

Through it all, Lloyd's loyally surged on.

There came a real test. It made Lloyd's name a byword.

It was horrendous, and it happened in the US of A. In 1906, San Francisco fell down. A terrible earthquake crumbled the place. People lost everything. When the dust cleared, they put in their claims. Insurance businesses everywhere wrung their hands in horror, for they'd go bust if they paid up on even a fraction for the poor San Franners. All over the globe insurance companies whined that they couldn't pay up on this claim or that claim because of the small print on their contracts . . .

Everywhere, insurers slipped away.

In the pit of despond, San Francisco stared poverty in the face. Ruined. Broke. It was the end.

Then, as the dust settled, there came a sterling one-liner across the Atlantic. In old London Town a gentleman quietly swilling his morning coffee at Lloyd's messaged a few calm words. One Cuthbert Heath, a Lloyd's man of the old style if ever there was one, sent a blunt instruction across the Atlantic on the fancy new electric telegraph to hirelings in the New World. It was world-shaking and utterly memorable. From his quiet little Lloyd's box, Mr Heath commanded his reps to pay *every single cent* claimed by the poor unfortunates in the Great

'Quake, *whatever the small print might say*. You insured with him at Lloyd's, kind sir, you were insured. Bounders might wriggle out from under, but mighty Lloyd's stood by its word. And that, said Cuthbert Heath, asking to please pass the loaf sugar, was that.

You can imagine. Relief abounded in the Americas. The consequence? Whole empires, royalty, global conglomerates, flocked to insure with Lloyd's of London. If you weren't 'A-One at Lloyd's' you ought not to be allowed into any respectable club and be off, you scoundrel you. Commerce at last had a trusty standard. Films were made extolling Lloyd's admirable virtues. Its motto was, of course, *Fidentia*. That's what Lloyd's sold. Confidence. If you were a Lloyd's man, you were a Name. 'Nuff said.

The only people allowed to become Names were gentlemen of standing. History records that you had to own the equivalent of a million in modern money. Actually it was much more, because so many of the UK population in those days lived from hand to mouth. Then times changed. Over the years, the amount of handy cash you needed was less than a third of what you insured. It was still, however, a posh mob.

One thing didn't alter, though. If you became a Name and insured somebody, you were in for every last cent. Down to the gold in your teeth 'and your cufflinks', as everybody jokingly used to say.

Nobody jokes like that now, because of Hurricane Hugo.

*   *   *

260

Remember I mentioned how the Almighty sometimes gets things cockeyed? Well, sometimes he gets things even worse.

As the 1980s bumbled along, God decided to have a field day with Planet Earth. Maybe we were looking too complacent, whatever. Bored, God roughed the world up. He foundered a vast ocean oil tanker here, caused a horrendous oil-rig fire there, and set in train disasters to blacken every front page. One especially grim event was Hurricane Hugo. Then the San Francisco earthquake returned, did a grim lap of honour. Claims beginning as a trickle became a deluge. Thousands of millions—count the noughts—were claimed, claimed, and claimed. The world wanted its insurance money.

No honourable telegraphed message this time. Why not? Was there a good—or maybe a bad—reason?

In the good old days when insurers stood by the words they uttered, you could become a Name by getting yourself put forward by someone as honourable and worthy as yourself, even. Should you be accepted, you were in. You dined there, and folk clapped politely as you entered a restaurant with the chairman, and respectfully stood as you took your seat. Your lady received precedence. It must have been marvellous, a world of honour cocooned in an honourable world.

It was all justified, in a curious way, for the Mother of Parliaments in London had, in its wisdom, decided that what was good for Lloyd's was good for the world. Mere mortals like you and me have to send in our income taxes on the dot every year, or we go to clink. Not so Lloyd's. 'Take

261

an extra year, old chap,' said Chancellors of the Exchequer to Lloyd's. 'Better still, take two or three years, and how is Elsie's riding coming along?' Lloyd's even got an extra extra perk. No kidding, they were exempt a little something called Law. Lloyd's got exemption from laws in every direction, sort of immunized by Lloyd's own parliamentary act. Cushty, as we ordinary fraudsters and conmen might enviously say out here. Cushty means money for the taking. It's how some define insurance. Not me.

In those halcyon days Lloyd's must have been heaven, a legal 'licence to print money', in the defunct jokey phrase. But some people in Lloyd's market were a new breed. They were sober professionals who'd salted away solid savings. Lloyd's had seven thousand at the start of the 1970s. In less than twenty years the 'names' almost quintupled. At first, all was rosy. Until Hugo, then Hurricane Betsy, then oil fields went wrong and ships glugged . . . The worst calamity of all was yet to come.

Asbestos struck. Actually, asbestos was trouble even before the 1950s. It wasn't until the 1970s, though, that incipient panic began. New Lloyd's investors, however, thrilled to become part of mighty Lloyd's, rolled in, signing gleefully on dotted lines. Prestige counted. Then horrendously huge claims washed in over the transom. Investors realized what they'd signed into. Many—that's many, many—faced ruin and some went down the pan. Royalty, ex-prime ministers, nobles, millionaire bankers, international celebrities bulging with cunny money, who had all jubilantly marched along in the profit carnival, now stared aghast into their mirrors of a morning wondering how they'd manage their penny cup of coffee today. Or ever again.

Some began lawsuits—against Lloyd's, no less, telling how they'd been lured by extravagant promise. Dark allegations were made, of official reports swept under the carpet, of Lloyd's ducking and dodging behind barricades of paperwork erected by dozens of lawyers. As the Millennium homed in, newspapers everywhere carried different slants on wild stories of supposed whispers on Walton Heath golf links, of conversations punctuated with nods and winks on the private yachts of moguls. As Americans say, it hit the fan, because unlimited liability means just that. Some fought through the courts and got massive damages against Lloyd's agents. Others wearily submitted and trudged off to live in sheds on handouts.

The media howled, thundered, yelled about cover-ups. New recruits to Lloyd's, finding to their horror that, far from sitting back and raking in the gelt, their purses and wallets were being relentlessly prised open by ever-increasing claims, began to squeal as the pain started.

The media went ballistic and demanded answers. Exactly what *did* happen, folk howled, to the Cromer report of 1969? Exactly *why* did the Mother of Parliaments, that stickler for law, on the feast day of St Apollinaris quietly slip Lloyd's that oh-so-valuable exemption from being sued? And how come the Bank of England's own special executive, a gent of renown and probity, whom the Bank forced into Lloyd's in the 1980s, got spat out like a pip? And so on, with emotional overstatement blasting everyone for everything.

263

Skullduggery was everywhere. And in Lloyd's.

Well, it would have been a mere storm in a teacup—okay, pedants, coffee cup—and we could have all got on with wondering about real life instead of the City's greed. Except that investors began to dive out of the windows, metaphorically and actually. Ask around, and everybody knows somebody who'd been touched by the calamity. Everybody everywhere has a cousin who was a once-wealthy Lloyd's investor, or making a claim for some prolonged ailment, or who was once cheerful but now is haggardly asking questions about the losses at Lloyd's that soared from mere thousands to billions. Heaven alone knew how many lawsuits ticker-taped down onto underwriters, insurance brokers, even ordinary agents in small town offices, but it was plenty. The terrible word fraud—normally reserved for humbler folk like me—was actually spoken. Folk meant Lloyd's.

Deaths began. Newspapers headlined that the suicide toll was to be laid squarely at the financial calamity's door. Some said ten deaths, twenty, then thirty. The Serious Fraud Office, an outfit that does Sweet Fanny Adams, will of course get nowhere as it peeps timidly round those solid double doors. Like those intrepid parliamentary teams that started investigating with drumrolls and fanfares—then finished up harrumphing into their gin and tonics before strolling out to the next round of golf.

And Lloyd's? Shrinking, shrinking.

Me, I worried about who was in for a penny or a pound. And who was in for every last cent. All very well to mull over commercial problems on some gigantic global scale, but not when you're worried about some lady you once painted.

CHAPTER TWENTY-EIGHT

We had a good day in Bristol—meaning that Peshy nicked a beautiful series of emeralds from a collector's job lot. I really wanted to see how the little dog did it. A Bichon Frise's ruff looks quite artificial though it's natural froth, and has nowhere else to hide anything. It can't bite its own collar off, for instance. So how did it manage to conceal whatever it picked up? See the problem? And how on earth *could* it lift things from a tray of gem stones it couldn't even see? BF is a midget, can't reach a table. And how, once the stuff was in its jaws, did the damned wolfhound . . . ?

Anyhow, good day for us in Bristol, but a loser for Merrimale Effend & Co, Ltd (Est. 1631 AD), Antique Auctioneers of that fair city. We won several watches, two small paintings, a set of earrings, and three pieces of Royal Doulton. I was disappointed she'd not stolen a collection of stickpins, Edwardian and late Victorian, that would have sold for a fortune, but you can't steal everything. (Well, actually you can, as I'll explain later.)

Job done, I left Alicia and Peshy resting and drove to East Anglia. I found Mel by three o'clock.

He was at the Fair Hair and Frolic in St Edmundsbury, Market Street. Or, rather, he was sitting beneath the market cross in a sulk while amused shoppers listened to the wails coming from inside.

'Listen, Mel,' I said, sitting beside him. 'Give me my ghost painting, and we'll do a deal, okay?'

What deal, I'd no idea. Worse, I realized uneasily that I'd called it my ghost painting. I'd no notion of what ghost. This is how you get talked into things.

'Just listen to that *riot*, Lovejoy.'

'Sandy having his hair done?'

Perm time was always Waterloo, girls resigning in tears and things thrown. I'd even seen the plod called to the Hair Poo in Short Wyre Street, with sirens wahwahing and uniformed officers piling out like Fred Karno's army. Once Sandy got going over his forelocks it was war. I can't understand this hair business with women. I suppose I include Sandy.

Mel wept. I looked away. They always nark me, him sobbing white-faced while Sandy hollers 'For ever, you hear me, world?' I think they're not grown up. Yet Mel and Sandy drive the cruellest antiques bargains. Twice I've seen this unlikely pair drive friendly dealers to destitution, Sandy cooing, 'Oh, the joys of usury in springtime!' and so on. Even Mel's teary episode here on the steps couldn't be taken at face value.

From inside the hairdresser's I heard a shrill howling. Something sploshed white gunge all over the window. I looked at the market clock. Soon he'd go nuclear. This is Phase Three. At least two assistants would be sacked, Sandy hurling coiffure implements after them. The growing pavement audience chatted contentedly, waiting for Sandy's big finish. Ten minutes at a guess.

'I'm seriously thinking of leaving him, Lovejoy. Wouldn't you?'

'Like a shot,' I said mechanically, quickly amending as his eyes went cold, 'Er, I mean I can't really understand your torment.'

'*You* people *can't*, Lovejoy,' he said with bitterness. 'Unless you're *deeply sensitive* like us, *aware* of the soul's funda . . .' et claptrap cetera.

Bored stiff, I saw Shell across the road looking in the window of that oh-so-posh antique silverware place that charges twenty per cent on credit card. Watch out for this, incidentally. It's called the mitt trick and is the worst kind of fraud, meaning a legal one. You don't find out you've been ripped off until you check your credit card. If you complain, you get reproach but no refund. They just give you the old patter, 'But, modom, you never asked about extra charges! So you agreed!'

I left Mel skryking and hurried across. 'What's good, Shell?'

She didn't turn, smiled at my reflection.

'Hello, Lovejoy. I heard you were on your way to see Sandy about your portrait thing. Is it really that good? Everybody's after it.'

Shell's nice. She isn't what you'd call pretty, lives in a houseboat with a bloke who composes chants for you to chant for ever more to other chanters. He even operates after-sales, new chants for old, should your first prove a disappointment. Believe it or not, he's cut a disc of chants, mostly the word 'Aw' in C natural. I like Shell. Maybe I'd like her bloke too if I knew what the hell he chanted.

'How's Chanter?' I asked politely.

'He's great,' she said happily. 'Oh, I know you think he's a waste, Lovejoy. But if chanting was the worst the world got up to—'

'It wouldn't be in such a bloody mess,' I capped

for her, smiling. 'What's all this about my painting, Shell?'

She tore her eyes away from the turmoil's reflection and turned to look. She was astonished.

'Are you telling me you really don't know?'

'Honest.'

'Sure you want to know, Lovejoy? Come dine with me, and I'll tell all.'

We settled into a nosh bar facing the market cross. She sips Earl Grey tea, and insists everybody else drinks the same because she hates calories. Joules might as well not have bothered in his Salford cellar, so we must all whoop it up on stained water. I always associate Shell with me trying to stop my belly rumbling. She even moves the tomato sauce out of your reach.

'No, Lovejoy,' she said severely, ballocking a waitress for depositing a welcoming bap. 'Calories define disease.'

'Food isn't all bad, Shell,' I pleaded, mouth watering, as some swine near by loudly ordered the entire menu fried to a sludge in delectable grease. 'Doctors say grub improves physique. Please?'

She lasered away the hovering girl, and quietly got down to business.

'I've got one of your ghost paintings, Lovejoy. The one that cow bought off you for a session in Manchester. Remember her?'

'Flintshire? That publicist?'

'That's her. You carried the can for her divorce.' Shell's voice became a hoar frost. I swear her breath thickened the air. 'I found it in a job lot three months back.'

What happened to Morwen wasn't my fault. On a holiday romp this Flintshire lady hired me to divvy a collection of jewellery, supposedly in antique settings. They were expensive gems set in real gold and platinum, but only modern rehashes. I told her. She went ballistic. In an agony of embarrassment, the jeweller sold her all sixteen at knock-down prices. She was thrilled because her manfriend was an avid gemstone collector. He was ecstatic because there were two morganites, one in an AMORE ring (the initial letters of the precious stones spell out that word, amethyst, morganite, opal, ruby, emerald). The language of gems was once as recognizable as a salvo to Edwardians, but is now mostly forgotten except by collectors. Look out for morganite, incidentally. Rare, named after some American banker, it's a faintly pinkish stone that sometimes looks almost colourless. It's a close cousin of emerald and aquamarine. Pink jewels are hell to distinguish, so if you don't know how to measure a stone's density (a good, near-certain marker) take along somebody who does. Morganites are lovely, always seem to be step-cut, and are often quite a size. Buy them, even if the setting's rubbish. You'll never regret it.

The trouble was that Morwen's husband (and I don't mean her manfriend) found them in her suitcase. Dearest Morwen claimed that a sex-mad antique dealer had given them to her, lusting after her flesh. Her dotingly thick hubby charged across the kingdom to brain me in a fit of Flintshire spleen. Luckily Big Frank from Suffolk, our champion serial spouse, was on hand—we were arranging his umpteenth wedding. He held the irate Taff at arm's length while explaining that every hotelier knew Morwen very, very well. Hubby collapsed into self-pitying woe and was never seen again.

Months later I was cited in Morwen's divorce. She got handsome alimony, alleging cruel marital inattention, and visited me on her next honeymoon. She still hadn't paid me. I'm always too embarrassed to remind defaulters who welsh—sorry—but Tinker bawled across Head Street to her that she was a chiselling bleeder. Quickly she bought a forgery I'd just finished. Her manfriend paid me on the spot. She went on to become publicity chief at some Camden Town publishers and has got fat as a blimp. Contentment of a more moral life, I shouldn't wonder. She separated after some cruise romance with a steward.

'Her taste in furnishings was dire,' Shell told me with satisfaction. 'Her stuff went unsold. I bought your painting.'

'Ta.'

'You know what I mean, Lovejoy.' She ordered another cup of tepid fluid. I watched it come, Shell's world of plenty. 'The woman's face is really lovely. You should be proud. I'd do a million if I could paint like that.'

'Then get on with it, love. Everybody's got imagination.'

She shivered. 'No, Lovejoy. Her eyes give me the creeps.'

'Eh?' I'd not looked at any of my Lady Hypatia portraits for yonks, not even in my mind's eye. I'd sold them, right? To eat, thereby supplementing these non-existent kilojoules the pretty Shell wasn't cramming into me. 'Why?'

From what little I remembered Lady Hypatia was a bit of all right. I was narked, but glossed over her features so I could concentrate on Shell. Well,

Ginny had one portrait, and with luck Tinker had salted it away by now. Shell had another. Two out of four. Thomasina Quayle's was number three.

Shell toyed with her spoon, perhaps wistfully wishing, as I, that it could be used for rice pudding, blancmange, porridge or soup, and so sustain life.

I heard a sudden commotion, guessed the reason. Which was as far as I got because Sandy burst into the caff wailing and throwing things and rushing towards me kicking chairs out of the way.

'That's him!' he howled, swooning yet managing to hurl a chair and break a wall mirror. Mel followed, pleading and weeping. 'Arrest that man!' Sandy shrieked. 'And that misshapen crone with him!' Which was a bit unfair. Shell's bonny.

'Sandy! Calm yourself!' was Mel's contribution.

Guessing what was coming, I left Shell to her repast. I got halfway out of the door before I was caught by two uniformed plod and dragged back to watch Sandy's storming conclusion. Mel was begging Sandy to remain cool, like he himself was a model of urbanity. I watched dispassionately, a little surprised that Sandy hadn't made more of an effort. Usually when he goes into a spectacular fit he hurls lotions across the thoroughfare. He acted his phoney epilepsy, though, always a winner. He got as far as dementia, but lost heart when he realized less than a dozen people were watching.

Tired out, I asked what I was collared for. The plod gave that mirthless smirk.

'You stole his antique portrait.'

'Me? But it's . . .'

'What you saying?' asked this uniformed grammarian.

'Nothing, constable.' Well, what could I say?

271

That Sandy's genuine antique portrait was a forgery, and I was the perpetrator? That I'd sold several?

They hauled me outside. As usual, bystanders lost interest. I was marched to Alicia's motor. They got my keys and lifted the lid. In it were two portraits of Lady Hypatia Parlayne, all my own work. For an instant I felt giddy, probably subnutrition.

'See?' Sandy shrieked, flinging himself to the cobble stones and writhing. He'd forgotten to foam at the mouth, I observed. 'It's there!'

'Thief!' Mel accused. 'Arrest him this instant!'

Now, if Mel had somehow slipped it into Alicia's motor after I'd gone in to see Shell, then whose was the other? Shell had one. Maybe, I hoped cautiously, one and one still equalled two? Except with my luck—

The ploddite intoned in sepulchral tones, 'Come along, lad.' I felt ailing. Things had gone wrong right from the day Mortimer had got me to Saffron Fields to meet that Susanne Eggers. A headache started.

'Wait.' The voice sounded so quiet and reasonable I couldn't see any reason to obey, but the plod stilled. I looked round.

Mrs Thomasina Quayle was standing on the pavement. Feet together, matching jacket and skirt, hat modest and lace gloves in a lovely pastel, she looked fresh from finishing school. I noticed two women giving her that cruel up-and-downer with which females hate somebody that little bit classier.

'Neither of those portraits is the one in question,' she said. The plod hesitated. Asking them to consider art was like making a marquee out of a thong.

Sandy, deprived of attention, made an instantaneous recovery and beckoned testily for minions to haul him upright. Mel obliged. Sandy strutted to face her, trailing his sheet. His head was a frothy brush, his mascara spread by false tears. He was of course attired in Lurex pantaloons and a silver bolero. One of his magenta high heels had broken off. He stood facing Mrs Quayle, spitting venom. He had to look up, being small.

'What do we have here?' he cooed, smiling sleet. 'Who're you, bitch?'

'I am Lovejoy's legal representative.' She displayed a card to the plod, slipped it back into a handbag made from the skin of the last dying reptilian representative of its conserved species. Sandy might not have been there. 'Are you arresting my client? If so, state your legal grounds forthwith.'

'An accusation has been made, miss,' one tried, losing heart.

'Supported by anything other than hysteria? Yes, no?' She was an impatient schoolmarm. The plod's grip weakened.

'This gentleman has accused—'

'Am I correct in assuming you mean a negative? If legal action is being taken against my client, please make it through proper channels. And,' she said in a voice that out-wintered anyone else's, 'please control this individual and keep the Sovereign's peace.'

She took my arm and led me away to where Shell was watching in awe.

'Mel!' Sandy screamed, falling into another fit. 'That mare called me an *individual*! Arrest her!

273

Constable! Mel, baby!'

'Good day,' this formidable lady said to Shell. 'I am Mrs Thomasina Quayle. Please inform me whether or not you are Lovejoy's friend, and if so in what capacity. If you are animose, please say.'

She waited obligingly. Shell glanced from her to me, and then said weakly, 'I was just trying to do Lovejoy a favour.'

'That's right,' I said. 'Shell's nice. She was going to give me back my painting.'

Mrs Quayle shut me up with a glance. 'Mrs Shell. Would you kindly accept my invitation to tea?'

Sandy, Mel and the plod were in retreat. I saw Mel slip the senior ploddite a note or two with a sleight-of-hand an honest man wouldn't have even noticed. Therefore my arrest might have been sham. God knows whether the coppers were genuine or not. I began to feel safe, maybe.

'Come to mine,' Shell said, gauging the newcomer. 'But let me leave first.'

My new ally agreed, and explained, 'How very wise! Mrs Shell means that we will not appear to be in collusion.' She added, 'Perhaps we should leave the market square by different exits, as further subterfuge?'

'Okay, love,' Shell said, giving me a look that asked if this bird was real or if somebody round the corner was working her with levers. 'Lovejoy knows the way.'

*　　　*　　　*

The boot of Alicia's motor locked on the two portraits, I drove out of St Edmundsbury heading north. There was no sign of Shell's motor.

For a long time I didn't speak.

When I was a youth, my gran once told me the following adage. A girl wants a man to make her a woman. The woman wants a husband to make her a wife. A wife wants a youth to make her a girl again. So life goes round.

At the time I simply took the crack at face value. Only years later did I wonder why life never asks what the bloke himself is after. Maybe that's the point, that everyone pretends that a man's desires are common knowledge, 'men are only after one thing,' etc.

Hell of an assumption to make about nearly fifty per cent of the species.

Try to guess what the next ten geezers you meet really *really* crave. I'll bet you'd get every single one wrong. I know I would. In antiques, however, you *have* to guess right every time. Guess wrong, you starve.

At the big roundabout where the Norwich dual carriageway slinks onto the old Roman road, I finally drew breath. 'What are you really, Mrs Thomasina Quayle?'

Smiling, she took off her hat and lace gloves, shaking her hair out like they do. 'Call me Tally, Lovejoy, when we're not in company.'

'You didn't even check the portraits,' I remembered.

'They're rubbish,' she said carelessly, watching the countryside slide past. 'Wake me when we're there, please.'

And slept with that curled grace women can do at a millisec's notice. I realized suddenly that my headache wasn't quite as bad. A good sign? Except sometimes I find the headache's less trouble than its cure.

The day had begun to chill by the time we arrived. You can't park next to Shell's houseboat. You've to walk a furlong, hell in wet because of brambles on the footpath but nice in sunshine because of bees and flowers. The houseboat's a converted longboat, barge as folk say to annoy watermen. No sign of life, though, which on board meant a prolonged drone from Chanter, hard at it composing new monotones in C natural.

Before we'd got there Shell was already hurrying, calling, 'Chanter? Darling? Are you all right?'

The place was locked. We wobbled up the gangplank. Shell let us in down a narrow gangway. Mrs Quayle was slick, looking everywhere. I noticed she felt the kettle, touched the half-drunk mug of tea. I went back up on deck to look back at our motors. No sign of marauders, except for a lone angler in the distance. There was a watercolourist painting at a portable easel. She wore a floral hat and a long elegant floral dress, a left-over Victorian perhaps.

'He'll have left a note for me,' Shell said, and plucked a paper from under the keyboard. It looked hell of a complicated gadget, for one note, but whatever turns folk on.

'People about,' Chanter had scrawled. 'Left to the nook.'

'Nook?' Mrs Quayle said sharply.

'It's our haven,' Shell said, her eyes shining. 'He's safe!'

She quickly checked that Chanter's drones were secure. This entailed waiting while she went

276

through a stack of tapes and discs. I got fed up. If her bloke was hale and hearty what the hell were we doing here? I almost burst out that the important thing was my portrait, but Mrs Thomasina Quayle stilled me with one of her radar glances. For God's sake, I tried to beam back in silent indignation, one lost moan would hardly count as nicking the Crown jewels. He'd got millions of the frigging things, could always drone out a few more.

'All present!' she cried, exultant.

'I'm so glad, dear,' said Mrs Quayle, still busily sherlocking round the boat's interior. 'Has the portrait remained safe also, do you surmise?'

'It's here.' Shell sounded surprised that we hadn't noticed it, and lifted it down from a slot in the ceiling. Until she did that, I'd thought it was a hatchway. I noticed Mrs Quayle colour slightly. She'd been caught out. I smiled to myself. We had a professional investigator in our midst, that's what we had.

'Is this it, Lovejoy?' Shell asked.

'Yes.' Even in the poor light I could tell.

'You have the newest devices, Shell,' our intrepid huntress remarked, taking the portrait.

I looked at the two illuminated screens, their small green lights and red staring things casting phosphorescent glows on our faces. Those colours always remind me of those flare matches that you lit fireworks with.

'Aren't they nautical, er, things?' I asked, then went red at my stupidity. A houseboat doesn't sail anywhere, does it, just stays moored.

'Chanter's music must be protected,' Shell said, serious as a girl learning her first skipping. 'I pay a fortune for the best systems. It's how Chanter realized the place was being watched.'

'Are they still there?' I asked nervously. Mrs Quayle gave me a glance of withering scorn. 'We'd best be going,' I said, on edge. Mrs Quayle took the portrait. I followed her off the boat and looked back. 'You not coming, Shell?'

'No, Lovejoy. I'll make my own way.'

We left her there. I stopped to wave. She waved to me. I felt slightly nauseated at the risks I was taking. I was the only one without a safe haven. Mrs Quayle was part of some team, so she was okay. Shell had her nook with Chanter.

She placed the portrait on the back seat and took the ignition key from me. 'It's reckoning time. Tinker will be worrying. Shall we go?'

'Tinker?' How the hell did she know Tinker?

'Such a nice man,' she said, reversing quickly away and barrelling us towards the road. 'I do rather think you ought to pay him. He needs more food and less alcohol. Have you considered an employment medical scheme?'

'I'll see to it, Mrs Quayle,' I said gravely.

Aye, I'd see to it by ballocking Tinker first chance I got. He's the biggest lead-swinger in the Eastern Hundreds, him and his sob stories. I'll bet he conned her out of a fortune in his campaign to drink the breweries dry.

'You ought to see that he has one pint a day, Lovejoy,' she continued, confirming my suspicions. 'An occasional drink does help his chest so . . .' etc, etc.

The forged portraits behind me burned my shoulders as if they were red-hot. I tried not to see Lady Hypatia's eyes looking at me. I had to ask

278

Mrs Quayle to stop a few miles north of Bures and was sick on the verge. She said nothing. Her silence made me feel worse.

That night I remembered Lady Hypatia.

*   *   *

I wasn't dreaming, yet I knew I was.

The Eastern Hundreds, like much of our tatty old kingdom, are addled with ancient titles. Arthur H. Goldhorn was Lord of the Manor of Saffron Fields, East Anglia. One day, Arthur's wife Colette decided to have her portrait painted.

Which is where I came in.

I painted her. I've already said paint the lady, love the lady. The inevitable happened. I went on my merry way, dealing, divvying. It was only years later that I heard Arthur had passed away. Little Mortimer must have been about twelve, something like that. Colette disintegrated, fell for sundry oafs and sharks. With my help, the estate came back to her. Finally I realized who Mortimer really was, if you follow. It wasn't easy.

Fool that I was, I assumed I'd walk straight back into Colette's affections. Rich again, she went off with a body-builder called Dang. Mortimer knew. The estate workers and villagers rallied round him, naturally. They thought me a pillock, also naturally.

It was afterwards, when I realized I'd lost Colette, that I sank into near oblivion. To earn enough to make a new start in antiques, I painted a few Cromwellian portraits, of somebody I'd made up. I invented a name for her, Lady Hypatia Parlayne. Her face was youthful. I sold the best ones.

Lady Hypatia was, I realized in my dreamery, Colette, who'd had Mortimer. And who, I told my dreaming self heatedly, I was never going to remember, so there. I woke in a bitter sweat realizing that my Lady Hypatias were all portraits of Colette. Colette raves endlessly in night clubs. And I really honestly certainly definitely never hoped the untrustworthy bitch would ever come back. If there was one bird I'd completely forgotten, it's she.

She sometimes sends Mortimer a birthday card. She doesn't get the date right. Pressure of life, I suppose.

But why did Susanne Eggers want the portraits? I guessed she was the one, from circumstantial evidence.

CHAPTER TWENTY-NINE

The wrestling match, like them all, was innocuous. For me it's not the atmosphere—smoke, sweat, ring riots. It's the women, as ever. I like to see them chat while bruisers are knocking six bells out of each other. Then if some specially grievous tangle appeals, they instantly shriek like banshees, clawing at some fighter's body should he tumble close. Weird.

Love it? Well, love comes pretty close. The women arrive dolled up to the nines. They take extra pains to glorify themselves, quite as if they're trotting out on some memorable date instead of a gory brawl in a toxic sweat. The ambience—I wish I knew what that means—is irrelevant. It's the violence that takes their fancy. Where I was born there used to be illegal cockfights. The saying was, 'Take your bird to see the birds, you'll have the bird by weekend.' I didn't understand it, being little. Now I do. Fight scenes stir passions.

I ditched Alicia, and went to see Tex fight.

*　　　*　　　*

Tex was already in the ring by the time I'd got to my seat. His speciality is the Triple Ripple, a move he concocted. He clasps his opponent—the referee will do if the script proves uncooperative—and climbs to the top rope, wriggles to and fro while the crowd yells, 'Ripple, ripple, *ripple*!' On the last syllable he flails over backwards, somehow firing the other bloke over his head to smash into the opposite post. Tex then strolls across to pin him to the canvas. Sometimes, though, Tex dawdles to take applause. The opponent then rises stealthily and smashes Tex down. The crowd bawls warnings, but Tex is so cocky that he's oblivious.

It sez here, as disbelieving folk cynically comment.

Wrestling is a con, one great scripted performance. I'm virtually alone in thinking this. Alicia was bitterly disappointed that I wouldn't take her, but she would have stopped the show in mid-grapple had she walked down the grubby aisle. She loves making an entrance.

Tex is on an antiques panel, has been for years, which is why I wanted to fix something with him. He owes me from having got him off the hook once. His missus died. He started what polite magazines like *Time* call 'substance abuse', meaning drugs. Easy to become addicted in the fight game, I'm told.

We met in a posh Oxford gallery. I'd come in out of the rain. The walkers—snobs who judge if a visitor is rich, or a duckegg like me without two coppers to rub together—were weighing me up. I heard a massive bloke, quite well dressed, protest as he was being taken in charge by two uniformed security officers. I thought the sight comical, because he could have minced both with one hand. I recognized him, Tex the Mighty Hex, wrestling champ.

'I only said it was crap,' he was grumbling.

'We were broadcasting,' the gallery supersnob complained, wafting this *hoi polloi* away like a bad smell. I then noticed the array of microphones, technicians swigging the cheap white wine and noshing the free grub.

'Excuse me, Sir Rollaston,' I said, going up to Tex. 'For being late.'

'Eh?' he asked. The action froze.

'I'm sorry, sir. The traffic here has worsened considerably since you were a Fellow at Corpus Christi. Is it the Klein?'

There was a Klein painting on the far wall. Kleins always do cause argument. It was simply a large canvas with huge swishes of blue across it.

'Er, yes.' Tex shook himself free. The gallery owner went into fawning mode and waved the security police off. 'The, er, Clean.'

'Klein,' I amended and led the way to stand in front of it. 'Yves Klein, Sir Rollaston, had a peculiar affinity for blue. He patented his own shade, called International Klein Blue.' Tex gazed at the picture. It looked like nothing on earth. 'He dipped women in it, then used them to smudge the canvases.'

Tex gaped. The gallery owner started a sales pitch of the 'Klein's imagery challenges modernity . . .' balderdash that shouldn't fool a whelk. I interrupted.

'I can see why you think it's not a patch on the two you already possess, Sir Rollaston. You're not seriously thinking of buying another? I wouldn't advise it, sir. Think of your Picasso . . .'

We escaped, the gallery boss trying desperately to woo Tex back to see the rest of his gunge. We had a drink round the corner. I told Tex I'd seen him fight once. Tex had to sniff some white crud using a straw while I had tea. He then had a gin and tonic. He was amazed that the gallery folk had taken my made-up prattle seriously.

'It's true, Tex. It's what Klein did. Died in Paris a famous man. Are those drugs?'

'They help, mate. Lost me wife.' He eyed me. 'Why didn't they bounce you? You look a right tramp.'

I flushed. 'That's because I've no gelt. You're a junkie because you've chucked the sponge in.'

He grabbed me by the throat and I flew across the caff, blamming tables and chairs as I went, finishing up slumped against the window. I rose, tottered out into the rain. Try to help folk, that's what you get.

There's a massive antiques fair near Newark, happens every so often. It starts early mornings among the queueing motors, and continues in fields. Hundreds of antique dealers go. It's a celebration of greed. I love it. You meet the world and his wife.

Tex was there. He pretended not to be watching as I divvied a few antiques for a rich American—there's no other kind—who'd hired me for the day plus com. This meant I'd get a percentage of the commission. His purchases, bought on my recommendation, would be valued by the average of three certified London dealers. The American finished buying about noon. Tex was there as I waited with the bags of handies, small portable antiques, for the Yank to fetch his motor. He shuffled a bit.

'Sorry, Lovejoy,' he said gruffly.

'Okay.'

'Were you hurt?'

'Aye.'

I'd had a bad shoulder for weeks. Doc Lancaster said I was a danger to my own health. I said not as much as he was. He got some physiotherapist, psychotically bent on breaking what Tex hadn't, to give me exercises. Doctors are sadistic swine. Their helpers are no better.

'I gave them up,' Tex said. 'I owe you. You done me a kindness in that gallery. You made me look at myself.' He glanced away. 'I'd lost my missus. Hard, when somebody dies.'

Well, it wasn't my fault, I thought, still narked.

'Want a job?' he asked as the American approached. 'I'm on an antiques club. We need somebody to divvy.'

'Maybe.' I was on my uppers, having just been given the sailor's elbow by Lydia, my erstwhile—and periodic—apprentice. She has the morals of a beatitude, can't accept that mankind is riddled with sinners. We'd parted over my forgeries of Colette

284

the ghost lady. I wasn't sure if I loved Colette yet, still, now, or ever had, but it felt like flu whenever I thought of her. Is that the real thing? I've no way of knowing.

'I'll send word.'

And he did. I got invited to suss out the antiques they bought. Once a week I'd go to a publican's wife in East Bergholt, who was the panel's paymaster. She stored the antiques in a warehouse by the river.

Lots of people do combined investments nowadays. And some, like Tex's mob, chip in to buy antiques. Not all are honest. I've already mentioned that some people (think Horse and FeelFree) make a fine living from defrauding such societies.

The trick among some groups, though, is to add an extra thrill. They think, hey, isn't it dull just buying antiques? Why not add a little spice? Let's gamble! So they challenge other antiques panels to see whose profits are greatest by the end of the year. Excitement! And then it's, 'Hey! Let's introduce a special prize—like, say, *the panel that gains the most profit next year wins everybody else's antiques*!'

You see the risk? It's not only that you might buy, say, a Chippendale chair that turns out to be worthless. The *real* risk is that you might buy with consistent brilliance, store up a magnificent stock of lovely antiques, and then lose out on the New Year's Eve valuation. You can fiddle a bit, but that's difficult because usually these panels can inspect each other's purchases as they go through the year.

Tex's panel won two years running, with my

285

help. I resigned because I got fed up. He tried bribing me, but I wanted a change. I hadn't seen him for a full year.

*   *   *

By the time he'd finished his grunting and hurling in the ring, I was outside reading in the caff. He joined me.

'Still a creature of habit, eh?' I said. He always has a bite after a bout.

'Let me, Lovejoy.' He paid for my nosh. I nodded ta. Never refuse a free calorie. 'Glad you came, actually. We've had an offer from two experts.'

'To help your panel?'

'Yes. A couple, Horse and FeelFree. They brought us some convincing testimonials.'

'Don't, Tex.' I looked for the tomato sauce but two all-in wrestlers on a neighbouring table had snaffled it so I smiled weakly and did without. 'They'll default. I've just saved you a fortune. Stick with Albina.' The publican's wife I told you about.

'We need expertise, Lovejoy.' He frowned. 'I think we're going to miss out this year. I've heard our opposition are doing superb buying. Got massive funds from somewhere, more than we could ever match.'

Tex's panel is a miscellaneous lot. There's a teacher, a road builder, two botanists trying to reforest Wiltshire, a doctor, a lady who breeds cats and is in love with a zookeeper. Antiques makes friends of all.

'Maybe I could help, Tex.' I went for gold. 'How about robbery?'

He looked his astonishment. 'I've never done anything like that.'

'No, Tex.' Sometimes I feel like I'm banging my head on a brick wall. '*You* needn't do it, see? *I'll* do it. You just add the antiques to your stash in the pub cellar, okay?'

'Will anybody know?'

'No,' I said brokenly to Dan Dare. 'That's the idea of robbery.'

'Are they all genuine?'

Talk about looking a gift horse in the mouth. I sighed. 'They're mixed. Like,' I said sharply, 'the assortment you usually buy.'

'Okay,' he said doubtfully, this great hulk of a bloke who routinely lobbed opponents hither and yon. 'If you're sure it'll be all right.'

'Just let Albina know they're coming.'

That was that. I left Reckless Ralph to his plate of egg and chips and drove to meet Alicia and Peshy. I'm sick of rescuing people. Except sometimes I don't manage to rescue some people at all.

*　　　*　　　*

The hospital told me Florence Giverill was up and able to walk haltingly with some sort of frame. I said fine.

*　　　*　　　*

Almost in a state of exaltation, we ran the sweep day after day. It became a marathon.

We switched from Ross-on-Wye (where Alicia did magnificently, stealing Victorian jewellery) to

287

Stourbridge (cameos, Chelsea enamels), then Stratford-upon-Avon (miniature paintings, antique gloves) to Birmingham (gems, mother-of-pearl) and back across the country to Sheffield and up to Leeds. Me and Alicia became quite a staid couple. Even the wolfhound didn't seem to mind my calling him Wolfhound any more. We started to run out of money because of the hotels, so I had to sell one or two antiques that Alicia and Peshy nicked (sorry, shouldered).

The trouble was, we were not alone. Every morning, under the door there was that cream envelope with the round sloping handwriting of Mrs Thomasina Quayle. And the tone of her brief messages became at first tart ('Lovejoy, this will have to stop . . .'), then finally resigned ('Very well, Lovejoy. However, you must take the consequences . . .').

The news from the hospital about Florence became even better, though more difficult to obtain. I ran out of relatives to pretend to be— quavery father, sad uncle, boozy brother—and finished up relying on Alicia to do the daily phone calls. Florence had made it to Rehabilitation by the time I reckoned we'd got enough antiques. I told Alicia we were done.

'Done?' She looked stricken, then composed herself. 'As in ended?'

'That's right, love. We send off the loot, then it's home time. We've made the Wanted pages, in the *Antiques Trade Gazette*!'

She looked truly downcast. Even Peshy seemed a mite saddened. I could see why, because after every theft I used to give him a special treat. They were little bone-shaped things that made him pong like a

288

stoat. He loved them.

Actually, I got queasy when Alicia tried showing me in the pet shop where to buy them, so she had to bring the treats in for me. I always made a fuss of the little sod even, in fact, when he hadn't nicked anything special at all. Once, he only fetched a shoelace, a particularly lean day, but I called him a hero and gave him two of the little stinking bone-things. He went into raptures.

Next morning, after a particularly hectic night of fare wells, I lifted the envelope from the mat and pocketed it as usual without letting Alicia see. After breakfast, I told her to meet Tex at his wrestling show in Lincoln.

'Introduce yourself, love,' I said. 'Stick with him all evening, even after he leaves the tournament. He'll need an alibi until midnight, okay?'

She was in tears. 'What about us, Lovejoy?'

'You and me, doowerlink, are just beginning,' I said mistily. 'And I do mean that most sincerely. Can I borrow your motor? I'll bring it back at two.'

Well, I needed it more. I think that deep down people like to share. She could always hire one. She had magic plastic, and I had none.

CHAPTER THIRTY

Cora is the best female burglar we have. Women are twenty per cent of all burglars, a fifth, save working it out. Most are men, except for shoplifters like Alicia Domander. I don't know the statistics on kleptomaniac mongrels, so I don't count Peshy. Not that women burglars aren't any good, because

289

when they happen along they're superb. Cora is a quality thief, only you've to choose the right job. To remind you, the ulk—robber's word meaning the place to be burgled—was Eleanor's garage in my lane, and the stuff already addressed to me c/o baby Henry's mum. If I'd wanted, say, the British Museum done over, maybe I'd choose myself, even, like I did once. Cora, incidentally, doesn't look like a cat padder, just a plain lass about thirty with freckles and long hair and neat feet.

'It's right up your street, Cora,' I told her. We met in a motorway service complex. She watches her bloke give out parking tickets. He's a traffic warden and she loves him. Could anything be more sickening?

'No, Lovejoy. It's right up *yours*.' I got the joke; it's my lane.

'Ha ha,' I said gravely. 'No hassle, love. Understand? The babby's safe, the lady's safe. The husband works the shore watch, so careful, okay?'

'I lift the tom from her garage. Then?'

'There's about thirty postal packages, some quite big, all addressed to me. Take them to Dedham. The publican's wife there keeps a cran for Tex.'

'Tex the wrestler? Oooh, I like him!'

A cran is a place to drop antiques—hole in a wall, derelict shed, an eel-catcher's pool, some old warehouse roof, anywhere nobody would think of.

'How much?'

This is typical. People don't trust anybody nowadays. Aged five, I'd been at school with her third cousin. I tried reminding her of this close family link but Cora has a heart of stone.

We agreed on a price. She said she'd take it 'on the arm', as antique dealers say for something owed. I watched her go. She never carries tools, always does a clean job. She used to be a convent housekeeper, even went into Holy Orders as a novice nun, but finally decided to forsake piety for a career in theft. I like happy endings. It takes character to realize the error of your ways. I should know.

That job arranged, I drove to the hospital, where to my alarm I learned that Florence Giverill had been discharged. The nurse gave me the address. I looked at it a long while before asking, 'You sure this is right?'

'Certain.' She eyed me. 'Only, she'll need help.'

'Is she still poorly?'

'Her and her husband went bankrupt the day of the accident. Bailiffs took everything, their house, savings. She's gone to her friend's. Take the slip road towards—'

'I know it.'

I ought to. It was my home.

She was asleep when I arrived. It was getting on for dusk, about the time Cora should be filing her jemmy and coiling her ropes, whatever she does. I deliberately didn't look down the lane. There was a candle burning in my window. Welcome home? I made a deal of here-I-come noise, and went in.

'Wotcher, love.'

'Lovejoy?' Florence sounded scared. She was on my one upright chair like waiting for an interview. 'I'm so glad to see you.'

'Brewed up?'

'Nothing works,' she said. 'No water, no electric, no telephone.' She caught herself. 'I'm sorry. I didn't mean . . .'

'Course you did. It's true.' I always joke at

penury. What else can you do? 'Here.'

I pulled out my divan and led her to it. She sank on it. I took off her shoes and gingerly lifted her legs, expecting her to yell but she didn't. Telling her to stay put, I drew water from the well in my frying pan. I filled my battered kettle and boiled it using petrol from Alicia's motor. Make a hole in the ground, drop in some petrol, light it—stand back—and balance the kettle over the flame. If I hadn't learned these tramp's tricks early on I'd not be here. We had tea.

Sensible of me to bring provisions on the way from the hospital, except I always forget something vital. Like, I'd no butter or margarine though I'd bought nine loaves. The thing about shopping is that I'm easily hoodwinked in supermarkets. Their come-ons con me: 'Special offer! Four for the price of two! Six for the price of three!' So I'd got enough skimmed milk ('Ten pack for the price of five!') to have a bath in. I'd got six fresh mackerel with no freezer to preserve them. And I'd to slog through ten cream cakes or let them go bad. See? I'm taken in.

It must be easy shopping for a family, but it's hard on your own. I keep finding necrotic fruit in nooks about the place, because of some special offers on bananas two months ago. I go all magpie, not having the sense to realize that I only ever need one bunch at a time because I've only one gob. Daft. Women are better at it but grumble more. I should remember what the Greeks used to say when their eyes got bigger than their bellies: 'Even Apollo can only eat once a day.' But out shopping I believe I'm really sensible. I've come home with enough to feed regiments believing I'd saved a fortune. I don't think I plan well.

Florence, recumbent, roused to cast an eagle eye on my bags of grub and creaked across to sort it through, complaining, 'You must work it out as you go, Lovejoy. Who needs four punnets of nectarines? And all these bottles of sauce?' I got narked and said she'd no right to come moaning and I was frigging tired. She looked at me and said she'd make us something. I showed her the firepit trick. She said it was primitive. What cooking isn't? I once worked as a kitchen scullion in a bad patch, and it was sheer carnage. She fried some eggs, and herself ate barely a mouthful. I'd bought five dozen.

My gran used to say, 'There's only two sorts, luv. There's them as do, and there's them as doesn't.' Meaning workers and drones. Florence was a doer. She swept the cottage, put my clothes in soak, washed up, went and cut bits off bushes until I asked her to leave my plants alone in case she made them ill. We had a spirited disagreement about pruning—I think it's cruel, she thought it necessary.

'I bury Timothy tomorrow, Lovejoy,' she said after a bit. 'I haven't the money.'

'St Mary's? I'll see to the cost, love.'

Her eyes filled in the candlelight. 'Timothy said to come to you if anything . . . I don't want to impose.'

'He was right.' I added a white lie, 'That was our arrangement.'

'Timothy was going to retire this year. He said we'd be in clover, until all this began.' She wept a while as I looked at the candle. 'He was so frightened. I'd never seen him like that. I asked

293

him to go to the authorities. He wouldn't. He said there was no way out. I loved him, Lovejoy. We were like children.'

What can you say? 'Stay here. I'll get the electric on tomorrow, and maybe the water and phone.'

'I'm so sorry. I'm a refugee.' She couldn't look. 'He didn't do anything wrong, Lovejoy. He wouldn't, not Timothy.'

'You don't need to tell me that, love.' I thought I knew most.

'I never thought we'd—I'd—be homeless. It's like the world has ended.'

For a moment I looked into her eyes. 'The old one has, love.'

In winter I sleep in a nightshirt of my grandad's. Other times I kip in my nip. Though winter hadn't yet arrived, for propriety's sake I donned Gramp's voluminous cowl when she was decently lying there, face averted, and slipped in beside her. They say the word spooning is a Yankism, from the way spoons lie among cutlery. Only lately has it come to mean lust-filled snogging. We spooned, then, meaning just lying there and drifting off. I'd forgotten candles—another winning safari round Bennick's Super Shop—so let my lone glim gutter to a faint red glow. Then darkness.

Florence lay there breathing unsteadily, under my arm. She shoved back against me, which was a bit unfair, though it was only for warmth because women are always freezing. Thermophilic, they say of plants, but I don't know a word for women. I can't work out why their knees and feet are always frigid, or why their breasts stay cool even on hot days. Maybe when something's inevitable you don't need a word for it at all? Like greed, to pick a

294

thought at random.

About fourish—I knew the time from the clipclop of Hawker's shire horse; it has to get up and be got ready to drag those pointless machines about the fields at dawn—Florence fell into steady breathing. It was only then that I let my mind off its lead to roam wherever it would. My eyes wouldn't shut, which was a pest, but then sleep doesn't get organized. I've always found that.

Timothy's funeral was in the morning, I warned myself sternly, so no vengeful thoughts. No vendettas, thank you very much. No itching to slay murderers. Peace, friends. The most I would allow myself tomorrow, no matter who turned up, would be a sad smile. I meant that most sincerely.

*   *   *

At six I rose, bathed in my tin bath—cold well water in my forgery—turned to grope for my towel and it was handed to me. Cora stood there, me naked. I yelped and clasped the towel.

'Morning, Lovejoy.' She eyed me as I dripped in my nip. 'Dry yourself, silly sod. You'll catch your death of cold. Anyhow, you're safe from rape. I'm angry.'

Standing shivering in the tin bath, I asked why.

'Eleanor's garage is empty. Not a box. The lock was broken.'

'Sure you got the right address?'

'Don't you dare.' She nicked the towel and turned me round to dry my back. Even so I modestly covered myself with my palms. Why on earth, when she was behind me? God didn't give us enough hands.

295

'Any idea who?' I asked.

'No idea. They knew their stuff, whoever they were.' She draped the towel over my shoulder. 'You pay, understand? One week from now, on the nail.'

'Course.'

'Want me to come in for a minute?'

'I've got a visitor, but ta.'

She left then. I didn't hear her motor, but by the time I emerged there was no sign. Like I say, Cora's a real pro. Inside. Florence was lying awake.

'Will you come, Lovejoy?' she asked.

'All the way, love,' I said, like it was Timbuctoo instead of a funeral at our village church.

CHAPTER THIRTY-ONE

What can you say about a funeral? Folk ask, 'Did it go well?' then go red realizing what they've said. There is no wellness in it. I worry that we haven't got the hang of politeness. I mean, those little tubs in bathrooms—what's the idea of them, exactly? Look in, they're empty. And bus tickets that accumulate in your pockets, the fluff in your trouser turn-ups, the grime you scrape from under your fingernails, what's the polite way to get rid?

And what to say when only me, Florence, and Tinker turn up to see Timothy off.

We warbled Bunyan's 'To Be A Pilgrim', the only hymn that matters. Tinker coughed all through, yet surprisingly sang in a good baritone, hardly any shale in clear tones. Eleanor crept in to the rearmost pew as the service started. She'd brought little Henry, who sang lustily along in discord, and whose belly parped during momentous silences. These caused Tinker to mutter, 'What the bleed'n hell's that?' looking round until I gave him the bent eye to shut it.

Tinker longingly eyed the kist where the altar wine's kept, disappointed there was no communion so we could all get sloshed in pious commemoration. I'd given him four notes so he could imbibe enough ale to sustain him during our grief. He stank like a brewery.

Still, he had attended. And nobody else had come. Note that, please, for future reference.

Hymns are trouble, I always think. If the congregation's massive, you're okay except when some pushy tenor or soprano reckons they're the bee's knees and outdoes everybody so we all shut up from embarrassment. If there's hardly anybody, like now for Timothy, your voice gets lost in the rafters so pigeons drown you out. It wasn't much of a service. There was no organist. The vicar had driven over from Hawkseley, very narked like we were a nuisance, his coffee ruined by thoughtless dead.

The coffin stood there on its trestles, a singular reproach. Only one wreath, that I'd got Tinker to bring. I always get flowers wrong, so told him to leave the choice to Pam in Sir Isaac's Walk. There's a whole language in blooms, isn't there, but working out what flowers mean only makes your eyes go wet at the wrong time—is there a right time?

The other hymn was Mrs Alexander's 'There Is A Green Hill Far Away'. It got the treatment from Henry, bawling on long after we'd done. Henry warbled his melody—Eleanor desperately trying to shush him—even as the vicar intoned the homily. He didn't know anything about Timothy, of course, too sloppy to check with anybody. I'd tried to speak to him but he'd hurried in with, 'In your places, please,' and given the service a Brands Hatch start.

For pall bearers I'd got four lads from the Treble Tile, me and Tinker making six. Carrying a coffin's hard. Our church has a trolley, donated by some kindly soul in 1847 so the poor could save on expense. It has only two wheels, but you put the coffin on it and push it among the gravestones as best you can. The grass isn't cut nowadays—it used to be in the past. Our own fault, really.

Luckily it wasn't raining. Eleanor and Henry came too. The lads lowered the coffin, Henry singing with gusto, his little belly working like tiny bellows, Eleanor trying to quieten him and smiling weakly when the vicar glared. I stood between Henry and the priest, who had a frigging job to do and ought to be getting on with it instead of showing he was a pompous prat.

The lads lowered the coffin and went. It left us six, seven if you count Timothy. I don't like staring in graves. I kept thinking the system's all off kilter. Surely God could have thought up something better than this? Get born, then some so-say accident cutting you off? It's barbaric. The vicar read a bit, shut his book with a snap, and reached to shake Florence's hand. Throughout it all, she'd stayed resolute. We dropped a handful of soil onto the coffin.

Then to my surprise Tinker stepped to the grave edge and cleared his throat, joining his hands like a child at prayer.

'Hang about, reverend,' he gravelled out.

'Tinker,' I said. I know he feels strongly about things, and didn't want Florence upset more than she already was. 'Come on, mate. We're done here.'

'Mr Giverill,' Tinker said, ignoring me and addressing the grave. 'Lovejoy'll do the buggers down as topped you, okay? Just so you know. God bless.'

'Mrs Giverill!' the vicar said, scandalized. 'Am I to understand from this that some threat . . . ?'

'No, reverend.' I tried to smile. 'My pal here is, er, the deceased's cousin. They were very close. Mr Dill only means the, er . . .'

'Arrangements for a headstone,' Eleanor put in calmly.

The silence spread until I obeyed Eleanor's prompting eyebrows and quickly cut in, 'Yes! That's it.'

Eleanor invited us all back to hers for tea and a wad. The vicar declined, stood there until I promised to settle his bill, which brought a beam to his face. We thanked him most sincerely for his indefatigable hard labour.

We set off down the lane, Tinker coughing his formidable cough and expectorating copiously into the long grass. Henry watched admiringly, doubtless longing for the day when he too could emit so much sound without being shushed all the time by a troublesome mother.

I was allowed to push Henry. I do this backwards, because he likes to see who's hard at it while he croons. He yelps with glee at passing dogs and bicycles, but goggles with most enthusiasm at wheelbarrows as we pass the allotments, his real favourites. I think he believes they're some kind of novel pram, on their way to collect a specially shaped infant.

Eleanor was kind. She'd seen that I was in difficulties over arranging a wake for poor Timothy. A lot of trouble, really, seeing she didn't know Timothy Giverill from Adam. People joke, don't they, that a funeral's only ham butties and a slow walk. She'd done sandwiches and a kind of Bakewell pudding—it's wrong to call it tart or cake. These functions, while obligatory, are a trial. Another instance of manners never telling you exactly what to do. We stood, not knowing whether to sit, until Eleanor said for goodness sake sit down. I got Henry. Florence went to make more tea. Tinker coughed, engulfed grub and drank down Eleanor's sherry while Henry gazed on admiringly.

'Was it all right about your things, Lovejoy?' Eleanor asked quietly. 'I didn't like to ask.'

She meant our nicked antiques that we'd posted to her.

'What time was it?'

'When they came? Ever so late, about ten o'clock. I'd just given Henry his half past nine change.'

Henry's head became a weight in the crook of my arm. He snored.

'Did they leave any message?'

'Yes. The elderly gentleman said he was sure you'd understand. Did I do right?'

'Course you did. Ta for all your help.' Elderly gentleman?

Tinker looked forlornly at me. The sherry bottle was empty. I gave him a couple of notes, told him I'd meet him at the Treble Tile in an hour. He brightened instantly and was off like a whippet.

Eleanor wasn't quite done. She glanced quickly at the door, listening as Florence did kettle magic, and asked quietly, 'Lovejoy. Are you and Florence . . . ?'

'No. She's bankrupt. Has nowhere to go.'

For the first time I realized I didn't actually know. Yet there had to be a record of Timothy's insurance work, because insurance is only writing down deals.

'She stayed at your cottage last night, Lovejoy,' Eleanor said frostily. Women have priorities, where enemy women abound.

'Her husband asked me to look out for her. He knew he was dying.'

Florence reappeared. Henry woke and went a spectacular red, grunting away, so we had to change him. Later, smelling like roses, he drooled my biscuits to a sog while I tried to slip myself some grub. Getting edibles past him is running the gauntlet because he collars anything mobile and drags it slowly to his mouth, salivating and grunting as he ingests it. He doesn't have much strength, yet always wins. He has the unshakeable conviction that anything moving ought to be in his mouth, at least on a trial basis, until something else gets a go.

Florence and Eleanor got on well after that. I'd been worried, because me and Eleanor sometimes made smiles and I didn't want anything to go wrong. The loss of all my nicked antiques was a disaster. I couldn't blame Eleanor. I'd not warned her, and anyway, what could she have done?

Old gentleman, though?

*   *   *

An hour later, I walked Florence to the cottage then hurried round to the Treble Tile to give Tinker his orders. Time I got a move on. My trusty barker was badly sloshed, but had news.

'The brigadier's got our stuff, son.' He was at the stage of bleary somnolence, just able to sit upright.

'You sure?' Even for Tinker this was swift.

'Farm lads seed him when they knocked off.'

I ought to have had the sense to ask.

That afternoon I tried to reassure Florence by simply being there. We walked about my neglected garden, fed the birds. I looked at the portraits unseeingly. Late afternoon, we had an improvised meal that Florence concocted. Not bad, but not enough stodge. I'd have to train her up.

We walked to the churchyard to check on Timothy. It takes a whole year before you can place a headstone. The little brown wooden cross looked lost, just his name cut into the bare sticks. I nicked some flowers from Eleanor's garden for him. Florence was scandalized, but I said reasonably that Henry only ate them anyway so I was in fact doing Eleanor a favour.

We went home. She told me everything she'd overheard about Timothy's dealings. It nearly almost practically all fitted. Nothing new. I wasn't angry, not really. Tinker saying his piece at the graveside was really wrong. He'd no right. I've found that people assume you're narked when you're quite calm inside and mean no harm to anyone.

302

CHAPTER THIRTY-TWO

The Officer's Club stands in the military part of town. It's been the garrison area, believe it or not, since before the Romans landed two thousand years agone. The Garrison Church dominates local streets. Within a few minutes' walk you see the military hospital, barracks named after victorious carnage, shops offering discounts to soldiers. You even see the odd tank.

And horses.

Now, I quite like horses, but aren't they great heaving things? Doctor Johnson said a horse was trouble at both ends and uncomfortable in the middle, at the time grumpily accepting a particularly expensive one as a present from his ladylove. All horses should live in a zoo, for children to feed, with fields where they could trot about if the mood took. Instead, there you are parked in a lay-by at Abbey Fields having a snog with somebody when she suddenly exclaims, 'Oooh, look! Isn't he lovely!' And trotting past the car's steamy window is a nag. Women go delirious over horses. If you see one when you're hungry for passion, you might as well drive her home and get back to antiques. Military nags belong to leftover cavalry. Somebody in the War Office still assumes that a dozen dragoons will rescue the nation should armoured divisions come clattering ashore.

Sitting on the stable windowsill, I watched Brigadier Hedge. He rode well, balanced stiffly forward like a pointer dog. He didn't bounce up and down like other riders.

'What's this, Lovejoy?' Sep asked. 'Joining up?'

He was watching me watching the riders.

'Nice things, horses,' I said idly. 'Just wondering if I should paint a Gainsborough forgery from this view.'

'You threatened murder at the Giverill burial. Tut tut. Haven't you heard there's laws against that?'

'There's laws against cruelty to people,' I said evenly. 'They don't work, either. Anyway, Tinker said it, not me. He was kaylied as usual.'

'A warning about Mrs Quayle,' he said casually. 'Steer clear of her, even if she is a friend of Sandy's. Let her chase red herrings like Ferdinand and Norma in their posh new antiques business. She'll never get anywhere.'

My mind went, eh? but I said nothing. Friend of Sandy's? The brigadier took two low hurdles, his mount's hooves thudding. Other riders cantered past the jumps, chicken.

'She's nowt to do with me.'

Sep was amused. 'The best her sort can hope for is to catch FeelFree and Horse pulling another antiques club scam. She'll never amount to much. You've to be a hard bloke like me to pull the crooks in.'

'Still macho, Sep? Surprised you're not here on your trusty steed.'

He snorted. 'Them lot? Chinless wonders. Ponces.'

He'd always been the same. I'd forgotten. In clink with him that time, I'd heard his endless grumbling about how unfair life was. Everybody else got promoted, while unspecified dark forces held him back. Life was treacherous. Sinister plots

304

got him turned down for the fire brigade, of all things. He'd flunked entry to the officers' academy at Sandhurst. Sep railed on until lads in adjoining cells had yelled at him to shut it.

'Mrs Quayle seems pretty sure of herself.' I was lost. I hadn't known she knew anything about Ferd and Norma, let alone FeelFree's antiques clubs.

'Her sort always do,' he said sourly. 'Silver-spoon bitch. Her daddy'll have shunted her into that job.'

What position did Mrs Thomasina Quayle hold, exactly? I wondered it suddenly.

'Maybe she hasn't come alone, Sep,' I said, innocently riling him.

'The frigging Aunties wouldn't run to that expense, Lovejoy,' Sep said, which made my heart sing.

Aunties is the nickname for the plod's meddlers in the antiques trade. They never do much, being too fragmented and uncoordinated. If Mrs Quayle wasn't one of their investigators, then she had to be from the Serious Fraud Office itself. Except the SFO only ever send one hunter at a time, never two. Which left Petra Deighnson unexplained. I now had all the bits of the jigsaw, but some didn't fit.

'Look, Sep,' I said quietly as the brigadier turned his mount for home. 'You helped me when that Yank Eggers tried to haul me in. I appreciate it. If I can put anything your way, let me know, eh?'

He looked at me in surprise, because he'd done nothing that day except bully me. He'd have done worse if Taylor Eggers had insisted. I could practically hear Sep's churning neurones. He finally stopped trying to think and opted for opportunity.

'Yeah. I slogged to get you out of that scrape,' he

305

said, convincing himself as ploddites do. 'You put something worthwhile my way, I'll see you right.'

'Right, Sep. I trust you.' Aye, as far as I could lob St Paul's.

He nodded and left, my comrade in arms. I saw his massive motor glide out of the riding fields, nudging aside smaller fry in the traffic. For a moment I wondered why the image disturbed me, but shelved the worry as Brigadier Hedge trotted up. The horse was breathing hard, possibly enjoying itself but maybe not. I once had this bird who rode in the Olympics. Horse mad, she raged at me for being unsporting when I said she should simply post her nag to Sydney, let it do its stuff there on its own. Riders are superfluous, as long as the nag knew how to climb onto the rostrum and hum the National Anthem. She gave me a day's abuse then left, taking her umpteen saddles, tackle, tons of linament and three cases full of jodhpurs. *Deo gratias.*

'Lovejoy, you're a month overdue.'

'I was away, Brig. Working.'

He was amused. Well, I would have been, if I'd just stolen all his antiques.

'Quite a collection you amassed,' he said, rolling in the aisles in a harf-harf sort of way. 'Would you like them back?'

I hadn't counted on this. 'What for?' I pondered my question, got it right second go. 'For what?'

He waited as jolly sporting types tottered by on their exhausted mounts.

'I made a suggestion, Lovejoy, remember? You and Maud. Become an item—isn't that the expression? I arranged a meeting that Friday. You defaulted. Having, ah, borrowed your antiques, I

306

now have a means of insisting on your compliance. Don't feed him anything, there's a good chap.'

His horse, spattering saliva everywhere, was nuzzling me for grub. Christ, I thought, the damned thing was worse than Henry, and he was a double-ended fountain. I was drenched in spit.

'I promise not to.' The beast's nose was like a sponge the size of a bolster. It had somehow stuffed it into my pocket. Thief, like its master. 'Look, Brig. Maud's married. I'm not allowed to betroth a lady who is wed. It's a law.' Lot of law about today.

He smiled a wintry non-smile.

'That's never stopped you from consorting with ladies similarly placed,' he said. 'The mayoress? The wife of a certain magistrate? The mother of Mortimer? I can't pretend to have them all off by heart, but I have a list.'

'What if I did?' I bleated, spirits failing. 'Start seeing Maud, I mean. Quaker's big in antiques. He might turn nasty.'

'That would be irrelevant,' he said, cold. 'Once you and Maud take up together, Quaker will leave the equation. Just mend your ways somewhat.'

He spoke carefully, glancing round from under his bushy eyebrows. I think these military types cultivate them to look like hoary old campaign veterans.

'Your conduct with other women must be proper. I couldn't allow you to roam freely quite as you presently do. Maud must be assured of your fidelity. However, should a temporary dalliance become essential in your antiques operations, then I should turn a blind eye.'

He amplified this for a few sentences, all
307

meaning the same thing: he'd neutralize Quaker's interest, and I should be Maud's constant paramour. I'd have to toe the line and not betray Maud's trust, unless it was absolutely essential for antiques. I heard him out, wondering uneasily whether he knew that Maud and me had made smiles in the past.

'Can I have my antiques back, Brig?' Pathetic worm that I am.

'Not without total agreement to my suggestion.'

'Right.' I tried my luck. 'I'm broke. I'd need—'

'Your credit is sound,' he said with a smile filled with sudden glee. Once a hunter, always a hunter. He lobbed me an envelope. It fell in the mud. More money? I must be worth it, but for what? 'Obey commands, Lovejoy.'

'Yes, Brig,' I said, like I loved subjection.

Not proud, I wiped the mud off the envelope. It held a good two months' money. I walked into town and caught Alanna at the broadcasting studios.

We drove to Vestry's barn, the place where he'd been found hanging by FeelFree and Horse. Something I should have done a long time back.

CHAPTER THIRTY-THREE

'Tinker's coming too?' Alanna asked, shocked, as I reached Benjie's Motor Caff. Tinker, wheezing and bedraggled, climbed in, the lorry drivers still swigging Benjie's outfall, whistling at Alanna.

'He's vital,' I told Alanna, pulling away and giving the drivers a regal farewell wave. 'What

308

about Vestry, Tinker?'

'Got a drink, Lovejoy?' The car filled with alcoholic fumes. He stank of dank.

'We'll stop soon,' I told him, like we were in the Gobi desert. 'Wotcher find?'

'Vestry was daft, son. Into a big export, after that Sotheby's cock-up. Lucy Ann summert. Remember that packing case?'

'Lucien Freud,' Alanna translated.

'Aye, luv.' Tinker sounded pleased. 'You're quite bright for a bird. Here, luv. Isn't that bint Marjorie your muvver? Lovejoy used to shag—'

Thank you, Mister Tact. I interrupted before Alanna could lob him out. 'What big export?'

'The Countess. Vestry'd bought one of her Grade A shipments to the Continong.'

'Who from?' Vestry *never*, but never ever, had funds.

It was all right for Alanna to hear, even though she was now grafted to her Cambridge plod. She knew enough about the local antiques trade to keep mum—sorry, no pun intended—or I wouldn't have asked her along.

The Sotheby's shambles over Lucien Freud's painting was famed in song and story, and had initiated more frauds than paltry. A simple enough mistake, but horrendous. Two Sotheby's whifflers blithely destroyed a packing case—only to realize, aghast, *that its contents hadn't been removed*. The contents? Tragically, an original work by none other than the great Lucien Freud. It was worth a fortune. Red faces all round.

Dealers rolled in the aisles, because everybody hates auctioneers. For weeks the lads went about saying things like, 'Get the picture, mate?' and falling about. Their joke meant that forgeries of the destroyed painting would instantly become available by the ton. It always happens, because who's to prove that the original *wasn't* destroyed? I call it the Anastasia problem. Once Anastasia did die—as she really really did that sad day at Ekaterinberg—impostors sprang up everywhere. Disproving a negative is hell.

'Some geezer from the Div. You knows him, Lovejoy.'

Footballers now, from the soccer divisions? Well, God knows they were rich enough to stash away antiques by the busload. In one ninety-minute Saturday game soccer players earn four times the average worker's yearly wage. I wonder about morality.

'Alanna. Your turn.'

'Vestry,' she began as I turned towards the coast road. 'Suicide, found hanged. Two antique dealers, FeelFree and Horse, were visiting him to propose founding a club for lady antiques collectors. The deceased wasn't in financial trouble, had good insurance, no debts. Divorced, one relative, a sister in Boston.'

Boston wasn't all that far. Me and Alicia had graciously included Neskett and Graceen's Auction Rooms on our sweep through Boston, Lincolnshire. A poor quality heist, though, except for one lattimo beaker. It was well worth Peshy's skill—wherever, I thought bitterly, the wretched glass had been salted away by the brigadier. Lattimo is milky white and virtually opaque. I don't like it much, though Venetian glassmakers claim that it looks like Far East porcelain. It doesn't, but collectors adore it. Greed promotes dross to art,

310

just as love makes a Venus de Milo out of a Plain Jane, and why not?

'Eh?' I asked. Alanna had said something that mattered.

'Your argument with Vestry's sister doesn't help one little bit, Lovejoy.'

'Eh?' I didn't even know Vestry's sister.

'Especially now she's extended her stay at Saffron Fields.'

'Eh?'

'Would you please stop saying that? I've never known a man so infuriating—'

'Not many left from the old Div,' Tinker said wistfully, sputum bubbling up. 'My mate Chalky White passed away last autumn. Frigging chest cold took him. Did I ever tell you about that twenty-five pounder he let roll over that sodding cliff in North Africa?' He gave a cackle that set him off coughing and trying to spit out of the car windows. I stopped in a lay-by.

'You lets me gullet get dry, Lovejoy,' he gasped, choking and wheezing. 'There a pub near here?'

Division as in armed forces, my brain finally reasoned, synapses clanging, not as in football. Alanna emerged to hand Tinker a hanky. A passing motor honked approval, the lads in it whistling. She has this effect.

'We'll stop at the next, Tinker,' I promised. I went to Alanna. 'Who's Vestry's sister?'

She stared, judging the extent of my ignorance.

'Mrs Susanne Eggers. You got her some actors for tomorrow.'

'Course,' I said brightly through a splitting headache. 'Just checking.'

So Vestry's antiques shipment was going to the

311

Continent via the Countess, as was decided by some old army geezer, bankrolled by Sandy who was funding Ferd and Norma, and back reeled my mind into a void where logic couldn't follow.

'How about we stop for a bite?' I said.

'Are you all right, Lovejoy?' Alanna asked.

'I was telling you about Chalky White and this twenty-five pounder,' Tinker resumed affably, splashing back through a puddle and getting into the car trailing a bushel of mud. 'There was our frigging battery on this bleeding cliff, see? The sergeant says—'

'I'll drive, Lovejoy,' Alanna said curtly.

Head thumping, I tried to doze while Tinker's incomprehensible tale rambled on between coughs. Alanna stopped at the Wig and Fidget in Pullingham where Tinker finally stopped moaning while he soaked up enough ale to bath in. Alanna admired the tavern's wisteria and nibbled an Eccles cake. I had sweet tea, three pasties and a stack of toast, and recovered. Not enough to take on Vestry's place, though.

It stood back from a stream. No access for the motor, just a footpath under an old cattlecreep arch. I was unprepared for the sheer rurality. Some maniac had set a stick bearing a notice in case we developed ideas of molesting the undergrowth: *Fritillaria Rare Do Not Disturb*, like some daffodil should make us all go on tiptoe. Alanna, of course, was in raptures. 'Lovejoy! Fritillaria! So called from its flower's resemblance to a Roman legionary's dice-shaker . . .' etc, etc. We followed the path, Tinker grumbling there wasn't a pub within miles and how did folk manage. For me, the depressing thought was, how soon everything was overgrown. Brambles, ferns, tendrils, you'd think nobody had ever been this way.

There stood Vestry's converted barn. I suppose once it had been a sort of stable, but now it was quite a grand house. Its beams and pargetry were restored, the leaded windows good if you like that sort of fake. A set of steps to the stream, and that was Vestry's house. We walked round. I tested the doors while Alanna tutted. Tinker saw the double doors of the workshop before I did, away from the building in a tangled grove. We made it, Alanna exclaiming as she laddered her tights on brambles, the creeping greenery no longer quite so delightful.

The barn didn't hold much. Every antique dealer has delusions of creative grandeur like, I'm told, screen actors get once they've played some bit part and see themselves mutating into directors. Similarly, antique dealers—basically furniture movers, nothing more—get the bug to improve antiques. If they buy a painting they'll cack-handedly try to add to it. A piece of furniture by Sheraton, they'll strip away the surface patina and leave it warping and scratched, then be narked when nobody wants to buy. For this barmy reason every dealer has a neffie assembly of brushes they can't use, jam jars of varnishes they don't know the properties of, and a few tools they couldn't wield in a month of Sundays. Against every dealer's wall there leans a load of old canvases, maybe some planks taken from some wardrobe that they dissected to extinction.

Vestry's was like that. I eyed the beam uneasily. Tinker coughed, spat, babbled, 'Yon middle hook's where he topped himself, FeelFree said.'

'Please, Mr Dill,' Alanna rebuked crisply. 'This

313

is the place of Mr Vestry's demise, let's not forget.'

There was an earth floor, no paving flags, nothing. Alanna winced when Tinker pointed out the marks on the floor where feet had scuffed while somebody'd cut Vestry down. I thought, what a lot of local grief. Ever since Vestry's sister Susanne Eggers had appeared, in fact.

'Is anything different, Alanna?' I asked.

'The stepladder's gone.' She shuddered. 'Vestry had been painting.' Indeed, one wall was whitewashed, nearly finished. 'He wore paint-stained clothes.'

'No ladder now. The Soco must've took it. Sep Verner?' Odd. 'See, I'm surprised FeelFree and Horse wanted to deal with him.'

Alanna gave me a moment's frost. 'Forgiveness is something you might learn, Lovejoy.'

Tinker said, 'You think it all comes down to shagging, son, but you're wrong. All comes down to money.'

Thank you, Beau Brummel. Hang on, though. 'Forgive who?' I asked. Then for clarity, 'Forgiveness of what, exactly?'

'Divorced people can be friends, Lovejoy, the consul himself said.'

Consul? I was looking at Vestry's canvas stack, pulling them away from the wall. Several had been 'cleaned'—meaning that some masterpiece had been sanded off so the canvas could be sold to passing forgers. Vestry sold me some. Genuine antique canvases are valuable, so never *never* throw them away, even if rotting to bits. New canvas undoes a forgery more often than bad painting.

'Who consul?' Grammar gone to pot.

'The   American   gentleman.   He   sent

314

condolences.'

'Decent of him.' The last canvas came away. It was my portrait of Colette as Lady Hypatia. I jumped away.

'In my radio interview.' She sounded proud. 'He promised me an in-depth interview on the American elections.'

'Why did he?'

She bridled. 'Because I have broadcasting talent, Lovejoy.'

'You're the best I've ever heard, love,' I lied. The trouble is that lying tends to grow, like an expanding verbal ladder getting riskier as it extends ever upward. 'Why'd he concern himself with Vestry?' I'd assumed I was the only person who was guessing right about the gorgeous Susanne Eggers.

She stared. 'Mrs Eggers was the consul's first wife, Lovejoy. They're still business partners. Names at Lloyd's. Head of syndicates. Vestry was their secretary. I thought you said you never miss my programme?'

'Well,' I said faintly, 'I can't remember everything.'

I took my painting and the scraped canvases, and we left the sorry place. I just asked Tinker to go over what deals Vestry had made before his passing. Tinker began a litany of deals, defaults, broken promises, sham antiques, humdrum sales, nothing anybody in the trade would think worth a light.

So why did somebody kill the poor duckegg?

*   *   *

Time passes faster than you think. I can remember

315

when actresses closed their mouths instead of acting with that half-idiot gape they all now assume shows inner dynamism. And when TV extras could dance instead of doing that embarrassed shuffle. And to when actors knew their lines, instead of reading prompt cards held off camera so they all look squinty. And to when police were reliable. And back when occasionally, just occasionally, people were innocent, sort of.

Now, though, everybody's got what Americans call an angle, a craving for sly money. And it always concerns antiques. Okay, we all know—and the plod condones—that the glorious bulb fields of Lincolnshire are farmed by illegal thick-sweat immigrant labour. And that priests and nuns aren't holy. And that teachers no longer know what the hell to teach, that parents are sometimes monsters and the honest social services neither honest, social nor services. Did folk ever really go out without locking their doors? Maybe they did, yonks since, but it's different now. Yet deep in me lingers a faint glim of hope that somewhere sometime somehow out there, maybe a huge fair-minded God thing will shazoom out of the ether and blam the baddies. Just maybe once, to give us all a prayer. You know the feeling. Let some avenging angel black the bully's eye.

It won't happen. It never will, never did, never does.

No good saying that the meek can inherit the earth, that virtue is and has its own reward. They can't and it won't and it hasn't. Shout for help, your echoes shout back louder. Shoot your one pathetic desperate arrow in this life, you get back a broadside. I had this stupid notion that the brigadier—officer and gentleman, after all—might simply want his daughter's eventual happiness like a true dedicated father.

'Here,' I told Alanna and Tinker. 'I've an idea. Drop me by that little quayside nosh bar. I'll see you at the Old Court coffee place. Make sure that Mrs Domander gets her motor back, okay?'

And walked to Quaker's bungalow along the riverbank. The brigadier, smiling, watched me approach from his picture window.

Smiles cost blood. I've always found that. But somebody had to work things right for once.

CHAPTER THIRTY-FOUR

Even before they opened the door, I felt like a suitor in *Emma*, seeing Maud standing there smiling. Her frock was new. She looked glammed up. In the background, Quaker gave me a wave, grinning. Was I expected? The Olympic fanfare was playing too loud—is there ever a time when it isn't?

'Come in, Lovejoy. Father's waiting.'

'Wotcher, Maud.'

Gingerly I went in, wishing I had flowers. But can a bloke call on another geezer's missus with a ton of daisies, when he's up to no good? Hardly.

'So kind of you to think of me, Lovejoy.'

Was it, when I hadn't? I followed her to her dad's adjoining door. A rowing boat glided by, then a small engined craft. Brig was watching the telly, horses leaping over sticks. On his side-table was a crime story, horses on the dust jacket. I'd sooner watch fog, but nags hook plenty of adherents. Can't fathom it.

'I'm so looking forward to the music, Lovejoy!' Maud enthused. 'I hadn't realized you liked English song cycles.'

'Neither had I.' What music?

'Oh, you!' She smacked out playfully, taking my answer for wit. 'Elgar's my favourite. Are they doing Peter Warlock?'

'Yes.' I gave the brigadier a challenging stare. Expose my ignorance, if you dare. 'Is it all right with Quaker?'

'Of course! He's delighted you're taking me. He's only interested in his old sports, though he'll be at the meeting afterwards.'

'Special dining invitation after the show, Lovejoy,' Brig said pleasantly. He blipped the telly off. 'Sit you down.'

His side-table was a French mahogany serving table, three-tier, one of a pair that me and Alicia Domander and little Peshy had nicked from Eness and Crow's auction yard in Cambridge. We'd had to load up outside St John's College during evensong, a triumph of commerce over theology. I felt truly narked. That table was mine by rights. He'd nicked all my stolen antiques from Eleanor's, then had it here as if it was his own. Stealing is immoral.

'Show?' This was the second mention of a show.

'The Quay Theatre. Safety regs, y'know. Demonstration first, then the music. Last, our meeting.' He harfed affably, shaking his head. 'You young folk, always wanting rations first, hey?'

'Silly me. Forget my head next.' I accepted a drink from Maud, a celebratory goblet so full of tiny umbrellas and toys I couldn't take a swig for

318

prongs getting up my nose. Brig's expression clouded as he checked a letter.

'See this? It's what civilization's up against.'

'Now, Dad, don't start. Lovejoy's only called about tomorrow.'

She looked good enough to eat, sitting on the couch with that smooth movement women do. Men sit down like a sack of tools, clumsy. I've only to walk into a room for things to start shuffling towards the edges of shelves ready to leap off, and valued vases to start tilting. Wary of spillage, I looked about for somewhere to place my glass. And saw a lovely little Victorian fede ring (means faith, trust in a loved one). A real lover's antique. I've a soft spot for them. I knew it instantly. Me and Alicia nicked it from Corridern's Auction, Scunthorpe. I'd checked the opening device myself. Describe it, a fede ring sounds almost impossible—how *did* craftsman get so much on a single small gold ring? Two hands often linked by pearls, with diamonds or rubies in the setting. They sometimes open, showing two hands clasping inside.

It was on the bottom tier of my mahogany serving table. Brig must be hoping to keep some of my—well, Alicia Domander's and Peshy's—stolen antiques for himself. I brooded on a plan to restore rightful ownership, meaning mine.

'Bad news, Brig?' I asked, swallowing my anger.

His face was grim. 'Purdey's the gunsmith has been taken over by a French firm. Guess what comes next.' When I shook my head, 'They're going to increase production, from sixty to eighty shotguns a year! Bounders, what?'

'As long as they keep it going, who cares?' I hate huntin', shootin', fishin', all those sporting

319

massacres. The implements are sometimes beautiful, but my experience is that carnage reduces merriment. Ancient gunsmiths' artefacts, like Purdey's weapons, are an instance. Lovely in a glass case, horrible in action.

'Standards, Lovejoy!' He was puce. 'Good God, man, they're not tins of beans!'

'What's this show?' I asked for diversion. Maud rolled her eyes in exasperation.

'Sandy's doing it,' Brig told me evenly. I almost spluttered. If he deplored Quaker, what on earth did he think of Sandy and Mel?

'Sandy's such a dear,' Maud said, smiling. 'His show's secret! Isn't he the one for surprises!'

Knowing Sandy, it would be a mad frolic, himself the centre of attention, embarrassment the main ingredient.

'What's it in aid of?' Like fowl pest viruses, charities abound in East Anglia. Like antiques auctions, too. I've never met an honest one of either yet.

Brig said smoothly, 'It's a London thing, Lovejoy. Let's hope it goes well for all our sakes.'

'Wotcher, Lovejoy.'

In wheeled Quaker with that electric hum. I said hello and was me taking Maud out okay.

'As long as you drive carefully!' We all fell about at the drollery, because the Quay Theatre was only a couple of hundred paces along the riverbank. You can walk the towpath to the side entrance. 'Did you hear about Morgan Motors?' His eyes shone. 'I'm driving their Formula One racer at Silverstone!'

'Brilliant, mate! Congratulations!'

This extra lunacy made me wax lyrical, saying

320

how marvellous but those risky hairpin bends and watch out for that Finland geezer who's champion. Quaker answered with axle ratios and drag coefficients. The brigadier kept a stiff upper lip throughout this nonsense but showed his screaming exasperation at his barmy son-in-law by rudely putting the telly back on to watch his bouncing nags.

'Have you been all right, Lovejoy?' Quaker asked. 'I heard you were in that accident, Timothy Giverill on the bypass.'

'Not in. Just nearby.'

'Lucky you.' He beamed. 'You're lodging his missus?'

Maud's attention came on me like a laser. I said, 'She'll be gone as soon as her relatives get organized.'

'And Tinker. Okay, is he?'

'Fine.' I thought, what *is* this? Blokes don't say such things. Keeping useless conversations going is women's talk, how's Jimmy's leg and did Constance's dance shoes prove right and all that. Quaker had never talked like this before.

'And your Mortimer. He in good health?'

'Who?' I tried to be casual, but gave in. 'Fine, last I saw.'

'Good. And little Henry? It *is* Henry and Eleanor who you're so fond of?'

'Fine, ta.'

'Good, Lovejoy. Pleased to hear it. No, Maud, I'll not have a drink.' She hadn't offered him one. He patted his belly. 'I've to watch the weight. No Schumacher octane tricks on us Morgan drivers!' And out he whirred, waving.

'Cheers, Quake,' I called after him, wondering

what that was all about.

Brig switched the TV off. Still looking for somewhere to put my glass down, I noticed something odd. The Victorian fede ring had vanished. I almost gaped but had the sense to simply tell Maud ta and pass her the drink like I was surfeited.

'Tell me about Mrs Giverill, Lovejoy. You asked her to stay?'

'Actually at a neighbour's, except during the day.' The lie got me out of it. 'She's still poorly from the crash, goes to out-patients.'

'Poor thing,' Maud said with that mix of sympathy and satisfaction that speaks volumes, while I wondered if I was the only one who'd not solved the Case of the Vanishing Ring.

Quaker hadn't been near it. I hadn't touched it. Maud was on the wrong side. The brigadier hadn't got out of his chair. Therefore . . . My mind found a fraction of explanation with relief, for who was the swiftest, slinkiest arch-thief in the kingdom? Who moreover was small and stealthy, and might creep in unnoticed on all four paws? No wonder Brig knew all about the antiques Alicia Domander had stashed for me at Eleanor's. Therefore Alicia and Peshy were here. And Brig and Alicia were Just Good Friends.

'What time tomorrow?'

Maud coloured slightly, deception now. 'It starts at seven-thirty, so just before that?'

'Right.' I watched her go.

'We'll have time for a gin and tonic first, Lovejoy,' Brig said.

'Maud might like to go somewhere else.' Me, testing the water.

322

Brig appraised me. 'Lovejoy. Your special talent is a matter of survival.'

'Whose?' The disappearing ring hadn't come back.

'Mine.' He spoke with the weight of years.

'I can't believe that.' I was shot by his glance. 'Not like you say it.'

'You think I'm immune?'

'No. But look at what I do.' I shrugged, made sure Maud hadn't reappeared, Quaker not lurking. 'Antiques is a grubby trade. Rooting through people's cast-offs. Rust and dust, to earn a crust.' I told him about Marjorie, queen of the rubbish dumps. 'She's our only grubber with style. I have no style at all. I scrape along by cadging. You said so yourself.'

'That's because you're stupid, Lovejoy.'

'Eh?' I said, narked. Even shame has its pride. Except the trouble with shame is that it's indivisible. It has no components, doesn't arrive in bits. And it has only one speed, flat out and total. Shame overwhelms you.

He leaned forward, eyes piercing. 'You could be a multi-billionaire. Why? Because you can divvy a single genuine antique among scores of lookalikes.'

He kept his voice down. A bloke like him, military background, would be aware of any bugging devices.

'It's not as easy as that.'

'You mean you're weak, Lovejoy. You give your divvy skill away to grope some bint. Or because you're sorry for a friend. Or to protect your by-blow Mortimer.' He stared me down. 'In my book that's utter stupidity. Well, those days are ended, Lovejoy. You are now subject to discipline.'

323

'Who says?'

'I do. Until further notice.' He added, not without a hint of regret, 'Everybody agrees.'

So I was enslaved for ever and ever? 'What if I refuse?'

'You will . . .' He searched for the right phrase, 'Be put down.'

Like a vet puts down sick cats? I gulped. He smiled, seeing cowardice.

'There is a positive side, Lovejoy. You will earn the undying gratitude of me and all my ilk.'

It didn't sound much. I'd got along pretty well without it so far. My expression must have shown because he leaned forward, keen to explain.

'Reluctance is all very well, Lovejoy.' He said it like my teachers used the phrase. When people say something's all very well they mean its opposite. 'You fail to understand the plight of my class.'

Here we go, I thought. His *class*? There's no such thing any longer. I used to know an old Polish soak who was mystified that one of our royal princes had failed some college examination. 'It could never happen anywhere else,' he said over and over in bafflement. I couldn't see why he was thunderstruck. 'Lazy little sod should have studied harder,' I'd told him in puzzlement. It was some time before it got through. Other countries weigh breeding with advantage. Middle Eastern professors' sons get an extra twelve per cent free marks in exams. But here, that's all back in thc Dark Ages except in romance stories. We've simply exchanged class for robber barons in council offices and government.

'There's no such thing any longer, Brig,' I said straight out. 'Class has been replaced by jacks-in-office with inflated pensions. We serfs get ballocked just the same.'

'Your . . . *sort* would think so.' He came near to a sneer. 'You have the arrogance of ignorance. Who keeps this world going, Lovejoy? Commerce, merchants, investors. People like me. We keep order, protect the lazy and indigent—fools like you, Lovejoy. Accept it.'

I already knew where his argument was leading. He too was a Name, a heavy investor in Lloyd's. His mob—okay, his clarrrsss—had gone broke because their chits were being called in. He and his pals were looking for a new profitable source of promissory notes, and they'd found me. I was to rescue them. They would stump up with the money gusher they'd get from antiques.

Maud was a carrot, and carrots didn't come any lovelier. My survival was another. Wealth—soon, I was sure, he would promise me a fortune—was a third. Other benefits? Possibly superb educations for Mortimer, Henry, Uncle Tom Cobley and whoever I favoured. The thought suddenly occurred: wasn't I suddenly important? Brig and his cronies evidently thought so. Except, who'd topped Vestry? And Bernicka?

What I felt at that moment was contempt. Brig had become a Name in order to reap easy profits year upon year. That's what insurance is. It's also why I don't trust it, and always tell folk never to insure. Now, the brigadier had to pay up. He didn't like it. So he wanted out, thought it unfair. The honourable thing would have been to simply keep his promise. Take the money in the good years, pay up in the bad.

'Play the game, Lovejoy. You'll be in clover.'

What he meant was, disobey and I was for it.

'Ta for the drink, Brig,' I said meekly. I'd not even tasted the damned thing. 'I'll do as you say. But . . .'

'Quaker?' He smiled. I was looking at a firing squad. 'He's just a clerk, Lovejoy. He will agree. Every step of the way.'

I left him watching his nags on the screen. *Step*, see? A jest, Quaker being in a wheelchair. Some joke to do with class, I expect.

*   *   *

If you're like me, you get dispirited. I made it as far as the Donkey and Buskin, where I stopped for pie and mash. I didn't begrudge the brigadier his authority—he'd doubtless sweated in the jungles or wherever in defence of the realm. He was entitled to peace in his advancing years.

Making me team up with his Maud? With *married* Maud? I felt shanghaied, to save his skin. I'd be under his thumb. That was too much. But he seemed all-powerful. No way out for the likes of me.

I must have been there, sunk in despond, for the best part of an hour, before I realized somebody was standing a yard away. It was the hulk from the Countess's Antiques Emporiana.

'Come wiv me, mate,' he growled.

The motor must have been a converted hearse. The Countess reclined on cushions inside, watching a television. The *Antiques Roadshow* was on, as drilled and rehearsed as ever. She smiled, crooked her finger. I felt my heart yearn.

'Drink, Lovejoy?' Her hand extended with a

326

clang of gold. She'd had diamonds set in her front teeth since I'd seen her last. The perfume was overpowering. Her cosmetics were trowelled on. Beautiful. That's taste.

'No, ta.'

'Lovejoy, would you help me?'

Time for defiance, rebellion against all these tyrants.

'Yes, Countess,' I said faintly. 'Anything.'

'Soon, I'll want you to do something . . . really special. Divvy some antiques that may or may not exactly belong to me.'

'I see.' My voice went hard to manage.

'Would you? No matter whose they were?'

Like Brig's syndicate? I thought it, but did not say.

'Yes, Countess.' Me, the hardliner.

'And could I depend on you for full . . . satisfaction?'

Three swallows later, I croaked, 'Yes, Countess.'

She squeezed my thigh. 'Then I'll let you go. For the moment.' She blew me a kiss. I sat transfixed, a hare in her headlights.

'When can I see you, Countess?'

'Later. Until then, Lovejoy.'

'Thank you,' I said like I'd received the most generous largesse, and got out. The motor drifted off down the road. I gazed admiringly after it, thinking that there went real class, not the brigadier's old-school attitudes. I caught the bus.

Where the hell was Tinker? Time was rushing to the meeting. I wanted at least one ally, and apart from Alicia Domander I'd no real hope of anybody who'd take my side. And now even she was joined at the hip to the brigadier.

327

CHAPTER THIRTY-FIVE

Odd what things fascinate people.

There's an American university offering millions, to anyone who can solve any unsolved mathematical problem. One is this: why do buses come in threes? No good telling them the old Cockney's joke: buses only come in convoys so they don't get torpedoed, ha-ha. That won't earn you the money. Another is this: why is it harder to discover a solution than have it explained? Seems simple to me, but brainboxes say no. If you can write down the mathematical proof, post it off. Honest, they'll send you millions. They think numbers are reasonable.

Others work with equal devotion doing wrong. It's sad, bad news. In antiques there's the doc job. (This is where you go into hospital, then antique dealers raid your house. And take everything.) If it happens to patients admitted to the same hospital then the crooked informant will be somebody in Reception who takes your details down. She tells her criminals the addresses of patients who are in for lengthy treatments . . . The plod are worse than useless. Ask the police to protect your house while you have your hip done, they'll simply go back to their snooker halls which, locals here joke, never get robbed. The box job's another version, when crooks strip your Aunt Agatha's house while you're at her funeral. (That's easier, needs no accessory other than the obituary columns.)

It was glimpsing Paul and his birds—still collecting for the hospice in the shopping

328

precinct—that made me remember somebody he'd mentioned. I crossed over, keeping a weather eye on his latest, an irritable sparrow the size of a sack.

'Wotcher, Paul. Okay to ask?'

He smiled, said hello. He was allowing a little girl to stroke a bird with white feathers. It looked a real gangster.

'That auctioneer you mentioned. Remember? He chandeliered me once, and there was that fuss. He used to stand help you collecting.'

To chandelier is when an auctioneer takes fake bids instead of from some legitimate punter. Auctioneers are always at it. I owed him.

He thought a minute, saying, 'Ta, missus,' every time somebody clanked a coin into his tin. Then, 'Nice bloke. Still lives in Dragonsdale. Lanny Langley-Willes. Big twitcher.'

He told me the address. I had the good manners to ask Paul about his missus. His face clouded.

'She gives her time to Aspirin, Lovejoy.' He glanced about, made sure no children could hear. 'I think it's the end for us, really. Pity.'

What can you say? 'Sorry, mate.'

He smiled bravely on, telling bystanders of his birds' evil predatory habits, letting them stroke their feathers. Some folk are just kindly made, and act holy all their lives. Other people, I've heard, aren't.

*　　　*　　　*

Money, like lawyers, absolves the killer. Enough money could beatify Stalin. It's a feature of civilizations. Countries in the throes of revolution do without the middlemen, go straight for the gun or famine. In it all, there stands the squeeze.

Squeeze is the old China Coast word for illicit money. You want a new dress design *before* the catwalk show? Easy. You pay squeeze to the guards, who let you in after nightfall so you can snap it and your seamstress run it up overnight. You want to leak that secret government report on Walsall's homeless? Slip squeeze to the printers, and behold a copy comes under your door! You want your handsome bachelor boss's private curriculum vitae? Why, a little squeeze paid to Elsie who does his dinners and, surprise surprise, his CV's on your desk! So now you can accidentally bump into him, all glammed up . . . and so on.

The hallmark of the squeeze? Nobody knows anything afterwards. When police hunt that somebody who stole those secret dress designs before the London Fashion Show, or filched that White Paper on the homeless, or let slip where your eligible boss went fishing, nobody knows anything. It's the old 'What, moi?' business, with the wide-eyed stare. Innocence rules.

It's everywhere. But mostly in auctions.

Think of the benefits. Suppose you knew the names and addresses of all the people who sent stuff in to an auction. You could casually meet them, then it's, 'Good heavens! I've just been looking for a piece of pure white-paste brilliant glazed Derby porcelain! My beloved sister collects post-1770s Derby ware! And you've actually sent it in to be auctioned? You poor thing. Auctioneers rook you, you know.' And quickly move on to, 'Look. Why don't I make you an offer? By the way, isn't your hair lovely! I've always admired women who wear blue / lemon / pink . . .' etc, etc.

Not only that, you could steal desirable items before viewing day if you get the catalogue early enough. Theft is always done for a flat fee, currently fifty zlotniks an item, unless there's something special about the antique. Incidentally, your hired thief will expect at least one item's fee as a tip if he does the job well. It's polite. Your thieves will then spread the word that you're a decent wallet to work for. Add one tip extra for every five antiques they steal. So if you want, say, ten antiques stolen from an auctioneer's, pay the thief ten times fifty zlotniks plus fifty times two— total six hundred for the transaction. They pay their own transport. Don't do it for them—you don't want to be implicated in any shocking robbery, do you? You're honest! And don't pay until you receive the stolen goods.

Er, I mean I *think* that's probably how it's fixed.

*   *   *

James Langley-Willes, nickname Lanny, once did me down. He was on the hammer in a famed Bond Street auction. I'd made a legitimate bid for a late eighteenth-century lady's work table. It was exquisite, slender legs with side drawers and a shelf (tier, dealers call this) low down between the legs. What I liked though was the sliding frame on its back legs. Lift, and a pleated silk screen rose to keep the heat of the lady's coal fire, so keeping her complexion pale and interesting. (This screen always suggests eighteenth century.) I'd raised four loans, two of which I would be compelled to actually pay off, just to buy this beautiful satinwood piece.

331

Lanny saw my final bid. *And ignored it!* Knocked the antique down to a lady friend.

White-hot with rage, I exacted revenge. It took me a week but was worth it. I hired Shammer—rhymes with hammer, a man of many voices—to contact Lanny and get him to sell a photocopy of the handwritten catalogue, for a high fee. It went like clockwork. Shammer gave me the catalogue that day. I went to see Mr Langley-Willes with a video showing him leaving the photocopy in a taxi for Shammer. And paying the squeeze. Lovely camera work by Yvette. She keeps the Thames toll bridge at Dartford.

He'd actually blubbered, begged, invoked his children—all at good schools—and his lovely wife who'd just started a costume-hire shop. Then, all but on his knees, he said something that placed his entire fate in my hands.

'Please, Lovejoy. Honest to God. I'll do anything. Think of the birds.'

'No go, Lanny.' Birds?

'Then it's suicide,' he said, broken.

'Eh?' I was startled. He really did look suddenly resolute, firm of purpose. Suicide, for birds? 'Look, mate . . .'

'No, Lovejoy.' Steadfastly he faced the charging hordes of Omdurman. 'You don't understand. I'm a four hundred.'

'Four hundred what?'

'A member of the Four Hundred Club.' Quietly he explained.

He loved birds. I said so did I. Only, women, migrating wrens, what?

'No, Lovejoy. Flying birds.'

Only then did I notice that his walls were

covered with photographs of our feathered friends. Hadn't even pictures of his family. A nutter.

'I'm what irresponsible people call a twitcher, Lovejoy.' He gave a you-rabble-don't-understand smile. 'Only those who record over four hundred different species are true birders.' A sad noble smile played around his lips, say goodbye to the old school, Carruthers. 'I was hoping to reach five hundred.'

'Different birds?'

God, that seemed easy. I'd seen thousands, millions. Maybe I'd been a champion birder for years and hadn't known. I sometimes have thirty birds at a time in my overgrown garden.

I'd heard of these twitchers, people who're daft on bird watching. I knew one lady who—you won't believe this—actually sold a Newcastle Light Baluster drinking glass, stipple engraved with a Dutch ship. It had four knops—bulges in the stem—and the Dutch engraver's initials were actually engraved on the pontil stub underneath the glass's foot. Rare, genuine antique. And why did the loon sell it? To buy a camera, so she could skulk in our sea marshes and photo swallows wading in the mud. Is that lunatic, or what?

'No, Lovejoy. Different species. Any fool can see a thousand birds any day of the week.'

Which narked me even more, because my birds are high quality. I've got some that sit on my shoulder for cheese, and I'll bet he hadn't. To stop him leaping off his balcony, seeing he looked so adamant, I went helpful.

'Look, Lanny. I'll bring details of some rare birds. You'll have your five hundred sparrows before Friday.'

333

He rose, his expression a pale, aghast mask.

'*Falsify?* You scoundrel!' He gave me a tirade of passionate denunciation.

Well, I gaped. Can you get the logic? Here was the trusted scion of famous London auctions—I won't mention which because Sotheby's and Christie's insist on anonymity—who'd ripped everybody off. Who now swoons because I suggest pretending that he's seen a robin. Do you believe some people?

He ranted on so much his missus came in. She left with the wife's resigned exasperation when she saw he was only on about his hobby.

The name for those accursed fraudsters who exaggerate the number of species that they falsely claim to have spotted? A stringer.

'There is no more odious wretch, Lovejoy. Detestable. Beneath contempt. Hanging's too good for them.'

Well, hardly. It was strange to see Lanny, with degrees all round the envelope, ready to face firing squads merely because his fellow twitchers might believe he'd spun a tale about some fledgling.

'It took me ten years, Lovejoy. I reached my four hundredth last Martinmas.' His eyes filled. 'The happiest day of my life. I was stuck two months on 399. I wanted to sell the wife's car last year to go to see a black-browed albatross, but she wouldn't give it up.'

'Selfish cow,' I joked, jollying him along.

He agreed, to my astonishment. 'Yes, she is. The Orkneys is a hell of a way.'

This was Lanny, famed auctioneer. To pay for my silence he gave me my expenses and saw that my next bid got preference three auction days running, until some of the lads began to mutter. I'd not seen him since. If anybody would know what big money was washing around, it would be Lanny. I decided it was time I renewed my interest in birdwatching. I might see something unexpected. You never know.

*   *   *

It was getting dark when I bowled up at Lanny Langley-Willes's house in Dragonsdale. Cars filled the drive. I went round to the rear, and walked into a group of enthusiasts. They all wore working overalls. Lanny's missus was serving roast something. The wine was out, Lanny the laughing host talking birds. Beyond, the acreage showed a miniature railway line, a small engine, a little carousel with fairy lights. Building a fairground?

'Here's Lovejoy!' he called, seeing me. 'Trust him to arrive at dinner break!'

I received nods and hellos. I accepted a glass of red wine that tasted of tannin. I praised it like you have to. Everybody was pleased at my judgement.

'We're excluding a 400 Club member, Lovejoy,' Lanny explained, his eyes warning me about divulging past secrets.

Vaguely I remembered that you got shot for reporting the wrong pigeons in Norfolk's Cley-next-the-Sea. 'Er, it's about that, Lanny.'

'You're not old enough to be a nancy, mate, are you?' some old geezer asked.

He sounded friendly enough, but I stepped forward to clock him one. Lanny intervened just in time.

'No, Lovejoy's an antique dealer, not a birder.'

335

He led me aside, chuckling. 'A nancy isn't a deviant, Lovejoy. It's one of the original birders. Nancy's Caff in Cley. It's where modern birdwatching started. We all used the caff's telephone. Now we use websited pagers.'

'Oh, good.' I made sure we were out of earshot of the others. 'Look, Lanny. Are you into insurance? Lloyd's and all that?'

'No.' His face clouded. 'I know some who are. Fingers burned lately.'

'And the auction houses?'

He sat on a low stone wall that fringed his herb garden, and lit a cigarette from a small sessile lantern.

'The American Justice Department's been gunning for the Big Two, Sotheby's and Christie's. The journals were full of it. Price fixing. Christie's decided to turn what here would be called Queen's Evidence. Asking immunity for blowing the gaff. Boss execs and chairmen resigned everywhere, to please the Yank Feds.'

'It's happened before, though?'

'Resignations? Don't you remember? Christie's chairman took a dive. Claimed those Impressionist paintings were sold when you-know-what.'

The Impressionist paintings weren't sold at all, so the market price was kept artificially high. Greed is what auctioneers' dreams are made of.

'And your pals?' I indicated his group, now passing bird photos around in the lantern light while Lanny's missus clucked, wanting them to scoff their grub.

'Only birders, Lovejoy. Promise.' He sounded offended. 'Heaven's sakes, one of them actually knew Emmett!'

'A copper?' I'd not heard the name before.

'He was the original twitcher—shook so much from cold and exhaustion when chasing a rare bird on his moped that he virtually had twitching seizures. Hence the nickname. Above suspicion, of course.'

So they were saints.

'Right. Tell your mates tara, Lanny. And your missus.' I paused. 'Lanny? If you hear anything about insurance defaults, let me know, eh?'

'Defaults?' His face clouded. 'I suppose you mean that consular man. Poor chap. He's in for everything. Friend of the brigadier. Has some relative locally. He formed an insurance syndicate of her friends.'

'Consular chap?'

'American. Divorced. Sommon was involved in some political scandal. That randy president's political party. Invested over his head. But, Lovejoy,' this epitome of honesty said in all seriousness, 'we shouldn't listen to vile rumour.'

'True, Lanny.' A thought occurred. 'Where are you getting the money to build this fancy fairground?' It was hell of a size, for a private garden.

'This?' He became proud. 'Our birders are chipping in. It's for the local infant school. When it's finished I'll assign that half of my plot to them in perpetuity. Think they'll like the engine? It's a model of an old Britannia.'

'Beautiful.'

'The wife approves,' he added, sighing. 'Pity she's not a birder. Did I ever tell you she wouldn't sell her car so I could go and see a black-browed albatross?'

'Well, nobody's perfect. Tara, Lanny.'

I left then, only realizing I still carried his glass when I reached the taxi rank. I swigged it dry, looked at it in the taxi's headlights. Modern. So I lobbed it into a nearby dustbin and went home. Fewer suspects now, thank God. I was down to a few thousand, if Lanny could be trusted.

CHAPTER THIRTY-SIX

One thing I've always got wrong is getting ready to go out. I once drove to a broadcast in Norwich in battered old slippers and didn't notice I'd no shoes on. Gran used to say I did it for attention. I think it's because I'm secretly worried sick.

This night I was different. Timothy's Florence had left me a note saying she'd gone to see the lawyer about her bankruptcy, ending it *With love*. No woman around when you need one, just good wishes.

Despite this, I spruced up. I found a tie and did my shoes with spit. I don't buy polish because it gets used up. Then I creased my trouser legs with two bricks and a steaming kettle. I tried to trim my frayed shirt cuffs with a razor blade but they finished up horrible so I turned them under with sticking plaster. I can never wash a shirt collar. After the first day, a black rim is simply there for life. Belle four years ago was the last one who could do it, get shirts clean I mean. She was lovely. Those ten Belle Days she turned me out like Lord Fauntleroy. It didn't last. She got exasperated, said I drove her mad, and went to Manchester to

338

become a concert cellist. She missed her vocation, could have run a lovely laundry (joke).

I did my teeth using plant pith, lots of it in my jungle. It's cheaper and cleaner than toothbrushes. Anyway, Paul Blondel the birdman says that waste toothbrushes choke seabirds in the Pacific, so I was doing my bit. Shaving's always a pest, razor blades so expensive. I did the old soldier's razor trick of honing a rusty blade by running it round inside a glass. I washed my one hanky and dried it on the kettle. I inspected my reflection in my plate. Gorgeous. I looked dynamite.

One worrying thing was Maud. Did she share Brig's dark intentions, that her husband Quaker should get the push and I take his place? She hadn't said anything. These mating games are always beyond me. Whatever happens between men and women is simply a fluke. Love, like family, is a lottery. I knew a bonny lady called Kitty, who married her bloke—a gambler and a thief—convinced she could reform him. Within a month she came a-weeping, asking me 'to set him up in antiques', like it was lending him a book. She went berserk when I said he wouldn't last a millisec. Later, he defaulted on his gambling debts, so the lads tailored him for a motorway robbery he hadn't done. He's currently doing a ten-year stretch. Mysteriously, his missus instantly flowered in his absence. Without a penny to her name, she has acquired a sports and leisure club in Brightlingsea. See? Luck.

Such thoughts warning me of possible mishaps, I smiled a glittering smile at my reflection, and went to meet Maud, the brigadier, Quaker, and any combination of others. I'd perhaps find out who his syndicate was. If Quaker kept out of the way, at least I'd maybe have Maud's company for a clandestine while. You never know. I caught the bus, shocked that my palms were damp. Shakily I dropped coins everywhere as I paid my fare, making passengers smile and raise who-is-this-oaf eyebrows. I said sorry, sorry, and stared at the shadows among the countryside's trees.

*   *   *

It was frankly dusk when I walked through the park among the Quay Theatre crowd. The rain had mercifully held off. The people were colourful— not as well turned out as me, I told myself jauntily. Mrs Thomasina Quayle was there in a smart evening dress contentedly chatting with Susanne Eggers and the mayor on the balcony. It overhung the water, illuminated with candles and flickering lamps. Copacetic, Consul Sommon would probably have said in American slang. He was there. I passed Taylor Eggers parking his motor. He waved. I waved back.

Music was playing. Coloured lights strung in the water. Boats glided under torches. Romance was in the air. A bonfire flickered, making amber fronds of the riverbank trees. One pity was the aroma of hot-dog stalls. First whiff, superbly alluring. When you get close, the stink is charred flesh. Nauseous. Like some auctions and lovers' trysts, entrancing at a distance then frightening close to. Tonight, though, no omens allowed. I'd get to the bottom of the whole thing.

'Evening, Lovejoy.'

'Hello, Olive.'

'Who's your lady for this gala evening?'

'You, if Lady Luck's kind.'

Very fetching, in slab Art Deco and a floral hat. 'Perhaps we can meet? I must see you.'

'Ta, love.'

And on I went, Burlington Bertie. I glimpsed her turning into the path of Taylor Eggers. Why did she want to renew acquaintance with him, when he'd bribed her with that duff Light Brown Reject pendant? Or was she going for his ankles? Or had she simply forgotten? Except, what woman ever forgets how she was slighted, or who by?

'Well, well,' said the Serious Fraud Officer, Petra Deighnson. 'Do I espy Lovejoy?'

She wore cobalt blue. I never really like trouser suits. Women don't look quite as fetching as they're supposed, though some think severe-cut slacks the height of femininity.

'You plod, always asking my help. Yes, I'm me.'

'Know who the original Police Constable Plod was?' She fell in, taking my arm, amiability itself. 'They say he was PC Rone in Studland. Isn't it Dorsetshire? Enid Blyton called him that in her children's stories.'

'SFO research, eh?'

She slowed me, smiling. 'Staying for the syndicate meeting afterwards?'

'Er . . .'

'I was hoping you'll be doing the antiques, Lovejoy.'

She indicated the stands that had been erected over the water. Everybody was there. Big Frank with his next spouse. Ferd and his Norma, both especially pally with the mayor. Peggy Price and Cromwell—he in full Puritan fig with tall white

341

collar and sombre black—and, surprising me, Ginny without Ox her driver-helper, though he'd be sure to be among the thickening crowds.

Petra Deighnson whispered confidingly as the crowd ooohed at fireworks hitting the darkening sky, 'I've seen the antiques' bills of sale. All legit, Lovejoy. Repro or genuine, they're honest.'

For a second I thought I caught sight of Mortimer, but it must have been my imagination.

'Legit? Honest genuine repro? You've a right porridge of words, missus.'

Shaking her off I said so-long and pressed through the crowd.

There's a pool that once was a wide water catchment into which the river flows. On the highest part of the bankside stands the Quay Theatre. It was once a mill. Barges and pleasure boats go by in summer. It looks really bonny with lanterns, streamers, floating lights and tableaux at carnival times. I'd spoken on its stage about antiques, back when I was trustworthy. I don't get asked now. I noticed Tramway Adenath's huge van—the flower gardener who was going to stab me with a dibble just because I'd ruined his garden centre, undermined his life campaign to restore Nature in a poisoned world. Selfish sod. He was carrying plants up the wooden staircase. His missus, the worldly Merry, was hauling greenery. Still together, then.

'He's coming! He's coming!' people exclaimed.

'No prizes for guessing who, Lovejoy,' Maud said, slipping her arm through mine. I was in vogue tonight. 'Sandy's refrain. Hear it?'

Through the gloam came the strains of Handel's *Water Music*. Cameras flashed leaving our retinas unusable. My vision cleared. A golden barge glided upstream, shaped like an enormous swan, with Sandy in flowing golden sheets in the prow. I felt really embarrassed. Even for him this was ridiculous. All around people were applauding.

'How wonderful! Look!' Maud pulled me so we could see this shambles better. 'Isn't Sandy brilliant?'

Shimmering sparklers made waterfalls on the surface. Lights rippled along the bulwarks, spotlights playing. Sandy stood in dramatic pose, his features set into an expression he probably thought regal. He looked a right prune. I said so. Maud was irritated and slapped at my arm.

'Don't be a spoilsport, Lovejoy! He's being Queen Midas!'

Queen Midas? Wasn't Midas the king of Phrygia? Who finished up wearing donkey's ears?

The golden swan was rowed by so-say slaves, except even among the crowd I could hear the electric motor that powered the barge. Nymphs in flowing robes hung gracefully in the rigging, showering the spectators with golden petals as the monstrosity floated to the Quay. The applause was deafening. Sandy would have loudspeakers supplementing the clapping. It would be just like him.

'What's it all in aid of?'

She gazed at me in amazement.

'The award, Lovejoy! The refunding of the town's syndicate!'

Unease took me. I tried to sound nonchalant. 'What syndicate?'

'Our town's investors, Lovejoy! It's been in all the papers!'

Her eyes shone with pure admiration. Not for me, for Sandy. But how could he fund anything? It must be a scam based on promises. That old one.

The great barge, with Sandy in his daft heroic pose above the colossal swan's beak, searchlights playing on him, serenely neared the theatre. People were running from across the car park, desperate not to miss the spectacle.

Slaves, skin oiled to shine in the lantern light, hauled on ropes. A line of chanting slavettes, flaming torches held aloft, approached to welcome the hero. All wore flowing silver dresses, their faces and arms painted silver, quite macabre. Jeremiah Clark's *Trumpet Voluntary* crashed out, deafening us as an extending staircase rose from the swan's neck. Sandy stepped onto the stairway, gesturing majestically to the crowds beneath. The music changed to *HMS Pinafore*. Sandy was carried, still in his silly stance, through the dark night air above us to the balcony. Some loons, doubtless paid by the indefatigable Mel, started up a chant, 'Sandy! Sandy!' The crowd took it up, drowning out the music.

Sandy ascended—not too emotive a word— giving queenly gestures, tears of exaltation running down his gilded cheeks. He would describe this for ever now, in pubs all over East Anglia: 'Did you see me . . . ?' He'd send photographs to us all, then try to charge us for them when we'd chucked them away.

'Nobody else could perform like this, Lovejoy!'

Maud's eyes glistened with moisture, adoring it. I kept looking for familiar faces. My erstwhile team of actors arrived, Tina leading them into the theatre. Jules was one. Conquistadores, on their way to new lands. I thought, once an actor, always.

On the balcony, the mayor—can you believe bloody politicians?—laid a golden laurel wreath on Sandy's brow. The background music burst into the Hallelujah Chorus from the *Messiah*. Lot of Handel about tonight, him and Gilbert and Sullivan busily adding to Sandy's majesty.

'Ladies and gentlemen!' the mayor shouted. 'Your saviour and mine, Sandy . . .'

Pandemonium. Ecstasy, the elation of people whose jobs were spared and wages secure. People all about shook hands and hugged. I bet they wouldn't give each other time of day on the street in the morning, but tonight was gala time. Mel—he must have run up the theatre stairs—held Sandy's hand aloft, champion boxer pose. Sandy bowed to the multitudes—see? Loaves-and-fishes talk gets even the most cynical after a bit. The crowd roared. I saw Tex the Mighty Hex like a beaming Alp, head above the crowd.

'He could finish up emperor,' I told Maud.

'Oh, stop it!' she cried. 'Enter the spirit of the thing! Come on. We'll be late.' Impatiently she pulled me through the throng.

'Lovejoy?' Mrs Domander took my other arm. She held Peshy. It looked even more smug than usual, but I noticed it darted nervous glances at the sky as more fireworks went off. 'Could I sit with you?'

'Ta for the offer but I've to see the brigadier and Quaker.'

Her lower lip trembled a moment, though it could have been a Shimmering Cascade that just then made silver firefalls from the theatre windows.

'Only, I need to hand over your notes from the

345

antiques sweep. Remember?'

Notes? We kept no notes. 'Did you get your motor back from Alanna?'

'Tinker brought it round.' Her mongrel snarled at me, not an all-time first. When did I ever do what it wanted?

'Good, love. Well, maybe tomorrow, eh?' I bussed her, carefully avoiding her wolfhound, and moved on.

'She's a pest, Lovejoy,' Maud said with satisfaction. We went towards the theatre with the crowd. 'You must watch her.'

Odd, though. I hadn't made any notes on our antiques sweep. Nor had she. And how had Tinker delivered her motor, when he'd no idea where she lived? Alicia was a wanderer. Local hotel owners give her a spare room, night and night about. It's pure chance where she kips. You have to leave her messages in the wall of Cramper Evans' ruined chapel. After the pubs close she calls on Cramper to find out which bedroom she'll lodge in, giving a new meaning to the term No Fixed Abode. The thought almost made me look back, but Maud urged me on.

'Look, Lovejoy! There's Quaker!'

I failed to see her husband. We reached the theatre foyer just as the commissionaires started to close the doors. Maud waved tickets. Others exclaimed in distress at being shut out. I felt smug: you poor inadequates are excluded, whereas I'm among the gentry. Satisfaction always quells sympathy.

'Where?'

'Gone on ahead,' Maud told me. One or two people said hello. Many more said hello to Maud.

346

She looked superb, radiant. I recognized the occasional face as we climbed the stairs, but Maud was the centre of attention.

'We have a balcony box, Lovejoy. We're not with the rest.'

New snobbery took hold and I went willingly. The auditorium was packed, newcomers filing in, a few discreet arguments starting up of the polite is-that-my-seat-madam kind. Clearly a festival scene made for rejoicing. Were these all investors? I heard glasses clinking, corks popping, laughter. The stage's red velvet curtain was glaringly lit. To each side, Tramway had placed potted white flowering almond trees, the sort that go red and look sore at the twig tips, like chapped fingers that need cream when you're little.

'Isn't this exciting?' Maud whispered, hugging my arm. She hadn't let go. I felt in chains, Lovejoy *in vincula*. 'This is what I've really been waiting for!'

'Who on earth went to all this trouble?'

Her smile dazzled. 'Why, me, silly!' she said, and my chest went cold.

The orchestra struck up, 'Three Little Maids From School Are We'. The curtains parted, and Sandy came on with Mel and, wrong guess, that toe-rag Dennis who'd tried to get the lads to hang me when this whole thing started. In gymslips, false pigtails, spectacles and blacked-out teeth, they sang the song doing hockey-stick actions. The crowd went wild. Maud fell about, thought it was a scream. I was trying to think, kept looking about the audience.

No sign of Alicia Domander or Peshy now, though Sep Verner was on the front row. The dignitaries were in expensive boxes, champagne flutes on the balcony rims. Where was Mrs Thomasina Quayle when I needed her? Instead I get Serious Fraud Officer Petra Deighnson across from us, smiling at the stage. Familiar faces everywhere, Jenny Blondel and her Aspirin, astonishingly with Paul the birdman. Wasn't he divorcing her?

Maud squeezed herself like women do when they're enjoying events.

'You'll not regret it, Lovejoy. I promise.'

'Will I not?' was the best I could do.

'We'll be happier than I've ever dared to hope, darling.'

Sandy's trio minced from the proscenium blowing kisses. Such hilarity. Usually the Quay Theatre is *Elektra* and one-voice Sanskrit versions of *The Cherry Orchard*.

The audience quietened. And on came Lanny Langley-Willes, another bad guess, smooth and wholly at ease with the world. Professional killers are. It's only amateur killers get the shakes. I saw Maud's eyes shining with rapture. It was a good night for her, everything coming just so. The house lights slowly dimmed and Lanny began to speak.

Like I say, you've got to admire class.

CHAPTER THIRTY-SEVEN

He spoke his introduction so calmly, with such accomplishment, that I almost came to share Maud's adoration. 'This is a celebration. Our backing syndicate is secure,' he began, immediately

348

raising his palms to quell the gratitude that rose from the audience. 'This gala night celebrates— let's not put too fine a point on it—*wealth*!'

The wave of admiration was too warm to be suppressed even by his grandiloquent gestures. The audience stood and cheered. Numbed, I thought, but this is East Anglia for Christ's sake. We don't *do* this kind of thing. This behaviour creates political coups, guerrilla warfare, bodies beside dusty roads. It simply doesn't happen here. Maud's eyes glistened. Everybody sat and rustled to stillness. Lanny's voice resumed quieter. He was good value, for a scam.

'I mean your wealth, the town's wealth. No!' It was a gunshot command for silence. The audience didn't move. 'Please listen.'

He stood in the spotlight, smart evening suit, tall, elegant, everything you'd want a leader to be.

'Our syndicate promised to underwrite your new developments—town centre, housing, leisure complex. Then.' He paused, voice mellifluous and falling an octave, and held it. 'Then the rumours began. People began to doubt. That the syndicate—*your* syndicate—was unable to stand by its commitment.' He sneered, holding attention, gazing round the auditorium.

'We are here tonight to renew our undertaking. We have a source of valuable antiques to back up every claim we ever have made.' His smile moved row by row. 'We present a short demonstration, more as entertainment than to convince. But you are bright enough to realize the consequences.'

'Isn't he wonderful?' Maud whispered. 'We were at school together!'

'Wonderful.'

349

'And to think Dad doesn't trust him!'

I looked at her in the gloaming thinking, eh? Lanny was going on, a master of timing. Doubtless all that bird watching.

'Four selected individuals—Tina is the leader—will face a range of items. They will each unerringly identify the priceless antiques from the fake. Now,' he smiled disarmingly, 'this could be a set-up. But you know the auction houses I'm associated with. I guarantee this little interlude is unflawed.

'Can I introduce Tina . . . ?'

Applause began, politely interested, as Tina led Wilhelmina, Larch the tree hugger, and Jules the ex-con on stage. They stood in line. The backdrop rose revealing an array of antiques on stands, on benches, maybe thirty or so in all. I felt one chime, a lone belling in my chest, from one direction but nothing much else. This scam was the goldie, the one deception that convinces when all else fails. So called from an old con trick that evolved back when people were easily hoodwinked. You'd show a seemingly gold statue, then allow the mark—the buyer you're tricking—to examine it, scrape off a sample for analysis. It's pure gold (of course). But it's only gold leaf, put there minutes before on the corner of the statue that you allowed the mark to touch, feel, use a microscope on.

'Look, love,' I whispered to Maud. 'I'll be back in a sec.'

'Now? Can't it wait?'

'I said I'd meet Florence. She's late.'

'Be sharp, then.'

Below, Lanny was describing the supposed antiques. His actors stayed gravely listening, occasionally glancing thoughtfully at the items. I

350

eeled out, hissing apologies like you do, and hurried down to the main entrance. The commissionaires were having a smoke, cigarettes cupped in fingers.

Tinker was nowhere. I whispered his name into the dark. Nothing. I'd throttle the idle old soak. I'd distinctly told him to be here. You can't depend on anybody. Okay, so I'd not paid him for a few months. Was that a reason to let me down?

'Good evening, Lovejoy.'

I jumped. 'Evening, Countess. Seen Tinker?'

'Yes.' She gave a throaty laugh. 'He had to leave.'

Her suited hulk who'd chucked me out of her Antiques Emporiana gave a snuffle of mirth. I could see their features only in the sheen of the theatre's foyer lights. Funny how still and quiet it was outside, when from inside there came the roaring of the audience. My actors, re-enacting my feeble scam with which I'd tried to please Susanne Eggers.

'Is Tinker okay?'

'Temporarily.' She moved. 'Come, Lovejoy. Stroll with me.'

'Countess, any other time—'

The hulk shoved me. Obediently I strolled. The Countess moved through a slice of silver light. She looked lovely. Other women would say she was too florid, tarty even. But what's wrong with tarty? Glamour's sensible when it's aimed in my direction. I call that real logic.

'Jules was mine once, Lovejoy.'

'I heard.'

'Like you, Lovejoy. Except, unlike you he leaped at my offer of . . . renewal.'

'I've had problems, Countess.'

She gave her throaty laugh. A bloke doesn't stand much chance. My resolve faded. 'Poor helpless Lovejoy. Your own scam is being used against you. You know that?'

'I'm guessing as I go.'

She sighed. 'It's my poor Russia. It always is poor Russia. You know, Lovejoy, Russia wounds herself. Tranquillity? Pshah! We Russians abhor it!'

'Look, er . . .'

'You know how to find tragedy? Follow the nearest Russian. With the instinct of a moth, he will dive into the flame with a cry of bliss.'

I'd heard her speak like this before. After we'd made smiles, she would become so morose that you became sad too. I found it hard to take. I knew her next line. No good explaining—

'—to the moth that it need only wait until morning, then it can enjoy all the light it desires. It simply seeks its catastrophic fate. All—'

'Moths are Russian?'

'You remember!' She gave a cry of delight.

'What do you want me for?'

'I want a little betrayal, Lovejoy. You and I will rescue a fragment of civilization from those barbarians!'

'Who?'

'Those in there,' she said with detestation. The hulk walked behind, feet going crunch crunch when we were on the greensward. Why did his steps go crunch? Mine didn't. The Countess's didn't. 'They will buy anything from those Muskovites. You know all Muskovites are oafs?'

'Not from St Petersburg?'

'Hah! You remembered!'

352

She turned. We were about two hundred yards along the riverbank, the theatre glowing like hot embers in the distance, lights reflecting in the water, the great gold swan barge still shimmering. The hulk stepped round us so he was behind.

'Moscow will sell anything. War loot. Rubbish. Dross from China. Among its shipments of garbage there will be some exquisite antiques. These they will sell without compunction. Icons. Furniture. Jewels. Porcelain. Holiness,' she added unexpectedly. 'The sanctity of generations, Lovejoy. And these idiots will buy them, to save their miserable skins.'

Wary of the hulk, I didn't heave a sigh of dismay. She wasn't speaking of merely one antique, or even of a trickle. She was talking of a tide, a great unstoppable flood. Out of control.

'Look, Countess. That syndicate has sources beyond imagination. The world is awash with money looking for a home—investments, antiques, securities. Russia has access to valuables. When unlimited money meets countless antiques, a deal is inevitable. That syndicate is nasty, so it's invincible.'

'Yes, Lovejoy.' She went calm. 'But we can *betray*.' Her face was in shadow as we began to retrace our steps towards the theatre. I could hear the smile in her voice. 'Our tactic!'

I can't believe these national characteristics. I once met a Yank who wasn't a millionaire. Unbelievable, but true.

'Got an idea how?'

'What were you and Tinker going to do, Lovejoy? Something truly pathetic, like try to upset the syndicate's first auction? Use your divvying talent to expose those infantile actors who're in there pretending they have the same unique gift?'

She made her explosive sound of scorn. It sounded an audible pout.

'Well, yes.' I was narked. 'It might have come off.'

'You think like a midget, Lovejoy! For true perfidy, you need my breeding, my genius.'

I'd thought I'd been really brainy, working out where the syndicate's first auctions would be held. They would do it in secret, of course, for a very specialized clientele of shady buyers. These things are easily arranged. They go on all the time, stolen stuff from country houses and auction rooms.

For something this big, though, all their items would have to be passed off as possibly tainted wartime loot, or antiques stolen from Asia Minor or India, the Persian Gulf states, the Far East, all those countries where embargoes had been placed on antiques. That would only be the start. Central and South America would come next within a twelvemonth, then West and Central African states would be denuded of their heritages. It was happening now, but disorganized. On the dripfeed, so to speak. This syndicate would establish regular channels.

She trilled a laugh. I wanted to see her face, her mouth. I always like to watch. Women have such mobile features, so expressive in laughter or dismay. And their eyes . . . What on earth was I thinking?

'You don't mean tell the Customs and Excise?'

'Silly!' I linked her arm through mine. 'I mean us! You and I! Not contemptible clerks.' Her old accent had come back to accompany her rage.

Contemp-teebell clerrr-kkess.

'Safely?'

She laughed. 'Safety is silly, Lovejoy. You know the Tsar's definition of safety? Safety is when you see the guns *before* they fire.'

Fat chance for me, then. I never even know what's happened afterwards.

'Who'll set it up?'

'You. Your skill is well known. Enough to be trusted by buyers.'

'Well, yes. If I know the buyers, and they know me.'

'I already have lists.'

The theatre music suddenly played. Doors opened sending huge swathes of light through the darkness. People spilled out onto balconies. Lights came on. Interval time, with celebration in the air. I could see the Countess's goon's silhouette. God, he was enormous. I was glad I hadn't made a run for it. Was I was better off taking the Countess's offer than trying to bubble the syndicate on my own? Maybe I'd save somebody's life. I'd not done too well so far.

'Right, Countess. Equal partners?'

Maybe I could start eating regularly, pay Tinker a fortnight's back wages.

She froze. There was enough light for me to see her face suddenly chill. 'Do not presume. I am nobility, Lovejoy. You are a serf.'

'Yes, Countess.'

Well, she was right, right? That we'd once been lovers wasn't to count. I heard a faint whirring sound. An electric motor? The river made a faint lapping sound. Doubtless some boat, perhaps a lucky lad drifting to bliss out there in the reedy

355

darkness, jammy sod. There was a series of soft susurruses among the bulrushes, the swift near-silent sort that you try to ignore but can't. Luckily the Countess hadn't noticed. It's always a bit embarrassing, others making love especially if you're with a bird. Dunno why. The velvety sounds stilled. The gentle whirring stopped. The lovers had clearly decided to stay there a while, switched off their engine. I didn't blame them.

The Countess had been explaining her fiscal policy, something about percentages. I dragged my attention back from passion.

'I shall apportion your share when the syndicate's brought down.'

'Who will you get to do the damage, Countess?' I asked humbly, as if I didn't know.

'There is a bandit, one Mr John Sheehan,' she said, cool. I warned myself off using that description in Big John's hearing. Or, indeed, anywhere on Planet Earth. 'My agent works for the syndicate. I placed him there very early. Almost, you could say, before the scam began. He is my contact with Mr Sheehan.'

Jules the actor? I thought but did not say. I vaguely wondered what might have happened if I'd not picked him at the audition. She'd have simply got a replacement. I'd only chosen him, I remembered with chagrin, from sympathy because he'd done porridge and was looking for a job. I must be transparent.

'What will you get out of this, Countess?'

'I shall not tolerate insolence. I am above such questions, Lovejoy.'

'Yes, Countess.'

Her amusement returned. 'However, since you

agree my demands, I reveal that I shall own one of those importing channels for myself.'

'I see.'

'It is not to be compromised by anyone.'

So I was to keep out of it while she made hay? Well, nothing ventured.

'Very well, Countess.' I was fed up with agreeing. 'Do I get Tinker back?'

'He is at the Marquis of Granby on North Hill.' The hulk's snuffle irritated me further. Her early hint that Tinker needed rescuing was a ruse. 'He is trinkink, Lovejoy. He was given money sufficient.'

'Thank you.' Thanking her for not marmalizing my barker? Pathetic.

'I shall let you know when we strike. Meanwhile, Lovejoy, join the celebrations. Maud is waiting. She is not for you. Such shoes, and that hair.'

'I think she's nice.'

She carolled laughter. 'You poor fool. You know nothing.' She sobered. 'Three weeks from now the Names will fall into bankruptcy when their illicit antiques import scheme fails. All their imports will be delivered to me. I shall celebrate.'

'What about the town, Countess?' I had some friends who lived in the area. They'd suffer. I didn't want her to bring the whole Russian mafia invading.

'Ah, you mean the developments, Lovejoy? The mall, the leisure, the housing?' She trilled. 'There *might* be other syndicates. They will take it over. As long as the terms are highly favourable. To me!'

'You've already worked it out.'

'Once I heard from your friend Quaker, that his father-in-law's syndicate—the one busily pretending in the theatre there—was close to ruin in Lloyd's insurance risks, of course I did.'

The theatre's two-minute bell sounded. The music was about to start celebrating the phoney success. She smiled, searching my face for doubt.

'My syndicate does not take unnecessary risks, Lovejoy. Greed is for peasants, not one such as I. One last thing, before we part.'

'Yes, Countess?'

'No disloyalty, no?'

'No disloyalty, yes.'

She simply remained there. The hulk strode for her motor. She didn't speak to me. The motor came. She embarked. It drove off in virtual silence.

The audience was returning. I went towards Maud, working up a smile.

CHAPTER THIRTY-EIGHT

In the main foyer a plain modern display case made me halt, though Maud was tugging me on saying we'd be late for the concert.

In it stood a terracotta head. I stared. It was a Nok figure. Just that. No notices, not a word of explanation. No guard, either. I'd never even seen one before, but I knew it could buy us all and leave enough for fish and chips on the way home.

'Wait, love.'

My breath was suddenly difficult. I stood. Folk went on past into the auditorium. Maud was on the staircase, fingers drumming on the brass handrail. I couldn't hear what she said for the chimes belling in my middle. I felt sick, malarial.

Hunting treasures is as human as greed. Look at

the so-called Rommel Treasure, ditched into the Mediterranean off Corsica in 1944. Every year, hunters with impossibly refined electronics seek these six packing cases of pure gold nicked from Libya's Tripoli and Tunisia during World War Two. Nobody succeeds, maybe because they look in the wrong place. (The Santo Antonio monastery is the nearest marker, if you want a try, and good luck.) But not all wealth is pretty.

There's a horridity in antiques. I swear some folk go for worrisome shapes and figures simply because they shock. A lady—lives up my lane— once did her living room out in purple flock wallpaper with dark scarlet corners, lampshades, skirting, rugs, cushions. It looked like the Inferno, but she proudly showed it off. Everybody thought her barmy. I thought it classy, because I liked her. Fine by me.

This antique head was different, though. I knew exactly where it had come from.

One of life's problems is the balance between greed and honesty. Think for example of the plight of some poor man whose country's in a hell of a state. Let's say he's a humble doorman at nothing more than a folklore museum. He's not been paid. The government's embroiled in revolution. People fleeing the city. Gunfire is heard at night, ever closer. (Now this is real, not made up.) What can he do? He has no friends in high places. His wife isn't from some rich clan, tribe. She earns a farthing cleaning, but the rich folk have fled in their Lagondas. His family's starving.

Then he thinks, our little frightened man. *He has the keys to the museum.* But tourists don't come any more. No coaches full of camera-toting

359

holidaymakers. His bosses are in Geneva or Acapulco. Desperately hoping to get paid, though, our little bloke still trudges in each day, unlocks the museum, crouches in the dust guarding his country's ancient treasures.

He's never felt so alone, so desperate.

He ponders. Inside, there's a ton of artefacts. Educated strangers travel thousands of miles to visit his shabby museum. They take photos with their expensive cameras, admiring the old-fashioned things.

What do these visitors admire? Why, one item especially: some manky old terracotta thing. It's a head, its features long, the chin showing a tufted beard, braided hair and tight, squarish ears. It wears a terracotta necklace and seems to be looking askance. Now, our little man squatting in the dusty doorway wouldn't give the thing the time of day. Also, aren't these old tribal statuettes ghostly?

Then up comes a bloke, perhaps the only visitor our doorman has seen since the troubles began. What ho, says the foreigner, can I see your museum? The little custodian's pleased. Maybe this stranger's arrival heralds a return to normality—wages, food, buses running again! Certainly, sir, in you go. Hoping for a tip, he eagerly shows the feller round. This conversation occurs:

Visitor: What a beautiful statuette!

Doorman: Foreigners admire it. It is old.

(Now, our little geezer thinks it's crud. But who is he to disagree?)

Visitor (sighs): My father has always wanted one. Unfortunately he is ill.

360

Doorman: I wish him better, with God's help.

Visitor: If only I could show this to my sick father! I would pay x dollars / euros just to borrow it for a week.

A gremlin alights on the doorman's shoulder and whispers how wonderful it would be. All that money! Who would know?

A week later, an unbelievably rare antique terracotta figure, such as this one from Nok in Nigeria, makes its appearance in London's showrooms and is sold for umpteen thousand. These figures, incidentally, look like nothing on earth. Mirthless, lips slightly agape, eyes triangular, necklaces of the same dulled earthenware. Yet one in pretty tatty condition will buy you a freehold townhouse.

This Quay Theatre piece was from Nok. I suppose I've made it sound really neff, but it's not. There's a plateau in Nigeria called Jos where these figures were made two thousand years ago. Collectors go mad for them, and pay fortunes. Why? Because they're the only real evidence that sophisticated sculptors were there that long ago. Sombre, almost menacing, they're not the sort of art you'd want on your sideboard, but dealers will kill for them. African travellers bring them into London, Munich, Zurich. Our dealers say, 'Notting Hill for illicit tribals.' They're not wrong.

'Whose is this, love?' I managed to get out.

She was smiling. 'I haven't the faintest notion, Lovejoy. I know Dad used to have one, but his was even uglier.'

The brigadier? One swallow doesn't make a summer, yet if his syndicate could display a Nok head with such cavalier abandon, unguarded in a foyer, it was a message, and such a message. No wonder the Countess wanted to supplant them. It was a sign to the knowing—look, see what we can get hold of any day of the week.

'Coming,' I said. I wanted to stick with her now. Obediently we went to watch the most dreadful concert of all time.

When it started the awful music made me nod off. The audience thinned, I noticed, many choosing not to return after the tacky excitement of Sandy's arrival and my actors' phoney antiques thrills. The songs were dross.

My mind kept going over what the Countess said. I was to help her, instead of the syndicate. She'd control the import of antiques. It was all the same to me. One tyrant's very like another. The only difference was that I'd get passion as a bonus from the Countess, not Maud. Promises, promises.

Maud sat with me in our grand box, everything going her way.

Several times I caught her looking at me with a frankly misty gaze, edging towards passion. She held my hand, even brought my arm round her. We were safe from gossipy eyes. We had champagne, too. I didn't touch mine because it gives me belly-wark. I'm lucky to be too poor to buy it. To please Maud I pretended to sip.

The singers came and went, warbling, wavering, shrilly vibrato up and down scales nobody but a deranged composer could love. The audience slyly began to drift faster. It was pretty poor. The orchestra had been replaced by a dud pianist. While some old dear screeched out a Britten piece I found my mind trying to work out the cost. Why the heck pay good money—if there is such a thing—for this sham?

I'm not keen on gelt. No, honest. I really do believe we think too much about it. Once you've got enough for bread and cheese, money's not a lot of use unless you're up to something. Maud was on fire. Her eyes met mine, ablaze with fervour. Was I worth all that?

Worry must have shown in my face because she leaned close to whisper, 'Don't worry, Lovejoy. We were meant to be.'

Between songs, I could hear the faint babble of some gathering in the ante-room. Possibly the orchestra and departing singers, leaving for their respective boozers. As the boring show ground on, though, the distant hubbub dwindled, until finally it too fell silent. The steam went out of our entertainers' performances. The audience drifted ever faster.

Sandy must have persuaded Brig's syndicate to stump up the money. It must have cost. The great swan barge, the dancers, slaves and slavettes, torch bearers, the fireworks. Not to mention the professional orchestra to start the proceedings. And decorations cost a pretty penny. I badly wanted to see Quaker. He'd tell me. If it was the brigadier's syndicate, the problem would be that much less.

'Where's Quaker, love?' I whispered.

Maud had her hand on my leg. 'He won't be coming.'

Who'd passed her that message?

A tenor was singing. I recognized him as a cricket umpire. Were we down to this, a musical of neffie warblers? No wonder people were vanishing in droves.

'And your dad?'

'Shhh.'

One newcomer crept in with that slow apology the body naturally makes when interrupting someone's performance. Florence Giverill, looking tired.

The show finally trailed to an end. By then only a scattered few were left. The applause was desultory. Some geezer came on to say ta and how marvellous. The curtain swished to with relief. The place seemed so hot. I wanted to wave to Florence but she was in the stalls below and didn't look up.

We went into the corridor. I kept looking about. No familiar faces now, just Maud's bright visage excited beyond what the evening deserved. It had been a mediocre show. She looked almost feverish.

'Let's have a drink on the balcony, Lovejoy.'

'Have we got time?' The place was closing fast. 'What about your meeting?'

She didn't hesitate. 'You're always so particular.'

The bar, usually so crowded, was almost deserted, just one barman washing glasses and tidying up. A couple had obviously sat out the last half-hour. They left as we entered. Maud put a note on the counter. I got the drinks and followed her out onto the balcony and stood beside her in the night air.

This was where Sandy's soaring staircase had risen from the swan barge on the river below. I looked over. All gone now. Fairy lights still adorned the riverbanks, but the fireworks had ended and the crowd dispersed. A last pair of snoggers glided below the bridge. Lucky bloke. I realized that I'd thought that thought about a lot of people tonight. Lucky others, not me.

'Isn't it blissful, Lovejoy?'

'Constable painted this stretch. He liked it.'

'And Gainsborough.'

Well, Gainsborough would, randy git. Hardly a blade of grass hadn't carried Tom G and his various birds at some time along his riverside. I didn't say this because the truth maddens women.

'When's the meeting?' I asked, to get things clear.

She leaned against the balcony, appraising me. The lights went out on the floor below, darkening the river. Probably last of the singers and ushers going home.

'Why are you so concerned about the meeting, Lovejoy?'

'The brigadier'll be narked if I make you late. And Quaker.'

'What's the difference? You can't come to it.'

She sounded mischievous, like she was setting me up for the laughter of others. I looked about. Nothing. Coloured lights downriver doused with appalling swiftness, leaving their imprint in my eye. The point was, I wanted to see who would be there. It was the last piece of the jigsaw puzzle. Whoever killed Vestry, drove Bernicka to suicide, and killed Timothy Giverill, was in the brigadier's syndicate. They were all responsible. Maybe it had been real democracy, let's take a vote, who's for executing Vestry, Bernicka, Timothy Giverill, show of hands? There's no telling when money rules.

I felt sudden pity for Bernicka, always worrying that her fifty-four years would show, crow's feet, her crazed love for Leonardo da Vinci, then dying like that. It simply wasn't fair.

'Can I lock up?' The barman came to the

365

balcony doors and started setting catches.

'Yes, fine,' Maud said, while I said no. 'We can go down the outer staircase.'

'It's regulations, see.'

He closed us on the balcony. I heard him shooting bolts along the doors. Reinforced, I now saw. I was ill at ease.

Cars started up, a door slammed. Voices called, a girl laughed, hurry up or Jane'll be late again, hahaha. Maud sipped at her glass. I didn't sip my drink, no wish for it. I find I only hold one because it's expected, don't imbibe as much as others want me to.

It wasn't like I was trapped. And there were worse fates than being encaged with a gorgeous bird like Maud. She placed her glass on the balcony rim and moved close. Her palm came on me. I gasped. Another choice taken out of my hands, so to speak. It isn't the same for women. They can simply say stop it, step aside and that's the end of the matter. A bloke can't. It's their power. My throat went thick. I managed to speak.

'How did you stop Quaker coming here?' I asked.

'I didn't. A friend did it for me.'

'Lanny Langley-Willes?' Had my voice gone higher? I don't usually sound breathless. Her hand kneaded me.

'Him?' Contempt, so soon? 'He just does a few valuations for Dad.'

Another one from the old regiment, hey? I couldn't speak. She held me in thrall, poets would have said. Somebody below called to check the main doors.

Was the Nok statuette still there? I wondered

366

why somebody had brought it in the first place. With this audience, there was unlikely to be an enormous amount of expertise knocking about. Or had somebody been watching, judging my reaction as me and Maud re-entered?

'Lovejoy, mate?'

I'd never been so relieved to hear Tinker's hoarse yell. Maud exclaimed in anger. Quickly I bawled down, 'Aye, Tinker. Up here.'

He called, 'There's a feller and two birds at the Drum and Flag.' I couldn't see him in the dark. 'Wants ter see you.'

That was a relief. I'd never wanted to escape from Maud before.

'Door open, is it? This balcony's locked.'

He chuckled, huff-huff-*huff* followed by a prolonged cough and a spit.

'You randy git. It's all shut. There's wood stairs. Pull the rope.'

'Tell them I'll be there in a minute.'

'Right, son.'

I heard his cough recede. Concealing my relief I turned to Maud and said I'd got to go, would see her after.

'It'll be Quaker, love. Him or the brigadier.'

'Go, Lovejoy?' She seemed to be sulking. I could see her face against the sky glow, not quite a silhouette. 'When we're partners for life?'

'Look, love. I want out from all this.'

'You—want—*out*?' Her hand slapped my head sideways. 'Don't you understand? I've made sacrifices to get that stupid obsessed dolt out of my life. To have you instead. And you say you want out?'

Her hand lashed me. I felt stunned, tried to back

away, stumbled over something, maybe bottles, a stool.

'Look, Maud. Nothing personal. But the Countess came in the interval. It's only a row between two syndicates. For money.' I sounded relieved even to myself. 'It's nothing important.'

'Nothing important? You're mad, Lovejoy! This means survival. Without your talent the syndicate will go under. People who've never lacked a thing in their lives. Not people used to poverty. People in responsible positions.'

'You mean posh folk should be protected from their own greed?'

'Yes!' she screamed, hitting out at me in fury. I ducked and weaved but still she caught me. I felt against the wall for the bloody rope, get out of this.

Then a bloke's iron grip took my arm. His voice said, 'Stop it, Maudie. I've got him.'

God, but I was relieved. Maud halted her assault. I could hear her breaths, fury in every waft.

'Thought you plod were never on time, Sep,' I gasped.

'No jokes, Lovejoy.'

'Sep?' Maud seemed puzzled. 'What are you doing here?'

'I've come to take Lovejoy into custody, Maudie. I have bad news. I'm sorry.'

'What bad news?' I sounded strangled. 'Tinker?'

Tinker couldn't hide, not with his cough. He's like a foghorn. So Sep must mean—

'Quaker's been found in the river, Maudie. He'd been bludgeoned and drowned. No hope, I'm afraid.'

'But—' Maud looked at me.

'Lovejoy slipped out, and so did Quaker. I saw

368

him. Lovejoy was seen coming from there. Then he went to sit with you. Alibi, see?'

'Me?' I bleated. 'I couldn't club anybody, Sep. You know that. Christ, I was in clink with you.'

'You're under arrest, Lovejoy. Don't move!'

'Sep,' Maud said. 'I don't know what you are saying. Where is Quaker? I want to see him.'

Maybe I could dart past the loon, find those wooden steps Sep must have used.

'Stand still, Lovejoy!' Sep yelled, coming at me swinging something.

I ducked, shoved Maud in front of me, stooping so he'd clout her instead of me. He did just that. I heard the crunch, something hitting her. She shrieked and went down moaning. Verner lashed at me and the world span out of sense. I actually heard blurs and saw Sep loom, arm raised.

A balcony door opened. A light came on. The brigadier stepped out, locking the door behind him. He was in full fig, regimental blues, medals, more brass than you'd see on a fender. From a carnival? How come he had keys? He held something long in his hand. It shone. But was he help, cavalry to the rescue?

'Verner,' he said quietly. 'That'll do.'

'I had to go for Lovejoy, sir. He was about to do for Maudie.'

'Eh?' I tried to stand, but Verner was too close.

'Stay still, Maud, Lovejoy.'

As if I'd want to move with a homicidal plod intent on battering me to death.

'I had to do it, sir,' Verner explained as if making a report, all calm. 'He'd some daft notion about coming clean to that Quayle tart, and helping the Countess's mob to take us over, do us out of our

369

scheme.'

'Stand by the balcony. I'll get Lovejoy up.'

The brigadier moved. Sep moved. I tried to crawl away behind the recumbent moaning mound that was probably Maud, to hide and let her take the brunt of whatever was coming. I thought maybe I could lob myself over the balcony, splash in the water below. Or was the vertical drop onto the quayside, where I'd smash my brains out on the flagstones—

Something swished. Hot wetness hosed across my neck. I screeched, wailed. The thing went swish, swish. Horrid spurts hosed my face.

A gurgle sounded near me. I clasped Maud and hung on, hoping the maniac wouldn't start swinging at his daughter while him and Verner came to some arrangement.

The brigadier grunted. Sep gurgled, tried to cough, failed. The balcony seemed to shiver a second, but it could only have been my imagination. Something heavy fell, thudding onto stones below.

Vertical. The drop was vertical.

Somebody close by—the brigadier, doubtless—shone a pencil torch into the balcony corners. There was blood everywhere. Maud was covered in it. The brigadier stood there, his expression calm. In his hand he held his sabre. It had surprisingly little blood on it at the tip, but the rest was gore, gore. Even the balcony doors' windows were liberally sprayed with a red cascade slowly trickling down the glass panes.

The brigadier stooped, looked at his daughter, then removed the door key and handed it to me.

'Do the necessary, old chap.'

370

'Eh?'

His face assumed a pained look. 'Insert the key in the other side of the door, if you please. Don't lock it. Then dial the police.'

'Where from?'

'Try the telephone.' He waited expectantly, then added, 'In the bar.'

I did as he said. Just told them to come fast, and bring an ambulance. They started asking me questions, bloody idiots, as if I knew anything.

'Good man,' Brig said. 'Bring Maud a cushion, Lovejoy.' As I turned, he asked conversationally, 'Oh, where did you leave Quaker?'

'I didn't touch him,' I croaked.

'I know,' he said with exhausted patience. 'You couldn't. He was on the opposite side of the river. Just remember that Verner said that, eh?'

'Right, sir,' I said, wondering what the hell he was on about.

He placed the cushion and sat down, cradling Maud.

'You can go, Lovejoy. You are irrelevant. Be prepared to answer their questions later. Be factual, please.'

'Right.' I hesitated. 'Do you want to get away, Brig? I'll think of something.' God. What if he said yes?

'No, Lovejoy. You fail to understand. Your perennial habit.' He gave a wry smile. Maud stirred in her father's arms. 'I am the principal Name. Therefore I must accept responsibility. Bankruptcy is now my duty.'

'Duty? But you might get out of it.'

'Duty is for doing, not evading. It is the possession of a gentleman.'

371

'Right, Brig.'

He meant he hoped I'd do mine, irrelevant as I was.

CHAPTER THIRTY-NINE

My jacket was hopelessly caked with blood. I found the bar's loos and washed some of the blood off. I didn't look presentable but when did I ever?

Maud was sitting up, shuddering. Her dad had draped his bloodstained jacket round her shoulders. He was seated beside her amid the gore. An execution scene. A couple of people were shouting up from below. Somebody had brought a torchlight, never still, flickering on trees.

'Is she all right?'

'A bad bruise.' The brigadier had wiped his sabre on his trouser leg—I saw the stripe it made—and sheathed it. First things first. 'Lucky I came, hey?'

'I'll go and find Quaker.'

'Be a good chap. Go down and let them in.'

No police as yet, though. I did as he said. Two astonished blokes, one in the uniform of a car-park attendant, coat of arms on his cap, were gaping aghast at me through the glass doors. I unlocked. They came in. One had two dogs straining at a leash, wanting ever more excitement on this unusual night walk.

'What the hell's happened?'

'I've called the police. It's upstairs.'

'There's a man dead out there,' the uniformed bloke said. It was beyond him. He wanted reason, like don't we all. 'Ted's there.'

372

'The lady will be all right,' I said, doing my best for his rational world. 'Her dad the brigadier's with her.'

'What do we do?'

'Ted minding the body, is he?' I said, walking past. 'Go on up until the police come.'

They went toward the staircase, dogs and all. Their relief was tangible, somebody telling them to do something and mentioning the police.

There's no bridge across the river until you reach the railway pub, then you get a choice of three. Too far. The theatre's lights were coming on, giving enough light to see the leisure boats. I unmoored one and rowed clumsily across to the opposite bank, left it there and walked until I judged I was opposite the place where I'd heard what I thought were lovers.

'Quaker?' I kept shouting. 'Quaker?'

Like a fool I'd not brought a flashlight. I did the best I could, flailing about the undergrowth by the towpath. Nothing. Then I heard it, a magic sound that almost brought tears of relief to my eyes. It was a long slow wheeze repeated until the ground shook. Tinker's cough. He thinks I don't know he still smokes. His snitch is always stained with snuff, which he's not used—honest, Lovejoy—for ten years, the lying old sod.

'Tinker?'

Answer came from across the river. Then lights, but from curtained windows. I recognized Maud and Quaker's house.

'That you, son?' And instantly into grumbles. I still couldn't see him. 'I found this lame bloke in the water like the brigadier said. I didn't get his wheelchair out. Sod that. Turns out the lazy

373

bastard's nothing wrong wiv him. Not a drop in the house.'

'Stay with him, Tinker. I'll be back.'

'Right. The brigadier get on all right, did he?'

'Aye, fine,' I said drily. I'd a mile walk into town.

'The brigadier said there'd be booze here but I found noffink. Any idea where he keeps it? This silly burke keeps showing me photographs of the Olympics.'

I walked on in silence.

*   *   *

The Drum and Flag is ancient, even as our local taverns go. Every so often some enthusiast dredges up proof that this pub or that hostelry was around in the ninth century, but we've some taverns encrusted in old Roman walls and they're still hard at it, serving their ale and nosh.

Ashamed, I walked into the light. It was still fairly crowded. I carried my jacket, and had turned my collar under. People must have assumed I was from the gala. The head waitress was standing at her podium, blonde, smart, thick spectacles, uniform. I asked for the Americans. A waitress conducted me to the alcove where the three of them were seated.

Consul Sommon smiled affably with that well-nourished bonhomie only millionaires can attain. I have a sneaking feeling that it puts the rest of us down onto some servile plane. Like society women, whose rich dresses do the same to the poor.

He was not quite sprawling—the sprawl is another characteristic of worldly power—on a couch. Before him, a long coffee table stocked with

374

drinks, food, enough to host a party. People all about talked, chatted, called to friends. Some TV match was on. Pleasant, everything safe, the town solvent for a generation. People were happy.

'Sit you down, feller. What'll you have?'

Friends, now he thought it all over.

'Nothing, thank you.'

The food looked stupendous. I looked away.

'May I offer you a shandy, Lovejoy?'

'Yes, please, Ms Deighnson.' Could I call her Petra?

'What the fuck?' said the consul. 'My drink not good enough?'

Grief is the only emotion insoluble in alcohol. I thought this, but did not say. He'd have demanded an explanation.

Petra Deighnson signalled a waitress and ordered me a shandy ('The gentleman likes his lemonade in first, please!'—the first I'd heard of it). 'You know, Lovejoy,' she went on quietly, 'half the trouble is that our country has never signed UNESCO's treaty banning the sale of archaeological treasures.'

'It's time you stopped these sales!' the consul exclaimed, his remark of course for public consumption. I've always found that those in public office want controls because they're on the right side of the barricades.

'Where will the antiques be exported?' I asked.

'You mean what, exactly?' she asked, her smile hardening.

Definitely not the question to ask Petra, for she was among friends. I wasn't.

'The consul's Nok-Jos terracotta in the theatre foyer isn't illegal here. A dozen antiques shops openly specialize in them.'

She almost winced. 'The Continent. The USA. It's a seller's market.'

'The United States is taking enormous steps to control traffic in illegal antiques.' The consul intoned the party line.

God, but politicians sound good. You have to admire them. They're really lifelike.

'You're not,' I told him, but pleasantly, like I too was their pal, part of the team. He'd recruited me at the Martello tower restaurant. He must take the consequences.

'The US of A has made enormous strides towards an ethical goal.'

'Famous museums throughout Africa are forced to display replicas of their own stuff.' The shandy came. I gulped it with what I hoped was decent slowness. La Deighnson ordered me another, adding her lemonade-in-first speech. 'It's unstoppable.'

Susanne Eggers was inspecting my jacket. I'd dropped it as I'd sat, casual man of the world that I was. She paled.

'Is that blood?'

'An accident at the fireworks.' They relaxed. 'You were saying, sir?'

'The US is against exploitation of Third World heritage.' He looked about for possible voters and placed his own drink carefully on the table. A portentous speech was coming on. 'We have a constant, definite, and determined policy of international cooperation . . .' and so on.

Petra Deighnson was a Name in Lloyd's. Nothing illegal there. I already knew that Susanne Eggers was the consul's former missus. They were still together. That too was allowed. Also, politicians transgress in ways that only Sun Kings and medieval popes were once able to. They also got away with murder.

Consul Sommon, a giant Name, had insurer's debts that were darkening his sky. Party politics deplore poverty. The only way for a man with political ambition was to get money. How lucky, I thought as his rhetoric bumbled on, that his position as an eminent diplomat provided him with the means to extort wealth. Contacts in embassies, favours for diplomats, his illicit antiques would bring a fortune. And it would be the very best sort of money, the untraceable sort.

Through the fenestrated wooden screen that shielded us from the *hoi polloi* I saw the head waitress at her podium. She'd made some sort of error and was laughing. A young waitress was laughing too, hand to her mouth in mock alarm, pointing to the ledger. I thought she looked a bit familiar, but not so you'd remember where you'd seen her last. I suddenly decided on a wrong tack.

'Is Mr Verner a friend of yours, Mr Sommon?'

The consul looked at Susanne. 'Yes. A business associate.'

I didn't really want to bring it up until the last person came in. It wouldn't be the brigadier. With his sabre or without.

'Only, I don't want any trouble.' I tried to look on edge.

He thumped me playfully.

'You're aboard with us now, Lovejoy. You've achieved your life's ambition! Being paid for what you like doing! There'll be no trouble from police, Lovejoy.'

Susanne was still unhappy about my jacket. Her unease had communicated itself to Petra Deighnson. I saw the latter look at my shoes. I'd rubbed the grubbier one on the back of my calf, like children do. I didn't glance down. Did it show blood?

'Have you cut yourself?' she asked.

'Somebody fell. I tried to help.' I'd wriggled to put Maud between me and a murderous maniac. Ever the hero. 'Did the antiques show go well, incidentally? I went out for a breath of fresh air while it was on. Too hot.'

'Yes.' Susanne described how well it had been received. 'They were all so good.'

She meant her actors were convincing enough to deceive the ignorant, and protect this ex-husband of hers.

'Anyhow, I'd already seen the show.' I said it like a gag, the last one-liner, smiling.

Mr Sommon hooted, choked. I had to bang his back.

'Your orders, sir?' Clear things up.

He opened his hands displaying largesse, the world his to be handed out to the deserving.

'I want three shipments a month to begin with, Lovejoy.'

'That many?' I stared, working it out. The man was off his trolley. 'Container loads? Four or five thousand antiques a month?'

'So?' His beaming smile faded. 'Jeez, Lovejoy. You're a freaking divvy. You've only got to say whether the antiques are genuine or not. Christ. You don't have to *work*.' He became mottled at the thought of idle bums who didn't slog ergs to achieve the dream. 'You've only to sit down and look.'

He had no idea. Only a divvy knows how sick you feel, the utter malaise. One divvying session ruins you for days. The headaches, the eerie disorientation. It drains. I once divvied a shipment in two days, several hundred pieces of antique furniture, for a French shipper. I'd taken it on soon after their one and only French divvy died. I didn't recover for a fortnight. He was old, lived in Brittany. Nice chap, very quiet. Normal people haven't a notion.

Thinking of how poorly I'd been that time brought my headache on. My temple thumped tribal paradiddles.

'How many, then?' Petra Deighnson, straight to the gelt.

'One container load in three weeks, for me to stay sane.'

'One? That's less than a thousand!'

'Keep your voice down, darling,' Susanne said.

She reached but her hand didn't make it. He drew away, eyes challenging me to mortal combat. Me, his only salvation, note, for the ghastly financial mess his greed enticed him into.

'Christ! Susanne's actors only needed ten minutes!'

Like other crooks, he'd begun to confuse reality and myth. The actors going through their paces on stage were acting rehearsed fiction. The import of antiques through his diplomatic channels was criminal reality.

'They were pretending,' I said patiently. Abruptly I was tired, sapped to exhaustion. 'It's me alone that would divvy your illegal shipments.'

'But—'

'If you think they can do it, hire them instead.'

'What he says is true,' Susanne said quietly. 'Remember? It's on the video movie Taylor made at Saffron Fields that day.'

He seethed, glared. A thwarted politician is an ugly sight. I wondered if Congress had a televised Prime Minister's Question Time like us. It's the nearest the electorate ever get to a straight answer. It's still miles off.

'One shipment a month would be better.'

'One a fortnight, Lovejoy.' He put the flat of his hand on the coffee table so hard the crockery jumped. 'And that's that. I already have one shipment here. You start tomorrow.'

'Right.' I gave in. If I'd guessed right, we'd not get to his bloody shipment anyway. Where were the Keystone Kops? I felt I'd done enough, got them all to speak the obvious.

'Can I have another drink, please?'

'Shandygaff, isn't it, sir?'

A waitress was already carrying a tray bearing a glass. Psychic? I looked up against the aura of my headache. I knew that face. The head waitress?

'And,' she said amiably to everyone, placing the drink in front of me, 'you are under arrest.'

Mrs Thomasina Quayle? I squinted up, dizzy now. Had her hair been that colour? And specs?

The tavern went silent. Four silent figures stood by our alcove, their bulk sending our nook into penumbral shadow. I recognized ploddites only a mother could love. They wore their arrest faces, an unsmiling satisfaction beyond ecstasy. The moment they lived for.

Petra Deighnson went white. She fumbled for her handbag, brought out a card.

'Don't bother, Petra,' Mrs Thomasina Quayle said calmly. She took the handbag. 'We'll look after this for you. Mr Dexter, please do the words.'

'Yes, ma'am.'

A plod stepped forward and intoned his gibberish. A small camera unit, videos busy at the wedding party by the tavern's entrance, had solidified into a steady focus on us. I was collared, every word got down on film.

While everybody expostulated—I'm a diplomat, I'm a SFO officer, I'm innocent, etc, etc—I drank my gill and wondered through my migraine if I'd got any friends left. Maybe they'd spring me.

Smiling, Mrs Thomasina Quayle placed a bill in front of me. 'If you'd care to settle up, Lovejoy, we'll be going.'

The bill? For one manky shandygaff? The police laughed and laughed, telling and retelling Mrs Quayle's crack to each other. Justice always triumphs—for the richest one per cent. I'd never been included.

Didn't look promising.

CHAPTER FORTY

By evening of the tenth day, I still hadn't recovered my spirits. Tinker came round endlessly. I was trying another Gainsborough portrait, still unable to get her eyes. Eyes are practically everything.

'Got ter snap out of it, son. We've work on.'

'What work?'

'Antiques. Ferdinand and his Norma. They've got landed with the Yank's shipment. Much got reclaimed by that African country. The rest, well, they don't know if it's gunge or priceless.'

'Tell them I'll divvy it for four fifths of its resale value.'

He cackled, falling about, blundering into my portrait. The easel swayed. I grabbed it. I'd been trying out the new water-miscible oils pigments. Disturbing how good they were.

'You're learning! Here, son. Say you want Norma as well. You used to. I'll bet she'd jump—'

'Tinker, mate,' I said wearily. 'Knock it off.'

'Consul Sommon has escaped justice,' Mortimer said. He helped me to right the easel.

'You burke!' I fumed, shaken. 'Where did you spring from? Stop creeping.'

Tinker laughed and almost spilled his beer. Five new tins were lined up ready. He perched on my stool, coughing. I raised a finger to stop him. He spat into his empty can.

'Leaves tomorrow. Diplomatic privilege.' Mortimer crouched against the wall like an Australian drover, one leg outstretched. 'You must make sure he does not profit.'

More orders? I sighed. 'The brigadier sent you to tell me this?'

'No. The brigadier will be exonerated from the death of Mr Sep Verner, but is a declared bankrupt. He and Mrs Alicia Domander now live together at the Garrison Riding Stables.'

'Do they now.' So much for love's loyalty. Sourly, I guessed that Alicia had been trying to warn me before that mad show.

'And Maud is well. Quaker is waiting outside, Lovejoy. I came to warn you.'

'Warn? Frighten me to death more like, stupid

382

little sod.'

'Consul Sommon will escape all penalties of the law, Lovejoy.' Mortimer sometimes sounds seventy years old. 'He caused your friend Bernicka's demise. And poor Mr Vestry, using Vestry's sister Susanne Eggers as his contact.'

'And Timothy Giverill? Sandy caused that. I was listening in the car.'

'You didn't listen closely enough.' Mortimer spoke like to a child. I was narked. I mean, who was the father here, him or me? I caught myself guiltily. Nobody suspected that, except everybody.

'Wotcher mean?'

'Accidentally, I overheard Mrs Thomasina Quayle discussing the issues with her staff,' Mortimer said with disarming candour. Accidentally? He'd probably hung from the eaves like a bloody bat, I'd bet.

'Which are?'

'The antiques the consul claimed from the imported consignment are already bonded for shipment to New York. He already has dealers bidding for them on the Internet. He will make a fortune.'

'Where are my portraits?'

Mortimer looked at Tinker, at the floor.

'Tell him, lad,' Tinker said.

'Lady Hypatia's portraits all have my mother's face, Lovejoy. It's she you keep painting.'

I said, 'I guessed. But—'

'Consul Sommon used to . . . see her on visits. He never came to the manor. He wanted them because he thought he could find her again. She's the reason Susanne Eggers divorced him. And why Mrs Eggers insisted on leasing Saffron Fields, and

383

wanted the portraits herself, to destroy.'

Poor Susanne Eggers, loving a twerp like him. Poor Sommon, still loving Colette Goldhorn. Poor all of us, always wanting something we haven't got.

'And he'll make a fortune, Lovejoy,' Tinker said, reproachful.

I thought a bit. 'Will he?'

'Mortimer's right, son. The bastard did for Vestry, Bernicka. Don't seem right, Lovejoy.'

'And Timothy Giverill,' Mortimer added quietly. 'Who was going to expose the illegal arrangement the Lloyd's syndicate had made with London auctioneers via Mr Langley-Willes. Sandy didn't know it would mean Mr Giverill's death. He thought Sep Verner would cause a minor traffic infringement, a warning. Instead . . .'

I already knew instead.

'See, Lovejoy,' Quaker said, entering slowly. I stared. He wasn't in his wheelchair. 'Somebody has to make sure that Consul Sommon catches it. Like,' he continued, looking round for somewhere to sit, finally opting to stand, 'like his schemes to sell fast to any dealer, crooked or otherwise. They're bidding high sums. I checked.'

'After murdering your friend Bernicka,' Tinker said. More reproach. He felt such deep sorrow that he had to open another two tins of ale.

'And Vestry,' Quaker reminded me. Everybody was reminding me, telling me I had to do something. Always me.

We all thought a bit, some more deeply than others. I couldn't help gaping at Quaker. I'd never seen him stand.

'Why aren't you dead in the bulrushes, Quake?'

'Sep Verner came ostensibly to wheel me to the

Quay. He shoved me into the river. Thought I'd drown. Then went to blame my death on you. I kept quiet, gurgled and splashed a bit.' Quaker smiled sheepishly. 'I'm no athlete. I was climbing out when Tinker happened by. Sep was crazy for Maud, always was.'

'Good old brigadier. He came armed. Ready to kill.' I can't manage reproach as well as other folk. Maybe they have the best target, in me.

'He says that. The plod thought his actions completely justified, protecting his daughter from attack by a deranged police officer.'

'The plod saw sense?' The world spun.

'That'll be the party line, Lovejoy. Right.' Quaker rubbed his hands, paused before leaving. 'Will you do it, then?'

'Do what?' As if I didn't know.

'One last job. Divvy the consul's antiques shipment.'

We all paused. I thought hard. The one thing that would make Consul Sommon pay any penalty at all would be . . .

'Are they at Ferd's? I've no motor.'

'I'll send my new driver.' Quaker smiled. 'My assistant can be trusted. He turned Queen's Evidence. Go now, Lovejoy.'

'Then I'll be in the clear?'

He grinned. 'I wouldn't go quite that far, Lovejoy.'

And he walked, as in one foot before the other, out of my overgrown garden. I'd always known he was fit, if loony, yet it was truly weird to see this normal man in full possession.

'Ready?'

Taylor Eggers poked his head into the

385

workshop. His eyes met mine. Sardonic again. I'd been right. A cuckolded husband always smarts, even at the point of vengeance.

So I drove with Tinker, very grand in Taylor's big black limo, to Ferdinand and Norma's splendid antiques farm.

My barker thought he'd gone to heaven because the motor had a minibar. He finished the spirits as we arrived. The ale he stuffed into his greatcoat pockets. Even then he was worried.

'Here, Lovejoy,' he said as Norma advanced smiling and Ferd dithered on his veranda. 'Don't get narked, son, but what if we get thirsty on the way back?'

*   *   *

The goods were bads. Most of the truly genuine antiques seemed to have gone. Doubtless Lanny Langley-Willes and his friends, or maybe Consul Sommon, had taken some in personal diplomatic baggage. Civil servants are always above the laws they make for the rest of us.

'Lovejoy!' Norma was more welcoming now. 'How lovely to see you!'

'Good to see old friends!' Ferd exclaimed, clapping his hands for his maids-of-all to bring victuals for his lifelong pals here. It was all so false.

'I've not long, Ferd. Aren't you due to ship the antiques?'

'Stansted,' he said, nodding. 'A godsend, that airport. So near.'

And yet so far, I silently finished for him.

'Let's get on, then.' I declined the frosted glass with the white wine, and went into the main stores.

A few dealers were drifting among the items. Some of the furniture felt good, and the cabinets of jewellery and small porcelains emitted really convincing chimes. I hardened my heart and went through into the cool, darkened room. Norma ushered me in, placing a stool. I asked for the air conditioning to be turned off. It always gets on my nerves. I also told Ferd to keep out, just let somebody bring each antique then clear off.

Norma wanted to do it. Ferd and Tinker went to talk over old times, Tinker ready to help the girls by imbibing whatever alcohol they might supply.

'Now,' I told Norma. I was already whacked, or does that mean killed in Americanese? I mean tired.

She started with a box of tribal crowns. These look absolutely home-made, almost from some infant school's dressing-up day. Gaudily coloured, supposedly a bird surmounting a tribal Yoruba crown on stalky legs. There were eleven. Genuine, looking like odd toys. Yet archaeologists would bite the consul's hand off to get them.

And bite the consul's head off, if they paid for genuine antiques and got fakes.

'Genuine,' I said. 'Yes, genuine. Genuine,' the chimes making me shudder so much I almost slumped from the chair.

Then tribal carvings. Three stools, unbelievable, for they were thrones.

'Genuine, genuine.'

It was so consistent I began to wonder if Consul Sommon was having me on. Or was the entire shipment authentic? One or two had museum stamps on, Lagos, Accra and others. One or two came from Kenya, Uganda, ancient Benin.

'Keep those faces and busts back, Norma.'

387

'Right, Lovejoy.'

She spoke with reverence, knowing she was in the presence of mysticism. On I went. She had a girl haul the old wrappings away, made swift notes of my judgements.

'This is the last,' she said after what must have been about an hour. I felt concussed. 'Just the seven heads and the bronzes.'

'How many?'

'Eleven in all.'

The statuettes from Nok-Jos and other villages on the Jos Plateau were formidably old, maybe nineteen centuries. The Benin bronzes were practically mint, after all these hundreds of years. I hate the small drilled holes along the chin. It's where, I think, they must have tied some dress garments to make the bronze heads more awe-inspiring back in those superstitious days.

This was the moment I'd come for.

The question is, what do you do when a killer is going to get away scotage free? I had, have, no right to execute. Death penalties are wrong. Everybody knows that. Yet raping whole countries, entire civilizations, mocks honesty. It's like mocking infants. It generates war.

Consul Sommon would return home—it would be the second flight from Stansted, his crates in the plane's hold. There in New York money would pour in, diplomats being beyond law.

But if the dealers paid him fortunes and subsequently discovered they were fake, what then? He'd be ruined. Maybe even worse?

'These last ones are fake,' I said. My voice shook.

'Fake?' She looked at them. At me.

'Fake,' I said firmly.

Her face paled. She tried to speak.

'But, Lovejoy. Mr Sommon has been accepting bids on the Internet. And some of them are from . . .'

She gulped. I too felt like gulping. I could guess who the serious bids were from, money laundering being what it is.

'Well, you did want me to help out,' I prompted.

'Lovejoy.' She sidled up to me. I mentally apologized to the authentic genuine statuettes.

'Yes?'

'Look, darling.' She bit her lip, tried again. 'Is there any way you could, say, provide us with the same number of genuine statuettes? I know you have contacts. Only,' she added, tears running down her cheeks, 'only, me and Ferd have come so far. We couldn't possibly go back to scrimping, living hand to mouth. Please?'

'You said I was no more use.' Well, I couldn't make it too easy or she'd suspect. Also, I was narked.

'Darling. You'll always be essential to *me*. You know that.'

'Right, love. I'll do it. Tell the airline your shipment will be delayed. I'll get you the genuine ones in three days.'

'Can't you do it sooner?'

'Sooner?' I cried, meaning every word. 'Casting Benin bronzes that quick? And terracottas like these? Honest to God!'

'Sorry, darling. I do understand.'

'I'll get rid of this dross for you, love. Possession of fakes will land you in it.'

'Oh, thank you, darling. Will I see you soon?'

That was it. Tinker loaded the eleven artefacts up in Taylor's limousine, and we drove them away to Eleanor's garage. As soon as Taylor Eggers had gone, we shifted them on wheelbarrows in the darkness. I ordered a load of common reproduction Benin heads and Nok-Jos terracotta figures from Sanko Deane Pitt's sheds in Southend. He always has a reasonable stock of fakes, though his Old Masters are truly rubbish since his girl from the Guildhall eloped with that Geordie heavy goods driver. I got Shammer—he of the many voices—to place the buy.

He asked, 'Who's the buyer?'

'Consul Wald Sommon,' I said.

'Do I give a phoney name?'

'No,' I said. 'Just as it sounds. And pay cash on the nail. Have them delivered to Stansted Airport for export to New York, okay?'

You can be slothful with genuine antiques, but fakes demand precision. Ferdinand and Norma, I said blithely, would know the address.

God help Consul Sommon. Well, I reasoned in a sad moment late that night, he shouldn't go round killing people.

CHAPTER FORTY-ONE

Stansted Airport is somewhat seedy. It's there because of a plot by politicians. Public enquiries ruled against the airport. Politicians promised that of course they'd not allow it to be built. Then they reneged. The politicians then made fortunes, the old wallet tango.

390

We stood like refugees in the wind, rain in the air. The Customs shed is marginally less drossy, but that's only because their turnover is faster, their authority absolute. It must be great to be a robber baron. The nosh is horrible.

'These the cases, ma'am?' some uniformed bloke asked cheerily. They always make cheerfulness sound ominous and agreement a crime.

'Yes.'

Thomasina Quayle was with Florence. I'd got Florence a thick coat from Eleanor. She was well wrapped, a cloche hat jammed on her head. She'd told me five times that she was perishing.

'Forms, ma'am.'

Mrs Quayle took an age filling things in. Only once did she pause, to ask me which of the two largest crates was which. I didn't hesitate. The one containing the fakes that Tinker had driven up from Sanko Deane Pitt's place the previous night was slightly larger and painted green.

'That big green one holds the genuine antiques,' I lied. 'Personal to Consul Sommon. His certificates . . .'

'We did the certificates.' Thomasina Quayle smiled fetchingly. 'You're absolutely certain, Lovejoy?'

Her joke. The Customs and Excise man laughed with a mortician's joviality.

'Yes. The smaller red one only has reproductions. To go to the African state.'

Me and Florence waited for the consignment to move to the aircraft. God, but these new planes are giants. Makes you wonder how they ever get up there.

'Lovejoy,' Florence said as we watched two officers on Mrs Quayle's team walk with the lady alongside the shipment. The big green crate was on a low caged trailer of its own. 'I heard yesterday about the reward.'

'Reward?'

'It's a lot of money. Even after legal expenses.'

'Whose reward?'

'Mine.' She went red. 'When I went to see the lawyer about the bankruptcy, while that Mr Verner . . . lost his life in that tragic fall. I actually called in at Mrs Quayle's office and revealed everything I knew about Timothy's insurance commitments, and to whom. She was very pleased, and went to the tavern to arrest you all.'

'Ta, love.'

'She promised that filming you all in the tavern alcove would exonerate you. She was so happy.'

'I'll bet she was.'

'You're not angry?'

'No.' I might have been stone dead, but not angry.

'Thank goodness!'

Standing by the smaller crate, its ancient antiques throbbing silently inside me, we saw the plane's hatch close. Mrs Quayle stood there, exchanging forms with Customs folk. Consul Sommon's worthless items were leaving in style.

'Lovejoy? What happens to these?' She indicated the smaller crate.

'It goes to the countries where the, er, originals were pinched from. As a memento.'

'Oh, Lovejoy! How sweet to think of that!'

'Well,' I said, because it really was kind of me. 'They'd have been so upset, losing their national treasures to that horrible killer, wouldn't they? At least these, er, reproductions are good enough to put on exhibition.'

'That's *so* charming. And at your own expense!'

'Well, sort of.'

I almost filled up. Except the developing countries would get the originals, and Consul Sommon the fakes. He wouldn't know it, of course, until enraged dealers came stalking him on some dark night, lift aside his office curtains, and just as he was talking on the telephone . . .

'Are you all right, Lovejoy?'

'Course I am, silly cow.'

'I'm sorry. You suddenly looked so pale. It must have been a strain, yet you've been so generous.'

'I'm okay.'

'Lovejoy,' she said shyly. 'I've decided to resume Timothy's work. Not insurance,' she added hastily, seeing me wince. 'His photography.' She gave a sad smile. 'It was his hobby. He was very artistic.'

Photography an art? Only maniacs think that pointing a lens and going *click*! constitutes the artistic expression of a lifetime.

'Timothy's bankruptcy assessors sent back his photographs last night.' I'd heard it come, but had been trying for oblivion, the state my mind was in. 'Two suitcases, negatives and prints.'

'Great,' I said bitterly. More gunge to clutter my little cottage.

The documentation seemed finished at last. Thomasina Quayle and her people came slowly towards us. Distantly, a plane took off doing that roar and sudden tilt. I hate flying, always get a terrible cold for days after. Doctors should study the viruses spread in aeroplanes' air conditioning, but the idle sods don't.

'Can I develop some of Timothy's prints for you, Lovejoy? As a present?' She tried a smile. Still, a start is a start. 'I can take your photographs. The antiques you find. I did all Timothy's developing and printing, right from when he began photographing his insured things.'

A tired retort was almost out when I suddenly thought, hang on. What was she on about?

'Photographs? Of all the antiques Timothy insured? Like what?'

'Well, everything. Old Masters, archaeology, furniture, the contents of mansions being sold up . . .'

Although I've always knocked photography as boringly dull, you have to admit that it is hugely profitable. In antiques, believe it or not. Remember two things. First, is this photograph authentic, and preferably a one-off picture of some notable scene, historical event, sports meeting, Queen Victoria, whatever. Secondly, and vital to those crazed photo collectors, *did the long-deceased photographer himself take and print* the photo?

There's a great modern photography scandal. It's the horror antique dealers call the Hine Shine.

Lewis Hine was a picture snapper. His photos are the most famous in the entire world. You'll have seen prints of those American workmen having their sandwiches on that unbelievably high girder? The building of the Empire State Building in New York? The legend—it might be no more than that—has it that Mr Hine dangled high in the air to take these snaps. The pictures almost make me dizzy just looking. Poster shops sell them. One original—repeat, original—print is worth a year's idle sloth on the Riviera. One of those much uglier sepia-coloured prints—supposedly enlarged by Hine himself—can go for the price of three years' cruising on the grandest ocean liner. Why? Because collectors want them.

For the genuine, developed-by-the-photographer-himself prints, that is.

Copies aren't worth a cent.

Okay, there's no real artistry involved—not as far as I'm concerned anyway—but maniacs will pay a king's ransom for a snap. I'd actually seen these photographs go at Sotheby's and Christie's for tens of thousands. Unbelievable, when you can borrow books of the same photos from the town library for nothing.

Well, that *was* the situation. Then somebody detected a fault. It's the Hine Shine. Something seemed wrong with the prints being sold of photos taken by Man Ray and Ansel Adams, whoever those worthies might be. Word was whispered round photo specialists, *Those prints might actually be modern reprints.* Horror!

Take a photograph. Stick it under a fluoroscope. Old photographs don't shine as much as prints made on new paper. There are books—wholly boring—on the chemistry of obrags (optical brightening agents, OBAs) that came in half a century ago. These chemicals stop modern paper from yellowing quite so quickly. The result is, modern photographic paper fluoresces differently. So if you're going to fake some 'old' photographs, print them on old rag-pulp printing paper. (Get the rags, incidentally, in bundles of old clothes from second-hand charity shops in every high street, and make your own paper. It's simple, takes a week to do, and you're in business. If you're a crook, that is.)

The tests are easy. The Hitler Diaries succumbed to similar tests, as did the drawings of Eric Hebborn, a forger of Old Master drawings who was a friend of mine and who really *was* a master faker. And the phoney Shroud of Turin.

All you need is a source of good photographs of the right objects, and somebody to do it. Then you can make a mint. I looked at Florence. Wouldn't it be churlish to refuse her kind offer? And didn't she need a kind friend, help her to get on with her life?

'Thank you, love. That's really kind.' I put my arm round her. 'Darling. I'd love some of Timothy's old pictures. Just as a memento.'

'Oh, Lovejoy. Would you really?' She looked at me. 'You're not saying that just to be kind?'

'No,' I replied truthfully. 'No. I'd really like them.'

'I'll pick his real favourites! He used to think they were quite valuable. I'll have them specially mounted.'

'Lovely.' I walked her to meet Mrs Quayle. 'Incidentally, can you do that nice old-fashioned sepia colouring? Only, my old auntie likes those. She's very sick. If I get some old paper, could you . . . ?'

'I'd love to!' she cried, recovering fast. Give a woman a job to do.

'Best say nothing to Mrs Quayle,' I improvised carefully. 'She might think you'd held back some of Timothy's possessions from probate.'

'I wouldn't do such a thing, Lovejoy!'

'I know that, darling.' I held her hands and smiled. 'Just between us.'

Mrs Thomasina Quayle approached. 'That's that. Now we can go. Are you all right, Mrs Giverill?'

'Yes, thank you, Mrs Quayle.'

Women spend half their time asking each other how they are. They never ask the bloke. Ever notice that?

CHAPTER FORTY-TWO

Thomasina Quayle walked with me to my cottage, Florence having been dropped off at the village shop.

'Your place isn't exactly a mansion, is it?'

'Never said it was.' I feel embarrassed when women stand watching me. I become an actor who's forgotten his cue. 'At least it's my own.'

'That's not quite true, is it?' She didn't smile, but inside she was rolling in the aisles. 'Your three false mortgages. Your two additional loans.'

'I'll get by.'

Mostly, I try to forget debts. They're a nuisance. She took a few paces, looked hard at the divan. It had been tidied by a skilled hand. Her eyebrows raised. I shrugged. Well, I'd no spare room, so there you go.

'What now, Lovejoy? You stay here, special friends with Florence?'

'No. I told you. She's off to her sister's in Cumbria.'

'I wouldn't bank on it.' She eyed me. 'When you get rid of your other obligations, Lovejoy, you might consider coming to lodge at my place. I mean if you get into difficulties. No obligations. I have a spare flat for . . . acquaintances. Rent free. By the water in Wroxham. I'm in the phone book.'

'I'm fine here, ta.'

'Only, I don't want this business to go on and on.' She faced me. 'Do you understand? No more trouble—Ferdinand, Tex, the brigadier, Horse and FeelFree, that queer Dennis, Jessica and her coven, so many rogues out there. And your Mortimer was helping tourists in the Antiques Arcade again yesterday. Your dealer friends are on the warpath.'

'I understand.' But board with the plod? I'd have to be pretty desperate.

'Let me know where you get to. Every single moment, Lovejoy.'

'Right.'

She sighed as if at some irritating child's foible. I went to see her motor glide off. Alone. I turned and yelped. Sandy stood there, weeping. Mel stony-faced beside him.

'You stupid burkes!' I yelled. 'You almost scared me to frigging death!'

'We waited in your forgery, Lovejoy.' Mel was furious as usual. It would be about something incomprehensible, as usual. 'Sandy is very upset.'

'Having killed Timothy Giverill?' I said nastily.

Sandy's tears became uncontrollable. Mel was white with rage.

'Lovejoy. Can't you see he's inconsolable?'

'He deserves to be, Mel. And so do you.'

'Lovejoy. I know I've been really careless, stupid.' Sandy plucked at my arm. I shook him off. 'But I've come to try and make it up to you.'

'How? Make up what? I'm still alive. Others aren't.'

'Didn't you know?' he said with sly innocence. 'Alicia Domander was the brigadier's housekeeper. They're off to Spain to live happily ever after. And that wretched mutt.'

'And FeelFree and Horse are gunning for you. And Dennis. And Big Frank from Suffolk. And Venison. And Roe Johnson—'

'I know, I know.'

'Mortimer's started up again. Divvying for tourists, so we dealers miss out. The dealers are on their way now, Lovejoy.'

'Hell fire.' I thought quickly.

'There's Margaret Dainty, of course.' Mel smiled, hugging himself. He'd be telling me he felt a delicious malice any moment. 'You could stay with your lame friend. Except her husband's home. I feel a delicious malice, Lovejoy.'

'They've already sent two dealers from Saxmundham to stake out Mortimer's hide in the marshes, Lovejoy. So that's out.'

'They're here!' Mel suddenly hissed. I dived into the kitchen alcove and pulled the curtain at the roar of cars.

'God help you if you tell them I'm here, Sandy!'

Not much of a threat. I went quiet. It's movement that's the giveaway, not stillness. I heard people come crashing to the door, somebody kicking it.

'It's only little me in here!' Sandy trilled. 'I'm waiting for Lovejoy. I've got six warrants here for his arrest.'

I thought, Sandy has six warrants?

'Listen, Sandy.' This was Smarts, he of the Victorian jewellery. I wondered what stupid things he'd be wearing, his head fronded with tiaras and earrings. I could hear him cling and tinkle like a Christmas tree in the wind. 'Tell us where the bugger is. *Je morteray il*, if I catch the sod.' Still trying to be French.

'I want him dead,' Jenny Blondel said. I just hoped she hadn't brought her erstwhile spouse Paul with his great hunting birds.

'Me too.' Aspirin, her bloke. 'I've lost two thousand from that Mortimer.'

Did you now, I thought coldly. I'll see you lose a deal more when I get out of this, mate. Even if you can do handstands.

'Find him for us, Sandy,' Willie Lott said. I went colder still.

'Do it fast, honey,' Jessica added.

The gang's all here, I thought in fright. They left slowly after sundry additional warnings. Car doors slammed. Engines started.

Silence. I waited until the curtain was lifted. Sandy stood there. He couldn't raise a sincere smile if he was paid.

'Well, Lovejoy? Deal?'

'What deal?'

'Your bitch with the disabled dress sense is due back any minute. Am I right?'

'Yes.' I peered timidly out of the window. The garden was clear.

'You can take her. But you stay where I say.'

'Right.' Promises don't keep.

'You stay on North Hill, Lovejoy. Our shop there's empty, under police wraps.'

'I thought they had it under surveillance?'

'That was only when Peter Myer was being a nuisance. He's in France with a sailor friend of mine.'

'Opposite Bea Willing's teashop?'

'She of the Princess Beatrice Canonization Fund. She'll be your eyes and ears, if nothing more!' He tittered. 'Bribe that little horror Polly to keep her trap shut.'

'There were police inside, spying. Polly told me.'

'That was only Sep Verner, doing his worst.'

'Maud's on her way to stay with you, Lovejoy. Quaker's left for London.' Mel gazed around the cottage. 'Pushy bitch will take you over. It'll be a mite crowded. And Tina's staking her claim, since her acting scam folded.'

'Deal,' I croaked.

'You'll divvy whatever antiques I send over during your stay.'

More orders. I swallowed. No way out.

'How will you get me there?' I knew Willie Lott would have some bruiser watching the lane.

'You can hide in Mel's van, with your antique bitch Florence.' He tittered. 'If Mel covers her up, she won't frighten the horses.'

One thing about Sandy, he never stops being vicious.

'Deal, then. Oh, one thing, Sandy.'

'Yes?' He felt on top of the world.

'I won't be able to pay you two rent until it's all over.' I saw greed light his eyes. I still hadn't forgiven him for being instrumental in killing Timothy Giverill, who'd simply been an innocent insurance man, if there is such a thing. 'Would you call us quits, if I mentioned to Susanne Eggers when I phone her tonight that you're the ones who helped to get Consul Sommon off the hook? He's going to make a fortune from his imported antiques. He'll be so grateful.'

His eyes shone. Mel looked at me with mistrust.

'No, Sandy,' Mel warned. 'Lovejoy's up to something.'

'What?' I said dolefully. 'I'm broke, have to hole up while thugs want to hang me. What can I do?'

'Don't trust him, Sandy, dear.'

'It's all *right*, Mel! Diplomatic immunity means nobody can touch him!'

'Then I'll spread the word that you two arranged everything for Consul Sommon.' I said it so kindly.

'Why, thank you, Lovejoy!'

'No need,' I said truthfully. 'Here comes Florence. Would you give her a hand with these two suitcases while I tell her where we're going to stay?'

'Mel, help the poor bitch, there's a dear.'

'And thanks, Sandy. You've been a real friend.'

'I have, haven't I? Incidentally, did you see my arrival as Queen Midas at the Quay? Wasn't I simply exquisite?'

'I thought it was Queen of Sheba,' I said pleasantly, as Mel went to take Florence's shopping bags.

'No,' Sandy said eagerly. 'I was like this *wonderful* Queen Midas. Gold was my *theme*, Lovejoy . . .'

I got ready to leave. Heaven alone knew when I'd see my cottage again.

'Thanks for everything, Sandy,' I said, giving the place one last look.

And God help you, I thought, but did not say.

*   *   *

In broad day, I stole into Bea Willing's teashop,

rear entrance from the alley behind St Peter's churchyard. I left Florence and Mel to carry the suitcases, in case I got spotted and had to make a run for it.

Little Polly sat on her stool by the cake counter eating ice cream. She watched me come. 'Mum? It's him.'

'Shut up, you noisy little sod.' Secret as the nine o'clock news.

'Mum! Lovejoy sweared!'

Across North Hill I could see my future abode. A tatty little antique shop, boarded up, the police yellow tape threatening you with all sorts if you went in. My heart sank.

'Hello, Lovejoy.' Bea was preparing her set cream teas, jam, scones, double cream, butter. 'Did Sandy tell you the arrangement? I send your food to you once you're over there. You don't move. You don't come here.'

'I know.'

A large presentation cake shaped like an ocean liner stood on the counter. Good enough to eat.

'Got some old dear along with you, I hear.'

'She's unloading my things in your yard.'

Bea smiled. 'That's my lad. How long will you be in there?'

'Few weeks, I expect. What's the ship?'

'That's the *Aphrodite*,' little Polly said. 'The cake's for its party.'

'Newly launched, first cruise tomorrow.' Bea checked the clock. 'Passengers are leaving the George at six.' She tutted, glanced out of the window. 'Those station taxis. I ordered him an hour ago, and he's only just arrived.'

A taxi drew up. I hefted the cake on its silver

stand. 'Want me to carry it out, Bea?'

'He'll lick it,' Polly prophesied with the untroubled serenity all infants possess.

'I'll do nothing of the sort,' I said indignantly, carrying the cake ship to the door.

'Don't be seen, Lovejoy,' Bea warned anxiously.

I smiled as Florence came staggering in with her two suitcases. I took the cake to the taxi, placed it on the back seat.

'Move up the road a few yards, mate,' I told him. 'I've a case.'

'That'll be extra,' the driver said sourly.

'Isn't everything?'

He gunned his engine and went up the hill a little. I went and took one of Florence's suitcases. Who'd have thought a load of old photographs would weigh so heavy? Well, she'd promised to give me some as a present, right? I could sort out which ones, as I travelled. It would save her bother.

'I'll just carry this across,' I said helpfully. 'No, it's fine. Nobody'll notice in the traffic.'

'Lovejoy's escaping,' Polly announced. 'I can tell.'

Little swine. I beamed at her. 'Back in a sec.'

I carried the case to the taxi, made sure it was beyond the view from Bea's teashop window, and loaded it in the boot. I got in.

'Where to, mate?'

'The George.'

'Going with that new cruise ship group, are yer?'

I thought for a second. 'That's an idea. Where does it sail from?'

'Southampton. I can do you a special rate all the way.'

Duty is for doing, the brigadier said. But I was

404

neither an officer nor a gentleman.

And wasn't it my duty to scarper when I was being hunted?

'You're on,' I told him. 'Stop at the George first, drop this cake off.'

'You got the money? It's quite a way.'

'Just get going.'

And sat back ready for the journey. The taxi could take the new one-way out of town.

Chivers Large Print Direct

If you have enjoyed this Large Print book and would like to build up your own collection of Large Print books and have them delivered direct to your door, please contact **Chivers Large Print Direct.**

Chivers Large Print Direct offers you a full service:

☆ **Created to support your local library**

☆ **Delivery direct to your door**

☆ **Easy-to-read type and attractively bound**

☆ **The very best authors**

☆ **Special low prices**

For further details either call Customer Services on 01225 443400 or write to us at

Chivers Large Print Direct
FREEPOST (BA 1686/1)
Bath
BA1 3QZ